Lieutenant Stanley Klubertanz of the Madison Police looked into the bedroom.

The bodies—what was left of the bodies—lay side by side on the bed, the sheets completely red with gore. Their heads both had been twisted around so that they were nearly backwards . . . . Their throats had been slit, and their stomachs and chests laid open, their organs spilling out in piles alongside them, and over the edge of the bed onto the floor.

Klubertanz's stomach flopped over; his mouth suddenly tasted like copper, and he could feel the sweat rolling down his forehead.

The sergeant had been right. This was no ordinary murder. It was more, much more.

LAST COME THE CHILDREN

DAVID HAGBERG

A TOM DOHERTY ASSOCIATES BOOK

This is a work of fiction. All the characters and events portrayed in this book are fictional, and any resemblance to real people or incidents is purely coincidental.

LAST COME THE CHILDREN

A Tor Book

Published by Tom Doherty Associates, 8-10 W. 36th St., New York City, N.Y. 10018

First printing, June 1982

ISBN: 0-523-48036-9

Printed in the United States of America

Distributed by Pinnacle Books, 1430 Broadway, New York, N.Y. 10018

This Book is for my father, Conrad.
Tho I hardly know him, I've always loved him.

"And the soul that turneth after spirits and after wizards, to go a whoring after them, I will set my face against that soul, and will cut him off from among his people."

LEVITICUS XX.6

"And he . . . observed times, and used enchantments, and dealt with . . . spirits and wizards; he wrought much wickedness . . . ."

II KINGS XXI.6

Part One
THE GATHERING
September

1

It was early September and too cold even for a Wisconsin fall. A northwest wind blew an icy rain into gusty sheets that shook the light poles, drummed against windows, and blew the stray bit of trash before it down a street or an alley.

A brooding, dark, fitful mood seemed to have come over Madison; cabbies snapped at their fares for no apparent reasons, bartenders were short with their drunks; and even the strippers at Horizon's, an eastside club, found it difficult to strut their stuff with any enthusiasm.

On the opposite side of the city, in an obviously expensive two-story colonial, a party was in its last stages as the hour approached two in the morning.

The woman had managed to drag her husband away from the wet bar, across the living room and into the vestibule, where she lost him again to a couple of his cronies who had been holding court half the evening on the staircase.

Her name was Cheryl Rader. Late thirties, medium height, pleasantly good looking in a midwestern sort of way. No guile. No cunning. A little too thin, cheeks a bit too angular. Impatience in her features now. She had told Frank not to drink too much. Not this evening. But he hadn't listened.

Elizabeth Surret, their hostess, who had been dispensing coats to the departing guests, touched Cheryl on the shoulder, then took her by the arm and led her away from the group.

"Do you want us to call you a cab?"

"I don't think so, thanks, Liz," Cheryl said, glancing back at her husband. "He usually lets me drive when he gets like this." Instantly she bit her tongue. Damn, she thought.

Lon Surret had started Solar Products, Inc., two years ago, and already the company was number three in the state in supplying solar heating equipment designs for commercial buildings. But the man and his wife were Republican, straight-laced Wasps.

"Excess," Frank would mimic his boss in a low-pitched voice, "is the bane of our culture."

Elizabeth patted Cheryl's arm. "Don't worry about it. We all know Franky. He's a go-getter. Needs to blow off a little steam every now and then. Lonnie was just telling me this morning how much he thought of your Franky."

Franky . . . Christ. Cheryl smiled uncertainly. "Thanks, Liz, I guess maybe he has been working too hard lately."

The older woman smiled patronizingly. "How are the girls?"

"Fine. Happy that school has started, if you can believe that."

"Our children always loved school," Elizabeth said.

Frank had turned away from the others as two more wives came out of the living room to collect their husbands, and Elizabeth went to the hall closet to get their coats.

"I was just going to mix myself another drink," Frank said, bleary eyed.

"We're leaving," Cheryl snapped a little too sharply. "You've had enough."

"You've had enough," he mimicked her, and the two men on the stairs chuckled.

Cheryl turned away to get their coats. Her ears were warm. Her husband had always been, as Liz called him, a "go-getter." But over the last couple of years, since he had started with Solar Products, he had changed somehow. Subtly. But the change was there. He had become somewhat sharper of tongue, easier to anger, less understanding. But most of all a change had come into his eyes. Or rather the expression his eyes held.

Part of that, Cheryl knew, was a direct result of his increased drinking. But which came first: the drinking which changed his moods, or his changed moods which caused his drinking?

Pressures of the new job, he would have said to her.

"You have to understand, babes, that this will only be for a couple more years. Just until we're over the hump. And then . . . ."

"And then what?" she would ask him at that point, but each time he would shake his head. It was as if he had some master plan that he could share with no one. Not even his wife.

She was about to turn around, but Liz caught her eye as if she was trying to communicate something. The look only lasted a moment, then disappeared as Frank was saying his goodbyes to his boss, and Cheryl turned around, a smile on her lips.

Lon Surret, a tall, stern-looking man in his late fifties, had come from the living room and was shaking Frank's hand.

"Glad you and Cheryl could join us this evening, Frank," he said, his voice rich, melodious. He turned to Cheryl, who had moved to her husband's side. "And if you ever want to give up this lovely wife of yours, you can send her over here."

Bullshit. The single word popped into Cheryl's mind, and it startled her because she had almost said it out loud.

Lon Surret kissed Cheryl on the cheek, and then they were pulling on their coats, saying their goodbyes to the other guests.

"I'm going to drive," she said as they stepped down off the porch into the wind and rain.

Frank took her arm without a word and together they hurried to their Citation on the street.

At the car Frank opened the passenger-side door for her, the interior light a haven in the pitch-dark night.

"Are you going to let me drive home?" she shouted.

"Nope," he said, and he went around to the other side of the car, opened the door, and slipped in behind the wheel.

"Damn it, Frank!" Cheryl could hear herself sounding like a shrew, but she couldn't help it. She got in and closed the door. He was drunk, the weather was bad and they lived across town. All they needed was for Frank to get an OWI ticket.

Frank started the car, then flipped on the headlights and windshield wipers.

"Lon will go through the roof if you get a ticket," she said reasonably.

He glanced at her as he slammed the car in gear, something menacing flashing in his eyes. "Fuck him," he said softly, and then turned back and pulled away from the curb.

It wasn't like him, Cheryl thought. The change had been there before. Growing over the past twenty-four months, but tonight the difference was more pronounced. Stark.

"Frank?" she started uncertainly.

"Enough harping, babes," he said. "I'm tired. I just want to get home and get to bed. Just don't harp. Ease up a little bit."

They turned at the corner and in a couple of blocks were on Verona Road heading back toward University Avenue where they lived, overlooking Lake Mendota.

Frank's driving was normal . . . if anything, slower and more cautious than normal, for which Cheryl was grateful. But she was upset, and at the pit of her stomach the worry that had begun gnawing at her several months ago returned in full force.

Forty, she thought. A hell of an age. Until now she had always dismissed the notion about midlife crises. Maybe for the losers. Or, as Frank would say, for people who didn't know what the hell they wanted out of life in the first place.

But not for us. Never us.

She snuck a glance at his profile. For some unfathomable reason the years were always much kinder to men than to women. Gray hairs, a few lines around the mouth and eyes and a thickening of the middle, were for a man sure signs of maturity, of character. For women they were certain signs of deterioration.

Was that it? She stared out the windshield at the rain-slicked streets. Had she failed to look eighteen for Frank? Was he looking for his own youth by capturing someone else's?

There was very little traffic at this hour of the morning. A truck up ahead, a car a quarter of a mile behind them. The traffic lights for the Beltline entrance flipped red while they were still half a block away as Cheryl turned again to her husband.

"I'm sorry, Frank," she said in a small voice.

He glanced at her, the expression around his eyes tight at first, but then he smiled, and shook his head. "I guess I behaved like a prick tonight."

Cheryl laughed, the relief sweet. It was her Frank. She leaned over in her seat to kiss him when, out of the corner of her eye, she saw the overhead traffic lights, still red, flash by.

"Frank . . . ," she started to say, but at that instant the interior of the car was flooded with an intense white light.

Headlights, the thought crystallized in her brain as Frank's side of the car erupted in a shower of glass and screeching, tearing metal, something slamming them over on their side, and then upside down.

Cheryl hit her shoulder on the roof of the car which was somehow directly beneath her, while overhead, through the shattered windshield, she caught a brief glimpse of the highway, sparks flying like a Fourth of July display, and she was in the back seat, wedged on the floor, as the car continued to spin.

Dust was everywhere. Something wet was in her left eye and she could smell the distinct odor of vomit. Yet she was in no pain as the car finally skidded to a halt on its top.

An accident. It had been an accident. Frank had run the red light. Christ, Lon would be mad, would probably fire

Frank. But the girls were all right. They'd be okay alone for a few minutes or so.

It was dark, but she could sense something directly in front of her face. Like fabric. Maybe the seat.

She yawned, and opened her eyes. Jesus, she had fallen asleep. There was something . . . .

Cheryl could hear sirens in the distance somewhere and she tried to turn her head. Then there were flashing red lights all around her. Strong hands were unbending her body, and there was rain on her face. Wind and rain.

Someone was talking in the distance, and she could hear a police radio blaring and hissing, and she was lying on a soft bed and a warm blanket was on top of her.

"Frank?" she could hear her own voice. She was embarrassed that they had caused so much trouble.

She turned her head as her stretcher was lifted up. Frank was lying on the street while a dark-haired man was pumping his chest. Another man in a white coat was racing toward Frank. He was carrying an oxygen bottle under his arm.

"Frank?" Cheryl cried, trying to rise up from the stretcher. "Frank!" she screamed. "He's dead! My Frank is dead!"

Frank Rader was drifting.

There was a very strong white light in the distance, through a heavy fog. He was aware that he was not alone. There were others here with him. Indistinct shapes, and shadows scattered along an undulating plain.

He had a sense of himself being in this place; he knew he was dead or dying. Yet he was also conscious—if that was the correct word—of being angry. Of feeling cheated.

"Franklin William Rader, it gives me the great pleasure to present to you the Presidential E Award, for excellence in service to industry and to your country."

He had a sense of acceleration. As if he was being propelled faster and faster through the vague shadows toward the end of the plain . . . toward the light that was at once comforting and frightening.

"Mr. Rader?"

"Yes."

"Your accountant is here, sir."

"Send him in."

"Mr. Rader, it gives me the great pleasure to announce that you've become a millionaire."

They were laughing at him, but he could not tell what it was about, although it was embarrassing.

The gun was in his hand and it was coming up. Surret was below him, his eyes wide, his nostrils flared with fear.

"Yes!" Frank screamed. "Yes!"

The white light began to recede faster and faster as the fog began to drift, and then blow away. In the distance, behind him, Frank could sense flashing red lights, rain on his face, and a woman screaming.

"Astaroth," he whispered.

Clinton Polk awoke with a start, his heart racing, his side cold with sweat as he carefully rolled over on his back.

His wife, Susan, sleeping beside him, was curled up in a ball, her breathing regular, her long, strawberry-blonde hair spilled around her head on the pillow.

For a long time he lay perfectly still, listening to the vagrant sounds of the house, listening to the rain and wind outside, until he became conscious of the fact he was cold.

He looked over at the clock radio on the nightstand, which showed it was just a few minutes after two, and tried to think: had he forgotten to turn the furnace up when he came home?

All in all it had been a fairly pleasant day . . . a pleasant week . . . except for the ongoing fight his department was having with the Board of Regents over funding for the project.

It had started to turn cool Thursday evening, however, and by yesterday afternoon the clouds had come in and the weather forecasters were calling for rain possibly mixed with snow.

"Damn," he said to himself as he threw the covers back and got carefully out of bed.

He tucked the covers back around his wife, grabbed his robe from the chair, and slipped it on as he stepped out into the upstairs hallway and groped for the light switch.

Finding it, he flipped the switch on, but nothing happened. He flipped it on and off several more times, but still nothing happened. The hall light must have burned out up here, he thought. But then, so had the light downstairs.

Strange. Probably a short somewhere.

He carefully moved down the corridor toward the head of the stairs and, trailing his right hand on the banister, carefully descended.

"Clinton?" Susan's sleepy voice drifted down to him.

He stopped and looked up over his shoulder, but he could see nothing in the intense darkness. "I'm going downstairs to get a drink. Do you want something?"

"It's cold," she called from her bedroom.

"I'll check the furnace," he said, and waited for her reply, but it didn't come, and he continued down the stairs.

They had been married only four years. He was forty, she twenty-seven. No children to bother with; they lived an orderly existence alone except for Bo, their black lab.

He was an assistant professor of molecular biology at the University of Wisconsin and had been fighting with the Board of Regents for the past couple of months for funds to carry out a research project. No one seemed impressed with his proposals and, as it had been put to him by one of the regents:

"Everyone is a little touchy at the moment about anything having to do with genetic engineering. Just bide your time for a few months, maybe as long as a year, and the money will be there, Clinton. I promise you."

I promise you, Polk thought. Three little words that invariably seemed to accompany lies and deceit.

It was even colder downstairs, and he wondered if a window hadn't been left open somewhere.

He started across the vestibule when he stumbled over something on the floor, nearly pitching forward in the darkness, just barely regaining his footing.

He backed up a step, then bent down and reached out with his hands, like a blind man groping his way forward, immediately touching a big ball of fur. The dog.

"For God's sake, Bo . . . ." The words died on his lips.

The dog's body was stiff and cold. It was dead.

Without thinking, Polk straightened up and went across the vestibule, where he found the light switch, and flipped it on. The hall lights, here and upstairs, came on. He went back to the dog stretched out stiff in the middle of the vestibule.

"Damn." He knelt down beside the animal again, and gently turned it over.

The dog was definitely dead. Had been dead for some time. There were no marks on his body as far as he could see, but it struck him as very odd that rigor mortis had set in so fast.

He and Susan had gone to bed around midnight, maybe a couple of hours ago at the most. At that time he had put the dog out, and had let him back in a moment later. Bo normally took his own sweet time for his nightly outing, but this evening the animal had come back whining and scratching at the door almost immediately.

And now he was dead. Apparently long dead.

Something else suddenly struck him, and he slowly turned and looked up at the light. It was on, as was the one upstairs.

What the hell was going on? A minute ago, upstairs, the lights wouldn't work. The switch was bad. Obvious.

The furnace clicked on and Polk could feel a warm blast of air coming from the hall register. He ran his fingers through his hair, tightened the belt on his bathrobe, and went back to the kitchen, where he unlocked the back door.

Back in the vestibule, he carefully picked the dog's body off the floor and carried it through the kitchen, out the back door and across the yard, where he laid it down in the bushes beside the garage.

It was bitterly cold outside, and the rain was beginning

to turn to snow as Polk went back into the kitchen.

In the morning he'd tell Susan. She had been very attached to the dog. Bo had taken the place of the child they'd decided never to have.

He relocked the kitchen door and for a few moments stood leaning against it. The dog had probably gotten into someone's garbage. Maybe rat poison. Yet, as far as he knew, rat poison would not induce a stiffening of the muscle tissue so fast.

Perhaps it had been some kind of a convulsive drug. Maybe someone had thrown out a prescription and Bo had gotten into it.

He'd take the animal to a vet tomorrow on the way to work. There was always the possibility that someone had deliberately poisoned it. An autopsy would show what had happened.

Polk went back through the house and in the vestibule checked to make sure the front door was locked. It was. And then he started up the stairs as the telephone rang, the strident sound startling him.

He answered it on the second ring. "Yes?"

"Clinton?" It was Cheryl Rader. Or at least he thought it was Cheryl's voice, although it was hard to tell. She sounded distraught.

"Cheryl? Where are you? What's happened?"

"Thank God you were home. There's been an accident. It's Frank. He's been hurt."

Polk looked at his watch, which showed it was just 2:15 A.M. "Where are you calling from?" he snapped.

"The hospital," Cheryl cried. "Madison General. Oh God, Clinton, it's terrible. I think . . . Frank . . . he's dead, I think. They won't tell me anything."

"Jesus," Polk swore half under his breath.

"Clinton?" Susan called from the head of the stairs.

"Listen, Cheryl, stay right where you are. Susan and I will get dressed and be there within fifteen minutes. Just don't panic."

There was a silence on the line.

"What's going on?" Susan called from the stairs as she

started down. "Who's on the phone?"

"Cheryl?" Polk spoke into the phone. "Cheryl, are you still there?" Silence. He slowly hung up the telephone and turned as his wife came all the way down the stairs, clutching her bathrobe tightly around her neck.

"It was Cheryl Rader."

"Has something happened?" Susan asked, instant deep concern in her eyes.

"There's been an accident, I think. She wasn't very coherent. Frank was hurt."

"Oh Christ, where are they?"

"Madison General. I told her we'd be right there."

"Oh, Christ," Susan said again, and she turned and headed up the stairs. "I knew something like this was going to happen."

"What the hell do you mean by that?" Polk asked, hurrying up the stairs after her. She didn't answer him.

In the dim light of the clock radio on the bookcase headboard, Fred Martin looked down at his sleeping wife.

One strap of her negligee had slipped down off her shoulder and, before he pulled the covers back up over her, he bent down and kissed the nipple of her exposed breast. She murmured something in her sleep and then rolled over.

For several seconds Martin stared at the back of her head, and then he turned, crossed the room and went out into the hall.

A night light shone softly from the open bathroom door, and for a moment he stared at it.

"What if there was a fire at night, Fred?" Marion had asked a few days after they had brought their new baby home from the hospital.

"What if we couldn't find our way out of the house?"

Was he smelling smoke?

"We'd have to make it to the baby's room, and then outside. We'd have to have a light."

Martin moved down the corridor to the bathroom and looked inside at the tiny night-light fixture plugged into the socket over the sink.

He turned and looked toward Jessica's door, every one of his senses straining, for an instant, for a sound or a sign that something was wrong.

Was he hearing a cough?

When one thing goes to hell, everything else follows suit.

Martin shook his head and padded, barefoot, down the corridor into the living room of their three-bedroom ranch-style house. He went immediately to the bar that was set up in the bookcase, poured himself a stiff shot of vodka and immediately drank it down, shuddering at the harsh impact of the liquor on his system. He poured himself another drink, then got a cigarette from the case on the coffee table. When he had it lit, he sat down in his favorite chair in front of the television set and closed his eyes.

"Christ," he said to himself as he inhaled deeply on the cigarette. "Christ." The plain truth was that he was frightened.

If they won . . . everything. Promotion, most likely to a full partner in Creative Sales, Inc. Big money. Maybe seventy-five or eighty thou plus a year. A new house. New car. The entire shooting match . . . including respect.

If they lost . . . if he lost . . . there would be less than nothing. No promotion, no money, nothing but jail.

Martin had never done anything really illegal in h life. Overtime parking. A U-turn once, a speeding ticket several years ago. But bribery of public officials was a criminal offense. Jail time.

And yet (why the hell was his life lately punctuated with that phrase?) the agency was not really cheating the city of Milwaukee. If they did get the industrial development advertising contract, they would do a good job. A good job at a fair price.

He heard the bathroom door close, and he opened his eyes. Marion must have gotten up.

Martin and his wife were both pushing forty and had been married only five years. After college he had spent his time and energy in the advertising business. There had always been plenty of women, despite his basic shyness, but never the right woman until Marion had come along.

Her story had been a sad one. She had married when she was twenty-five, and had two boys, three years apart. Seven years ago her husband and both boys had been killed in the crash of a light airplane, leaving her for a full year under psychiatric care.

Their friends had been concerned about them having a baby so late in life, but both Martin and his wife had desperately wanted a family; he because he wanted to be a father, and she in some respects because she wanted to replace the family she had lost.

He had to smile despite his worries. Having Jessica was wonderful. Better than he had thought possible. And now that they had her, there were no second thoughts, no doubts, only gladness.

The toilet flushed, and a few moments later he heard the bathroom door open.

"Fred?" his wife called from the back of the house.

"In here," he said softly.

She stopped just within the living room. "What are you doing out here? Can't you sleep?"

"Just got up for a cigarette," he said. He loved her very much at that moment. If Marion's personality had to be summarized in one simple sentence, it would have to be that she was a woman genuinely concerned about others.

"Are you coming back to bed soon?"

"In a minute," he said.

She started to turn away, but then came back. "Are you all right, Fred? Do you feel okay?"

"I'm fine, Marion. Go on back to bed, I'll be right there."

"Okay," she said, and she disappeared down the corridor.

Martin stubbed his cigarette out in the ashtray, then drank the rest of his vodka, got up and set the glass back on the bar. As he was about to turn away, Marion screamed, the sound piercing, animalistic in its intensity.

His stomach flopped over as he raced for the corridor, bouncing off the wall. "Marion?" he shouted, but she continued to scream.

For a moment he thought she was in the bathroom, and perhaps had fallen, but then with a sick feeling he realized that her cries were coming from Jessica's room.

A crash of lightning lit up the room for just an instant as he came through the doorway, and he could see clearly that Marion was clutching their baby in her arms as she screamed.

The thunder came then, powerfully rattling the windows, shaking the house as he leaped across the room to her.

"What happened?" he shouted. "What's wrong?"

"Jessica!" she cried. "Oh God . . . Jessica . . . our baby! She's dead!"

It was impossible. It was a dream. And yet the way she was holding the baby Martin knew that it wasn't . . . that it was really happening to them.

Suddenly he became very conscious of time. It was racing by too fast. Crib death. Suffocation. A hundred things passed through his mind.

"Give her to me!" he shouted.

Marion tried to back away. "She's dead . . . ."

Martin roughly grabbed Jessica from her arms, turned and raced back to their bedroom, where he hit the light switch and laid the baby on the bed, Marion right behind him.

"Call the doctor," he snapped as he hurriedly undid the baby's sleeper nightgown.

The baby's face was blue, her little chest still. He laid his ear to her chest, but he couldn't hear anything over Marion's crying.

"Shut up," he screamed, looking up. "Call the doctor. Now!"

Gently, but with shaking hands, he applied a regular pressure to the baby's chest with two fingers. Once, twice, three times, and then down on his knees beside the bed, he pried her mouth open, and placed his mouth over her entire face and blew gently. Her chest rose. He lifted his head up and Jessica's tiny chest fell. A moment later he blew into her mouth and nose again.

"The doctor," he shouted almost hysterically when he looked up the next time. Marion stood directly behind him, quiet now, her hands over her mouth to stifle her sobs.

Again he blew into the baby's mouth, released, and blew again.

"Please . . . Jessica . . . please," he half mumbled to himself. Time was speeding by too fast. He was aware not only of the lifeless child, but of Marion behind him, of the storm outside, of everything.

He applied the rhythmic pressure to the baby's chest again, five times, and then continued the mouth-to-mouth resuscitation, but it wasn't working. He knew it wasn't working. The deep blue coloring on his baby's face had not changed. Jessica hadn't sputtered. Hadn't moved. They needed the doctor. The rescue squad.

The telephone on the nightstand next to him rang, the sound seemingly louder than the thunder, and Martin reached out and grabbed it.

"Get off this phone!" he roared.

"Frank's been in an accident!" Cheryl Rader's voice came over the phone.

"Get off this fucking phone, Cheryl!" Martin screamed. "Send an ambulance out here. Our baby needs help!"

"It's Frank . . . I think he's dead . . . ," Cheryl's voice screamed.

The ambulance, its red lights flashing, its siren wailing, screamed off South Park Street and raced up the curved driveway to the emergency entrance at Madison General Hospital.

A doctor and two nurses were waiting with a Gurney bed, and, even before the ambulance came to a complete halt, they were yanking open the back door.

Stan Shapiro, the ambulance attendant riding in the back with Frank and Cheryl Rader, knew his job well; he had been doing this sort of thing now for almost eleven years. He pulled the oxygen mask off Frank's face, firmly moved the wife out of the way, and helped the nurses get the man's body out of the ambulance.

"Vitals are all steady now!" he snapped, shoving the ambulance stretcher aside as Frank's body was expertly flopped onto the wheeled bed. "His wife needs help!"

One of the nurses stayed behind to help Cheryl, while Shapiro raced with the doctor and other nurse into the hospital, down a very short corridor and into the emergency room itself.

The doctor ripped Rader's shirt open. He hooked his stethescope into his ears, and laid the pickup on Frank's chest.

An intern had moved an EKG monitor next to the bed, while a nurse was taking Frank's blood pressure, and another was moving in with a rollabout cart loaded with bandages and other supplies.

"I want an ECG put on the man, stat, and set me up a saline drip," the doctor snapped. "Blood pressure?"

"140 over 90," the nurse said, reading the figures from the indicator on the cuff bulb.

There was a commotion in the corridor as Cheryl Rader was led in. "Frank!" she screamed.

The doctor looked up. "His wife?"

Shapiro nodded.

"Was she injured?"

"I don't think so."

"Take her to three. Get Larry down here to look at her," the doctor snapped, and he turned back to Frank as the nurses were cutting away his jacket and shirt, and then his trousers.

A large angry bruise had already formed across Frank's chest where he had struck the steering wheel, and blood seeped from a cut on the left side of his forehead.

The heart monitor machine's leads were attached to his chest, and the machine turned on, as another of the nurses was attaching several leads to his head, connecting him to the electroencephlograph, and the intravenous saline drip was inserted in his left arm.

Shapiro stared for a long moment at Frank lying on the table, then turned as his partner Bruce Ahern hurried in from outside.

"How is he?" Ahern asked.

"Looks like he'll be okay."

"What?" the other man asked, coming up to him. "I thought he was . . . ."

"So did I," Shapiro said shakily. Together they went to the ward secretary's cubicle and signed in, handing across a copy of their patient pickup and release forms.

"Your ambulance out of the way?" the secretary asked, stamping the forms.

"Sure is, Pat," Bruce Ahern said. "Someone else coming in?"

"Should be . . . ," the pretty young woman said, but her telephone console buzzed, and she turned away and picked up the phone. "Emergency room," she said, listening a moment, her mouth tightening. "Yes," she said, then cleared the line and hit the hospital paging line.

"Dr. Blue from pediatrics, Dr. Blue from pediatrics to the emergency room, please," her voice sounded from the ceiling speakers throughout the hospital.

Before she had repeated the message a second time, a young doctor and two nurses wheeling a small rollabout table raced down the corridor to the emergency entrance as an ambulance came screaming up the circular driveway.

Shapiro and Ahern stepped around the corner from the ward secretary's cubicle and watched as an infant was loaded on the table and brought into the emergency room, one of the nurses helping the distraught parents past the ward secretary and into the waiting room, where Cheryl Rader had just been taken.

"Oh, God . . . Cheryl," the woman cried, and Cheryl Rader jumped up from where she had been sitting, and the two women fell sobbing into each other's arms.

"Let's get the wagon back, it's been a long night," Ahern said, and Shapiro looked up at his friend and nodded.

"Yeah," he said. "I could use a cup of coffee."

As they passed the open emergency room door, Shapiro looked inside. A nurse was cleaning and bandaging Frank Rader's cuts, and it just didn't make any sense. Shapiro had been certain that the man was dead. Dead beyond revival. Yet now it looked as if he was going to be all right.

At the outside door a small BMW sedan screeched to a halt, and a man and woman jumped out as Shapiro and Ahern walked down the driveway and climbed into their ambulance.

The rain had stopped, finally, and the sky had begun to lighten to a leaden gray by the time Clinton and Susan Polk helped Cheryl Rader out the emergency door and down to where their car was parked. The air outside smelled clean and fresh compared to the antiseptic atmosphere of the hospital, and all three of them were glad to be away.

Polk helped the two women into the car and then came around to the driver's side, but before he got in he looked back up at the hospital and shook his head.

This night had been incredible, and it would take them months to recover from it, if they ever did completely.

And now what would Marion do that her new baby was dead? This morning, and probably for the next twenty-four hours or so, she would be under sedation, in her own little world. But later, when she came out of it, she and Fred were somehow going to have to face the fact that their baby was dead. Somehow, they were going to have to live with it. And Polk felt that it would be impossible for them unless they had the help and the support of their friends.

He opened the car door and climbed in behind the wheel. His wife and Cheryl were both in the back seat, not saying a word, just staring straight ahead, waiting to be taken home.

Traffic was very light at this hour of the morning: a police car, a couple of trucks, and a few early-shift workers heading sleepily to their jobs.

The streets were rain slicked, and at the Square, downtown, Polk had to swing out, away from a couple of tree limbs that had apparently been blown down in the storm.

"I knew something like this was going to happen," Cheryl said softly.

Polk looked at her reflection in the rearview mirror. She seemed on the verge of collapse.

"Frank is going to be all right," Susan said.

"The doctor said he could come home in a couple of days," Polk added, but Cheryl was shaking her head.

"I mean about Fred and Marion's baby," she said.

"Hush, now," Susan said. "We're going to get you home and put you to bed."

"The twins . . . ?" Cheryl said, her voice rising.

"I called them. Everything is all right. They understand."

"Oh, God," Cheryl cried, holding tightly onto Susan. "How is Marion ever going to handle this, Susan? How?"

"We're going to have to help her. Her and Fred. That's all."

"What kind of night has this been?"

What kind indeed, Polk thought frowning, remembering their dog, Bo. It had been a crazy night. He was very glad it was nearly over.

When they reached the Raders' home on the west side of town, just off University Avenue, Polk pulled the car into the driveway, then helped the women out.

Together they started up the walk to the pretty, two-story colonial, when the front door opened and Dawn and Felicity, the Raders' pretty, thirteen-year-old twin girls came racing down the walk to them.

"Mom, mom, are you all right? Is daddy okay? It's been on the radio! Mrs. Surret called and said if you needed any help she'd be right over!"

The girls shouted and danced around their mother, both of them talking at once.

Cheryl drew back for just a moment, but then the girls' enthusiasm and concern seemed to act as a tonic that she needed.

"Everything is going to be all right," she said to them.

"When's daddy coming home?" Dawn asked.

"Tomorrow or maybe the next day."

"What are they doing to him?" Felicity asked. "Did he break something?"

"No," Cheryl said. "He got a few cuts and some bruises. That's all."

"Then why does he have to stay in the hospital so long?" Dawn asked.

They had reached the front door, and Susan stepped aside as the girls helped their mother.

"The doctor wants to make sure he doesn't have any injuries inside. They have to watch him for a couple of days," Cheryl said.

Just inside the vestibule she turned. "Do you two want to come in for some coffee?"

Susan shook her head and glanced at her husband. "No, we're going back home. It's been a long night."

"I've still got to get to work sometime before noon this morning," Polk said.

Cheryl came back to the door and hugged Susan and Clinton. "Thanks for being there with me tonight," she said, her eyes moist.

"I was up anyway when you called," Polk said.

An odd expression came into Cheryl's eyes. "I didn't call," she said.

"Of course you did . . . ," Polk started to say, but Susan nudged him.

"Really, Clinton, I didn't call anyone. The ambulance drivers brought us to the hospital, and a few minutes later you two showed up."

"It's all right," Susan said. "It was probably the hospital."

"It must have been," Cheryl said. "You sure you two don't want to come in for some coffee?"

"No, thanks, Cheryl. I think you'd better lie down and get some rest now," Susan said.

"Sure, and thanks again, you two. See you later today?"

"Of course," Susan said.

For five of Stan Shapiro's years as an ambulance driver and attendant, he had been working with Bruce Ahern. Both men had served as medics in Vietnam, both had originally come from the West Coast, and both had decided on the quieter life in the Midwest.

They had met at the university where they both had taken classes, had struck up a friendship, and finally a couple of years ago had moved into an apartment together to share the rent and utilities.

Both of them were gentle men, kind, generally soft spoken. Part of that was because they had been born that way, but another, even larger contributing factor to their gentleness was a reaction to the oftentimes extreme violence they were witness to.

Together they had pulled people from wrecked automobiles, had scraped up remains from the street, and had saved dozens of lives with their quick thinking.

As another result of their work together, they knew each other better than most friends. Their relationship was a very special one. And this morning each knew that the other was bothered.

"The man was dead," Shapiro said. They were seated across the table from each other in the break room at the Capitol City Ambulance Service Center on King Street.

"You're damned right he was dead, Stan," Ahern replied. They had driven back from the hospital in silence, and had checked in without a word to each other. But now they could no longer hold their silence.

"Jesus Christ, he was as cold as ice," Shapiro said shakily, letting himself go. "I don't know why I even tried the resuscitator."

"I felt it, too," Ahern said, his eyes wide. "So what happened?"

"I don't know. But no one would ever believe us if we told them."

"But that's impossible, isn't it, Stan? I mean if he was cold, there would have been no way for him to come back. Isn't that right?"

Shapiro nodded uncertainly.

"Then we were dreaming. That's all."

"Twenty minutes from the time of the accident until we got there. That's no dream."

"What are you trying to say, for Christ's sake?" Ahern shouted, jumping up. He looked down at his friend. "They'd put us away for this, man. Jesus H . . . ."

Shapiro looked up at him, his eyes moist. He shook his head. "Lots of things don't make sense, Bruce. We learned that in Nam."

"You're saying just forget it?"

Shapiro nodded.

Ahern shook his head. "Never."

2

It was Sunday afternoon when Cheryl Rader picked her husband up from the hospital and they headed home in a loaner station wagon from their insurance agent. Over the weekend the storm had passed, leaving in its wake beautifully clear skies and a crisp, early-fall day.

"How do you feel, darling?" Cheryl asked as she drove.

Frank had not said much at the hospital, and she was worried about him now. He seemed so morose.

He looked over at her. "Sore," he said. "I feel like I've been run over by a truck."

Cheryl forced a smile at the very bad joke. "Are you sure you're okay, honey?"

"Shit," Frank said, looking away. "I really fucked it up, didn't I? I mean, if I had let you drive, none of this would have happened. Christ, I could have killed you."

Cheryl reached out with her right hand and caressed Frank's cheek. "It'll be all right. The girls are excited about you coming home. They baked a chocolate cake for you."

Frank looked at her again, and Cheryl flinched inside. There was something different about him. A heaviness, a sadness. But he smiled. "They must have been worried."

"Out of their minds," Cheryl said. "But everything is going to be fine now."

"Did Surret call?"

Cheryl shook her head. "But his wife phoned twice. She was over yesterday afternoon to make sure I was okay."

"I probably won't have a job to go to, once he finds out what happened."

"How will he . . . ?"

Frank cut her off. "The cops were up yesterday afternoon. I've been ticketed."

"For what?"

"Drunk driving."

Cheryl was confused. "I don't understand," she said.

"Don't understand what?" he snapped in anger. "How the cops could prove that I had been drinking? It's simple, the hospital authorized a blood alcohol test while I was unconscious."

"But that's not right."

"You're goddamned right it's not right, the pricks." He looked away. "I could go over there and blow the entire place away."

"Frank!" Cheryl said sharply.

Frank shook his head and turned back to his wife, a lopsided grin on his face. "Besides the fact it's going to cost me a few hundred bucks, Surret just might fire me."

"I know, but don't add to our problems by getting yourself worked up. It won't help."

"Right," he said dryly.

They passed the University's Camp Randall Stadium in silence, and Cheryl turned west on old University Avenue. The traffic was heavier here nearer the school.

For her, fall was always a time of beginnings, not endings, as it was for many people who lived for summertime. She had always enjoyed school, especially college, where fall meant a new round of friends, new classes, new social activities. September for her meant new projects, shopping for sweaters and knit hats.

But not this year, she thought, sneaking a glance at her husband. She had a premonition that Frank was going to go through a very bad time this fall. The accident was only a part of it. If he lost his job, she didn't know how he would react, or how long it would take him to recover.

On top of all of that was the news about the Martins' baby. She had debated telling him earlier, at the hospital, but somehow had not been able to bring herself to mention it. And now was certainly not the best time. Frank seemed so . . . down, so different.

"It's too bad about Fred and Marion," he said, the

sound of his voice startling her.

She looked over at him. "What do you mean?"

"I mean about their baby. What the hell did you think I meant?"

"I . . . ." Cheryl was at a loss for words.

The expression on Frank's face softened, "Sorry," he said. "I guess I'm a little uptight right now. Things were just starting to get good at work."

"Everything is going to be all right," Cheryl said.

He nodded. "Yeah. But I damned near dropped my teeth when Susan told me about the baby."

"Susan?"

Again Frank nodded. "She was up to visit me yesterday afternoon."

"I didn't know that."

"She just dropped by to see how I was. I guess she assumed I already knew about Fred and Marion's baby. It's just so goddamned unfair. Christ, everything she went through seven years ago, and now this?"

Friend or not, she should not have bothered Frank with something like that, Cheryl thought.

"We're all going to have to help," Frank was saying.

"Help?"

"Yeah," he said. "They're going to need their friends now more than ever before. On top of this, I think Fred's been having some troubles at work."

"Marion hasn't said anything."

"No," Frank said. "I don't think either of them would say anything. Maybe we'll have them over for cards on Wednesday, as usual."

Cheryl was shocked into silence for a moment. "Frank?" she said. "Wednesday . . . the baby's funeral is that day."

"I know," he said. "Families and friends usually get together afterwards. Why not some cards? We've been playing cards every Wednesday night for nearly two years. Why not this Wednesday? It would certainly help them forget."

Not by playing cards, Cheryl wanted to scream. But she

was too sick at heart to say anything more than, "I'll see."

For an instant it seemed as if Frank would blow up, but then he calmed down again. "Give them a call, anyway," he said. "Call Clinton and Susan, too. Just see what they say."

Creative Sales, Inc., occupied a full floor of the First Wisconsin Bank Building, a fourteen-story edifice of green glass on downtown Madison's Square just across from the State Capitol building.

Fred Martin stood on the street corner in the shadow of the building, waiting for the traffic light to change. He wanted to get away. To run away and hide so that no one could see what had left his heart, what perhaps had never been there.

But there was nowhere for him to hide. Everyone around him, even the people on the street, in the passing cars, everyone had to know just by looking at him the terrible burden of guilt that was beginning to build inside. Beginning to throb like an uncontrollable wound.

The light changed, and he trudged mechanically across East Washington Avenue, toward the ramp where he had parked his car this morning.

Marion had come home from the hospital yesterday, but had slept most of Sunday afternoon, had been up for a few hours, then had gone back to bed.

This morning when the alarm had woken him he had automatically risen, shaved, showered, and then dressed.

Breakfast. Had he eaten breakfast? Walking now, he wasn't sure.

His memory of this morning came to him in fits and starts. He remembered getting up, but he didn't remember driving downtown. He remembered walking to the bank building, but he did not remember crossing the lobby.

The first startlingly clear thing that he remembered was stepping off the elevator on the tenth floor. The receptionist had looked up, then had half risen out of her seat.

"Mr. Martin . . . ," she had sputtered.

She knew! Christ, she knew!

"Morning." He hurried past her desk, down the corridor and ducked into his office.

His heart was pounding nearly out of his chest. If the receptionist knew, there was only one way she could have found out. And that was by reading it in the expression on his face. In his eyes.

Words of sorrow. Condolences. Sympathy. Half the staff had tromped through his office, so that he hadn't been able to work. The Milwaukee Mayor's administrative assistant was out, and so was the city's chief engineer. No luck there.

"Go home, Fred," the words echoed and re-echoed in his mind as he reached the corner of Hamilton Street, and stopped.

"Milwaukee . . . ." he had ineffectually protested.

"There's no contract that important. I want you to leave right now. I'll call Marion and tell her you're on your way."

He had closed his office, gone down the corridor, past the receptionist, down the elevator and outside. It seemed as if his life was speeding up, catching up with him, and when he finally looked up, he was pulling into his own driveway with absolutely no clear idea how he had gotten home.

When he had the car parked and the engine shut off, he buried his head in his hands and cried. For his dead child. For Marion and all that she had lost. And for himself. For what was happening to him.

He was too frightened to run, and too frightened to stay, and he didn't know if he could handle it much longer without help.

But what kind of help? And where could he seek it? And would they sympathize with him, or would they look at him as Marion had looked at him Saturday morning?

He sat up, and held his hands up in front of him. If he had known more about CPR, maybe he could have saved the baby. Or if, instead of going into the living room for a drink and a cigarette, he had checked on Jessica first, then maybe he would have been on time.

Slowly, mechanically, he got out of the car, trudged up the walk and let himself in.

The house was quiet; Marion was probably still in bed. He crossed the living room and went down the hallway to their bedroom.

The bed was unmade, but Marion was not in it. He moved silently down the hall to the bathroom and looked in, but she wasn't there, either.

Then he turned and looked towards the baby's room. The door was open, and now he thought he could hear a soft mewing, almost like the sound a kitten might make.

Very carefully, one step at a time, Fred moved to the open door, and looked inside.

Marion was sitting on the floor next to the crib. She was still in her nightgown, her hair disheveled, and she held onto the crib's barred sides with both hands as the tears streamed down her cheeks, and a soft mewing sound came from her mouth.

"Marion?" he said softly.

She turned and looked up at him. "Where did you go?" she asked, her voice barely audible.

He came all the way into the room, looked down at her for a moment, and then sank down next to her, his legs folding beneath him.

"Fred?" Marion cried, and she reached out for him.

He took her into his arms, and together they cried, yet part of his mind seemed detached from the rest of him. In that section of his brain he knew that, after all of this, he did not care that his baby was dead. He could not find the grief in himself for their lost child. The funeral had already been set for Wednesday, and yet he could find no room in his heart for sorrow. Only guilt. Guilt for not checking on the baby sooner. Guilt for not being able to save her life. And most of all, guilt for not feeling any grief.

"I'm going to see a psychiatrist," he said. "I don't think I can handle this much longer."

Marion pulled away slowly, and looked into her husband's eyes. "What is it, Fred? What in God's name is wrong?''

''Why can't I be sorry my baby is dead?'' he cried, the words torn from deep inside his heart.

It was three o'clock in the afternoon when Madison Police Lieutenant Stanley Klubertanz parked his thirteen-year-old Alpha Romeo coupe at Madison General Hospital. It had turned out to be a lovely fall afternoon, but Klubertanz was not in a particularly good mood.

Earlier in the afternoon he had gotten a telephone call from Brenda Wolfe, the assistant district attorney, asking him to stop up for a little chat.

''Something up, Brenda?'' he had asked. There had been something in the tone of her voice.

''Could be, Stan, but we're going to have to handle this through the back door, at least for the time being. Come up and I'll explain.''

Over the past few years he and Brenda had worked together on one thing or another. In fact, three years ago when his wife had divorced him and had taken their two children out to Los Angeles, she had mentioned Brenda's name as one of the reasons.

But, for better or for worse, his wife was doing fine in L.A. as a department store fashion buyer. The kids were both doing fine in school. He had gotten a letter just last week that Sylvia was seriously considering remarriage. Wonderful guy. Loves the kids, kids love him.

He hadn't known at the time whether she had sent him the letter to gloat, or was merely being considerate, for a change. He still hadn't decided which, and had twice nearly broached the subject with Brenda, but hadn't.

She had been waiting for him outside her office in the City-County Building, upstairs from the detective division, and she had shown him inside without a word.

''Business or social?'' he asked, slumping down in a chair.

She went around behind her desk and sat down. ''Business of the nastiest kind. Only, this time, I hope like hell I'm wrong.''

Klubertanz sat forward. Brenda was a good-looking woman in her mid-thirties. Her husband had run off with her best friend five years ago, and for a time she had turned off on all men. Until Klubertanz, she had never been on a date since her divorce.

She opened a file folder, extracted a sheet of paper and handed it across. "Death certificate for Jessica Martin, a three-month-old baby."

Klubertanz quickly scanned the standard form. Names, address, dates, times. Cause of death: suffocation. Not *accidental* suffocation. He looked up, his jaws tightening. "There's a reason Maxwell sent this up to you?"

Brenda sat back in her chair, obviously choosing her next words with extreme care. "The baby suffocated. That's all he could tell me without an autopsy."

"Without an autopsy," Klubertanz repeated softly. There was a very cold feeling in his gut. "Lay it out for me, Brenda."

None of this is official, Stan. Not yet. For now it's between you and me. Agreed?"

Klubertanz nodded.

"A friend of Maxwell's, on the staff at the hospital, has some questions, that's all. I talked this over with them, and then phoned John McDonald, the hospital's counselor. He's agreed to meet with you this afternoon."

"Who's this friend of Maxwell's?"

"The emergency room physician who was on call the night the baby was brought in."

"You want me to go over and talk to them. Unofficially."

"Something like that."

"Are you going to seek an autopsy?"

Brenda turned away and looked out the window of her fourth-floor office, toward Lake Monona a couple of blocks away. "Depends upon what you come up with, Stan," she said. She turned back. "I'm going to have to depend upon your instinct. If you think we should seek an autopsy, I'll do it, but I'm going to try to convince the judge to have it done immediately. This evening, and without the parents being informed.''

''So that, if nothing comes up, the body can be released to the funeral home tomorrow?''

''Exactly,'' Brenda said.

''You're skating on some pretty thin ice, Brenda.''

''Damn it, don't you think I know that?'' she snapped, trying to keep her voice low. ''But, for Christ's sake, we're talking about possible murder here! An infant's murder.''

''What about the parents' background?''

Brenda shrugged. ''The mother is as good as gold, which really doesn't mean anything, but there might be something with the father, Fred Martin. He's a VP at Creative Sales, an advertising agency here in Madison. We've had a couple of complaints about some deal he's cooking up in Milwaukee. Nothing yet we can bring action on, but we're watching the situation.''

''Politics and child killing do not necessarily follow hand in hand,'' Klubertanz said dryly.

''Just look into this for me, would you? As a friend.''

''Sure,'' Klubertanz had said. He had left her office shortly after that and had driven directly over to the hospital to meet with McDonald and the attending doctor, William Bush.

On his way up in the elevator he thought about his own children, Stewart and Melissa. They were seven and eleven. It had not been so long ago when they were three months old. And thinking about them, thinking about holding their tiny, very dependent bodies in his arms, made him angry.

Child molestation was nothing new. Hell, it happened all the time, and would continue to happen. But it made Klubertanz sick at heart to envision an adult inflicting fatal wounds on a helpless child.

The elevator doors slid open on the tenth floor, and Klubertanz stepped across the corridor to the receptionist's desk. She looked up and smiled pleasantly.

''May I help you, sir?''

''The name's Klubertanz. I'm here to see John McDonald.''

"Yes, sir," she said, picking up her telephone. "He's expecting you. One moment, please." She dialed a number and a moment later it was answered. "Mr. Klubertanz is here, sir," she said. She nodded. "Yes, sir," she said and she hung up the phone. "Down the hall, sir, third door on your left."

At McDonald's door Klubertanz knocked once and went in. The secretary looked up at the same moment McDonald came out of his office.

He was a tall man, impeccably dressed in a three-piece suit. There was a grim expression on his face.

"Lieutenant Klubertanz?" he said, coming across the room.

"Right," Klubertanz said, and they shook hands.

"Doctor Bush is on his way up. Care for some coffee?"

"No thanks," Klubertanz said, and he followed the hospital's attorney into his spacious, well-decorated office where they sat across from each other at a small conference table.

"How much has Brenda told you about this situation?" McDonald started when they were settled.

"Nothing other than there may be a question about the death of an infant here on Saturday morning."

McDonald seemed to study Klubertanz for a long moment before he spoke. "You must understand the hospital's position."

"I do," Klubertanz said. He sat forward. "I'm here unofficially for the moment, merely to talk with you and Doctor Bush. If, among the three of us, we think an autopsy is indicated, then I'll make that recommendation to Brenda. It'll go no further than that for now."

McDonald seemed somewhat relieved. "Good," he said. A minute later Dr. William Bush, a young man in his early thirties with long flowing mustaches, came in, and McDonald introduced him.

"Bill phoned me on Saturday afternoon," McDonald explained to Klubertanz, and then he turned to the doctor. "Why don't you repeat what you told me?"

The doctor glanced down at his hands, then looked up

directly into Klubertanz's eyes. "The baby . . . the Martin infant . . . was murdered," he said. "I'd bet almost anything on it."

Klubertanz's gut was suddenly tied in knots. "What makes you think that, doctor?"

"I've seen plenty of crib deaths, and even accidental suffocation. Believe me, it happens all the time."

"But?"

"But this one was different. There were slight bruises at the back of the child's head and neck, and I'll bet an autopsy will show a twisting of the spine where it attaches to the base of the skull."

"Showing what?" Klubertanz asked.

"Showing that someone held a pillow over the baby's face with one hand, while holding the back of the baby's head with the other."

The office was silent for a long moment. "Are you sure, doctor? Absolutely sure?" Klubertanz asked.

The doctor shrugged. "As sure as I can be without the results of an autopsy."

"Could it have happened accidentally?" Klubertanz asked. "Could the baby's head have gotten caught in the bars of its crib? Something like that?"

Doctor Bush nodded slowly after a hesitation. "It's possible," he said. "But unlikely, I think."

Klubertanz looked at McDonald, sighed heavily, then stood up. "I'll get back to Brenda this afternoon. You should have your court order to perform an autopsy by early this evening."

It had probably been poison, the vet had said, but he could not be absolutely sure. Clinton Polk found a parking spot half a block down from the Madison Police Department, got out of his car, locked it and hurried down the street.

But who the hell would poison the dog? Bo had never been a nuisance. He had never been a barker, never gotten into other people's garbage, as far as Polk knew. So why poison the dog? Unless it was a crazy.

Susan had taken it hard when he had told her, and yet she had not seemed surprised. Just as she had not seemed surprised when they had learned that Frank and Cheryl had been in the car accident.

Disturbing.

As Cheryl had said when they brought her home from the hospital yesterday: "What the hell kind of a weekend was this?"

The front desk of the police department was busy with uniformed officers coming and going. Behind the long booking counter was a large, glassed-in room filled with electronic equipment—radios, Polk supposed—manned by half-a-dozen men and women in uniform.

He approached the counter, and for a moment hesitated. One of the sergeants came up to him.

"Yes, sir?" the man said. He seemed harried.

"I want to register a complaint," Polk said.

The sergeant pulled a clipboard filled with forms over to him. "Name and address?" he said tiredly.

Polk gave him the information and the sergeant quickly wrote it on the form.

"Nature of your complaint, sir?"

"It's my dog," Polk said, and the sergeant looked up. "Someone poisoned him."

"Are you sure?"

"Reasonably. I brought the animal to our vet this morning for an autopsy. He thinks it was poisoned."

"I see . . . ," the sergeant said. "When did this happen?"

"Sometime late Friday night or early Saturday morning."

"Why didn't you call sooner?" the sergeant asked. He had stopped writing on the forms.

"I wanted to make sure first," Polk said. This wasn't going right. He suddenly felt foolish.

"I don't know if there'd be anything we can do for you, sir . . . ," the sergeant started, but a tall, husky man in civilian clothes had come up to the counter, and he interrupted.

"What's the trouble, Smitty?"

"You look at it, Lieutenant. This is Mr. Polk. He says his dog was poisoned."

"When?" Klubertanz asked, holding out his hand for the clipboard. The sergeant gave it to him.

"Late Friday night or early Saturday."

Klubertanz quickly scanned the sergeant's notes, then looked up at Polk. "I'm afraid there isn't much we can do for you, Mr. Polk," he said. He put the clipboard back on the counter. "Do you have any other pets, or children?"

Polk shook his head. The sergeant seemed harried, but this one seemed to have the entire world on his shoulders.

"I shouldn't have brought my complaint here."

"On the contrary," Klubertanz said. "We'll make sure the patrol unit for your area is on the alert. And although we may not be able to help you now, if it happens again to someone else's pet in your neighborhood, we may be able to do something."

"But probably not," Polk said.

Klubertanz shrugged. "Probably not," he said. "I hope you understand."

"I do," Polk said. "Thanks anyway."

Cheryl Rader stood at their darkened living-room window in shocked silence as Frank walked down the block and disappeared around the corner. He was limping slightly, his hands were stuffed deeply into his pockets, and his jacket collar was turned up against the chill evening wind.

"Frank," she said, half to herself. She reached up and traced a pattern on the window glass with her right index finger, then leaned forward and laid her head on the cool glass.

The girls were upstairs, watching TV in their own room, and Cheryl supposed they were just as frightened and confused as she was. She knew she should go up to them, to comfort them, to tell them that daddy would be all right, and yet she could not move herself away from the window.

It had started this afternoon. He had asked if she had called Fred and Marion yet to invite them over for cards after the funeral on Wednesday. She had been thinking about it ever since he had made the suggestion Sunday, and she had found the idea in very bad taste. She told him so, and he blew up.

Thinking about this afternoon now made her shiver. Frank had literally gone berserk for a couple of minutes, smashing glasses and bottles in the liquor cabinet, throwing magazines and books around the living room, yelling about how everything was going to hell, even his own wife.

He had calmed down after a while, and had been very apologetic, even charming; the old Frank. The girls had been outside during that outburst, but they hadn't been so lucky this evening. At the dinner table it had happened again. For the same reason.

"I'm not going to invite them anywhere for cards," Cheryl had said firmly. "I just can't. Not the day of their baby's funeral."

The girls were watching the play of emotions across Frank's face. But he didn't say anything at first. For a few moments Cheryl hoped that he was coming around, that he was understanding what she was saying to him.

"They're going to need our help, Frank. But not that kind of . . . ."

Frank jumped up from his chair, knocking it over, picked up his dinner plate, food and all, and threw it across the room at the wall.

"Fuck you, broad!" he screamed, and then he had turned, stomped through the house to the hall closet where he had grabbed his jacket, and then had stormed outside.

"Frank," Cheryl said his name softly as she began to cry by the window. "What's happening to you?"

3

Klubertanz had spent half the night dreaming about his children in trouble. They were drowning in a gravel pit, falling off a cliff, crashing in a car, their little bodies crushed, and finally a faceless man was strangling them, their faces turning blue, and the telephone rang.

He sat up with a start, his body greasy with sweat, and for the first moments he had trouble orienting himself to place or time.

But then, slowly, he held his watch up to his eyes and read the luminous dial; it was a few minutes after three in the morning. The phone rang a second time.

He swung his legs over the edge of the living-room couch, and stumbled across to the phone hanging on the wall in the tiny kitchen.

"Yes," he mumbled, still half in his dreams.

"Lieutenant Klubertanz, this is Sergeant Crebbs, dispatch," the familiar voice came over the phone.

"What have you got?" Klubertanz ran the fingers of his left hand through his thick brown hair.

"Double homicide. Should I call the captain?"

The sleep fully left Klubertanz's brain. "No," he said. "Not yet. Give me what you have and I'll get out there."

"It's an apartment house at 215 West Mifflin. Neighbors called it in a half hour ago. Eighty-two was out there and they went to investigate and found the bodies."

"Shots?"

"No, from what we can gather the neighbors said they heard someone crying."

"Who's out there?"

"The coroner is on his way, and I dispatched the BCI van. Thirty-seven and fifty-eight showed up for backup."

"I'll be there in ten minutes. I don't want anything disturbed."

"Yes, sir," the dispatcher said, and Klubertanz hung up, went into the bathroom and splashed some cold water on his face and ran a comb through his hair.

The remains of a TV dinner in its foil tray still lay on the coffee table and, as he stepped into his loafers and headed for the door, he had to shake his head. Basically, he was a slob, not even making it into his bedroom last night. His bad habits and worse hours were among the reasons Sylvia had left him.

He hurried downstairs and out the front door to where his Alpha Romeo was parked, tossing his gun and jacket in the passenger seat.

From what Klubertanz had read, Madison had been a sleepy college town in the forties and fifties. But all that began to change when the university grew too big. First came the drug subculture during the sixties, then the anti-Vietnam war movement in the seventies had placed Madison in the national news almost daily for a couple of years. The bombing of the Army Mathematics Center, the burning of the American flag on campus.

From a sleepy little college town, Madison had grown, along with the university . . . too large, too fast. And the city, like the college, had its growing pains. Murder among them.

Traffic was almost nonexistent at this hour of the morning, and Klubertanz made it to West Mifflin in a little over five minutes.

The BCI van had already arrived and was parked next to three squad cars, their red lights still flashing. A city ambulance and a civilian car which probably belonged to one of the assistant coroners were parked across the street. A small knot of people had gathered in front of the shabby, two-story apartment house, and to one side a television news crew had already set up its lights and was filming an interview with someone.

Klubertanz parked just behind the van, got out of his car and was pulling on his shoulder holster and jacket when one of the uniformed officers whom he vaguely recognized came over to him.

"The lab people have started their photographs and dusting. The coroner is waiting for you to release the bodies."

Klubertanz glanced at his name tag, and then headed toward the building. "All right, Wallace," he said. "What about the neighbors who made the call?"

"Just over here, sir," the cop said. "Do you want to talk to them first?"

"Sounds like a good idea," Klubertanz said. "IDs on the victims yet?"

"Yes, sir," Wallace said. He pulled out his notebook and flipped it open. "Stanley Shapiro, Bruce Ahern. Both white males. Shapiro was thirty-six, Ahern thirty-five."

They had come around the BCI van, its back doors open, and approached one of the squad cars, next to which stood another uniformed police officer and two college-age girls dressed in bathrobes and slippers. One of them had her hair up in curlers.

"This is Lieutenant Klubertanz," Wallace said, and the girls turned around, their eyes wide. Frightened. It was the neighborhood. More rapes and murders here than anywhere else in Madison. Cheap rent.

"Which one of you ladies made the call?" Klubertanz said, keeping his voice soft.

The girl with the curlers started to raise her hand, then felt foolish about it. "Me," she said in a small voice.

"Why'd you call us?"

"They were crying," she said, almost crying herself.

"People cry," Klubertanz said. "No reason to call the cops."

"No, they were crying like they were hurt or something," the other girl said.

"I see," Klubertanz said. "So then you called us?"

Curlers shook her head. "We went upstairs first, we see what was wrong. We knocked on the door and asked if they needed any help, but they wouldn't answer. They just kept crying."

"But then they stopped, and we got scared, so we called

the . . . you guys," the other girl said.

Klubertanz looked up at the house. The lights were on in the upstairs windows; several people were moving around up there.

"Did you know them well?" he asked, turning back.

"Sort of," Curlers said. "They were nice. Gentle, you know."

"Gay?" Klubertanz asked.

Curlers lowered her head. "Yeah," she said. "But they were nice."

Klubertanz nodded his head. "I'd like both of you to stop down to my office later today. We'll need your statement. Okay?" He pulled out a business card and handed it to Curlers.

"Sure," they both said.

Klubertanz entered the building, then started up the stairs. One of the lab men, his face white, sweat beaded on his upper lip, was coming down.

"That bad?" Klubertanz asked. The other man just nodded.

At the head of the stairs was a short corridor with two doors leading from it. One of them was open and, even from here, he could smell the stench of human defecation. He took a deep breath, held it a moment, and then let it out slowly as he moved down the hall.

Half a dozen men were at work in the small, tastefully decorated living room, and a couple of them looked up as Klubertanz stepped through the door, but no one was saying anything. To the right was a kitchenette, cut flowers in a vase on the tiny table. And to the left was an open door from which a camera strobe flashed once, then again.

Don Maxwell, the Dane County assistant coroner, came out of the room a second later, grim lipped. He spotted Klubertanz.

"Haven't touched anything yet, Stan," he said. "But as a huge favor to me, be quick in there, will you? I want to get this over with."

Klubertanz glanced again toward the open bedroom door. "Any preliminary guesses on cause of death?"

"Shit," Maxwell swore. "A two year old could tell you what they died of from just looking at them."

Klubertanz turned his gaze to the young doctor. "Yes?"

"Disembowelment," he said, "among other things. Broken necks. Ruptured hearts. Suffocation. Their penises were cut off and stuffed down their throats." He shook his head.

"They were homosexuals."

"I figured as much," Maxwell said, "but this isn't any love-triangle murder."

"No?"

"No way, Stan. Whoever did that in there was nuts. I mean completely insane. Another Charlie Manson."

"I'll make it quick," Klubertanz said, steeling himself.

The stench from the open bedroom door was bad in the living room, but just inside the bedroom itself, it was nearly overpowering. Klubertanz gagged despite himself.

The police photographer took a last photograph, then turned and left. Klubertanz was alone with the most gruesome sight he had ever seen in his life.

The bodies—what was left of the bodies—lay side by side on the bed, the sheets completely red with gore. Their heads both had been twisted around so that they were nearly backwards, and from the doorway Klubertanz could see the raw meat of their genitals sticking out of their mouths. Their throats had been slit, and their stomachs and chests laid open, their organs spilling out in piles alongside them, and over the edge of the bed onto the floor.

Klubertanz took a step farther into the room, but then his stomach began to flop over, his mouth suddenly tasted like copper, and he could feel the sweat rolling down his forehead. He turned on his heel and went back out, all the way into the corridor, where he took several deep breaths in a row.

Maxwell had been right. This had been no lovers' quarrel. It was more, much more.

It was just noon when Cheryl Rader pulled the station wagon into Frank's parking slot at Solar Products, Inc., in Femrite Drive.

Frank had come home late last night, but he had gotten up early with the girls and had fixed pancakes, something he had not done for several months.

At breakfast he had been bright, and in very high spirits, a paper sack on his head like a chef's hat, as he flipped the pancakes and sang opera in a deep voice.

Dawn and Felicity had loved every minute of it, and had gotten into his mood so much that they sang opera with him, dancing around the table as they laid out the plates and silverware.

They had gone off to school at eight, kissing their father goodbye. Cheryl had been in the kitchen, loading the dishwasher, when Frank came in dressed in a suit and tie.

"Off to the salt mines," he said, kissing her on the neck.

She turned around and did a double take. She had assumed he would stay home at least another day or two. "You're going to work?"

"Sure," he said, pouring himself a cup of coffee to take with him. "Bill Myers is coming by to pick me up. Should be here any minute. I thought you might need the car today."

"Are you sure you're feeling okay, honey?"

"I've got a little bit of a headache, and I'm still sore as hell, but I'll manage," he said. "I can't sit around here wondering how Surret is taking all this. It's driving me crazy."

A few minutes later, when Myers' Honda Civic had pulled into their driveway, he had kissed Cheryl on the cheek and had left, his step light, a smile on his face.

But at eleven thirty Frank had telephoned from work that he was taking the rest of the day off, and asked Cheryl to come and pick him up.

He came out of the office building now, spotted her and started across the lot. He was limping, and he held his head at a funny angle.

Cheryl slid over to the passenger side of the car, but he came to that side and opened the door.

"You drive,' he said in a choked voice, his face screwed up in a grimace.

"What's the matter?" Cheryl said, fear rising inside her.

"My goddamn head is splitting apart!" he snapped. "I told you I was having headaches. Jesus."

Cheryl slid over behind the wheel. Frank got in the car and softly closed the door.

"Do you want to see the doctor?" she asked.

"Yes," he said, his head slightly cocked. "Just drive carefully."

"All right, honey." Cheryl swung the car out and headed back into town.

As she drove she kept glancing over at her husband. It was obvious he was in pain, and his complexion seemed sallow. She could see that he was holding himself against it. He seemed like a little boy, hurting, in need of comfort.

"Was everything all right at the office?" she asked.

Frank looked at her out of the corner of his eye. "Surret was out of town. He won't be back until later in the week."

"Does he know . . . about the accident?"

"Yeah," Frank said. "There was a race down there to see who could tell him first."

They made it to South Park Street within fifteen minutes, and Cheryl pulled into the lot at The Doctor's Park Center, a block from Madison General.

By the time she was out of the car, Frank had already darted out and was halfway across the lot to the entry; she had to hurry to catch up with him.

Together they went inside, up to the fourth floor, and entered the half-filled reception room.

The nurse looked up and smiled. "Good morning, Cheryl. Mr. Rader."

"Is Doctor Manklin in?" Cheryl asked.

The nurse looked at the chart. "He's with someone

right now."

"It's Frank," Cheryl said. "He's been having terrible headaches since the accident."

"Are you in pain right now, Mr. Rader?"

Frank carefully nodded his head.

"I'll fit him in right away, then." The nurse wrote something on a slip of paper and got up. "Just have a seat, Cheryl," she said. "Come with me, Mr. Rader."

Frank followed the nurse down the corridor, and Cheryl sat in one of the easy chairs, picked up a magazine and started leafing through it.

It had been too soon for Frank to return to work. She had known something like this would happen if he pushed himself. And yet, it had become impossible to tell him anything. The slightest provocation would send him into a rage. The girls were frightened, and Cheryl was deeply worried.

Forty-five minutes later, a nurse came out into the reception room. "Mrs. Rader?" she called.

Cheryl jumped up and went across to her. "What is it?"

The nurse smiled. "Doctor Manklin would like to speak with you for just a moment." She showed Cheryl into the doctor's office.

A couple of minutes later the doctor came in, softly closed the door behind him, and sat down behind his desk.

"What's wrong with Frank?" she asked.

"Nothing terribly wrong, Mrs. Rader," the doctor said. He had pulled out a prescription pad, and wrote something on it. When he was done, he tore the slip off and handed it across to Cheryl. "Get that filled right away. It's for a fairly strong tranquilizer."

"All right," Cheryl said. "But what's wrong with Frank?"

"Besides a few bumps and bruises, nothing more than an aftermath shock," the doctor said. "Fairly common in cases like Frank's."

"I don't understand."

"Your husband was clinically dead for two or three minutes, Mrs. Rader. He is suffering from nothing more than the shock of it, the realization that he was technically dead for a short period."

"Is there . . . ." She couldn't complete the sentence.

"Brain damage?" the doctor asked. She nodded. "No, or at least there's none evident. If you're concerned, I could set up an appointment for him with a neurologist. But I don't think he'd find anything. Frank is in good health. His headaches and nightmares are nothing more than the result of shock."

"Nightmares?" Cheryl asked.

"He hasn't mentioned them to you?"

"No. What kind of nightmares?"

"He didn't go into any great detail," the doctor said thoughtfully. "But from what I gathered he's been having the same dream every night, sometimes more than once in a night, in which he has just died, and is being drawn toward some kind of a strong light in the distance. He's frightened. Just as he is about to see what's beneath the light, he wakes up."

"Does he need a psychiatrist?" Cheryl asked, sitting forward.

"I wouldn't advise it, Mrs. Rader. At least not for the time being. Try the Valium for a couple of weeks, and keep him home from work at least until next Monday."

He rose, and Cheryl did too.

"He's getting a shot now which is going to make him very sleepy. Get him home as soon as possible, and put him to bed. Don't be surprised if he sleeps through until morning."

"We have a funeral to attend tomorrow afternoon," Cheryl said. "Can he go?"

"He may be a bit dopey, but physically he'll be all right. But . . . is it necessary he attend the funeral? It could bring on a fit of depression."

"Our best friends lost their baby," Cheryl said. "We're obligated."

"I see," the doctor said. "I'm sure he'll be all right."

"Thanks," Cheryl said, and she left the office.

Klubertanz' office in the Madison Police Department's Detective Division was a glassed-in cubicle on the basement floor of the City-County Building. He had been swamped with work most of the morning, including giving a brief press conference on the double homicide last night: names, occupations and a watered-down version of the cause of death.

Later in the morning the girls who had heard Shapiro and Ahern crying had shown up to give their statements to a police stenographer. They told Klubertanz that they had given notice, and were moving back on campus, into the dorms.

"Not a bad idea," he had told them. They were nineteen or twenty, with a freshly scrubbed look about them. He wondered if his daughter would look the same when she was their age.

He had sent out three teams of leg men to nail down the ambulance drivers' backgrounds, their friends, relatives, associates; and fill in a minute-by-minute chart of their last forty-eight hours.

Mundane. Routine. Basic police work.

The photographs and BCI van lab work results on the apartment were promised for this afternoon, and he expected that Maxwell would be phoning soon with the results of the autopsy.

Someone knocked once on his door, and he looked up as Brenda Wolfe came in. She was smiling.

"Slumming today, counselor?" Klubertanz sat back in his chair.

She closed the glass door behind her. "I had a hunch you'd forget," she said. She perched on the edge of his desk and looked at him, her eyes bright, guileless. He thought she was a pretty woman.

"Forget what?" he asked.

"It's noon, Stan. Lunch. Remember? You promised to take me to lunch today?"

"Oh, Christ," Klubertanz said, jumping up and looking at his watch. It was nearly twelve thirty. "I'm sorry, Brenda. I've been socked in all morning."

"Ahern and Shapiro?" she asked, the smile leaving her lips for a moment.

Klubertanz nodded.

"Anything promising?"

"Not a damned thing yet. And I've got a feeling this one is going to take a while."

"Well, I've got one bit of good news for you."

"I can use it," Klubertanz said, coming around his desk as he straightened his tie and rolled down his sleeves.

"McDonald called me from the hospital about the Martin baby."

"What'd they find out?" Klubertanz asked.

"The doctor was wrong. It *was* an accident," Brenda said. "They found bits of paint from the crib's bars at the base of the baby's skull. The poor thing evidently got her head caught between the bars and a pillow."

Klubertanz shook his head. "I'm sorry for the parents," he said, thinking about his own children. "But I'm glad it's not going to have to go any further than this. No one wins in a child molestation case."

The telephone on his desk rang, and he picked it up. "Klubertanz."

"This is Maxwell," the assistant coroner's voice came over the line. "There's going to be a delay with the autopsies on the ambulance drivers. Thought I'd better call and let you know."

"Anything I should be aware of?"

"Bunches," Maxwell said, "but we're just not sure yet. We should be ready by tomorrow morning, maybe early tomorrow afternoon. I just don't know."

"Can you give me a hint?"

"Yeah," Maxwell said. "But you wouldn't believe it. I don't, yet. It'll hold until tomorrow."

4

It was dark. There was a chill in the air, and the tiny room smelled of incense. Sister Francine Colletta, a diminutive nun of twenty-six, awoke with her heart pounding and the feeling that something was pressing down on her.

For a long time she lay in the darkness, listening to the sounds of her long-familiar room in the residence hall of downtown Madison's Good Shepherd Church. Over the loud ticking of her cheap alarm clock on the nightstand, she could hear the wind blowing rain against the glass.

"There will never be loneliness in the ordinary sense of the word, when you have the love of a living God in your heart," she had been told in school.

She had believed it then, as she believed it now. And yet she missed her mother, and brothers, and especially she missed her father—his wide gentle eyes, his smells of wool sweaters, pipe tobacco, and leather.

Lying there, Sister Colletta pictured her family as she had seen them at graduation three years ago. Their eyes uplifted. Sad, proud smiles on their faces; pride that she had become a Catholic nun, sorrow that they had finally lost their little girl.

She was lonely, God help her. She was. And yet she could not help it.

She sat up, threw the covers back and swung her legs over the edge of the bed, her feet finding her slippers and stepping into them. The room was ice cold and she was shivering by the time she pulled on her robe.

She was a small girl, five feet three and barely a hundred and five pounds, but she was perfectly proportioned, and had a pretty, scrubbed look about her.

She opened the door and stepped silently out into the dimly lit corridor, hurried down to the residence chapel, and slipped inside.

A half-dozen votive candles were lit in their holders to the right of the tiny altar beneath the statue of the Virgin Mary. A single dim light over the altar itself cast a soft glow over the crucifix on the back wall.

She stared up at Christ's figure on the cross, tears coming to her eyes as she dipped her fingers in the holy water by the door and crossed herself.

"Yours will be the vows of poverty and obedience," her Mother Superior at school had told her. "Chastity and faith. As a nun you will wear a gold band on your ring finger, because in truth you will be wedded to Christ."

But it was lonely at times. Cold. Frightening that the remainder of her life still stretched in front of her with no assurances that she would be able to maintain the goodness of a Mother Superior.

She went forward, knelt at the altar rail, and looked up at the crucifix. Somehow, she still couldn't pray. Her heart still pounded wildly in her chest, her breathing was shallow, and the heavy feeling still pressed in on her.

"Merciful Jesus, help me in my hour of need," she spoke the words softly.

The candles flickered in a chance draft, and without really knowing why, she crossed herself, got to her feet and hurried out of the chapel, back into the corridor.

Her parents had come down from Bay City two weeks ago, for a visit, and Sunday morning, before they left, they had attended mass with her in the main church.

Sister Colletta headed that way now, down the stairs and out into an enclosed courtyard.

It was raining very hard as she dashed across the courtyard, and then into the side doors of the church. A flash of lightning, followed a second later by thunder, rattled the stained-glass windows and reverberated through the huge sanctuary.

Softly she padded down the corridor, her heart pounding, and entered the nave from one of the doors by the confessionals.

From this angle she could only see the side of the altar; she could not see deeply enough into the apse itself to look at the magnificent wooden crucifix that hung from the ceiling far overhead. But she wanted to see it. She needed to kneel before it, and draw the same comfort from the figure she had drawn when her parents had sat next to her two Sundays ago.

She crossed herself again with holy water, and started slowly toward the middle of the church, her head bowed, her hands held together in front of her.

"May the homage of my service be pleasing to Thee, O Holy Trinity," she prayed.

There was a dark patch of something on the floor directly in front of her, and Sister Colletta stopped, her heart pounding even harder. It was blood. She could see that it was blood.

She bent down to dip a finger in it. A shadow cast itself directly in front of her, and she looked up, her own blood running instantly cold, her heart skipping a beat, and her throat constricting so that she could not scream, or even move.

A man, or an apparition, stood in front of her, his arms crossed over his bare chest, a malevolent grin on his lips. On his head and over his shoulders he wore some kind of shaggy fur cape, the figure of a goat's head at the top. He was nude from the waist down.

Something woke Cheryl Rader from a deep sleep. She opened her eyes and looked over at the clock on the nightstand. It was shortly after 3:00 A.M. Rain was spitting aginst the windows. As she turned over, she automatically reached out for Frank, but he wasn't there, and she sat up.

"Frank?" she called. Then she saw him.

He was seated on her dressing-table chair, in front of the windows, dressed only in his pajama bottoms, his face buried in his hands. It sounded as though he was crying.

Cheryl threw the covers off, scrambled out of the bed and hurried around to him. "Frank, what's the matter?"

she asked. She reached out and touched his shoulder. His skin was ice cold, and she recoiled.

"Frank?" she said in a small voice.

He mumbled something indistinct, and Cheryl knelt down in front of him. Gingerly she reached out to pull his hands away from his face, but for a moment she could not bring herself to touch him.

"It hurts," Frank mumbled.

"What hurts, darling? Is it your headache?" The doctor had said he would probably sleep until morning.

"The pain. I want it to go away. I can't stand it."

"Do you want your medicine, Frank?"

"Make it stop."

Cheryl jumped up, hurried into the bathroom, and with shaking hands opened the Valium tablets the doctor had prescribed and shook two out.

She ran some cold water in a glass, and then hurried back into their bedroom. Frank had not moved, and was still mumbling about the pain.

"Here's your pills, darling," she said. She set the water glass down on the windowsill and, holding the pills in one hand, reached up with her other and pulled Frank's hand away from his face. His skin was still ice cold, and horribly clammy to the touch.

She drew his hand down to his side, then pulled his other unresisting hand away from his face, and when he looked up at her she almost screamed.

For a moment he was not Frank. For a terrible moment she was looking into the eyes of a stranger whose face was contorted into a mask of pain and fear. But then it passed. His features softened, melting back into her Frank.

"There," she said shakily, placing the tablets in his hand. "Take these right now; they'll make your headache go away."

She turned for the water glass, but Frank had already put the pills in his mouth, chewed them once and then swallowed them.

Cheryl put the water back, then helped Frank up from the chair and over to the bed. She pulled the covers up over him, sat down beside him, and brushed his hair away from his forehead. "It will be better in just a little while. But you have to sleep. Let the pills work, Frank."

He was looking up at her, and although he was Frank again, Cheryl had the feeling that there was no recognition in his eyes.

"What's happening to me?" he croaked.

Cheryl wanted to get into the bed and snuggle close to him, to comfort him, but she could not bring herself to do it. He was too cold, his skin almost oily.

"Sleep now," she said. "It will get better. I promise you." she said. "We'll see the doctor again. It'll get better."

Frank's eyes fluttered and then closed, and after a while his breathing deepended and the grimace that had contorted his face went slack.

For a long time, Cheryl stared down at her husband, worry, concern, confusion in her mind. Something had changed him. And she decided that she would take the doctor's offer to set up an appointment with a neurologist.

After a while she got up from the bed and went over to the window, where she picked up the water glass. She looked outside, but for a moment what she was seeing did not register. It didn't make any sense. When she awakened, it had been raining. She was sure of it. The wind had been blowing the rain against the house.

But the streets were dry! No breeze rustled the trees! It had not rained!

Monsignor Dominic Ferrari, dressed in his vestments, stepped outside, into the chill morning air, clasped the rosary entwined in his fingers, and started across the courtyard to the church.

Behind him he could hear the soft shuffle of seven other priests heading for morning mass. It was just 6:00 A.M., and this was a seven-day-a-week routine.

Comforting, Msgr. Ferrari, a man in his mid-sixties, thought. The Church and her rituals were a comforting oasis in a world of crises.

Sometimes as many as twenty priests attended morning mass here at Good Shepherd, but in the fall, at the beginning of school, with all the other projects that traditionally were begun then, the numbers dropped for a time.

Sad, Msgr. Ferrari had always thought, that his own brothers couldn't find the time in their schedules for a simple mass. It was the wellspring of his peace of mind, of his direction and reassurance, and of his reaffirmation of faith.

In Amelia, his small hometown north of Rome, he had been an altar boy. And from the first time he had participated in the mass, he had known a comfort that went beyond ordinary words.

Through Mussolini's era, his faith had never wavered, nor had it been shaken when he was sent away from his beloved Italy, here to the United States, twenty years ago.

One of the younger priests stepped ahead and opened the side doors to the church and the others filed in, Msgr. Ferrari in the lead.

At the doorway to the nave, they stopped a moment in silent prayer, then softly moved into the church, dipping their hands in the holy water and crossing themselves before they started, heads bowed, to the altar.

Monsignor Ferrari was the chief administrator for church activities and programs in this section of Madison, and his work included the direction of a dozen social workers, two family psychologists, and the staffs of two parochial schools, as well as this church itself.

His days were never dull, never completely peaceful, and certainly never free from strife. For him it would have been inconceivable to begin a day without mass, just as it would have been impossible to live without food or water. The offertory was his reason for existence.

"We offer Thee, O Lord, the chalice of salvation," he prayed, head lowered, "beseeching Thy clemency that it may ascend before Thy divine majesty with the odor of sweetness for our salvation and that of the whole world."

"Merciful Jesus," someone behind him said, and Msgr. Ferrari was confused. The words did not belong.

"My God!" someone else said, much louder. Monsignor Ferrari looked up, angry with the unreasoning sacrilege, ready to lash out, but then he saw it, and he could feel the blood rushing to his face, his knees suddenly weak.

Sister Colletta, or what remained of her nude, mutilated body, was tied, spreadeagle, to the crucifix hanging from the ceiling above the altar. Her blood had splashed down on the white linen altar cloth, and for a long moment Msgr. Ferrari simply could not believe his eyes. It was a sight from hell.

His heart fluttered in his chest, his breath came in ragged gasps, and he could feel his bowels loosening.

He tried to speak, but nothing would come out. He crossed himself, repeatedly, until strong hands took him by the arms, and physically turned him away.

"Quickly, brother, call an ambulance," someone was saying, and Msgr. Ferrari looked up; one of the younger priests was issuing orders.

"Call the police as well."

Priests were running away down the aisle, *running in the church*, as the others led Msgr. Ferrari back out into the cool morning air.

"Are you all right, Reverend Father?" someone was asking him. It was his heart. They were worried that he would die.

He managed to nod his head.

"We'll take you back to your quarters," the priest was saying, but Msgr. Ferrari managed to straighten up and pull away from their grasp.

"If the police are coming, I will see them," he said in a surprisingly clear voice. He half turned to look back at the church entrance, and then he shuddered. Five hundred years ago such a thing was conceivable. But today? Here? Impossible.

As the ambulance carrying the body of the young nun pulled away, Lt. Klubertanz closed his notebook and pocketed it. For a time he stood quietly in the courtyard, listening to the sounds of the city through the gate that opened on West Washington Avenue. Murder never made any sense, but this one was worse than most. Meaningless. Brutal.

"Busy week," someone said behind him. Klubertanz glanced to his right; Don Maxwell had come out of the church, lit a cigarette, and tossed the match aside.

"What do you make of it?" Klubertanz said softly, holding his anger in check.

Maxwell shook his head. "I'm the coroner, you're the cop."

Klubertanz waited. Although he didn't know Maxwell on a social basis, they had worked together for the past couple of years, and had built up a mutual respect and trust.

"If you want me to tell you that this is the work of the same crazy who snuffed the two ambulance drivers, you're going to have to wait until this afternoon. I might have something for you then."

"No hints?"

"Like I said before, Stan, bunches, but we're just not sure yet. It's sorta crazy."

Klubertanz knew enough not to push the man, not this early in the investigation, but when he had seen the nun's body hanging from the crucifix, he had felt instantly and very strongly that this was the work of the same person who had killed Ahern and Shapiro. He didn't know yet why he felt that, but the connection was there, nevertheless.

"I'll be in my office after lunch," Klubertanz said. "Call me as soon as you can talk."

"Sure thing," Maxwell said.

Klubertanz went across the courtyard and entered the residence hall. A priest just coming down the corridor directed him to Msgr. Ferrari's office at the front of the building.

His secretary was in the outer office talking on the phone; Klubertanz waited respectfully until the young priest was finished.

"I'd like to speak with the Monsignor," Klubertanz

said.

The priest looked up at him, grim lipped. "You're Lieutenant Klubertanz?"

Klubertanz nodded.

"The Reverend Father is waiting for you," the priest said, getting up from behind his desk, and opening a wide wooden door. "He's here," he said, sticking his head inside.

"Send him in," a frail old voice came from within, and the priest opened the door wide.

Monsignor Ferrari was getting to his feet as Klubertanz entered the huge, well-decorated office. The priest softly closed the door behind him.

"Please sit down, Monsignor," Klubertanz said.

" 'Father' will be sufficient," the old man said, sinking back into his chair. He was wearing a black hassock with white buttons up the front, and a skull cap on the back of his head. His face was pale, and his hands shook.

Klubertanz took a seat across the wide, leather-topped desk from the prelate, and for a moment both men just looked at each other.

Finally, Klubertanz spoke. "If this is too painful for you, Father, I could come back later."

Monsignor Ferrari gestured with his right hand. "You have your work to do, my son. The sooner you have what information you need, the sooner you will be able to start."

"I have most of what I need, Father," Klubertanz began, "but it would be helpful for our investigation if I could see Sister Colletta's personal file."

"A copy will be provided you," the priest said.

"I'd also like permission to speak with her friends and coworkers here."

Monsignor Ferrari nodded. "You may speak with anyone you wish." He bowed his head, unable for a moment to continue.

"I know this is difficult for you, Father. Perhaps it would be better if I returned later."

The priest looked up, a defiant expression in his eyes.

"Centuries ago, things . . . like this were common."

"How so?" Klubertanz asked.

The priest glanced away for a moment. "During the dark ages, there was a persecution of our people. Witchcraft, demonology, evil . . . all common. We were the target."

Klubertanz pulled his notebook out and flipped it open to the last page, checking what he had written.

"There was an inscription on the floor of the altar."

"Yes?" the priest said. Klubertanz had the momentary impression the old man knew what was coming.

"It's in Latin, I think."

"How was it written?"

"What do you mean, Father?"

"Was it written in . . . blood?" the old priest said very softly.

Klubertanz nodded, and the priest seemed to turn even paler. He held out his hand for the notebook, and Klubertanz handed it over.

Monsignor Ferrari pulled a pair of wire-rimmed glasses from a pocket in his robe, carefully put them on, and then looked down at what Klubertanz had copied. The sixteen words had been written in the young nun's blood in large, bold letters on the marble floor of the apse just in front of the altar table.

"*Haec commixtio, et consecratio Corporis et Sanguinis Domini nostri* . . . ," the old priest began softly in Latin, but he could not go on. He laid the notebook down, took off his glasses and wiped his eyes with a badly shaking hand.

"What does it mean, Father?" Klubertanz asked. "What do the words say?"

"Are you familiar with the Catholic Mass, Lieutenant?"

"Only slightly."

Monsignor Ferrari nodded, but Klubertanz noticed that he carefully avoided looking down at the notebook. "The main point of the mass is the symbolic recreation of the Last Supper, at which our Lord consecrated the bread they ate, telling His disciples that it was His body, and consecrating the wine they drank, telling them it was His blood. We celebrate it with wafers of unleavened bread and red wine. Communion, it is called."

Klubertanz nodded, but said nothing, allowing the priest to gather his thoughts.

"At one moment in the mass, the priest breaks the wafer and it is comingled, as we say, with the wine. Body and blood. A prayer is said then. The most sacred . . . ." He had to stop.

Klubertanz held his silence. He could feel the hairs at the nape of his neck bristling.

"In English, we would say: May this commingling and consecration of the body and blood of our . . . Lord Jesus Christ, avail us who receive it unto life everlasting."

"Is that what is written, Father?" Klubertanz asked.

Monsignor Ferrari shook his head. "Instead of 'unto life everlasting,' the Latin says 'unto eternal damnation.'"

A chill played up Klubertanz's spine. "Any other differences?"

Monsignor Ferrari took a deep breath and let it out slowly, as if he was girding himself for a very difficult task. "Substituted for the words 'our Lord Jesus Christ,' are . . . ." He stopped again. "Are *'Domini nostri Astaroth,'* . . . our Lord Astaroth."

The priest crossed himself, closed Klubertanz's notebook and handed it back.

"What is Astaroth?" the detective said.

"In demonology, he is said to be the destroyer. The evil one. The devil, or one of his archangels."

"Witchcraft?"

Monsignor Ferrari seemed on the verge of collapse. "Someone said all or part of a black mass on our altar," he managed to stammer, and he buried his face in his hands and began to weep.

5

Clinton Polk stood next to his wife and the Raders as the pitifully small coffin was lowered into the grave. It was a lovely afternoon. The sun was shining and a light, warm breeze blew from the southwest.

"Dust to dust, ashes to ashes," the minister intoned, as Fred Martin held his wife in his arms. She was crying, although the doctor had given her a sedative, but Fred was stony faced.

Clinton's wife, Susan, linked her arm in his as she dabbed at her eyes with a handkerchief, and he could feel the lump rising in his throat.

"We return the soul of the baby Jessica Martin, O Lord, to your care for everlasting happiness . . . ."

There were only a few cars parked below on the road through this section of Roselawn Cemetary, among them the hearse, the funeral-home limousine, the Raders' station wagon, the Polks' BMW, and half-a-dozen others belonging mostly to relatives of Fred and Marion.

There had been no time, Polk thought, for little Jessica to make friends, to have acquaintances, to have past loves, or brothers and sisters, or any of the other rewards of a long, full life. None of that was represented here. Only a cheated fate.

Polk thought briefly about his own mortality; wondered about his own funeral, and what it would be like; who would attend, and what words would be said afterwards.

He looked down at Susan at the same moment she looked up. She shook her head slightly, more tears coming, and then looked away.

The minister closed his book and came around the open

grave to the Martins, where he said something to them, holding Marion's hand.

Words of condolence, of comfort, Polk thought. And yet, what could he say to help? What could any of them say?

As the others started back down to the cars, Susan broke away and went over to Marion. Along with Cheryl, they moved slowly toward the path, and Polk waited for Fred to come over. Frank had moved to the open grave and stared down into it.

"Are you coming to the house, Clinton?" Fred Martin asked.

Polk looked away from Radar, and into his friend's eyes. There was something there, or rather some lack. Not enough grief? Worry? Or was it guilt?

"Are you sure it's what Marion wants?" Polk heard himself asking. He felt detached.

Martin was nodding. "I think she needs to be with friends right now. I think we both do."

Polk reached out and squeezed Fred's shoulder. "Sure thing," he said. "We'll follow you over. Are Frank and Cheryl coming too?"

Martin looked over at Radar by the open grave. "I think so," he said. "I hope so." He looked back. "Frank wants . . . wanted to have us all over tonight. To play cards."

Polk was dumbfounded. He had forgotten about the crazy call he had gotten yesterday, but he had never suspected that Frank would have been stupid enough to call Fred and Marion.

"There's something wrong with him," Martin said. "Something different."

Polk glanced at Radar again. He had been too wrapped up in his own problems recently to notice anything wrong with his friends. But standing there now, looking over at Frank, he couldn't help but wonder. Since the accident Frank *had* been different. Distant. Moody. Strange.

Rader looked their way, almost as if he knew they were staring at him, glanced once again into the open grave and then came over to them. He had a bewildered look in his eyes.

"I'm sorry, Fred," he said, his voice choked. "For you and Marion. I wish . . . ."

"I understand," Martin said softly. "Thank you."

For a minute they were all silent.

"I want to apologize for yesterday," Rader said. "To both of you. I don't know what got into me. I just thought that maybe we should all be together tonight."

Something *was* wrong with him, Polk thought. It seemed almost as if he was in pain. "Are you all right, Frank?"

Rader nodded. "I'll be okay. It's just that I've been getting these . . . headaches since the accident."

"Are you seeing a doctor?" Polk asked.

"Yeah. He gave me some Valium. Doesn't help the headaches, they just make it seem like I'm floating."

That was it, Polk thought. It was because of the pills he was taking.

"Marion and I thought we'd have you all over to the house now," Martin said, "but if you'd rather not—"

"It's all right," Rader said. "We'll follow you over."

"You're sure?"

Rader nodded. "That's what friends are for."

Together the three of them went down the path. Cheryl and Susan were waiting by the limousine; Marion had already gotten in the back seat. Both women hugged and kissed Fred and then he climbed in beside his wife. Frank closed the door, and the limousine pulled away.

"Are you and Frank going over there?" Susan asked Cheryl, who looked at her husband.

"I think so," she said.

"We'll follow you and Clinton," Frank said.

As they drove across town Polk asked his wife how Marion was holding up.

"I don't know. It's too soon to tell, I guess."

Polk had not told her about Frank's crazy suggestion that they get together for cards tonight. It would have worried and upset her. But now he wondered if he shouldn't ask Cheryl about it.

"How's Fred taking it?" Susan asked, breaking into his thoughts.

"I don't think he's accepted it yet. But he'll come through all right. It's Marion I'm worried about."

"I know." Susan stared moodily out the window. "I guess it was pretty bad when she lost her first husband and boys. And now this." She shook her head.

Polk reached out and patted his wife's knee. She looked at him, her eyes wide, and a little moist.

"We're okay, aren't we, Clinton?" The question startled him.

"What do you mean?"

"I mean about the lab. Your grant is going to be continued, isn't it?"

Polk's jaw tightened as he thought about it. Administration and science never seemed to mix. They were like oil and water together. Yet the administrators were the ones holding the purse strings. "We'll know in the next few days," he said.

"What if it doesn't go through?" Susan asked.

"Don't worry about it," he said, wondering for just a moment if he even wanted to continue. Did he really want the project to go through? Did he? He managed a smile. "Worst comes to worst, I'll sell out to the Philistines, and go to work for Dow, Monsanto, Lilli or someone like that. Big bucks. Regular vacations. New car. The whole bit."

"And you'd be miserable."

Polk stopped himself from snapping that he was miserable now, so what difference would it make, and they drove in silence the rest of the way to the Martins' pretty, ranch-style house.

The limousine was parked in the driveway along with several other cars, so Polk parked on the street. Frank and Cheryl pulled up a moment later.

"Let's not stay very long, okay?" Polk said. "I'm a little tired."

"Me too," Susan said. "I didn't sleep worth a damn last night."

They started across the street, expecting Frank and

Cheryl to be right behind them, but the Raders held back by their car.

"You two coming in?" Polk called.

Cheryl looked over. "Go on in, Clinton, we'll be right there."

For a moment Polk looked across at them, a funny feeling playing up the base of his spine. Frank had his back turned to them, and was looking at something down the street. Polk glanced that way, but there was nothing there except a couple of parked cars, and at the end of the block a stop sign.

He shrugged, and he and Susan went up the walk, rang the bell and let themselves in.

The gathering was subdued, and although Cheryl and Susan had wanted to do the coffee-making and serving of sandwiches and snacks, Marion wouldn't allow it.

"It's my house and my guests, I'll do it," she had said stubbornly.

"Once she stops, it's going to hit her right between the eyes, poor dear," her sister from Detroit told Polk.

Fred was at the bar mixing drinks. Except for the fact no one was smiling, and the noise level in the room was low, this could have been a party.

Each time Marion came in from the kitchen, everything in the room stopped, until she had filled coffee cups, laid out more food or emptied an ashtray or two. When she was gone, conversations began again, and Fred continued mixing drinks.

It was strange, Polk thought. Strange and uncomfortable. And he felt very much out of place.

He got a refill on his brandy and water from Fred, and moved across the room to where Frank was seated by himself, staring morosely toward the opening to the hallway.

"How're you doing, Frank?" he asked, perching on the chair next to his.

Frank jerked almost as if he had been hit, but he did not look up. "It happened in there," he mumbled.

Polk didn't quite catch it, and he leaned forward in his chair. "What's that?"

"In there," Frank said a little more closely. "The baby. She was killed in there."

Polk's stomach flopped over. "Jesus," he swore, looking around to make sure no one else had heard it, especially not Marion or Fred. "What the hell's the matter with you?"

Frank suddenly jumped up from his chair. "In there," he said loudly.

Everyone in the room stopped talking and looked up.

Polk got up, set his drink down and grabbed Frank's arm, to force him to sit down, but Frank pulled away and rushed across the living room and down the corridor.

"The baby was killed in here," he shouted at the top of his lungs.

Polk raced after him; Fred dropped the liquor bottle he was holding.

"The baby!" Frank screamed. "My God, the baby!" He had reached the baby's room, where he barged through the door and stopped just inside.

Polk reached him a second later, Fred and the others right behind him.

"Frank?" Polk said, stepping closer.

Rader turned to face them all, his face white and beaded with sweat, his eyes wide and filled with fear, his mouth contorted into an ugly grimace.

"The baby!" he screamed again. "The baby was killed here! Oh God, can't you see?"

"Frank?" Cheryl cried, pushing through the knot of people at the door.

Frank backed up a step, his eyes fluttered, and he grabbed at his head with both hands and sank to the floor, crying in pain and agony.

Outside it had clouded up and it began to rain but no one noticed that, nor did they notice Marion, who stood at the end of the corridor, her eyes wide, her right hand to her mouth as if to stifle a scream, as she stared at her husband standing in the doorway with the others.

It was just past 5:00 P.M. when Klubertanz arrived at the Dane County Morgue, parked his car and hurried up the steps and inside. It had been a lovely day, weatherwise, but he was tired from his interrupted sleep of the last two nights, and in a sour, foul mood.

Murder was bad enough. But three of them within a twenty-four-hour period, and all of them gruesome, was just too much to take.

Maxwell was waiting for him just outside his office, a strange, pensive look on his face.

"I waited all goddamned afternoon for you to call," Klubertanz snapped, his leather heels barking hollowly on the marble floor.

"Sorry," Maxwell mumbled.

"What the hell gives? Two-hour lunches?"

"Take it easy, Stan," Maxwell said. "I wasn't about to call you until I was completely sure."

"So now you're sure . . . ."

Maxwell was shaking his head. "No, I'm not. None of us are."

"What are you talking about?" Klubertanz asked. He had been feeling strange ever since he had been called out on the Shapiro-Ahern murders. The feeling had come on again at the church, and now it was like a big bass drum booming in his head.

"Let's go downstairs," Maxwell said. "I'll try to explain what we've come up with . . . or haven't."

They went down through a metal door marked NO ADMITTANCE, and along a long corridor with gleaming, white-tiled walls and highly polished floors.

Maxwell led the way through a set of swinging doors into a large room, one end of which was dominated by refrigerated body drawers. A steel rollabout table, a white sheet folded neatly on it, was standing beneath a large plateglass window that opened to the viewing room. The window was blocked now by curtains.

Klubertanz had been down here more than once. He had never liked it, and he liked it even less now.

Just inside the door was a steel desk with a single chair behind it. Maxwell opened one of its drawers and took out a bottle of bourbon and two coffee cups.

"Drink?" He asked opening the bottle.

Klubertanz looked toward the body boxes and shrugged. "Why not? You're going to take your time telling me whatever it is you're going to tell me, anyway."

Maxwell poured whiskey in both cups, handed Klubertanz one, then picked up the other and took a deep drink of it, shuddering as the whiskey went down.

Klubertanz did the same, then sighed deeply. "I'm here, Don."

Maxwell managed a nervous smile, and seemed to think for a moment about what he was going to say. "What do you know about death, Stan?"

Klubertanz started to protest, but Maxwell held him off.

"No, I'm serious. What do you know about death? I'm talking about clinical death."

"The courts haven't figured that one out yet."

"I know," Maxwell said, nodding his head. He glanced over at the body boxes. "They're all dead in there," he said softly, and he turned back. "There's two kinds of death . . . somatic and molecular. The first is nothing more than the cessation of normal functions. Heart stops. Lungs stop. Brain waves go flat."

"Put them on a heart-lung machine, and they're technically not dead . . . at least as far as the law is concerned."

"Right," Maxwell said, "which leads us to molecular death, which is when the individual cells of the body cease functioning. No electrochemical actions. No heat produced. The body cools. Putrefaction begins, unless we hold it back for a little while with formaldehyde."

"All right, I'm with you," Klubertanz said. He took another sip of his drink, the liquor warming his insides. The room was chilly, and smelled nauseatingly of antiseptic and something else he didn't want to think about.

"Which brings us to our problem," Maxwell said softly.

"Shortly after somatic death—true somatic death—when the individual cells begin winking out in molecular death, a number of the body's natural acids begin accumulating in the tissue. The protoplasm in the cells begins to coagulate, and what we call rigor mortis sets in."

"The body gets cold and stiff."

"Yeah," Maxwell said thoughtfully. He looked up a moment later. "Rigor mortis doesn't always happen. Sometimes it takes as long as a day, but it takes at least hours."

"Not a very reliable method of determining time of death."

"Totally unreliable," Maxwell said. He placed his cup firmly on the desk. "The problem with Ahern, Shapiro and Sister Colletta is placing their time of death with any degree of accuracy."

"I'm not following you," Klubertanz said. "Witnesses heard the ambulance drivers crying. You showed up a few minutes later. Maybe an hour elapsed."

Maxwell was nodding. "Both of them were stiff. Cold and stiff. Huge accumulations of acid in the body, and in every tissue we tested, the protoplasm had coagulated."

"What are you saying, Stan?"

"Rigor mortis had set in at least twelve, maybe twenty-four hours, before we arrived."

"Impossible."

"Agreed. Digested food in their stomach put their time of death around the time the girls called us. Maybe an hour before we arrived."

Klubertanz was having a difficult time with this, but he knew what was coming. "And the nun? It was the same with her body?"

Maxwell nodded. "Some of the tissues in her body had already begun to rot. As if she had been dead for thirty-six hours."

"Impossible."

Again Maxwell nodded. "You're damned right it's impossible, Stan, but the tests don't lie."

"Run them again."

"What the hell do you think took us so long?" Maxwell shouted. "We ran the goddamned tests a dozen times. Every time, we came up with exactly the same results."

Klubertanz finished the liquor in his cup, grabbed the bottle, and poured himself and Maxwell another drink. "Is there anything you know of, Don, any condition or drug, that could cause those symptoms?"

"Plenty. We tested for them as well. Negative."

"You're the coroner; what are you telling me?"

Maxwell was silent as he perched on the edge of the desk, his cup cradled in both hands. "I'm establishing the time of death according to witnesses and the other symptomology of the body. Stomach contents, coagulation of the blood and things like that. And I'm listing the cause of death in each case as numerous massive injuries."

"How about the rigor mortis?"

Maxwell looked up and shook his head. "No way, Stan. That's between you and me, and that's as far as it's going to go." He took a sip of his drink. "Every cause has an effect. I've seen an effect for which there is no known cause. But it does give us one safe bet."

"Which is?"

"Whoever killed the ambulance attendants, also killed the nun."

6

It was Monday. The girls were at school and Frank was at work. The incredible week had come and gone. Cheryl Rader sat drinking coffee at the kitchen table, smiling. Everything was going to be all right now. Finally.

Wednesday night they had taken Frank to the hospital, and all day Thursday the neurologist had run tests on him, with totally negative results.

On Friday they had gone out to a movie, stopping for a pizza later, and over the weekend Frank had recarpeted their basement rec-room, pressing the girls into service, while Cheryl did the fetching of everything from carpet glue to beer and pop.

Yesterday he had telephoned Fred and Marion to apologize for his bizarre behavior after the funeral, and when he got off the phone he was smiling, and his eyes were moist.

"What'd they say?" Cheryl had asked him when he came back into the living room.

Frank had come over, sat down next to her on the couch and put his arm around her. "We all thought Marion was the one who would be needing the help and understanding?"

Cheryl nodded.

"Well, she's the one giving it out." He'd shaken his head. "God, I was such an asshole." He had looked into Cheryl's eyes. "She said it was all right. Told me to forget about it, and told me to hurry up and get better from the accident. She said that they missed me."

Cheryl felt a warm glow thinking about it. She had her husband back, and the Martins were going to be all right after all.

She drank the last of her coffee, rinsed the cup out at the sink, and headed upstairs to start her housework. She was halfway through the dining room when the front doorbell rang.

A salesman, she thought, going to the door. They always managed to show up when her hair wasn't fixed, no makeup, ratty old housecoat.

The bell rang again just as she opened the door. "Not interested . . . ." She choked off the words.

Marion Martin stood on the doorstep, a strange, unsettled look in her red-rimmed eyes. Her hair was a mess, her lipstick smeared, and she was dressed in a sweatshirt, jeans and a pair of sneakers. She looked like hell.

"Good God, Marion, what's wrong?" Cheryl said, taking her friend by the arm and leading her into the house.

"I have to talk to you, Cheryl," said said, her voice husky. "We have to talk."

"Of course we will," Cheryl said, leading Marion into the kitchen, where she poured coffee for both of them.

"Have you got anything stronger?" Marion asked. "Something to put in the coffee?"

"Stronger?" Cheryl realized what her friend wanted. "For God's sake, Marion, it's only nine o'clock in the morning."

"I know," Marion said, hanging her head. "It's just that . . . ."

"Just a minute; I'll get you something," Cheryl said, and she hurried to the living room where she rummaged around in the liquor cabinet, coming up with a half-full bottle of Almadén brandy.

She was frightened now. It wasn't like Marion. At parties her friend hardly ever had more than a couple of drinks, and those weak. In fact, it was a friendly joke with all of them. They'd mimic her: "Make it a light one."

Back in the kitchen, she poured a little brandy into Marion's cup, set the bottle on the counter, and then took her seat. Her friend sipped noisily at the laced coffee.

"Now what's happened, Marion?"

"I don't know, Cheryl."

"What do you mean, you don't know?"

"It's so crazy. It's just different. I don't know what to do, or what to say or who to turn to." Marion closed her eyes for a second, took a deep breath and let it out slowly.

"Is it about the . . . about your baby?"

Marion nodded. "And Fred and Frank."

Something clutched at Cheryl's gut. "Wednesday afternoon, Marion . . . Frank is sorry, he didn't know what he was doing. The doctor said it was because of his accident."

Marion stared at her, no warmth in her eyes. "It started out with Fred," she said, as if she hadn't heard Cheryl. "He's been worried about his job. Some advertising contract they've been having trouble with."

There was something wrong, something very wrong. Cheryl could feel it thick in the air, and she wanted to tell Marion to go away and leave her alone. The weekend had been so pleasant. Please, dear God, she thought, please don't change that.

Marion was continuing, her voice still husky. "Before the funeral, Fred told me that he thought he was going crazy. Said he thought he should see a psychiatrist."

"Because of his work?" Cheryl could not help asking.

Marion shook her head. "Because of our baby. He said he couldn't feel sorry that she was dead."

Cheryl bit her knuckle. She didn't want to hear this! But she couldn't help herself.

"He didn't go to a psychiatrist, though, Cheryl. Instead, he talked to your Frank."

"Frank?" Cheryl mumbled. She was cold.

"Frank filled his head with insane gibberish. Yesterday on the phone. And Fred is beginning to believe it. We argued all night."

"What kind of gibberish?" Cheryl asked.

"It's about our baby. Frank told my husband that he knew a way to contact our baby."

Cheryl stared at her friend. Fear. Confusion. Worry. And an ache beginning deep inside her.

"He wants to contact our dead baby!" Marion suddenly screamed. "My God, the man is insane!"

"Marion . . . I . . ." Cheryl started, but Marion cut her off.

"Fred is beginning to believe he can do it. He almost had me convinced this morning, Cheryl. What can I do?"

"Frank couldn't have said that. Are you sure you heard Fred correctly?"

"Don't say that to me! Jesus Fucking Christ, Cheryl, *don't say that to me!*"

Cheryl's heart was pounding out of her chest. She didn't know what to say or do. What was happening? What in hell was happening?

It was shortly after 10:00 P.M., Monday, when Clinton and Susan Polk returned from the movies. He was tired, but pleasantly so. For a change, everything had gone smoothly at the lab. Three test results they had anxiously been awaiting had come back positive, which indicated they were heading in the right direction.

The words of his major professor ran through his mind: "There must be years of hard work before a breakthrough of any significance comes about." Well, he had put the years in, and now it was time for that "significant breakthrough."

They were so close he could feel it. Just a little more time. A little longer with the funding. They had weathered all sorts of storms: the annual budget dry-up; the general lack of trained, dedicated personnel; the sudden addition of a teaching load last year; and the brief whirl or negative publicity when the newspaper discovered that the Genetic Research Lab was playing around with cloned viruses. All of that had come and gone, each year the project growing a little larger, a little stronger. But now the Regents had stepped in and were fiddling with the flow of Washington money.

He was staring into the open refrigerator without really seeing the contents, when Susan came in from the living room.

"Should I put on some coffee?" she asked.

He pulled out a can of beer. "Not for me," he said,

closing the refrigerator. "I'm going to drink this, then take a quick shower and go to bed."

"Tomorrow's the big day?" she asked.

He nodded. "The Regents met this evening. Willis said he'd have their answer for me first thing in the morning."

She got serious for a moment. "What happens if they cut off your funding?"

Polk shrugged. "Like I said, sweetheart, I'll probably go to work for one for the big chemical companies."

"I'm serious, Clinton," she said.

"So am I," he said, opening the beer. "Our money will last through the end of this phase, which we should complete before Thanksgiving. After that, I'd be on my own. I'd probably wait until after the end of the semester and then start looking."

"Is that—"

The telephone rang. Susan answered it. "Hello."

Clinton took another drink of the cold beer. Susan turned toward him.

"Yes he is, Doctor Willis," she said. "Just a moment." She held the phone out to him, and Clinton put his beer down on the counter, went across the room and took it from her.

"Good evening, Doctor Willis," he said pleasantly. Willis was his department head.

"I'm glad I caught you home, Clinton," the older man said. "The Regents finished up just a couple of minutes ago."

"What'd they do?" Polk asked, his heart accelerating.

"Well, I've got some good news and some bad news," Dr. Willis said. "The general feeling is not to continue your project."

"Did they read my report?" Polk asked, suddenly angry. "Do they realize just how close we are?"

"Simmer down, Clinton. That's the bad news; I did say I had some good news as well."

Polk waited.

"Although they're disinclined to continue your project, they decided to table it for further study."

"Which means what, Doctor Willis?"

"Which means they're giving you a little more time to strengthen your case," the older man said. "It's up to you now to convince them that the project is not only important, but that it poses no danger."

"Danger to whom?" Clinton said, trying his damndest to control his anger.

"In Farnsworth's words, they're afraid that there'll be an accident. Someone will inadvertently dump one of your creations down the drain, and some kind of a monster will grow in the sewers."

"Christ," Polk said. "They *didn't* read my report. Every virus we work with is genetically tagged for a lifespan of less than twenty-four hours."

"Exactly," Willis said. "But Farnsworth wasn't budging. A lot can happen in twenty-four hours, he said."

Polk wanted to argue his case right now, but he knew it came down to the simple fact that if he wanted the project to continue, he was going to have to coddle the Regents. It meant another round of report writing, even more time away from his work.

"Thanks for calling, Doctor Willis," he said, managing to maintain his control.

"It's not the end yet, Clinton," Willis said. "I want to see you in my office first thing in the morning. We'll put our heads together and see what we can come up with."

"See you in the morning," Polk said.

"You know, I believe in what you're doing just as much as you do. It's work that has to be done. And will be done."

"Yes, sir," Polk said.

"See you in the morning, then. Good night."

"Good night." Polk hung up. For several long seconds he just stood there, until Susan broke the silence.

"Well?" she said.

"They didn't axe the grant money, but they're still thinking about it."

"That's wonderful, darling," she said, coming across

the room to him.

"Just a stay of execution," he said glumly. "They want me to plead my case."

"Then plead it, Clinton."

Polk shook his head. "I don't know if I want to anymore!"

"Don't be a silly goose," Susan said. She took him by the hand and led him out of the kitchen. "When you finish with them, they'll not only extend your grant, they'll probably double it."

Together they went upstairs. As Clinton took his shower, the hot water streaming down on his body, he tried to let his mind relax, tried to stop the worry from eating at his gut. But it was a losing battle, just as the battle with the Regents would eventually be lost.

Damn it, he had a real contribution to make to science. To pure science, not the technology of products that industry was so interested in, and certainly not the middle-of-the-road course the Regents advocated.

When he was finished, he dried off, brushed his teeth, and then the bath towel wrapped around his waist, went back into the bedroom.

Susan had turned the lights low, had flipped the covers back, and was lying nude in the bed, a lascivious smile on her face.

She had a lovely body; long, well-shaped legs, a slightly rounded tummy and large, perfectly-formed breasts. Her nipples were hard, and Clinton had to smile despite his worry.

"That's your answer for everything, isn't it?" he said gently. He didn't feel like having sex, but she obviously did.

"Take that silly towel off and come to bed, Clinton," she said, her voice husky.

He hesitated a moment, and she rose, came over to him, pulled the towel away and led him back to the bed, where she made him lie down on his back. She was all over him, kissing his neck and his chest as she moved her pubis up and down his leg, but he wasn't responding.

Without the grant money, he'd be finished at the university. There was no need for a scientist without a project.

"Clinton?" Susan whispered.

He reached down and caressed her back. "I'm sorry," he said.

She kissed his belly, then his legs, and finally took him in her mouth, but still he could not respond. There was no way he could go to work for industry. And without the stature a successfully completed project would give him, there would be no other opportunities for him.

"Oh, God," Susan moaned, rolling over, her legs squeezed tightly together.

"I'm sorry," Clinton said. "I'm sorry."

Early the next evening Susan answered the doorbell. Clinton had come home from the university in a foul mood, his arms loaded with IBM printouts and lab books, and after dinner he had closeted himself in his study, working on the "stupid, kissass" report.

Frank Rader was standing on the doorstep, a cardboard box in his arms. "Hi, Susan, is Clinton at home?"

"Sure," she said, surprised. "Come on in."

He kissed her on the cheek, then went into the living room. Aftershave lotion or cologne. Very nice, Susan thought as she closed the door and followed him.

"Didn't Cheryl come with you?" she asked.

Frank had set the box down by the coffee table, and when he turned around he was grinning. "No," he said. "I just stopped by for a minute. How about fixing me a drink, and then get your husband out here? I have something for you."

"What is it?" Susan asked. On her way to the liquor cabinet she eyed the box. Its flaps were closed, and she had no earthly idea what it might contain. But she loved surprises.

"Not until I have my drink, and Clinton is out here," Frank said. He seemed to be in a very expansive mood, almost joyful.

"How about a straight brandy?" Susan asked.

"That'll be fine," he said, sitting down on the couch and stretching his legs out.

She poured him his drink and brought it across to him. "Just a hint?" she asked.

"Not a clue." Frank sipped at his drink. "Now go get Clinton. Hurry up."

Susan went back to the study and stuck her head inside. Clinton was at his desk, the lab reports spread out in front of him.

"What do you want?" he snapped.

"Frank's here. He's got something for us."

"Frank?" Clinton said, putting down his pencil. "What the hell does he want?"

"He's got something for us. Come on."

Grumbling, Clinton followed Susan back out into the living room.

Frank's grin widened. "You can get back to your work in just a minute, Clinton," he said. "But first of all I want you and Susan to open this box. It's a little present."

"How are you feeling?" Clinton asked.

"Never felt better," Rader said. "Now go on, open the box."

Susan reached down to pick it up.

"Don't pick it up, just open it," Frank said.

She knelt down beside the box and gingerly opened the flaps. A small black muzzle, with a tiny red tongue, licked at her fingers, momentarily startling her, but then she had the box all the way open, and a tiny black lab puppy fairly exploded out into her lap, piddling all over her in its excitement.

"Clinton!" Susan squealed in delight.

"What the hell?" Polk started, but Frank cut him off with a smile.

"I heard about what happened to your dog, so I thought you two needed a replacement."

Clinton had gotten down on the floor. The puppy leaped off Susan's lap and raced around in circles, jumping up to lick his face, then racing to Susan and back again.

"He's darling," Susan said.

"Then you'll keep him?" Frank asked.

Clinton nodded. "That was damned nice, Frank."

Rader got to his feet. "Cards tomorrow night. Eight o'clock, my place?"

"I don't know," Clinton said, and Susan immediately thought about the afternoon of the funeral.

"Are you sure?" she asked.

"Absolutely," Frank said. "Fred and Marion will be there. And I think we all need it. It's been a hell of a week and a half."

"We'll see," Clinton said after a moment.

"Be there," Frank said, and he left, closing the front door behind him.

A few seconds later Susan could hear his car starting up, and then drive away. She turned to her husband.

"Did you tell him about Bo?"

Clinton looked at her, a strange expression on his face. "No," he said. "I thought you had."

7

There are moments when absolutely everything is as perfect as it will ever get, and lying back in her warm bath, Marion Martin felt that this was one of them. For the first time in two weeks, she was at peace with herself and her surroundings.

No worries. No strife. Even her grief was beginning to fade around the edges, especially if she did not focus on it. And she no longer felt guilty about her outburst in front of Cheryl. It was all a dream now.

Retreat from reality, a psychiatrist would have called it, and she would have agreed. But for the moment, just this moment, it was wonderful.

Dreamily she thought about how it had been a year ago, when she was pregnant with Jessica. There was happiness and joy in her life. Expectation. Plans for the future.

She languidly turned her head as Fred appeared at the open bathroom door.

"We're going to be late," he said, shattering her peace.

Marion sighed deeply and sat up in the tub. "I'm not going, Fred." She turned away, not able to look him in the eye.

"Yes, we are," he said. "They're our friends, and we're going to be with them tonight." He came the rest of the way into the bathroom and sat down on the toilet, his arms resting on his knees. "It's exactly what you need."

"No," she said defiantly. She wanted to scream.

"You've been brooding around this house ever since . . . ever since the funeral. It can't go on."

She turned to him, angry. "You want to go over there so Frank can fill your head with insanity. Is that what you want?"

"For Christ's sake, Marion! All I want is to get you out of the house. Play a little cards. Have a couple of drinks, a few laughs with our friends."

"I don't feel like laughing."

Fred hesitated a moment. "I've already accepted. They're expecting us. Susan and Clinton will be there, too."

The grief, the sorrow, the worry all came back to her in a rush. "Frank Rader is crazy, but you're worse if you believe what he says," she snapped.

"Bullshit," Fred said softly. He got slowly to his feet, turned and shuffled, like an old man, out of the bathroom.

"Fred?" Marion called. What had she done? "Fred?" she shouted again, but there was no answer. She climbed out of the tub, hurriedly dried herself, then threw on her bathrobe and went out into the hallway.

She went into the living room, but he wasn't there. Through all of this she had been selfish. She realized that now for the first time. *Her* baby had died. *Her* world had been crushed. *Her* grief was all encompassing. *Her. Her. Her* . . . .

She hurried back down the hall to their bedroom, but he wasn't there, either. Jessica was his first and only child. Their doctor had recommended no more children.

The kitchen, she thought as she went back out into the hallway, but then she stopped, her eyes straying to the baby's room. The door had been closed. But now it was open.

Slowly she forced herself forward, toward the open door, and the closer she came, the more vivid her memory of that night became. It had ben raining. Thunder and lightning. That's what had awakened her. That's what she told herself, but it wasn't true.

"Fred?" she called in a weak voice.

Just before the doorway she stopped, unable to take the last two steps. Unable to bring herself to look inside at the crib.

"Fred?" she called out a little more loudly. Her knees

were weak, and her eyes were misting.

"I'm here," Fred said from behind her, and she spun around, her heart thumping, as he came down the hall to her. He had a drink in his hand.

"Where were you?"

"In the kitchen," he said. "I needed some ice." He looked beyond her to the baby's room, then back at her. "Did you go in?"

She shook her head, afraid to look over her shoulder at the open door. Afraid what it would do to her.

"Put the crib in the garage, Fred," she said.

His eyes narrowed, and she could see that he was having just as hard a time as she was, but he didn't say anything.

"Please?" She felt as if she was fighting for her life, her sanity.

"All right . . . tomorrow," he said.

She shook her head. "No, tonight. Right now," she said. "I'll get ready while you're doing it. We'll go to Frank and Cheryl's. Tomorrow we'll cover the wallpaper. Put some paneling up. I'll get new curtains."

Fred took his wife in his arms. "Take it easy, darling," he said.

She was shaking, frightened of the deep black thing that lurked at the back of her mind, ready at any moment to emerge and completely engulf her. Now she was crying, the tears streaming down her cheeks, her entire body wracked with sobs. It was the first time she had let herself go since their baby had died.

"That's right," Fred was saying, the words meaningless but his tone comforting. "That's right, darling, let it all go."

"You're jealous, Clinton! Jesus," Susan Polk said. She looked at his reflection in the vanity-table mirror.

"Bullshit," Clinton said, his back to her as he rummaged in his bureau drawer for a pair of socks.

They had been arguing since shortly after he had come home from the lab around five thirty. At first he had been adamant about not going to the Raders' tonight for cards, but Susan had put her foot down, and he had finally, reluctantly agreed. Yet he could not stop arguing, finding fault. Nit picking.

"Then what's the big deal?" She turned in her chair to look directly at him. Their new puppy, which they had named Puppy, was cringing by the door, where it had piddled.

Clinton had found his socks, and straightened up to face her. "It's no big deal," he said, obviously fighting for control. "It's just that I find it a little odd that one of my colleagues tells me he saw my wife and friend having lunch together, but when I get home my wife doesn't bother mentioning it."

"You have lunch with your little lab assistants damned near every day of the week."

"Yeah, ten of us at a time. And I work with them."

"Frank and Cheryl are our friends!" Susan shouted, exasperated. The puppy whined. "I was shopping downtown, happened to run into Frank and he invited me for lunch. What the hell is wrong with that?"

"Nothing," Clinton snapped. "Not a goddamned thing." He glanced at the puppy. "And the goddamned dog has pissed all over the floor again." He stalked off into the bathroom and slammed the door.

Susan stared at the door, listening to his running water in the sink, and she knew exactly what the problem was. It had happened to them a couple of times before. It was the sex thing.

Whenever a lab project of his was going sour, he would turn off on sex. Not only would there be a lack of interest, he would become unable to perform.

She got up and went across the room, where she patted the cringing puppy, then opened the door so that it could go downstairs.

Back at the vanity table, she looked at her reflection in the mirror. No lipstick, mascara only on one eye. Very sheer bra and bikini panties.

There was a thirteen-year difference in their ages that most of the time made absolutely no difference to their relationship. And yet, if she was honest with herself, she knew that the difference was there, and would become more pronounced as they grew older.

Just how honest did she want to get with herself, she reflected. Honest enough to admit that she had married Clinton because he reminded her of her father?

Susan shuddered now, thinking back to when she was sixteen and had her first sex. Her father had found out about it. He had simply made an appointment for her with a campus doctor for a pelvic examination and a prescription for birth control pills.

She had thought he would be disappointed in her. But he hadn't been. He had been wonderfully understanding; gentle with her feelings.

And then he had died, and there was Clinton, so much like her father. The same mannerisms, the same gentleness. And she had fallen head over heels in love with him.

The toilet flushed, bringing her out of her thoughts about the past, focusing them on the present.

How honest did she want to be with herself? Honest enough to admit that she had jumped at the chance to have lunch with Frank Rader? Honest enough to admit that she found him sexually attractive?

She and Frank had flirted during lunch, in a kidding manner.

"Don't let Clinton find out about our meeting like this," Frank had laughed.

"I won't tell him as long as you don't breathe a word to Cheryl. Hell hath no fury like a woman scorned," she had quipped, and they both laughed.

It had been an innocent, chance meeting. Or had it?

The bathroom door opened and Clinton came out, a sheepish grin on his face. She turned around to him.

"I'm sorry," he said.

"Me, too," Susan said, a wave of love for him washing over her. Yet there was a tinge of guilt there, too. "I should be flattered that you were jealous of me."

Something flared in his eyes, but then the gentle grin returned. "It's been a bitch, that grant thing hanging over my head. I just can't think straight."

Susan got up and put her arms around him. "It's barely seven," she said huskily. "We've got plenty of time." She was moist already, and she could feel her nipples hardening.

"Not now . . . ," Clinton said, his voice choked.

Susan ran her hands up and down his bare back as she moved her body against his. God, she needed him now. "Clinton. Please."

"I can't," he said.

"Let's try, honey," she said, nibbling at his earlobe, kissing his neck. "Let's just try."

He pulled away, and looked down at her, an expression almost of anguish on his face. For an instant she felt a stab of pity for him, but that made her angry. Not so much at him, but at herself. She knew that eventually he would come out of this by himself. And she also knew that when she worked herself up like this, there would be nothing for her but frustration.

She turned away and went back to the vanity table where she sat down, her knees together, her heart beating rapidly.

Clinton remained where he was standing, and as she looked at him in the mirror, she recalled the cologne Frank Rader had been wearing the night he had brought them the puppy. He had also been wearing it today at lunch.

8

Cheryl poured herself a cup of coffee as the twins argued about who was going to rinse this time, and who was going to load the dishwasher.

It was shortly after 6:00 P.M. Frank had gone down to the basement directly after dinner with the admonishment that the girls were to help their mother. But they seemed incapable of doing anything without an argument.

"I rinsed last night," Dawn screeched, holding the box of soap out of her sister's reach.

"Yeah, well, I scraped *all* last week," Felicity cried in a piercing voice.

Cheryl turned and glared at the girls, exasperated. They were good kids, their only major problem being their age. At thirteen they were right in the middle of adolescence. Periods. Icky boys versus yummy boys. Andy Gibb, the Bee Gees and Scott Baio. Bras. Bikini underpants inscribed MONDAY, TUESDAY, WEDNESDAY. *Seventeen* magazine. *Seventeen* was their Bible. If it wasn't in *Seventeen,* then it was wrong or gross.

"Mo-th-er," Dawn wailed.

"Enough," Cheryl snapped. "I want the arguing to stop, I want the dishes washed, and I want this kitchen cleaned before I come back downstairs."

"But it's . . . ," Felicity started.

Cheryl cut her off. "Felicity Ann!"

"Yes, mother," her daughter said, and Cheryl turned to Dawn, who also said, "Yes, mother."

"You girls can help lay out the snacks," Cheryl said, her voice softening. "I'm sure there'll be some left over. You can watch the TV in the rec-room."

"Dad says we have to stay in our room tonight when

company comes,'' Dawn said. Although they were identical twins, Dawn, who had been born first by four minutes, seemed to be the older, more mature of the two of them.

''When did he tell you that?''

''Just before supper. Can we take the little TV up with us?''

Cheryl went to the door that led down to their finished rec-room and opened it. The lights were on.

''Frank?'' She stared down the stairs.

''Don't come down here,'' he shouted up at her, and she stopped.

''What are you doing?'' she asked.

He came to the foot of the stairs, a grin on his face. ''It's a surprise,'' he said brightly. ''Now go on back upstairs and get ready.''

''The girls said you wanted them to stay up in their room tonight. We're not going to play cards down there, are we?''

''Nope,'' Frank said, his grin even wider. It was as if he was excited about something.

''Then . . . .''

He cut her off. ''Go on. Get out of here. You'll find out soon enough.''

Cheryl hesitated, but then turned and went back up to the kitchen, where she refilled her coffee cup.

The girls had obviously been listening to the exchange. They had bright, expectant looks on their faces.

''What kind of a surprise, mother?'' Dawn asked.

''You've got me,'' Cheryl said. ''I guess we're all going to have to wait until your father lets us know. Now get busy with this kitchen; I'll be down in fifteen minutes.''

The Polks and Martins would be here at eight, which left Cheryl less than two hours to shower and change clothes, then come down and prepare the snacks, get the bar ready and make the house presentable.

She didn't mind the extra work, but she had been surprised that Fred and Marion had accepted Frank's invitation. Yet, on reflection, she was glad they had. It had been a couple of weeks now since that terrible night, and all of them needed a life. Especially Marion. Cheryl only hoped that her friend would not bring up her crazy story again. It was frightening.

The girls were staring at Cheryl, and she realized that she had been daydreaming. She smiled. "What are you two waiting for?"

Dawn bounded across the room, threw her arms around her mother's neck, and kissed her on the cheek. "I love you, mom," she gushed.

Felicity was right behind her, and she hugged and kissed her mother.

"What's this all about?" Cheryl asked, a warm, comforting feeling spreading from her middle.

The girls grinned impishly.

"Oh no, you don't," Cheryl said, laughing. "You two are going to do the dishes."

"We know that, mother," Dawn sighed theatrically. She looked at her sister, who shrugged. "It's just that—me and Felicity been talking—about you and dad."

Cheryl's heart skipped a beat, but she said nothing.

"It's just like it used to be," Dawn said. "I mean with daddy." She shrugged.

"Daddy isn't crazy anymore—" Felicity started.

"Retard!" Dawn snapped. "We just want you and daddy to be happy, mother."

Cheryl didn't know whether to laugh or cry. Instead, she nodded, seriously. But the moment was broken then, and the girls went back to the dishes.

After a moment Cheryl left the kitchen and headed upstairs.

Frank *had* been happy all day, but his mood had seemed a little off key. He had seemed *too* animated, too quick to make jokes. And he had been secretive. The girls had loved it. Cheryl hadn't. It seemed phony.

In the bedroom, she sipped her coffee, then set the cup down and looked at herself in the mirror. Christ, crows' feet already, and gray hair that was almost impossible to keep up with, no matter what tint she used.

She went into the bathroom and looked at herself again, this time in the full-length mirror on the door. She stepped back and turned sideways, pushing her tummy in with both hands, then letting it out.

Not really all that bad, she told herself appraisingly. Ass just a little too big for her liking, tummy a little too full, and thighs just a little too thick.

She closed the door all the way, then slowly undressed, tossed the clothes down the laundry chute, and stepped into the shower. Turning the water on as hard and as hot as she could stand it, she let the spray stream down on her chest and stomach, her muscles relaxing, her skin tingling.

It had been two and a half weeks now since the accident, and she and Frank had not made love in all that time. She hadn't really given it much more than a fleeting thought over the past eighteen days, but for some reason it hit her strongly now.

They had always had a warm, loving relationship in bed. Frank was gentle and understanding. Maybe not as in tune with her needs lately but still a good mate.

She missed the sex part at night when the girls were asleep in bed, the house was quiet and she would snuggle close to him. In the dim light from the clock radio, his long, dark, well-muscled body never failed to excite her. Even as the thought of it did now.

She missed him inside of her. It was as simple as that. Yet she knew damned well that the neurologist would say that it was nothing more than another of the reactions to the accident, and would fade.

But she wanted him now. Right now, this very minute.

She was finished in the shower five minutes later. Wrapping a towel around her wet hair, she opened the bathroom door.

Frank had just come in to the bedroom. She stopped in her tracks.

"Is that what you're going to wear tonight?" he asked, grinning, almost as though he was drunk.

Unaccountably, Cheryl felt the gooseflesh rising on her arms and legs. "I thought I might," she said, trying to keep her voice light.

Frank continued to stare fixedly at her for several long seconds, and she felt uncomfortable under his gaze.

''What's the matter?'' he asked, sensing her mood.

She shook her head. ''I'm cold.''

''Put some clothes on, then.'' He chuckled, sat down on the bed and took off his shoes. The strange feeling in the room was suddenly broken.

She crossed over to him and, taking his face in both hands, bent down and kissed him on the lips. He gently patted her buttocks.

''I'm not finished downstairs yet,'' he said when they parted. ''I just came up to take a quick shower and shave.''

''We've got the time . . . .''

Frank shook his head. ''Nope,'' he said. ''Later, maybe.''

''Then don't drink so much tonight; you know how you get when you do,'' she said, biting her lip the moment the words were out of her mouth.

Frank's expression darkened. ''Maybe you should serve tea,'' he snapped.

She stepped back as he stood up. ''I'm sorry, Frank. I didn't mean it the way it sounded.''

''Oh?'' he said, raising his right eyebrow.

''Frank?''

He brushed past her, went into the bathroom and, without bothering to close the door, undressed and stepped into the shower.

''Goddamn it,'' she said to herself as the shower began. She pulled out some clean underpants and a bra. ''Goddamn it to hell.''

The Martins were the first to arrive, a few minutes after 8:00 P.M., and as Cheryl let them in, Fred gave her a kiss on the cheek, a big smile on his face, but Marion held back.

''Go on in, Fred,'' Cheryl said. ''Frank should be up in a minute.''

Fred went into the living room, leaving his wife and Cheryl alone for a moment in the vestibule.

"Are you feeling okay, Marion?" Cheryl asked. She was concerned for her. They had not spoken since the morning Marion had come over with her wild story about what Frank had supposedly been telling her husband. She looked a little wan now.

Marion nodded, the motion birdlike. "Did you talk to Frank . . . about what I told you?"

"Last night," Cheryl lied. The right moment had never presented itself to her, and in a way she was glad it hadn't.

"What'd he say?"

Cheryl looked directly into her friend's eyes. "He said he was sorry. He was just trying to help."

"Help?" Marion had raised her voice, and instantly lowered it. "Help? For God's sake, it's made Fred crazy."

"I'll talk to him again," Cheryl said firmly. "But I'm sure Frank won't say anything more about it."

Marion glanced toward the living room. "Fred is going to insist," she said, and looked back into Cheryl's eyes. "I'm frightened for him."

"Don't be," Cheryl said. "Everything will be all right. You'll see."

Marion wanted to believe it, Cheryl could see it written clearly on her face. But she could also see that Marion was skeptical. And she couldn't blame her.

Frank had just come up from the rec-room as the two women entered the living room, and he rubbed his hands together, the smile back on his face.

"What'll it be, guys?" he asked. "Vodka and sour, Marion? A light one?"

Marion had to smile, despite herself, and Fred chuckled. "Make her the light one," he said. "But I'll take anything and water, just as long as there's not much water."

"Coming up," Frank said. As he mixed the drinks at the little bar next to the fireplace, the doorbell chimed.

"I'll get it," Cheryl said. She went back out into the vestibule.

"Give me a bloody Mary, light on the hot stuff," Susan

Polk said as soon as Cheryl opened the door. Clinton stood just behind her, and he smiled. "Are we early?"

"No, you two are just fashionably late."

Clinton was wearing a light sweater and tweed sport-coat, but Susan was dressed in designer jeans, high heels, a sheer blouse and nearly transparent bra, a light jacket over her shoulder.

"You're going to drive Frank wild," Cheryl quipped, just a tinge of cattiness behind the remark, and Susan laughed.

"You can call me the *femme fatale,*" Susan said, flouncing past Cheryl into the living room. "Now, where's my drink?" she called out.

Clinton raised his eyebrows in an attempt at mock despair, but Cheryl could see that something was really bothering him. "I don't know what the hell I'm married to, at times."

"If she gives you too much trouble, you can always sleep on our couch tonight," Cheryl said lightly, linking her arm in his and leading him.

"What the hell are you trying to do, professor, seduce my wife?" Frank called from the bar.

"You're damned right I am," Polk said. "And it looks as if I might get lucky tonight."

Again Cheryl got the impression that there was something in Clinton's voice that wasn't quite right. He crossed the room to Frank, got a brandy and water, and then sat down across from Fred and Marion.

Susan had her bloody Mary, and she was perched on the arm of an easy chair by the fireplace. When Frank turned around Cheryl couldn't help but notice that his eyes strayed from her face to her breasts, the nipples just slightly visible, back to her face, and then he smiled. Clinton had noticed it, too, and his jaws tightened.

But then the moment passed and Frank came across to Cheryl and handed her a Rhine wine and seltzer. He had at least a triple shot of straight brandy, no ice, which he held up in a toast.

"To the future, with good friends," he said seriously.

Cheryl glanced at each one of their friends. Fred was smiling. Marion seemed worried. Clinton seemed as if he was on the verge of anger, and, unless she was terribly mistaken, Cheryl was certain that Susan was enraptured with Frank.

"To friends," Fred echoed, raising his glass. "These past couple of weeks would have been impossible without you."

Everyone sipped at their drinks, the mood subdued, but then Susan broke the ice.

"Say, guys, do you know what Frank did for Clinton and me this week?"

"No, what's that?" Cheryl heard herself asking.

Susan smiled. "He didn't tell you?" she asked, and she wagged her finger at Frank. "On top of everything, he's modest, too."

"What was it?" Fred asked.

Susan turned to him. "You know that someone poisoned our dog, the night . . . a couple of weeks ago. Well, Monday Frank came over to our place." She paused for effect. "He brought us a puppy." She looked at him, smiling. "We've named it Puppy."

"Yeah," Clinton said dryly. "The damn thing piddles everywhere except on the newspaper. Thanks a lot, Frank." He raised his glass.

Everyone laughed. Cheryl thought it was a lovely gesture, but she wondered why Frank hadn't said anything to her about it.

For the next hour, then, everything seemed to go reasonably well, as the drinks began to do their work, slowing them down, making them all relaxed, and a bit more mellow. It was crazy, but the later it got, the stronger the feeling became in Cheryl that something was about to happen. She would not have been a bit surprised if Clinton got up and punched Frank in the nose. All through the evening he had been unable to keep his eyes off Susan's breasts. And the more he looked, the more Susan seemed to love it.

It was just ten thirty when Frank finished telling a very

bad joke that elicited only a few bored chuckles. Frank got to his feet. He had drunk a little bit too much, but he still seemed in control.

"Enough of this nonsense," he announed.

"Cards," Clinton said. "It's about time. I don't think I could handle another of Fred's stories."

"Have another drink, Clinton my boy, and my jokes are guaranteed to get better," Fred quipped.

"No cards tonight," Frank said. Everyone looked up at him. Cheryl felt a strange little thrill run through her stomach. "I've got something different planned for tonight."

"Frank?" Cheryl said uncertainly. Fred was sitting forward on the couch, and Marion's complexion had turned pale.

"Guaranteed to amaze and delight you," Frank continued. He set his drink down and turned to his wife. "Keep them up here for a couple of minutes, then bring them down to the rec-room."

"Frank?" Cheryl said again, but he had turned and hurried out of the living room. A second later they could hear him tromping down the basement stairs.

"What's going on, Cheryl?" Clinton asked, and she turned to him.

"I don't know," she said. "He wouldn't let me see what he was doing. It's some kind of a surprise."

Marion got up and came over to Cheryl, where she bent down and, in a low, frightened voice, asked, "This doesn't have anything to do with what he's been telling Fred, does it?"

"I honestly don't know," Cheryl said, looking up into the woman's wide eyes.

Marion straightened up. "I think I'd like to go home, Fred."

"What's going on?" Clinton asked, also getting to his feet.

"He's just got something goofy planned, you know Frank," Cheryl said. "It's nothing to worry about. Honestly."

"She's right, honey," Fred said, getting up. "It'll be okay."

"You can come down now," Frank called from downstairs.

"I want to go home," Marion insisted.

Cheryl got up and took her hand. "Frank is just going to play some kind of a silly game," she said. "Honestly. He wouldn't try to hurt you. It's just his way of entertaining us. He's trying to make us forget our troubles."

"I think I'm going home, too," Clinton said.

Susan had put her drink down, and she came across to them. "Don't be rude," she said irritably.

Both Clinton and Marion looked at Cheryl, and she felt as if she was being backed into a corner, but there wasn't much she could do about it. "Please stay," she said.

Clinton didn't seem very happy, but he finally nodded, and Fred took his wife by the arm, and she nodded as well.

"He's probably going to show us those dreadful home movies he took two years ago at the house up in Door County," Cheryl said, leading the way through the dining room. "If he does, I'll divorce him for sure."

The basement door was open, and from downstairs there was a dim, flickering light reflecting off the paneled walls. The stairway light was off.

"Frank," she called down. "What did you do to the lights?"

"Mood, my dear," Frank's voice came from the rec-room. "Come on down."

Cheryl looked at the others, shook her head, and then started down the stairs, trailing her right hand on the banister.

At the bottom, she turned the corner into the rec-room. The sight that greeted her stopped her in her tracks.

"My God," she said.

The couch and two easy chairs had been arranged in a semicircle across from a card table, behind which Frank stood. He was dressed in black choir robes. In the middle of the room, evidently painted on the carpeting, was a five-sided figure. At each corner of the figure a black candle, in a small holder, flickered, its feeble light reflecting off a plastic model of a human skull at the center.

"Come on and sit down," Frank said, gesturing to the couch and chairs.

"Frank, for Christ's sake," Cheryl snapped.

Fred was peering, wide eyed, over Clinton's shoulder; Marion was still on the stairs, refusing to come around the corner.

For a moment they all stood in silence, the grin finally fading from Frank's face. But then he finally shook his head.

"The hell with it," he said. "I was just trying to have a little fun. We need a laugh."

"This is fun?" Cheryl said, her voice rising. What in God's name was happening to him? Or was she crazy?

"Come on, you party poopers," Susan said, pushing past Cheryl and Clinton. "Let's at least catch the first act."

She stepped around the pentagram, and sat down in one of the easy chairs.

"Come on," Frank coaxed, his smile back. "Step right up. The next show begins in one minute," he called out in a sideshow barker's voice.

"You're certifiably nuts," Clinton said, coming the rest of the way into the rec-room. He sat down on the couch, and a moment later Cheryl joined him, Fred and a very frightened Marion right behind her.

After they were all seated, Frank went over to the door and closed it. When he turned around the smile was gone from his face. He took something that looked like a burned piece of toast from his pocket, held it overhead and started slowly back to the card table as he began chanting in a low, ominous voice: "I will take the bread of Hades and will call upon the name of my Lord, Astaroth."

Susan tittered and Marion closed her eyes. Cheryl simply could not believe what she was witnessing.

"Oh Astaroth, I am not worthy that Thou shouldst enter under my roof, but only say the word and our souls here tonight shall be healed. May the body of our Master,

Astaroth, preserve our souls into life everlasting."

He had reached the card table, and he turned now to face the others. Cheryl could see sweat gleaming on his forehead as he looked up at the blackened bread. She wanted to jump up, turn on the lights and put a halt to this nonsense. But she could not. She could do nothing more than sit, gape mouthed, and watch her husband.

"What shall we render unto our Lord, Astaroth, for all the things he is about to render unto us?" Frank called out, still staring up at the bread. "I will take the sacrifice of eternal bliss and call upon the name of Astaroth for Clinton Polk's research grant, that the Regents may see his way."

Cheryl sensed that Clinton, seated next to her, had stiffened, but still she could not take her eyes off Frank.

"I will take the sacrifice of eternal bliss and call upon the name of Astaroth for the infant Jessica Martin so that she may yet know her parents."

Marion gasped, the sound very loud in the dark room.

"And for me, Oh my Lord Astaroth," Frank shouted, "I will take the sacrifice of eternal bliss and call upon your name for my salvation!"

He laid the blackened crust reverently on the card table, pulled something from a cardboard box at his feet, and then straightened up.

"I will give praise to Beelzebub and Leviathan and to Asmodeus the temptor," he shouted. Over his head he held a small black rabbit by the ears. The creature was struggling and kicking. Cheryl felt her heart racing nearly out of her chest, her breath coming in short gasps.

"I will give praise and call upon my Lords and Masters, and we will be saved from our enemies!" Frank screamed.

A flash of lightning, followed by a crash of thunder, shook the house as Frank slammed the rabbit on the table. Something in his other hand flashed in the dim candlelight and when he raised the rabbit overhead a second later, its blood spurted from a slit throat.

"Asmodeus!" Frank shouted. "Astaroth! Lucifer! May this blood preserve our souls unto Your service for life everlasting."

The rabbit jerked powerfully one last time, then its hind legs twitched for a few seconds, and finally it was still.

Cheryl's heart began to slow down, and she caught her breath. Frank laid the dead rabbit in the box beneath the table, and he stood there now, blood all down the front of his black robe, looking at them, a silly grin on his face.

"Oh, Frank," Cheryl said softly, her heart aching for him.

"I heard her," Fred said, getting up. Marion stifled a sob, and together they shuffled across the room, opened the door and went upstairs.

Susan's eyes were wide, but instead of being troubled, she seemed thoughtful, almost dreamy. Clinton got up and took his wife's arm, and they headed for the door.

"Frank?" Cheryl said a minute later. "Are you all right?"

"Yeah," he said, the smile gone from his face. "Go on upstairs. I'll be up in a minute."

"We've got to talk . . . ," Cheryl said, but Frank savagely cut her off.

"Get the fuck out of here!"

She got up and, without looking back, went out of the rec-room and started up the stairs, tears welling up in her eyes.

Fred and Marion Martin drove home in silence, both of them deep in their own thoughts.

For Marion it was as if something monstrous and black had descended upon her, blocking out all of her senses, making it seem as if she was locked in some dark vault.

For Fred, the opposite was true. For the first time since their baby had died, he felt alive; he was acutely aware of his surroundings. Frank's ceremony had not been macabre; it had been thrilling, and somehow reassuring.

He parked the car in the driveway, then helped Marion out of the car, up the walk and into the house.

When he had the door locked, he turned to his wife and took her in his arms. She was shivering.

"Please hold me, Fred," she said shakily. "Please hold me."

They kissed deeply, and when they parted Fred looked into her eyes. "I love you, darling," he said.

"I love you, too," Marion replied, her voice hoarse.

He led her across the living room, down the hall and into their bedroom, where beside their bed he methodically undressed her, then picked her up and laid her atop the bed covers.

She watched as he undressed, letting his clothes fall to the floor, and then he came to her, kissing her neck and her breasts, and soon they were making love with more passion than either of them had ever known.

Clinton Polk had always felt that his gift, which set him apart from most other people, was his ability to view the world objectively.

But as he locked the kitchen door, turned off the lights and went into the living room, he knew that he would never be able to see Frank as anything but crazy.

What the man had done tonight, the spectacle he had made of himself, was beyond what any rational person could accept.

Frank needed to see a psychiatrist. And Clinton would tell Cheryl just that, tomorrow.

Susan had put some soft music on the stereo in the dark living room. He came around the corner stopping a moment until his eyes adjusted, and then he could see her clearly where she stood across the room, and he went to her.

She came into his arms, and they danced for a few minutes, all thoughts about Frank Rader, about the lab, and about the university's Board of Regents leaving his mind.

And then, somehow, they were on the floor, and Clinton was pulling her jeans and panties down around her knees as she pulled open her blouse and ripped off her bra.

"Oh God, Clinton . . . hurry, darling . . . please,"

Susan cried.

Clinton tore his clothes off, and then he was inside her, her arms and legs wrapped around him as he pounded deeper and faster, his entire life reduced to this single act.

It was after 1:00 A.M. when Cheryl Rader slipped out of bed and put on her robe. She still felt the tingling afterglow of lovemaking, and as she looked down at Frank's sleeping figure, she felt a wave of love intermingled with the fear she felt for him.

Softly, she left the bedroom and went to the twins' room, where she opened the door. They were both sleeping soundly, pop cans, potato-chip and pretzel bags strewn on the floor with their clothes.

She hoped that they had heard nothing tonight. This all had been difficult enough without that.

She closed the door, turned and padded down the hall to the stairs, and went down.

Frank had told her that he had cleaned up the mess in the basement before he came up, but the pentagram had been painted on the carpet, probably ruining it. That, combined with the candle wax, and the . . . blood from the poor rabbit, would mean they'd probably have to tear the carpet up and throw it away.

At the basement door, Cheryl hesitated a moment, but then took a deep breath, let it out slowly and flipped the light switch on. She had to blink against the sudden brightness.

Slowly, she went down the stairs, and at the bottom she steeled herself before she stepped into the rec-room.

For several long moments she just stared, unable to believe her eyes.

The furniture was back in its proper place. The card table had been folded and was lying against the wall. And the carpet looked fresh and clean. Brand new. No stains. Nothing.

Cheryl went all the way into the room, and got down on her hands and knees on the floor, her face inches away from the carpeting.

Nothing. There was nothing. The carpet was brand new. It wasn't even wet where Frank would have had to clean it.

Nothing, Cheryl thought, looking up. She got to her feet and shook her head. Maybe she was going crazy. Maybe it was her.

It was as if a chill wind was passing over her as she left the rec-room and headed back upstairs to bed.

Part Two

ALL HALLOWS EVE

October

1

It was a lovely fall afternoon when Stanley Klubertanz parked his Alpha Romeo on the sprawling campus of the University of Wisconsin and headed on foot to the Department of Psychiatry Building.

Since the first spate of headlines about the sensational murders last month, the newspapers had given them a breather.

Some breather, Klubertanz thought morosely. Since he had been assigned full time to the investigation, he had gotten absolutely nowhere.

He had talked to dozens of known sex offenders. Most of them had alibis. Three of them had readily admitted to the murder of the young nun, but they didn't know the details of the crime. They were lying. As usual.

He had interviewed the nun's colleagues, her teachers at school, and finally her parents. All that had only deepened the mystery. There was absolutely no reason for anyone to murder her.

He had switched his investigation then for a time to Ahern and Shapiro. Beginning with their war records, he had worked his way forward to the night they had been murdered.

Although they had been homosexuals, they had been quiet types. They had each other, and never had been interested in playing the field, it seemed. They seldom went to the gay bars, didn't belong to any of the gay clubs, nor were they card-carrying members of the Gay Liberation Movement.

They were both clean. Again, he had drawn a complete blank.

He rounded the corner at Lurch Court, crossed the narrow street, entered the front door of the U.W. Psychiatry Department, and trudged upstairs to the second floor.

No leads, he thought. No direction. Nowhere to turn.

"Keep plugging at it, Stan," Capt. Miller had told him this morning.

"This is a tough one," Klubertanz said. "Christ, we don't even have a motive. There was absolutely no reason for those three people to be murdered. None."

The captain shrugged. "I thought we had established that from the beginning," he said. "I thought we had pegged in on a crazy."

"Yeah," Klubertanz said.

"Well then, how about Osborne at the University? What'd he have to say?"

"He agrees one hundred percent," Klubertanz said. He had talked with Osborne two days after the murder of the nun. But all he had gotten was the usual psychological profile crap. The drivers' murderer had a grudge against doctors or against anyone in white. Perhaps a wife or mother or some loved one had needlessly died because of a mistake someone in white had made. And the nun? Probably the work of someone with a grudge against women. She was raped, after all.

No help. No help. None.

Captain Miller had closed the master file, and handed it across to Klubertanz, his sign of dismissal. "Like I say, Stan, keep plugging away at it. Your man is out there. Sooner or later he'll make a mistake, and we'll nail the bastard."

"Yeah," Klubertanz said, taking the file and getting to his feet.

"Anything else?" Capt. Miller asked.

Klubertanz shook his head. "I'll just get back to work. There are a number of things I still haven't run down."

"There you are," Miller said. "Something will turn up."

Later that morning, Klubertanz had telephoned Osborne, and the man had set up a two o'clock appointment. It was just that time now.

Osborne's office was large, and incredibly cluttered with several thousand books in floor-to-ceiling bookcases, atop file cabinets and a library table, on chairs, on the floor, and piled in dusty corners. Klubertanz knocked once and went in.

Doctor Bruce Osborne, a man in his early fifties, had been staring out the window toward the lake. He turned around and squinted.

"Stanley Klubertanz," he said, a soft British accent in his voice. He was originally from Chicago, but had spent a couple of years in England, and had affected the accent. It lent him an air of authority.

"Thanks for seeing me on such short notice, Doctor." Klubertanz shook hands with the psychiatrist, and then they both sat down.

Osborne reached out for his pipe and began filling it from a humidor on his cluttered desk, but his eyes never left Klubertanz's.

"Something is worrying you, Stanley," he said matter-of-factly. "Something new?"

Klubertanz shook his head. "It's still Ahern, Shapiro and Sister Colletta."

Osborne's eyebrows rose. "You've definitely combined the three of them, then? You suspect the same murderer?"

Klubertanz wanted to tell Osborne the business about the rigor mortis that Maxwell had confided to him, but he held his tongue. Osborne was a psychiatrist, not a physiologist.

"We think it's a distinct possibility," he said instead. "So far we've come up with nothing, so I thought I'd start all over again, under the assumption that all three were killed by the same person or persons."

Osborne had his pipe lit, and he was nodding thoughtfully. "This, of course, did not come out of the clear blue sky. You have a reason."

"Yes," Klubertanz said. He lit himself a cigarette as he

gathered his thoughts.

"But it's giving you some trouble," Osborne was saying. "In fact, I'd hazard the guess that you haven't even discussed this with your own people yet."

"Only with a priest," Klubertanz said.

Again Osborne raised his eyebrows. "That bad?"

"He's Monsignor Ferrari, from Good Shepherd."

"I see," Osborne said. He puffed on his pipe. "Monsignor Ferrari had something significant to say that led you to think all three murders were committed by the same person?"

Klubertanz sat forward, deciding the only way he was going to get any help from Osborne would be if he was totally honest with the man. "What do you know about witchcraft and demonology?"

The question seemed to startle Osborne and he took his pipe from his mouth. "Not terribly much," he said. "But enough to realize that people who believe in it have exhibited some highly selective behavior."

"Murder?"

"Indeed," Osborne said. "They would consider it sacrifice."

"Is it possible that there is such a person or persons here in Madison?"

Osborne shrugged. "Why not? But if you're going to want my help on this, Stanley, you're going to have to tell me everything. I can't work in the dark."

Klubertanz stubbed out his cigarette in the ashtray, and pulled out his notebook, turning to the page where he had copied the inscription that had been written in the nun's blood on the altar. He read the English translation for Osborne.

"It sounds like some kind of a prayer."

"It is," Klubertanz said. "Monsignor Ferrari says it comes at the point in the witch's black mass when a sacrifice is made. A blood sacrifice."

"An attack on the church," Osborne said thoughtfully. "Yes, I can understand that." He blinked. "But then, where is the connection with Ahern and Shapiro? Was there the same writing in their apartment?"

"No," Klubertanz said. "The murders were very similar and within twenty-four hours of the nun's."

"I don't buy that," Osborne said. "You're either clutching at straws . . . in which case I'd advise you to back up; or you're holding something from me. If that's so, I'm not going to be able to do very much for you."

"There is another connection," Klubertanz said after a long hesitation. "But I can't talk about it at this point, except to say that it has something to do with the condition of all three bodies."

"All right," Osborne said. "What is it, exactly, that you want from me?"

"I don't believe in the supernatural . . . or at least I don't believe in ghosts, and things like that. What I'm asking you, is, what kind of a person does? And is it possible for a number of people to have the same intense emotions?"

"Mass hypnosis," Osborne said. "Look at Jonestown in Guyana, if you want answers on group hysteria. But your other question . . . what kind of a person believes in witchcraft . . . is somewhat more intriguing, and certainly more difficult."

Osborne tamped his pipe and relit it. "I can recommend a couple of books for you, but you're going to find that for as many authors on the subject that you'll read, you're going to get as many totally different opinions on the subject. No one really knows for sure."

Klubertanz was disappointed, and yet he had not really counted on any significant help from the psychiatrist.

"From what I've read, there have been no serious profile studies done on the subject. But I might make a few guesses . . . none of them too helpful, I'm afraid."

Klubertanz waited for him to continue.

"I'd expect the person you're looking for would be very ordinary. The only bizarre aspect of his or her psyche would be this belief in the occult."

"Ordinary people do not commit such methodical murders."

"Oh, but they do, Stanley," Osborne disagreed. "It depends upon their beliefs. Such as a belief in the United States. Quite ordinary young men become very efficient killers."

"War and soldiering," Klubertanz said.

"How about a belief in the state penal codes that allows capital punishment? The man who pulls the switch is doing his duty in one state, and yet a few miles away, across the border, he would be considered a murderer."

"You're talking about death and killing for the good of a higher authority. Not the kind of murder I'm investigating."

"Again, you're wrong, Stanley. Witchcraft is a religion, just like Catholicism, Judaism and Mohammedanism. Consider what has been done in Iran in the name of religious beliefs. Your murderer, if he or she is involved with witchcraft, could very well be operating under what he feels are orders from a higher authority."

Klubertanz looked down again at his notebook. "*Domini nostri Astaroth.* Our Lord Astaroth." The destroyer demon, Msgr. Ferrari had called him. The higher authority?

"Still," Osborne said pensively. "I'd put my money on a deeply disturbed person or persons, acting out their hate fantasies."

2

Clinton Polk's laboratory was in the Biochemistry Building, across University Avenue from Camp Randall Stadium. It was in a large, airy room, with tall ceilings and huge windows, and was furnished with half-a-dozen lab tables in addition to several pieces of sophisticated research equipment. Toward the back of the room was a small, glassed-in cubicle, which served as Polk's office and as a general planning and strategy room.

Polk had just arrived, and even before he had a chance to take off his coat, Gil Mortensen, one of his lab assistants, came across the room, a grim expression on his face.

"We've got troubles, Doctor Polk," Mortensen said.

Polk hesitated by the door to his office, and glanced past the young man, toward the large culture cabinet along the far wall. Ten other student assistants were standing around it.

"Didn't any of them take?" Polk asked.

The young man shook his head. "They all took. There is spotting in every dish."

"That's impossible."

"Yes, sir."

Everything had been working the way it was supposed to. Polk had begun to feel good. Even the Regents had begun to come around, extending his grant at least to the end of the semester, with the promise that they would seriously consider continuation.

But over the past few days it had all seemed to fall apart.

"Set up the mass spectrograph, and give me three dishes at random . . . ," Polk started, but something in Mortensen's eyes stopped him.

"I was excited about it. Couldn't sleep, so I came down around six this morning," Mortensen said. "I went ahead and began the analysis."

"And?" Polk asked.

"I ran six cultures through; they all came up the same. No DS 19."

"Impossible," Polk said, his stomach tied in a knot, and a black rage welling up inside of him. "Impossible," he shouted. "What the hell happened? The enzyme was clearly labeled for the entire batch this time around. Jesus Christ, it was even mixed in with the soup. It couldn't have been left out. It could not have been. I prepared it myself."

Mortensen shook his head. He seemed embarrassed. The others had stopped what they were doing, and had looked around.

"The experiment log is blank at that entry position," the young man said.

"That, too, is impossible," Polk shouted, his anger threatening to take control. "I never forget the entries."

"No, sir," Mortensen said.

"Well, then . . . ," Polk started to say, but the words were choked off in his throat. He *never* did forget the lab book. Never. If the book was empty, the enzyme had not been added to the mixture that had been placed for culture in the petri dishes.

He turned away and looked into his office. He had taken the enzyme out of the refrigerator. He had brought it down to nuclear science for tagging.

Jesus. It hadn't come back. He had forgotten it.

He looked back at Mortensen and the others, and shook his head. It was impossible. It was incredibly sloppy and absent minded. "Not good science," his major professor would have called it.

"Clean it up," he said in a hoarse voice.

"Yes, sir," Mortensen said softly. "Do you want to run the experiment again?"

Polk nodded. "Yes, we'll have to run it again," he said. He turned and went into his office, where he took off his coat and then telephoned the Nuclear Science Biolab downstairs.

"Polk here," he said when he got an answer. "Is my DS 19 ready?"

"Sure is, Doctor," a young woman said. "We refrigerated it for you overnight. We thought you wanted it yesterday."

"I'll pick it up later this morning." Polk hung up the phone and sat down.

Beyond the glass windows of his office, his lab assistants began clearing the ruined cultures out of the temperature-controlled cabinet. Six hundred cultures, he thought. Six hundred possibilities for the answer he was looking for, all ruined.

Why? Never in his career as a scientist had he made such an incredibly stupid blunder. If one of his lab assistants had made the same mistake, he would have fired the person on the spot.

All of his students had gathered around Mortensen at the culture cabinet. They were talking and gesturing. Probably laughing at him. Probably condemning him.

At length Mortensen broke away and hurried across to Polk's office. His face was animated, almost flushed.

"You've got to see this, Doctor Polk," he bubbled.

Polk rose. "What is it?"

"Secondaries. We've got secondaries."

"What?" Polk asked, coming around his desk. His heart was beginning to accelerate.

"They must have been developing from the time I looked at them. But every culture spot is developing a secondary mold. Probably because the tagged DS 19 was left out."

Polk hurried with the young man out of his office and across the lab. The others parted respectfully to let him through. A dozen of the small, clear glass dishes had been removed from the cabinet, and in the center of each of the primary molds that had formed on the agar was a tiny spot of pale green and yellow. A secondary mold. One growing from the first.

Polk tried to make his excited brain slow down. They had been looking for at least one secondary all along. For months they had been working on it. Only now, because of a stupid mistake, it looked as if the entire batch was active.

"Incredible."

"All right," he said, loosening his tie and pulling off his jacket. "We've got a lot of work ahead of us, starting right now." He rolled up his shirtsleeves and pulled out several more of the petri dishes from the cabinet.

"We'll separate and label them all," Mortensen said.

"Carefully," Polk cautioned. "I want no cross-contamination here. None whatsoever." He turned to one of the girls. "Vicki, I want you to take the scrapings as they come and separate the cytoplasts in the centrifuge." He turned to Mortensen. "Then I want the reactive ones mounted, tagged and dyed. We're going to run the mass spectrograph, the electron microscope and the gas chromatograph. I don't care if it takes a year, we're finally on to it."

The excitement was high in the room.

"No mistakes," he cautioned. "We're not going to botch this." He had a fleeting thought about his own mistake with the DS 19, but then it faded as they began their work.

It was late, and traffic on the Interstate Highway from Milwaukee was light. Soft music was playing on the radio, and Marion Martin felt as if she was in a protective cocoon. It was warm and comforting, and she wanted it never to end. She wanted to burrow deeper down into her seat, Fred beside her, darkness outside, and the dim light from the dash inside.

She stared at her own distorted reflection in the windshield, and wondered how other people saw her. Short. Mousy. Weak willed. And frightened most of the time.

Fred reached over and patted her on the knee, but she didn't look over.

"Peppinger was practically eating out of my hand," he said. "Did you see that, hon?"

"Yes," Marion mumbled. She didn't want to talk.

"Tired?"

Marion sighed. "A little."

"We'll be home in half an hour. But Jesus, Marion, we're going to get the contract. It's actually going to happen."

Two days ago Dwight Peppinger, an administrative assistant to Milwaukee Mayor Marshall Burns, had invited them to a little get-together at the mayor's home in Milwaukee.

It had gone smoothly, Marion had to admit. They were all friendly, gracious people, especially the mayor's wife, who refused to be called Mrs. Burns. "Please, dear, call me Dorothy."

"You should have been there when we all went into the study. They practically fell all over themselves, lighting my cigar, getting my drink. 'Are you comfortable, Fred?' 'Sure there's nothing else we can get for you, Fred?' My God, you should have heard them."

Her makeup had smeared, but it didn't matter now, she thought. The evening was over. Please, dear God, let it be over. Please.

"This contract is going to cost us plenty, but once we've got it, we'll make up what we spent, in spades."

What he was saying began to penetrate Marion's awareness, and she turned to him. "What?" she said. "What did you say?"

He glanced at her and smiled. "You haven't heard a thing I've said, have you?"

"About the contract, and spending a lot of money to get it," she said. "What did you mean, Fred?"

Fred suddenly seemed uncomfortable. "It's done all the time, hon. Just don't talk about it with anyone. Not even Cheryl or Susan."

"What's done all the time?" Marion asked. She had a sick feeling. She had thought he was going to bring up Frank Rader and his crazy ideas, but this, now, was something different.

"You know," Fred said, hedging.

"No, I don't know. What are you talking about?"

"It's no different than taking someone to lunch on your expense account."

"Bribery?" she said.

"Don't ever say that, Marion! Good Lord. Bribery. Of course it's nothing like that."

"Then what are you talking about? What have you been doing?"

For a long moment Fred was silent, apparently concentrating on his driving. They passed a semi up a long hill, and when they were back in the right-hand lane, he glanced at her.

"It's simple," he said. "Milwaukee wants an industrial development program. Worldwide. Big bucks. Creative Sales is the company for the job. We're geared up for it. We know Milwaukee and its needs. We understand the market. We know that, and they know that."

"Then you'll get the contract," Marion said.

"It's simple, but not quite that easy," Fred said. "Besides convincing the City Council, we've got to convince at least two dozen department heads in order to put the pressure on Burns to sign the contract."

"So you bribe . . . I mean, you do something nice for all of those people?"

"Not all of them. Just a few key people. The people who make the decisions. The people whom everyone else follows."

"Like Peppinger?"

"He doesn't give a damn about Milwaukee. All he wants to do is line his pockets."

"And you're lining them."

"We need the contract, Marion. Creative Sales needs it or we'll go under. I need it for my own self-esteem."

It was bribery, Marion thought. On top of everything else, Fred was leaving himself open to criminal prosecution.

"I'm sorry you asked," Fred said glumly.

"So am I," she said. "And I'm not going to any more

of these get-togethers, either. I don't want to be a part of it."

"It doesn't matter any longer," Fred said.

"Are you getting out?" Marion asked, a slight hope springing up inside of her.

"No, but I'm not going to have to do these things any longer. The contract is going to be formally signed within a few weeks. Peppinger assured me. It's just like Frank said it would be."

The words took her breath away, leaving her light-headed. Fred believed that Frank's bizarre ceremony last month had something to do with his success. It was insane.

Once again she sank down in her seat, thankful for the protective darkness outside, and stared at her reflection in the glass. What was happening to them? To Fred?

3

"Let's go; we're going to be late," Frank Rader called from downstairs.

Cheryl had just finished in the bathroom. "Get the van out, I'll be right down," she called.

"Well, hurry it up," Frank snapped, and a moment later Cheryl could hear the door open, then close.

The house was quiet, except for the faint sound of the girls' television set playing. She turned and hurried down the hall to the girls' room, where she knocked once and entered.

Dawn and Felicity had made themselves a pot of hot chocolate a few minutes ago in the kitchen, and they were sprawled out on their big double bed now, dressed in their pajamas, freshly scrubbed, watching television. They looked up when she came in.

"Are you going now, mom?" Dawn asked.

"Yes, but we're not going to be very late. So I want this television set off and the lights out no later than ten o'clock."

"Mom," Felicity whined.

"Tomorrow is a school day," Cheryl insisted. "Ten o'clock, and I mean ten."

"Yes, mother," Felicity said.

Cheryl remained where she was, looking down at the girls. They were so beautiful. So innocent. And clean and new. She did not want to go to the Martins' tonight. She didn't want to leave the house.

"What's wrong, mother?" Dawn asked.

Cheryl managed a slight smile, and she sat down on the edge of the bed. Felicity scooted a little closer.

"Did I ever tell you two that I loved you?"

Both girls beamed. They liked it when she got like this.

"Well, if I haven't, I'll tell you now that I do. Bunches."

"Oh, mom," both girls gushed, and they hugged her.

When they parted, Cheryl's eyes were slightly moist. Sometimes it was impossible to contain all the love she felt for them. Love, mixed with pride, and hope for their future.

She got up, kissed both of them on the cheek, and then went to the door. "Ten o'clock," she said in an effort to be stern.

"Mother, what about daddy?" Dawn said before Cheryl could open the door.

"What about him?"

"Will he be all right?" Dawn said. "I mean, he's been sorta different, you know."

"Scary," Felicity said timidly.

Cheryl came back to the bed and sat down between them. How could she tell the girls that she had the same fears about their father? "The accident was very bad, you both know that."

Both girls nodded. Their eyes were wide.

"The doctor said it would take daddy a while longer to get better. But we've all got to help. We've all got to understand."

"Does he hurt?" Felicity asked.

Cheryl squeezed her. "Yes, I think he does. Very much. But he'll get better pretty soon. Just watch and see."

"He's so pale," Dawn said. "And his eyes look funny."

"I know," Cheryl said. She ached inside. "I know. But he'll get better. Promise."

She hugged them both, kissed them one more time, then got up and went to the door. "Ten o'clock," she said.

"Good night, mother," both girls chirped.

"Good night," Cheryl said. She hurried outside and climbed into the blue Chevy van that Frank had insisted they buy with the insurance money from the accident.

The engine was running, and Frank flipped on the headlights and then backed out of the driveway.

"What the hell took you so long?" he asked peevishly.

"I was tucking the girls in."

Out in the street, Frank glanced over at his wife. "Shit," he said. "I didn't even say goodnight to them."

"That's all right. They understand."

Something flashed in Frank's eyes. "Were they in bed?"

"Yes. They had the little TV upstairs, and some hot chocolate."

"We won't be late."

"I told them that." Cheryl stopped. "Don't you feel well?"

"A little headache."

"Why don't you see the doctor again?"

Frank looked at her. "Don't you mean, why don't you see a psychiatrist?"

Cheryl was flustered. "Frank, I . . . ."

The expression in his eyes softened. "Things'll get better. You'll see. I just need a little more time."

For what, Cheryl wanted to ask, but she held her silence, and, as Frank drove across town to the Martins', she drew inward to her own thoughts and fears.

Their lives had become fragmented since the strange ceremony that Frank had performed last month. Certain things were normal, others were not.

They were making love regularly now—which was wonderful—yet at least once a week Frank went to work late, and came home early. He was not pushing as hard as he had been. It was as if he no longer cared about his job.

His behavior with the girls was even more bothersome. He had been a very attentive, loving father, but over the past weeks it seemed as if he was barely aware of their existence. Like tonight. In the past he would never have forgotten such a simple thing as saying goodnight to them.

At first the girls had been worried sick about his strange behavior. But that worry was beginning to develop into confusion. Should she send them away to a private school?

Just for a semester?

They had talked about it last year, but then had decided to wait a little longer. So it wouldn't be something out of the clear blue sky.

Frank parked behind the Polks' BMW in the Martins' driveway, shut out the headlights and switched off the ignition. He sat there a moment in the darkness, gripping the steering wheel with both hands, staring at the house. The lights were on in the living room and kitchen, and Cheryl could see their friends inside.

"What is it, Frank?" she said softly. Her heart was pounding.

He turned to her, worry in his eyes. "I hope they're not still mad at me for . . . what I did last month."

"You apologized. They understand," she said.

"It was just a game," he said. "Like a ouija board, or reading palms . . . something like that."

Cheryl reached out and touched him on the cheek. "No games tonight," she said. "Just cards."

He nodded. "And if I drink too much, you can drive," he said. He took the keys out of the ignition and handed them to her. "Deal?"

"It's a deal," Cheryl said.

"I love you."

"And I love you, darling." She leaned across the center console and they kissed, his lips warm. Responsive. Her old Frank.

They parted, and Frank got out of the van, hurried around to her side and helped her down. Together they went up the walk, but before they could ring the bell, the door opened and Fred was standing there, a drink in hand and a grin on his face.

"We were watching you two out there," he said waggishly as they came into the house. "And now we know why you bought that van. You're just a couple of kids who want to make out in the back."

Susan and Clinton were seated on the couch across the room, and she laughed. "I tried to talk Clinton into buying one of those sex wagons," she said. "But his idea of roughing it is martinis by the Holiday Inn pool, and a king-sized bed with a vibrator in the room."

"That's definitely roughing it," Clinton said, smiling. "The Hyatt Regency is more to my liking."

Marion seemed a little pale, and there were dark circles under her eyes, but she managed to smile. "We didn't know if you two were going to make it. We were going to start without you."

"Oh, no, you don't," Frank said. "I'm feeling lucky tonight. Poker's in my blood, and I'm going to be leaving here a hell of a lot richer than I am right now."

"Oh, jeez. Is this the pride that goeth before the hard fall?" Fred quipped.

"Only if I don't get a drink," Frank said.

"Water on the rocks for Frank," Clinton said, a slight edge to his voice, and they all laughed again.

It wasn't natural, though. Cheryl could feel an underlying tension in all of them.

Fred mixed them drinks, and after half an hour of light chitchat and snacks, they went into the dining room where the regular table had been shoved aside, and a six-sided, green felt-topped game table had been set up.

They took their places. Clinton opened the deck of cards and began shuffling them as Fred mixed them all another round. When he returned with the drinks and took his place, Cheryl cut the cards and Clinton dealt them out.

"Five card draw, doubles or better to open," he said.

"Quarter ante?" Frank asked, passing a couple of rolls of quarters across the table to Cheryl.

"Sounds good," Clinton said.

Cheryl wasn't really concentrating, and she drew badly, not improving her hand, but she stuck with it, matching the bets and raises nevertheless, and losing the first hand to Susan, who had come up with three queens against her husband's three jacks and Frank's two pair.

Marion and Clinton weren't playing well either, and after an hour it was evident to Cheryl that Fred, Susan and Frank were the only ones having a really good time.

It seemed that Fred was waiting for something to

happen, waiting for Frank to say or do something. And she recalled that Frank had supposedly filled his head with that nonsense about contacting their dead baby. The night that Frank had staged his ceremony, Fred had actually said that he had heard their child. Cheryl had forgotten the remark until now, and looking at him gave her a little chill.

Susan, on the other hand, was obviously flirting with Frank. And it made her a little sad that her friend would even consider something like that. She could see that Clinton had noticed it as well, and as the evening progressed he became more and more taciturn.

"Are you going deer hunting this year, Frank?" Clinton finally asked, in an effort to break his own mood.

Frank looked up from his hand and shrugged. "I don't know. I haven't even got my license yet. But if I do, it won't be up north with the guys from the office again."

"How about your little shack up in Door County?" Fred asked. Neither he nor Clinton were hunters. "You could open that up."

"That little twenty-four-room shack would be a bitch to heat in the winter, but if the hunting was any good up there I might give it a try." Frank laid two cards face down on the table as Susan dealt their draws. "Two," he said when it was his turn, and as the cards were dealt to him, he picked them up and inserted them into his hand. "If I go hunting at all this year, it'll probably be around here. I thought about scouting around over the weekend if the weather is good."

"How can you do it, Frank?" Marion asked.

Frank looked up at her. "Scout around?"

"No, I mean actually kill a little deer?"

Frank took a moment to answer, and everyone at the table was looking at him. "Well, first of all I don't kill little deer, only grown-up ones. Second of all, unless the deer population is controlled by hunting, much of the existing herd would starve to death. And thirdly, I only kill animals I intend eating. No different than the steaks you have for dinner, Marion. It's just that you don't actually participate in the kill."

Cheryl couldn't help thinking about the rabbit that Frank had killed last month. She presumed he had thrown the carcass away that night, and had not eaten it.

"It still bothers me," Marion said. She glanced down at her cards, then turned them face down on the table. "What time is it getting to be?"

Fred looked at his watch. "A little before ten."

"Anyone hungry?" Marion asked.

"Starved," Susan said.

"Bite-sized steaks?" Frank quipped.

Marion wanted to flare, Cheryl could see that, but she smiled a second later. "Broccoli and cauliflower for you, Franklin Rader," she said. She pushed away from the table and got up. "This hand of mine?" she said, tossing her cards down on the table. "Burn it."

Everyone laughed, the tense mood of a few moments ago broken. They all were trying, including Frank, and for that Cheryl was grateful.

They finished out their hand, Fred winning this time with a full house, and then they all went into the living room where he mixed them drinks.

Frank stood by the fireplace; he raised his cool glass to his forehead and half closed his eyes.

"Headache back?" Cheryl asked.

"Yeah," he said, glancing at her, and then he turned to Fred. "I hope I didn't upset Marion with all that talk about deer hunting."

"Not at all," Fred said. "But don't be too surprised if she corners you one of these days and takes you to task for it. I don't think she's ever forgiven you for that year when you called us all over to your house to see the deer you had killed. We had figured on seeing a bunch of steaks and roasts all bundled up in your freezer, not the carcass hanging from the tree in your back yard."

Frank chuckled. "Venison is just like beef. It has to be aged for a few days or so."

"I know, but it was quite a shock for Marion."

"She was quiet that afternoon," Frank said.

"Quiet hell, she damned near lost her lunch."

Frank set his drink down on the mantel. "I'm sorry Fred, but I'm going to have to go home."

Cheryl jumped up. "Are you all right?"

"This headache is blowing the back of my head off. I've got to take a couple of pills and go to bed. Tomorrow's a big day at work."

Marion had come from the kitchen, carrying a tray of small pizzas. She looked from Frank to Cheryl. "You two aren't going already, are you?"

Cheryl crossed the room to her, and pecked her on the cheek. "Frank's headache is getting worse. He has to get home to bed."

"I'm sorry, Frank," she said. "Have you been seeing a doctor?"

Frank nodded. "Right along, thanks. I've just got to get to bed now."

Marion looked down at the pizzas on the tray, then set them down on the coffee table. "Pepperoni and Italian sausage. Just for you," she said.

Frank managed a grin. "I'll take a rain check."

"You'd better drive," Frank said when they were outside. He got in the passenger side of the van.

"Did you bring any of your tablets with you?" she asked, starting the van and flipping the headlights on.

"They're at home."

Cheryl backed out of the driveway, then headed across town, driving carefully to minimize the motion for him.

All the way home they didn't talk. Cheryl concentrated on her driving, glancing at her husband every now and then, and Frank rode with his head back against the seat, his eyes closed.

It was shortly before 11:00 P.M. when they pulled into their garage. Cheryl shut off the lights and ignition.

Without a word, Frank went out to the driveway, where he stared down the street toward the corner.

Cheryl came out of the garage, closed the door, and took Frank's arm. "I'll run a nice, hot bath for you," she said.

He turned and looked down at her, his eyes strange, almost luminous in the dark. "That's all right," he said softly. "I'm going for a walk."

Cheryl was confused. "Are you sure?"

"Of course I'm sure," he said. She saw that he was on the verge of losing his temper; she let go of his arm.

"Is your headache better?"

"Some," he said, glancing down the street toward the corner. "I just have to get some fresh air, that's all."

"I'll go with you . . . ," she started, but Frank exploded.

"Go to bed, goddamn it! I want fresh air, not company!"

Cheryl backed up a step. "I'm worried about you," she said in a small voice.

"Don't nag me," he said through clenched teeth. "I told you everything would be all right soon. Now don't nag."

He turned down the driveway and onto the sidewalk, disappearing around the corner at the end of the block.

Cheryl shivered and hugged herself against the cool night air, and after a while she turned and went back into the house, her eyes moist, her stomach fluttering.

4

Klubertanz sat across the table from Brenda Wolfe, picking at his salad, his linen napkin on his knee, his mind a thousand miles away. She had been saying something to him. Was saying something. The other diners at the Top Of The Park restaurant in downtown Madison were laughing, eating, drinking, enjoying their evening out. But not Klubertanz.

Brenda was saying something to him. Something that required a response. He looked up at her. She was smiling sadly.

"I knew this was going to be a bust even before I agreed to meet you up here," she was saying as he finally focused on her.

She took a sip of her wine and set her glass down as Klubertanz was raising his. He could feel his cheeks flushing.

"I'll never talk you to bed this way, will I?" he said. He sipped at his wine, and set the glass down.

"I even brought my overnight bag," she said without rancor. "Tonight could have been the night, lieutenant."

"Sorry, counselor," Klubertanz said, looking at his salad, his hunger completely gone. He pushed his plate away and beckoned for a waiter.

When the man came he ordered a brandy straight with no ice. "How about you, Brenda?"

She shook her head. "The wine will do. I'm at least going to get a good meal out of this."

When the waiter was gone, Klubertanz reached across the table, and covered her hands with his. "I'm sorry," he said with feeling.

The crooked smile that he loved in her creased her cheeks now. "So am I," she said. "I could have my dinner in front of the television and have a better shake than this."

Klubertanz sighed deeply. He was tired. Mentally fatigued. So many dead ends. Nothing seemed to fit. And yet everything did.

He realized that he had been drifting again, and he looked up.

"You look as if the entire world was on your shoulders, Stan," she said. "Care to talk about it?"

He tried to dismiss her offer with a shrug, but she insisted.

"No, I mean it. I bring my problems to you. How about asking me for help? We women make awfully swell partners, you know. Feminine intuition, and all that. Feminine logic?"

The waiter came with the brandy. When he was gone again, Klubertanz picked up the snifter in both hands and rolled the liquor around in the glass. "Ahern, Shapiro and Sister Colletta."

"Department giving you a hassle?"

Klubertanz shook his head. "Not really. Miller tells me to keep plugging away. Something will come up."

"And it will."

Klubertanz looked into her eyes. "The three murders are related."

Brenda raised her right eyebrow. "That the official line?"

"If you mean has the connection been made on the investigation logs, no it hasn't."

"But you have."

"I have," he said, lowering his head a moment. When he looked up, Brenda was studying him intently. "We'll talk, but not at dinner. It'll keep."

"I'll drink to that, on one condition," she said, once again raising her wine glass in a toast. Klubertanz lifted his brandy glass. "You'll join me for dinner. And I do mean join me."

"A bargain."

They both drank, and then talked about inconsequential things such as the movies they had both intended to see, but had missed; the quality, or lack of it, on television; and even the weather; it was promising to be "one bitch of a winter," in Brenda's words.

After their soup came prime rib for him, a small fillet for her, with more wine, more light talk with little or no substance.

"Dessert, sir?" the waiter was asking Klubertanz finally.

Klubertanz looked up and shook his head. "Not for me. Brenda?"

"No," she said.

"An after-dinner drink?"

"We'll have it at the bar," Klubertanz said. "I'll take the check now."

"Yes, sir," the waiter said.

Klubertanz paid, left a respectable tip, and then got up and helped Brenda with her chair. Together they crossed the dining room and sat down at the bar, behind which were tall windows that looked across the square on the capitol dome. The granite and marble edifice, with its gold statue at the top, was bathed in soft lights, and after they had ordered their drinks, they both sat looking across at it.

"Beautiful," Brenda said.

"Yes, it is," Klubertanz agreed.

Brenda turned to him, her face softly glowing in the dim light, and he wanted to reach over and caress her cheek, kiss her.

"Thanks for the dinner, Stan, but I think that's as far as it's going to go for us tonight," she said.

He had to smile. But she did not.

"You've got what you think is a triple murder on your hands, and you're having trouble with it."

"Do you want the long, or the short version?"

"The short version. We'll flesh it out from there."

He lit himself a cigarette as he tried to organize his

thoughts.

"Most of what we've come up with on Ahern and Shapiro and the nun has been sent up to the DA's office. Have you seen any of it?"

"I glanced at the pile. Pretty gruesome."

"Did you happen to look at the autopsy reports?"

"Didn't have to," Brenda said. "The photographs were enough."

"The time of death on all three of them may not be quite accurate."

"What?" Brenda asked. "Maxwell was the signing officer, wasn't he?"

Klubertanz nodded.

"Then what are you talking about?"

Where to begin, he wondered briefly, looking at her. How to approach it? From the beginning?

Slowly, Klubertanz told her everything he had learned to date, including the negative results of their roundup of known homosexual offenders as well as rapists, along with the testimony of witnesses in Shapiro's and Ahern's building who swore they had heard the two men crying, and witnesses at the church who had seen Sister Colletta entering her room around 10:00 P.M. But then he backtracked to his meeting with Maxwell at the Dane County Morgue, and their discussion of rigor mortis.

In the telling, he could see that Brenda was having a difficult time accepting what he was saying, just as he had had a hard time swallowing it when Maxwell had first told him.

"That's impossible," she said.

"Yes," Klubertanz said, nodding patiently. "Nevertheless, half a dozen tests on each of the three bodies came up with the same results. And Maxwell isn't the kind of man who would pull that kind of a stunt."

"Why wasn't it on the autopsy report, then?" she asked, sharply. "Why the hell wasn't a coroner's jury ordered?"

Klubertanz looked away momentarily. "It was a case of the scientific data not fitting the known circumstances."

Brenda thought about that a minute. "Then it's nothing more than a glitch in Maxwell's equipment, or even his procedures. Maybe he's slipping. Who knows? But you've got to be reasonable about this, Stan."

"My sentiments, exactly, but I'm not finished."

Brenda looked into his eyes for a long moment. "I was afraid you were going to say that."

"There was an inscription on the altar beneath the nun's body. It was written in blood."

Brenda was grim lipped. "I saw it in the reports, but it didn't seem to make much sense."

He told her what Msgr. Ferrari had explained to him about the ritual of the Catholic mass, and the offering of the bread and wine as a recreation of the last supper, including the prayer that was said by the priest during this portion of the mass.

"Written on the floor in Sister Colletta's blood was a parody of that prayer. Instead of paying homage to the Lord, or to Jesus Christ, the prayer paid homage to Astaroth."

"What's Astaroth?"

"In demonology, he is said to be the destroyer demon."

"A spook?"

"A demon that someone in this city apparently takes very seriously."

Brenda sat back in her seat and toyed with her drink for a moment. "The writing on the floor was in Latin."

"Yes."

"A priest?"

"Possibly. Osborne guesses it could be a priest."

Brenda thought about that. "But you don't," she said.

Klubertanz shook his head. "But don't ask me why. It's just a feeling at this stage."

Again she hesitated. "So where's the problem for you, Stan? What's giving you fits?"

"If it's not a priest . . . and that's a small enough group to check quite easily . . . then I would suspect it would be a crazy. But Osborne disagrees."

"It would have to be someone crazy to mutilate their

bodies like that."

"Not necessarily. According to Osborne, anyone involved in black magic or the occult could conceivably work himself up to that level."

"What level?"

"The black mass. Human sacrifice."

Brenda turned away and gazed across at the capitol dome, as if she needed something real as a counterpoint to what she was being told. When she looked back, there was a sympathetic expression in her eyes.

"I imagine you're checking the libraries to see who is displaying an interest in the occult."

Klubertanz nodded. Four of his people had been working on that until Capt. Miller had pulled them off. "Libraries, as well as bookstores and mail-order houses. But the numbers are approaching the thousand mark. There's a lot of interest in this town."

"Even that's not your problem, though, is it?"

"No," Klubertanz said. "I can accept the possibility that someone out there is involved in a parlor game that's gotten out of hand."

"But?"

"But the condition of the bodies. The rigor mortis. If I accept witchcraft as an explanation, then I'll have to accept the fact that it works . . . that it's real."

It was barely 11:00 P.M. when Klubertanz dropped Brenda off at her westside apartment.

"Keep in touch," she told him, as if they lived in separate parts of the world, which in a way they did.

He drove back downtown, but instead of heading back to his apartment, he swung over to Good Shepherd Church, where he parked across the street from the rectory and offices.

There was a dim light over the front door and another over the gate that led into the courtyard at the side of the church.

Klubertanz sat in the darkness, watching the church, wondering exactly what had gone on there last month.

After a minute or two he got out of his car, pocketed his keys and went across the street, letting himself in through the courtyard gate. It was mostly dark here, with even deeper shadows around the buildings and beneath the trees. The fountain at the center had not yet been turned off for the winter, and its bubbling and splashing was a comforting sound. Restful. Yet there was fear here. Thick. Almost palpable.

To the left was the residence hall and administration building. At the back of the courtyard was the school, and to the right the mammoth church rose high above everything else, its tall, stained-glass windows dark.

Klubertanz moved silently away from the gate, passing the fountain, and reached the walkway that led from the residence hall to the side entrance of the church.

Sister Colletta had come this way. In her nightgown, robe and slippers. They had found her clothing neatly folded on one of the pews near the altar. No rips, no blood.

At length, he turned and headed softly across to the church, where he let himself in, taking care to make absolutely no noise.

The doorknob had been dusted as a matter of routine. Mostly smudges, only three clear prints. Useless. Totally useless.

He went down the corridor, walking up on the balls of his feet so that he would make no noise, and entered the nave from a door that opened near the confessionals.

Several rows of candles were lit on either side of the altar, and a small light shone near the front of the church. The vaulted ceiling drew his eyes upwards. A feeling of space. Of peace. Of security.

What had Sister Colletta come looking for that night? Solace? "Well adjusted." "A flower of a nun." Those were the terms the other nuns and priests used to describe her. Her mother felt that she might have missed her family, but what young woman away from home does not?

Slowly, he moved deeper into the church, past the statue of the Virgin Mary, a rack with votive candles beneath her, finally stopping where he could see the hanging crucifix suspended above the altar.

It was a new one. Modern, stainless steel. The old hand-carved wooden one had been destroyed. It had been desecrated, and therefore had to be burned.

"She came here for comfort," a voice came from his right.

Klubertanz swung around, his hand reaching for his shoulder holster. Monsignor Ferrari got to his feet from where he had been sitting in one of the pews half-a-dozen rows back.

"You startled me, Father," Klubertanz said.

Monsignor Ferrari slipped out of the pew, genuflected slowly, painfully, and then joined Klubertanz in front of the altar. He was dressed in a long, thick, off-white hassock, buttons up the front. He looked about ten years older than the last time Klubertanz had seen him.

"I come here every evening," the priest said.

"Why?"

Monsignor Ferrari smiled. "To pray. What else?"

Klubertanz was embarrassed. "I'm sorry . . . I didn't . . . ."

"That's all right, my son," the priest said, taking Klubertanz's arm. "But let's leave this place first, before we talk."

Arm in arm they shuffled across the church, past the confessional booths, down the corridor and then out to the courtyard.

"I love this garden, even in the winter. Except, then I miss the fountain," Msgr. Ferrari said.

They went across to one of the stone benches and sat down. For a long time they just sat there, listening to the gentle sound of the splashing water.

Finally Klubertanz broke the silence. "You say she came to the church for comfort, Father. Comfort from what?"

"I don't know," the old priest said. "We all need comfort at one time or another. She had come often to the church to pray. For continued faith, perhaps. For strength.

For goodness."

Klubertanz glanced toward the church.

"You're troubled."

He turned back to the priest. "I believe that whoever murdered Sister Colletta murdered two men the night before."

"Shapiro and Ahern?" the priest asked. "I read about them in the newspaper. But why do you suspect their murderer was the same?"

Klubertanz told the priest about Maxwell's findings, and then what the psychiatrist, Osborne, had told him. By the time he was finished, the priest's complexion had turned sallow and his breathing seemed rapid.

"Then, it's true," Msgr. Ferrari said.

"What's true?" Klubertanz asked, a chill playing up his back.

Monsignor Ferrari turned to him, his eyes intense, almost glowing with their own light. "There is a gathering of witches here. I know it now for a fact."

"How do you know it?"

"The ritual murders."

"The work of a crazy person," Klubertanz said, finding himself taking the opposite side.

Monsignor Ferrari shook his head. "I've spoken with other priests in the area. In the past few weeks every single Catholic church in Madison has been entered and the altars desecrated in one way or another."

"Have they reported it to the police?"

Monsignor Ferrari nodded. "Vandalism. It happens all the time."

"Why just Catholic churches?" Klubertanz asked. "And why desecrate the altars?"

"Witchcraft and Satanism have selected Catholicism as their main target almost from the beginning. Nuns and priests are especially prime targets, as are our places of worship. As I told you before, the witches' black mass is nothing more than a travesty of a real mass, the words Lucifer, Asmodeus and Astaroth being substituted for the Father, the Son and the Holy Ghost."

That was it, then, Klubertanz thought, looking again toward the church. It was as if battle lines had been drawn. Yet he was having trouble accepting it. "I can't believe in it. I can't believe in demons and witches and black magic."

"Do you admit the existence of good and evil?"

"That's what I do for a living."

"God personifies good, and if you admit that, you must admit a personification of evil. The devil. Lucifer. His archangels."

"It's . . . . " Klubertanz couldn't finish.

"Fantasy?"

Klubertanz nodded.

"No," Monsignor Ferrari said simply. Klubertanz found the certainty of the man's knowledge as comforting as its implications were frightening.

5

It was Wednesday again, a week and a half before Halloween. Outside, the weather was cool and very crisp. The weathermen were predicting increasing cloudiness over the next few days, with a possibility of some light, scattered snow by the weekend.

At the Polks' home, Clinton had laid a birch fire in the fireplace, and the house smelled good. Warm. Cozy.

Susan had dressed in silk lounging pajamas, and although she had concealed the fact from her husband, she wore no underclothing tonight.

She had no idea why she had dressed this way, except that, for a change, she felt deliciously devilish. Almost evil.

They had not made love for the past seven days, and after the previous weeks of lovemaking almost every evening, she was very frustrated. She had the vague idea at the back of her mind that flirting with Frank might make Clinton so jealous he would do something about it. What that something might be, she had no conscious idea, but she had her fantasies.

Fred and Marion showed up just at eight, and after Clinton had mixed them both a drink, and they were all settled down in front of the fire, Fred asked if Frank and Cheryl were coming.

"As far as I know, they are," Clinton said. "I had lunch with Frank yesterday. He seems a lot better."

"I certainly hope so," Marion said.

"What do you mean?" Susan asked.

Marion looked at her, and then at Clinton. She was wearing a skirt and blouse, her hair was done up nicely and she was wearing a touch of makeup. Except for the expression in her eyes, she looked a lot better than she had for a long time.

"He's been kind of crazy lately," she said.

"You mean that business at his house last month?" Clinton asked.

Marion nodded. "I did some reading on it," she said somewhat timidly.

Fred looked at her in surprise. "Why'd you do that?"

"Because of you."

"What do you mean?"

Susan felt uncomfortable with the conversation, but she was at a loss for words at the moment.

"You were starting to believe what he was saying."

"It was nothing more than a parlor game, for God's sake, Marion," Fred said. He glanced at Clinton and Susan. "But you have to admit one thing."

Marion said nothing.

"Right after Frank's little game, the Milwaukee thing came through."

"You can't tell me that . . . ."

"No, listen to me, Marion. The Milwaukee deal looked like it was going to be a bust. But all of a sudden everything got switched around."

Susan felt a little chill play up her spine. Clinton had told her what had happened at the lab with the cultures. It had been a mistake that, nevertheless, was turning out to be a major research breakthrough. And she could see that her husband was thinking the same thing.

"Maybe there is something to it, after all," she said.

Marion jerked, almost as if she had been slapped. "Come on, Susan. You can't be serious."

Susan shrugged. "I don't know."

"Well, I do," Clinton said. Everyone turned to him. "I've done some reading on the subject as well."

"When?" Susan asked, surprised.

"Last week. I went down to the university library and looked at a couple of books."

"And?" she asked.

"It's called mass hysteria, or mass hypnosis. Frank's little ceremony was part of what's called a witch's black mass."

Marion shrank back in the couch, but Fred's eyes were bright.

"Fred and I both reacted to it in a positive manner. Just like a pep talk at half time. Unconsciously, we were charged up. As a result, Fred gets his contract, and I've made a possible breakthrough."

"It was disgusting," Marion said.

"I agree," Clinton replied. "But it was powerful, evidently powerful enough to affect Fred and me."

The doorbell rang, and Susan got up. "It's probably Frank and Cheryl."

"I don't want to talk about this with Frank," Marion said urgently.

"Take it easy, Marion," Fred said. "No harm was done."

"We're just going to play cards tonight," Susan said. "Promise."

She left the living room and opened the front door just as the bell rang again. Frank and Cheryl stood on the porch.

"For a minute there I thought you were just going to let us stand out here for the evening," Frank said, smiling. "Are we late?"

"No." Susan stepped back and let them in. "Fred and Marion arrived just a couple of minutes ago."

Frank kissed her on the cheek and her stomach fluttered. He was wearing the same aftershave lotion as the last time.

Cheryl kissed her on the cheek as Frank went into the living room.

"How is Marion?" Cheryl whispered.

Susan closed the door. "A lot better. I think she's finally beginning to accept it."

"Good," Cheryl said. She seemed tired, or worried about something.

"Are you okay?"

Cheryl looked sharply at her. "I'm fine," she said. "Do I look bad?"

"No. I'm just a worrywart."

The two of them went into the living room, where Clinton was pouring Frank a straight brandy.

"What can I get for you, Cheryl?" he asked over his shoulder.

"A glass of wine," Cheryl said. She sat down on the couch next to Marion, and patted the woman's hand. "Haven't seen you since last week. When are you coming over for coffee?"

Marion managed a slight smile. "Tomorrow, maybe," she said.

"I'll make a coffee cake."

Clinton poured her a glass of wine and brought it over to her, then sat down next to his wife. Frank stood by the fireplace.

He was dressed in dark slacks and a thick turtleneck sweater. Virile, the single word popped into Susan's head. But she kept herself from taking the thought any further.

"We were just talking about what a good week we've all had," Clinton said. "How about you, Frank?"

Frank smiled. "I had a great week, too. Got a lot done."

"Solar energy is the thing these days," Clinton said. "I think you got in the right business at the right time."

"Oh, that," Frank said off-handedly. "Work is going pretty well too, I guess."

Susan wondered what it was he had accomplished if he wasn't talking about his work, but Marion's eyes had widened, and she bit her question off. Instead, she quipped, "Well, if this evening is like our other card sessions, we're all going to have a couple of drinks, and then be subjected to some very bad jokes."

They all laughed.

"You've cut us to the quick," Frank said. "Hasn't she, Fred?"

"To the quick," Fred agreed. "And I had half-a-dozen new jokes all set for tonight. You should hear the one about the two Swedes."

"Oh, no, you don't," Cheryl said. "I'd rather lose at cards."

Susan got to her feet. "I'll vote for cards right now," she said, winking at Cheryl. "It's up to us girls to win tonight; maybe it'll keep the guys quiet."

"Not a chance," Frank said.

They all rose then, and Susan said, "Go ahead downstairs; there's a tray in the fridge I've got to bring down."

"And I'm going to the bathroom," Frank said. He went through the dining room as the others filed down to the basement rec-room.

Susan went into the kitchen, got out a large tray of hors d'oeuvres she had made up earlier in the afternoon and pulled the plastic wrap off as Frank came out of the bathroom near the back door.

She looked up and smiled.

"Need any help?" he asked.

"I can manage," she said. "Just get the door."

As Frank passed her, he said, "I like the outfit," and he patted her on the ass.

She had just started to pick up the tray, but she turned around. "Frank!" she snapped.

He stopped in mid-stride and he was looking at her, his eyes bright. "I'll be damned," he said softly.

She stared into his eyes for a long moment, not sure whether or not she should be offended. But deep inside she was enjoying it. "You'll be damned, what?"

"If you ran around like that at my house, we'd be in bed all the time," he said. He took a step closer. He was smiling, and Susan was very conscious of his after-shave, and of her heart, which was pounding nearly out of her chest.

"Run around like what?" she said. The others would be waiting for them. Christ, if Clinton decided to come upstairs right now . . . .

Frank reached out and touched her right breast with his fingertips. She flinched but didn't move away. "Run around with nothing on under your outfit."

She glanced over her shoulder at the kitchen door. Frank caught the motion of her eyes.

"They're downstairs," he said softly. "We've got a minute."

"For what?" she said, a catch in her voice.

"To make sure," Frank said. He unbuttoned the front of her silk lounging pajama top. She wanted to pull back, to push his hands away, to tell him to stop, but she could not. She could only look into his eyes.

He had three of the buttons undone, and he reached inside and cupped her left breast in his hand, then stepped closer, bent down and took the nipple in his mouth, the pleasure coursing through her like an electric shock, making her knees weak.

"For Christ's sake, Frank," she moaned. "Not here, like this."

He straightened up and took her into his arms, and she could not stop herself from pressing her body against his, and she could feel that he was hard. Deliciously big and hard.

"Jesus, Frank," she said, breathing hard.

They kissed deeply, his tongue darting inside her mouth, his hands on her buttocks, pressing her against his hardness.

"What the hell are you two doing up there, having an orgy?" Clinton called from downstairs.

Frank looked down at Susan and smiled. "You're goddamned right," he called out.

Susan giggled.

"Well, hurry it up. The cards are hot," Clinton said.

"So am I," Susan said.

Frank released her, then took the tray as she rebuttoned her top, and together they went downstairs.

"I've left some money on the counter," Frank quipped, setting the tray down on the buffet.

Everyone laughed, but as Susan took her seat across the table from Frank, her eyes briefly caught Cheryl's, and the communication was instant. Susan was almost a hundred percent certain that Cheryl suspected that something had gone on up in the kitchen.

Clinton was dealing the cards. "The usual. Five card draw, a pair or better to open," he said.

"Come on, ladies," Fred added. "Let's see just how good you're going to play tonight."

All through the evening Susan found herself avoiding Cheryl's eyes. And Frank wasn't doing anything to help the situation. He could not keep his eyes off her. Every time she looked over at him, he was staring at her. At first it made her terribly self-conscious, but after awhile she began to enjoy it, no matter what Cheryl thought or didn't think. Twice she missed her bet, as she fantasized lying nude next to Frank. The first time they were on the kitchen floor upstairs with everyone else down here. But the second time they were on a deserted beach. It was early evening, the stars were out, the moon bright, and the weather warm as they made love.

"It's a lovely outfit, Susan. Is it new?" Cheryl was asking.

Susan blinked. "Got it last week," she said.

"Nice."

"That's not all that's nice," Susan wanted to say, but she bit her tongue.

"Dawn is Cheryl's mink, and Felicity is my Ferrari," Frank quipped.

Instantly a silence fell over the room, and they all turned to Marion, whose complexion had turned white. For a long moment Frank looked confused, but then what he had said seemed to dawn on him, and he turned red faced.

"Christ, Marion, I'm sorry," he said.

"It's all right," Marion said, tears starting to come to her eyes. She got up.

"Me and my big mouth," Frank said. He seemed very contrite. "I'm really sorry, Marion."

She looked at him, shook her head, then turned and went upstairs. Cheryl jumped up, glared at her husband and then followed Marion.

"It wasn't your fault," Fred said. "You didn't do anything intentional."

"I'm really sorry. I don't know what to say."

"How about a drink?" Clinton said, getting to his feet. "I know I can use one."

"Me, too," Fred said, and Susan nodded.

Clinton went upstairs to get more ice, leaving the three of them alone.

They both stared at Frank, and Susan found herself wishing desperately that Fred would get up and go to the bathroom or something. She wanted to be in Frank's arms again. She wanted to feel his hands on her body.

"Next week we're going to meet at my house," Frank said softly.

Fred nodded, and Susan could feel that she was moist. God, she needed him.

"But not on Wednesday," Frank was saying. "We're going to meet a week from this Saturday."

"Saturday night is fine with us," Fred said, and Susan nodded. He was going to be wonderful in bed.

"You're going to have a little trouble this coming week with the Milwaukee contract, but it's nothing to worry about," Frank said. Before Fred could react, he turned to Susan. She felt like she was going to melt. Her breasts ached. "Clinton's going to have some trouble at the lab. Nothing major, but he'll weather it. Our only problem right now is sex. None of us have had any sex lately."

"How in the hell did you know that?" Fred asked. Susan's heart was pounding.

"Saturday night," Frank said, ignoring the question. "After that everything will be fine."

"That's Halloween," Fred said.

Frank looked at Susan, a slight smile playing across his lips.

"All Hallows Eve," he said. "It will happen then."

"What will happen then?" she asked. It was almost as if she was in a dream, as if she was living one of her own fantasies.

"Whatever you'd like, Susan," he said. "Whatever."

6

Early the next Saturday morning Frank Rader dressed in corduroy slacks, a wool shirt, and his hunting boots and vest, and then tromped downstairs while Cheryl feigned sleep.

She opened her eyes, but remained huddled beneath the blankets, listening to him moving around in the kitchen. He was whistling.

Outside the window, the sun was bright in an absolutely clear, blue sky. The leaves on the trees had turned, most of them a muted gold or silvery brown, but others brilliant reds and oranges.

It was a perfect sort of Midwestern day, the kind that had always made Frank happy. Hunting season would open soon, and before long she would be making his sandwiches and coffee for his weekend forays into the fields and woods.

Fall had always been an up time for Frank. He was a tweed and sweater person. An outdoors man.

She heard the girls getting up, using the bathroom and racing downstairs. She closed her eyes tightly, trying to block out the sun and the ordinary Saturday morning sounds of her family. She was confused and frightened.

Since Wednesday, Frank had been in good spirits. Free. Easy going. Generous. There were no black, angry moods. Maybe the neurologist knew what he was talking about. Maybe the aftershocks from the accident *were* finally beginning to fade. Yet so much had happened that she was afraid to believe that Frank was actually getting better.

"Let's go sleepyhead," Frank called up from the front hall. The girls laughed.

Cheryl opened her eyes.

"Come on, mom, dad's got pancakes on the table already," Dawn called.

Someone came up the stairs in a rush, and Felicity burst through the bedroom door and leaped on the end of the bed. Her face was animated, her eyes bright.

"We're going out in the woods! Dad says we can help look for deer signs! We can help him pick a place to hunt!" Felicity bubbled.

"Right now, this morning?" Cheryl asked. Frank hadn't said anything to her about it.

"Right now, mom! Soon as we finish breakfast. Come on."

Cheryl sat up in bed and tousled her daughter's hair. "Go on and have your breakfast. I'll be right down."

Felicity scooted off the bed, and for a moment she looked seriously at her mother. "You're not going back to sleep, are you?"

Cheryl laughed and shook her head.

"Promise?"

"Scout's honor," Cheryl said, holding up three fingers.

"Hooray!" Felicity whooped, and she ran out of the room, shouting, "Mom's up. Mom's up."

Cheryl got out of bed and went to brush her teeth. When she was finished she looked at herself in the mirror. Something she had been doing a lot, lately.

Something was going on between Frank and Susan Polk. Or at least it had been on Wednesday night. It had been obvious from the expression on Frank's face when he and Susan had come down together from the kitchen. And it had been like a gigantic neon sign illuminating Susan's. The woman had been flushed, and for the rest of the evening, she and Frank had not been able to keep their eyes off each other.

Cheryl hung her head. Why, she asked herself. On top of everything else, why this now? It wasn't fair.

"Your pancakes are getting cold, mom," Felicity shouted from the foot of the stairs.

"Coming," Cheryl called over her shoulder.

The girls were as agile with their affections as little

puppydogs. They could be beaten one day, and the next bubble over with love and enthusiasm, with nothing more than a mile to set them off.

Cheryl shook her head. Frank was her husband. She would stick by him.

She dressed in a pair of wool slacks, a sweater and sneakers with thick white socks, threw on some lipstick and a little foundation, and then went downstairs to the kitchen where Frank and the girls were just finishing their pancakes.

Frank jumped up when she came in, poured her a cup of coffee and a glass of orange juice, and brought her a plate of pancakes that had been warming in the toaster oven.

"About time you got up, lazybones," he quipped. "We thought we were going to have to come up and drag you out of the sack."

The girls squealed with laughter, and Cheryl had to smile. "A lady needs her beauty rest, you know," she said, winking at the girls. They loved it.

"Oh, no, you don't," Frank said. "Look at me; I got less sleep than you." He made a funny face.

Cheryl couldn't help herself. She laughed out loud. For a moment she was totally relaxed; the knots in her stomach disappeared. She had her husband back.

"All right," Frank said, clapping his hands together. "Cheryl, you finish your breakfast. Girls, I want you to do the dishes. And I'll get the van out of the garage."

"Shall I pack a lunch?" Cheryl asked.

"Nope. I'm taking us out for lunch. Now, let's shake a leg; the day is wasting."

It was only a few minutes past 10:00 P.M., and already Clinton Polk was bored. There were at least three dozen people, most of them drunk, at the "department blow-out," as these get-togethers at Dr. Willis' home were called. And every time Polk attended one of them he swore he'd never come back to another. But each fall and each spring they talked him into it.

Gil Mortensen, his lab assistant, came across the large

living room to where Polk was leaning against the door-frame near the front vestibule.

"Hiya, Doctor Polk," he said, slopping some of his drink down his front.

"Looks like you're having a good time, Gil," Polk said dryly.

Mortensen waved his glass around. "Ol' Willis sure puts on a nice party," he said thickly.

"There's coffee in the kitchen," Polk suggested.

"No," Mortensen said. "Monday through Friday I'm yours, screw-ups or no screw-ups. Sundown Friday comes, and I'm on my own."

Polk's ears turned red. The little bastard. But he managed a smile, nevertheless. "See you bright and early Monday, then."

Mortensen stood there weaving back and forth, blinking, but then he shrugged and wandered off.

Clinton let his eyes roam around the room, finally spotting Susan sitting crosslegged on the floor with eight or ten other department wives.

She was beautiful. And at times he ached so badly to have her that he could hardly stand it. And yet, when they were in bed together, he often couldn't perform. It was frustrating for her, but even more frustrating for him.

The DS 19 experiment, the ongoing battle with the Regents over funding, and sex . . . or lack of it.

Clinton raised his glass to his lips and drank. It was turning out to be one hell of a fall, with winter promising to be just as bad, or even worse.

"All alone, Doctor Polk?" a girl said from behind him.

Polk turned around to look into the eyes of his lab assistant, Vicki Karsten. She was a tall, willowy girl, nearly his height, who always wore tattered blue jeans and sweatshirts around campus.

Tonight she was wearing a short knitted dress with a very wide, open weave. Her blonde hair reached to the middle of her back. And she was wearing makeup. She had her coat over her arm.

Although Clinton hated stupid women, and Vicki was

not particularly bright, she looked stunning this evening.

He glanced over her shoulder, but there was no one behind her. "Where's your date this evening?"

She smiled demurely. "I'm here stag tonight," she said. She looked across the living room. "This is a drag."

"You can say that again," Polk said.

Vicki looked at him. "I was just on my way out when I spotted you standing there all alone."

"You're not leaving already?"

The girl smiled again and shrugged. "Maybe not," she said. Her eyes were large, and deep blue, her cheekbones high and delicate, and her complexion unblemished. She was probably twenty or twenty-one at the most, Polk figured, and yet he found himself slightly tongue-tied in her presence. It was as if he was a kid all over again.

"I wanted to tell you how sorry I am about the way the experiment is going," she said after a moment.

Polk shook his head. "We're not going to talk about the lab tonight."

"Okay," she said. "But I wanted you to know that I think you're a great scientist."

"Thank you," Polk said. His knees felt rubbery.

"Let me hang up my coat," the girl said. She turned and laid her coat on the hall table atop a pile of others.

Polk hadn't moved, and when Vicki turned around she caught him staring at her legs. She smiled.

"I'm going upstairs," she said. "To fix my makeup." She crossed the hall and started slowly up the stairs, and Polk watched her ass, and the way the muscles rippled at the back of her legs.

At the top she looked back down at him, then disappeared down the upstairs hall.

Polk turned and looked back across the living room. Susan was still seated with the group of wives, and it looked as if she was in some kind of a heated discussion.

No one else was paying any attention to him, and after a couple of guilty seconds, he slipped into the hallway, set his drink down on the floor beside the stairs, and slowly went up, his right hand on the banister, his knees weak now.

This was all unreal. It wasn't really happening. Most likely he had misread her interest in him, and she'd be offended. Worse yet, she might even find him funny.

At the top, he stopped and looked down. No one had come out of the living room. No one had missed him.

When he turned around, Vicki was just coming out of the bathroom.

"Doctor Polk," she said.

"Call me Clinton. Please."

She nodded, but instead of coming toward the stairs, she turned and went down the hallway, opened one of the bedroom doors and went inside.

For several seconds Polk stood rooted to his spot. He knew he should turn around, go back downstairs, and retrieve his drink, but he couldn't.

He moved slowly down the hall, and just before the open door, he stopped again. What the hell was he doing? Christ, what the hell did he think he was doing?

He went into the bedroom just as Vicki was stepping out of her dress.

"Close the door, Clinton," she said softly.

With fumbling hands Polk closed the door and then watched as the young girl took off her flesh-colored bra, the nipples on her small breasts erect, and then panties, the small tuft of hair at her pubis a light, wispy blonde.

She came across the room to him, put her arms around his neck and kissed him deeply, pressing her body against his.

At first he didn't quite know what to do with his hands, but then he put his arms around her and caressed her incredibly soft back, letting his hands slide down to her firm buttocks, pressing her against his erection.

"Oooh," she said, looking up at him. Her lips were parted slightly; she moistened them with her tongue.

"Are you sure this is what you want, Vicki?" Polk said, his voice husky. It was a stupid thing to say.

The girl giggled, disengaged herself from him, and then went to the bed where she lay down on her back, her legs spread slightly. "It's up to you, Clinton," she said.

Polk stared at her lovely body for a few seconds longer, and then began taking his clothes off.

Still, he had the feeling of unreality. None of this could be happening. Others on the staff at the university had their stories about the young, willing grad-student assistants, but he had always dismissed such tales as mostly bullshit.

When he was undressed, he went to the girl on the bed, and soon they were intertwined, her body firm and wonderful, and he lost himself in her, forgetting for the moment about everything: the lab, the funding and especially Susan.

He almost came when he entered her, she was so tight and he was so excited.

"Yes . . . yes," she moaned. "Oh God . . . deeper . . . harder."

And then they were making love, with more passion than he had ever thought he was capable of. She was moaning and kissing him on the face and neck, her long, muscular legs tightly wrapped around his back, and he could not believe this was happening.

"Oh God, yes. Fuck me. Fuck me," the girl was crying. "Harder. Please . . . harder . . . ."

And finally he was coming, his entire body shuddering, and he was pushing himself deeper and deeper inside of the girl, and she squeezed her legs around his back to meet his thrusts.

He let out a long sigh of relief, his entire body relaxing. Vicki opened her eyes and looked up at him, a smile on her moist lips, her arms around his neck.

"I'm glad I didn't leave the party," she said softly.

"Me, too," Polk said, but he was embarrassed now, and he only wanted to get dressed and get back downstairs.

He reached down and kissed the girl on the nose, and then withdrew as she let her legs slide off his back.

When he rolled over, off the girl, he glanced up at the door. Susan was standing there, a drink in hand, a contemptuous smile on her face.

Marion Martin, finished in the bathroom, turned off the light and went back into the bedroom. Fred was already asleep, the clock radio above his head playing soft music.

One week from tonight was Halloween. This afternoon Fred had informed her that they would be going to the Raders' for a party that night. Fred had vehemently denied that Frank was planning anything, but Marion knew as well as she knew her own name that something would happen. Something like the last time.

Yet Marion knew that she was losing her resistance. Something was going out of her. Fight. The will to survive. Whatever. Standing next to the bed, looking down at her husband, she knew that she would go to the Raders' next Saturday night. She knew that she would endure whatever it was Frank was going to do.

She took off her robe and climbed in beneath the covers.

Fred didn't move, and before she turned out the light she leaned over and kissed him on the lips. In sleep he seemed composed. Peaceful.

Yesterday and all today had been pure hell for him. The Milwaukee contracts, which should have been in the mail by midweek, had not arrived. Fred had tried to call Peppinger, but the man had been out. So had the mayor.

"They're avoiding me," Fred had said fearfully last night after work. "Christ, I'm way the hell out on a limb, and now they're avoiding me."

Marion reached over and shut off the radio, then lay back on her pillow with a deep sigh.

Two months ago they had been happy. But then, in one night, it had all fallen apart.

She rolled over, squeezing her eyes shut against the tears welling up in them. Against the thoughts of Jessica. Against the suspicion that had been tormenting her. It wasn't fair, she thought. It just wasn't fair.

7

Lieutenant Klubertanz had spent most of the morning in Middleton, a suburb of Madison, where the body of an eighteen-year-old girl had been found in the woods near Lake Mendota. Two young boys, hiking around the lakeshore, had found the partially clad body.

At first he had been worried that it was connected with the other murders, but it hadn't been the same.

Maxwell's best guess was that she had been dead at least three months, had been raped, and then strangled. It was a routine murder, if murder could be routine, and Klubertanz found himself strangely grateful that it was so.

Back downtown he would have Missing Persons start a trace on the girl. Maxwell had promised a complete workup on the body, including a dental chart, by late afternoon. Once she had been identified, they could begin tracing her movements up to the time she disappeared.

They would find her murderer. He had no doubt of this one. No doubt at all.

He parked his Alpha Romeo in the police garage beneath the City-County Building, and took the stairs up to the duty room. The half-dozen officers there all stopped what they were doing and looked up. It reminded Klubertanz of the day Kennedy had been shot. They all had the same vacant look in their eyes.

He stopped in mid-stride. "Mind telling me what's going on?"

Captain Miller came out of his office and motioned him over.

"What's wrong?" Klubertanz asked, crossing the room, his gut churning.

"Inside, Stan," Miller said.

Klubertanz stepped past the man, into his office, Miller coming right behind him and closing the door.

"Have a seat," the captain said. He went around behind his desk, but Klubertanz made no move to sit down, and Miller remained standing as well.

"You have some bad news for me," Klubertanz said.

Miller nodded and looked down at his desk. "I'm afraid I do, Stan. The worst kind of news."

"Spit it out."

Miller looked back up, but he seemed to have a hard time meeting Klubertanz's eyes. "It's your ex-wife, Sylvia."

Klubertanz's eyes narrowed, and his first thought was that she was suing him for an increase in child support. But that didn't make any sense. She wouldn't have called the department. "What'd she do?"

Miller shook his head again. "Christ, I don't know how to tell you this, Stan."

"Straight out, captain," Klubertanz said, steeling himself now for something very bad.

Miller took a deep breath. "Your ex-wife and your two kids, Stewart and Melissa, were in a car accident on the Pacific Coast Highway. Just a couple of hours ago."

"Car accident?" Klubertanz said, not understanding at all. "The kids should have been in school. Sylvia should have been at work. Are they all right?"

Miller hung his head, and Klubertanz took a step closer. "Are they all right, goddamn it?"

"I'm afraid they're not," Miller said after a long hesitation. "They were all killed. Sylvia evidently lost control of the car. It went off the road, crashed, then burned."

Klubertanz just stared at the man, but he was not really seeing him. Instead he was back in time. He remembered when each of the children was born, and he remembered little incidents in their lives. When Stewart first walked. Melissa's first words. The long weekend he babysat them while Sylvia visited her mother in Chicago. A thousand and one little details, snatches of memories, raced through his mind, along with a very clear picture of the day he came home from work to find Sylvia gone, and a legal notice of separation from her lawyer in his mailbox.

"Josh has taken over your case load," Captain Miller was saying. "I want you to go home now."

"I'll have to go out there," Klubertanz heard himself saying. But his own voice seemed a long way off.

"Of course, Stan," Miller said, coming around the desk. "Take a week or two, whatever you need. The California Highway Patrol has the incident report. I'll telephone them that you're coming."

Klubertanz looked beyond Miller, out the windows. It was a lovely fall day. Halloween would be here in five days. Sylvia had written to him a couple of weeks ago that Stewart and Melissa were looking forward to trick-or-treating.

"I'm sorry for you, Stan," Miller said, and Klubertanz looked back at him.

"Thanks," he said, and he turned and shuffled out of the office.

As he crossed the duty room, the other officers mumbled their condolences.

Then he was in the stairwell, his feet a hundred miles below him, and finally he was in his car, pulling out of the sub-basement garage, and turning down the street, the day bright and very beautiful.

What the hell was Sylvia doing out on the highway with the kids on a Monday morning? It didn't make any sense. Where the hell was she going?

He headed toward his apartment on the other side of town, his driving mechanical, his mind a kaleidoscope of thoughts and impressions.

"For Christ's sake, Syl, California's no place to raise kids."

"The Midwest is?"

"It's a hell of a lot safer here than out there."

"I don't know what the hell you're bitching about, you're never home to see them anyway. I might just as well be raising them alone."

All the words. All the futile arguments. Were they what

had driven her away from him? Were they what had caused him to lose his children?

As a young cop just out of the Police Academy, Klubertanz had spent a two-year stint on traffic. He had had his share of accident calls. Scraping bodies off the roads, torching crushed people out of demolished cars, bones and guts and tattered clothing, and blood, always incredible amounts of blood.

The worst, of course, were the accidents in which fire was involved.

Somehow he was parking in front of his building, stumbling up the stairs and letting himself into his apartment. When he had the door closed, he leaned back against it and closed his eyes.

Why? The question screamed in his brain. Jesus, Syl, why did it have to happen?

Stewart and Melissa were seven and eleven. At that age, children were supposed to be immortal. The idea of death was unthinkable. They had the rest of their lives ahead of them. School. Jobs. Love. Discovery. So much.

After a time, Klubertanz opened his eyes and went into the kitchen, where he poured a stiff shot of whisky and tossed it down. The liquor burned in his throat, but instead of loosening the knot in his stomach, it made it worse. He poured himself another anyway, then picked up the telephone and called Republic Airlines. He made reservations for the evening flight to Los Angeles.

Sipping his drink, he went into the bedroom, pulled an overnight bag down from his closet, and tossed in some clothes.

When he was done, he sat down on the edge of the bed and looked at the photograph of Sylvia and the kids that he had taken three years ago.

He reached out and picked it up so that he could look closer at their faces.

They had never taken a lot of photographs; there never seemed to be the time. Now there would be no more photographs.

He stared at the picture for a long time before he put it

back on the night table. Then he took his bag into the living room and set it down by the door. He went back into the kitchen, where he poured another drink.

He wanted to be with someone now. Brenda would understand. She would know what to say. What to do. And yet, the larger part of him resisted that as totally unfair to her. Their relationship wasn't ready yet to handle a burden that even he was having trouble with.

He looked at the phone, but shook his head, then sat down at the kitchen table, the bottle of whiskey in front of him, and began to cry for his dead children.

8

Cheryl stood in her robe at the stove, cooking eggs for breakfast. The girls were still upstairs in the bathroom, and Frank was in the basement, doing something with the furnace.

It was Friday, and so far Frank's mood had continued on an even keel. He had not been snappish all week. The change was wonderful.

The only dark cloud on her horizon was the Halloween party Frank had planned for tomorrow night. He had not mentioned it to her, but yesterday Susan and Fred had both called to say they would be there.

Last night she had asked Frank about it, and offhandedly he had admitted that he had invited everyone over for drinks.

She had almost asked him if he was planning on doing something bizarre like he had last month, but she had kept silent.

''Come on, girls, breakfast is on,'' Cheryl called over her shoulder as she slid the last eggs onto the platter and set it on the table. ''Frank?'' she called.

''Be right up,'' he called from the basement.

Four slices of toast popped from the toaster, and as Cheryl buttered them, she thought about tomorrow night.

A year ago, she would have had no doubts about it. A Halloween party with their friends would be fun. But now, after everything they had gone through, after the changes in Frank, she was nervous about it.

But everything was back to normal. This week had been wonderful. The aftermath shock from the accident was over, or at least it seemed to be.

''The filter was all clogged up, that's why we didn't get

any heat last night," Frank said, coming up from the basement.

Cheryl turned around. "Did you fix it?"

He smiled. "I put a new one in," he said, crossing the kitchen. "I'll clean up and be right down."

"Roust those girls out of the bathroom," Cheryl called after him.

"Aye, aye, captain," Frank quipped, and he was gone.

She could hear him a moment later banging on the bathroom door. "Let's go, girls, chow's on. Come on."

Normal sounds, Cheryl thought, standing there with the butter knife in one hand. At last.

After awhile she sighed, finished buttering the toast, and then got the milk out as the girls came bounding down the stairs.

"Morning, mom," Dawn said, pecking her mother on the cheek.

Felicity had snitched a strip of bacon from the plate, and she munched it as she came around the table and gave Cheryl a greasy kiss on the cheek.

"Sit down and eat your breakfast before it gets cold," Cheryl said, and the girls noisily took their places as she poured coffee for herself and Frank.

"You were snoring last night," Felicity said peevishly to her sister as she helped herself to the bacon and eggs.

"No, I wasn't," Dawn said. "It was you."

"It wasn't me. I heard you all night."

"Yeah, well, you were farting," Dawn shouted.

"Dawn Rader!" Cheryl snapped, coming to the table. She had to suppress a giggle.

"Well, she was, mother. It was gross."

"It's a natural function that we're not going to talk about at the breakfast table," Cheryl said, trying to keep her voice stern.

"Well, it wasn't me," Felicity said smugly. "But I know who it was. D-A-W-N."

"You're so infantile," her sister mocked.

"Sounds like World War Two in here," Frank said, coming into the kitchen and taking his seat.

"They're your daughters," Cheryl said, laughing. "I can't do anything with them."

"Well, mother, it was disgusting . . . ," Dawn started, but Frank cut her off.

"Either one of you farts here at the breakfast table, and you'll both be eating all your meals in the bathroom. Bread and water."

"Daddy," Felicity protested, but Frank silenced her with a stern look.

"Any more and tomorrow night is out."

Cheryl dropped her toast on her lap. "What?" she said.

"Oh, daddy, you spoiled it," Felicity said.

"What about tomorrow night, Frank?" Cheryl asked, staring directly into Frank's eyes. He had a strange, far-away expression on his face, and it gave her gooseflesh.

"Daddy said we can come to your Halloween party tomorrow night," Dawn said.

"No," Cheryl snapped, still looking at Frank. He was grinning now.

"But daddy said we could," Dawn argued.

"Just to show everyone their costumes," Frank said reasonably.

Cheryl was confused now, and she turned to her daughters. "I thought last year was your last trick-or-treating?"

"It was," Frank said. "But haven't you noticed them moping around the house for the last couple of weeks?"

Cheryl turned back to her husband, but didn't say a thing.

"Saturday, when we were out in the woods, we had a little talk. I told them that if they made costumes, they could come down and show us. Just for a few minutes. I thought they could have some pop and some pretzels and then go back up to their room."

Cheryl's mind was spinning. Last year she would not have objected to the girls showing their costumes at a party. What was she afraid of now?

He had held the black rabbit over his head while he chanted those strange words. And then he had slammed the poor creature on the table and had cut its throat. It wasn't something she wanted the girls to see.

"I don't know . . . ," she said.

Frank reached over and patted her hand. "Don't be such a worrywart. They're not really coming to our party. They're just going to show off their costumes."

Cheryl looked from Frank to the girls, to their expectant expressions. "Finish your breakfast," she said to them, and she picked up her coffee cup with shaking hands.

For twenty minutes after Frank and the girls had left the house, Cheryl remained at the kitchen table, drinking her coffee and thinking. The last time Frank had pulled his little stunt in the rec-room, it was as if he had completely lost control. He had become someone else.

If Frank killed another rabbit, in another bizarre ceremony, the girls would not be able to handle it. It was as simple as that.

They were at the highly impressionable age. Such an experience could scar them for life.

Cheryl got up from the table, finally, and began rinsing the dishes and loading them into the dishwasher. Perhaps she was being melodramatic. Perhaps she was being a fool. But she could not shake the uneasy feeling growing inside of her.

Drying her hands on a dish towel, Cheryl went to the counter where she kept the address book and looked up her sister's telephone number in Minneapolis.

Harriet had married a civil engineer from Milwaukee, and eight years ago they had moved to Minnesota. They had no children, and enjoyed occasional visits by the girls. For the twins, the seven-hour Greyhound bus trip was a big adventure, and Harriet and her husband spoiled them rotten while they were there.

Cheryl stared at her sister's telephone number. She had never done anything behind Frank's back before, and she knew he would be hurt, and probably angry. She suspected she was being foolish; nothing was going to happen at the party tomorrow night. And yet . . . .

She took a deep breath, then picked up the phone and

dialed the number.

The bus left a little after four, she remembered from the last time they had gone up there. She could pack the girls' bags, pick them up at school and get them out of town before Frank got home from work. When he discovered they were gone, it would be too late for him to do anything about it.

But after that, after this weekend, what would she do? Her sister's number began to ring. If Frank held another of his strange ceremonies tomorrow night, and it made him crazy like before, something would have to be done with the girls. She couldn't send them north every weekend.

Her sister answered the phone on the fourth ring. "Hi, Harriet, how would you like to have your nieces for the weekend?"

Fred Martin felt like a drowning man clutching at straws as he waited on the phone for Peppinger. The man had been "out" or "in conference" all week, and had not returned any of his calls.

Peppinger was obviously avoiding him, but why? The contracts had been ready for more than a week, their bid had been fixed as the lowest, and both Peppinger and the mayor had assured him that it was just a matter of minor administrative procedure for the go-ahead.

"Could you hold just a moment longer, Mr. Martin? I think Mr. Peppinger will be off his other call momentarily," Peppinger's secretary said.

"Sure," Fred answered, and at that moment his boss, Roland Friedan, came in.

"Did you get ahold of Peppinger yet?" he asked softly.

Fred held his right hand over the mouthpiece. "On the line with him right now."

Friedan smiled broadly, and sat down across the desk from Fred.

"I was getting a little worried there for awhile," the man said.

I still am, Fred wanted to say, but he held his tongue, and Peppinger's secretary was back.

"Mr. Martin?"

"Yes," Fred said.

"I'm terribly sorry, sir, but Mr. Peppinger asked me to tell you that he will be on this conference call for some time. Can he telephone you later this evening, or tomorrow?"

"Yes," Fred said, unable for that moment to look his boss in the eye. "Do you have my home phone?"

"Yes, sir, we do."

"Fine," Fred said. "I'll wait for the call."

"Very good, sir," the woman said, and she hung up.

Friedan had a dark look on his face, and Fred heard himself blurting into the telephone, "Yes, I'm authorized to sign the contracts."

Friedan sat forward.

"No. You can tell him that if I receive the contracts tomorrow, or even Sunday, I'll sign them immediately and return them by courier service directly to his home."

Friedan was smiling.

"No trouble . . . no trouble at all," Fred said, and he hung up the telephone.

Friedan got to his feet. "Goddamn it, Fred, it looks as if you actually pulled it off. Sonofabitch."

Fred got to his feet, and Friedan pumped his hand.

"If the contracts aren't here over the weekend, I'm sure they'll be here Monday or Tuesday."

Friedan was shaking his head. "Think positive. You've got to think positive," he said. "The moment they come in, give me a call. I'll stick around town this weekend."

"That's not necessary . . . ," Fred said, but Friedan cut him off.

"Oh, yes it is, Fred," he said. "You may know that this contract will put us over the hump, but since you're going to end up a full partner very soon anyway, you might just as well know the entire story." He had stepped a little closer, and he lowered his voice now. "Without this contract, we're going under. And that's as plainly as I can put it."

"I didn't know for sure," Fred mumbled.

"No one knows," Friedan said. "It's the only reason I've let you work this deal the way you have. Our necks are all on the chopping block. This either goes through or we'll probably all be up on charges. Don't forget it."

"I won't," Fred said glumly. "I won't."

Tomorrow night was the party. Frank had warned that there would be a minor hitch with the Milwaukee deal, but he had also promised that after the weekend everything would go smoothly again.

"After this weekend we're going to have it made," Friedan said, going to the door. "We'll have it made."

"I think you're right," Fred said, looking up and managing a weak smile.

"I *know* I'm right," Friedan said, and he left.

Alone and isolated in his own thoughts, Clinton Polk parked his car in his driveway, shut off the engine and climbed out. The day had turned overcast, and a chill northwest wind blew, scattering leaves and promising an early snow.

But Clinton noticed none of that. At the lab the DS 19 fuck-up, as they were now calling the botched experiment behind his back, had been going from bad to worse. Out of a total of six hundred cultures, they had now checked 547, all with negative results. Nor did the last 53 cultures promise anything different.

Gil Mortensen had quit first thing on Monday, Willis had asked for a full report on the experiment, Vicki Karsten was out with the flu, and Susan had not said a single word about the incident all week.

All day Sunday she had curled up with a book in front of the fireplace, while Clinton went down to the lake with their puppy.

Then on Monday everything had seemed near normal, except for the fact that Susan had slept by herself in the guest room.

But in the morning, and then in the evening, she was pleasant. Even chatty. Until she headed off for the guest room overnight. It was driving him crazy, and yet he did not have the guts to bring it up himself. Nor did he think he had the right.

He went inside, hung his coat in the hall closet, then entered the living room. Susan was mixing a drink at the bar, and she turned around when he came in.

"Sit down," she said pleasantly. "I'm fixing you a drink."

"I don't want one," he said.

"Sure you do. You're going to sit down, have yourself a drink, and listen to me. I have something to say to you."

Clinton's stomach flopped over, and he sank down in an easy chair near the fireplace. Susan had started a birch fire, and it was pleasant in the room.

She brought him his drink, then sat down on the arm of his chair.

He looked up at her, his insides twisted with guilt. But what could he say? Christ, there was no excuse. She had caught him in bed with Vicki. There simply was no excuse.

"It's been a rough week for you, darling," she began. "But I wanted you to stew in your own juices before I said anything to you."

"I'm sorry," Clinton said, unable to look her in the eye. "I don't know how it happened. I'm sorry."

"There's nothing to be sorry about," Susan said matter-of-factly.

He wasn't sure that he had heard her correctly, and he looked up.

"Silly," she said, brushing her fingertips on his cheek. "Don't you think I know what you've been going through these past months at the lab? Don't you think I understand the kind of pressure you've been under?"

"What do you mean?" he said, dumbfounded.

"All I'm trying to say to you, Clinton, is that I understand about Friday night."

"Christ," Clinton said, looking away. "I don't know what happened."

"I do," Susan said, and he was compelled to look up at her. "You were drunk and horny, and the little bitch wiggled her ass in front of you. If you hadn't jumped her,

I would have been more worried about you.''

"I don't understand . . . ." He stopped, the words choked off by his confusion.

"You don't understand what, darling?" Susan asked.

He shook his head. He wasn't hearing this. He had to be dreaming.

"What don't you understand?" Susan insisted.

"You," he blurted. "I mean, I went to bed with another woman, and you're taking it this way."

"Girl," Susan said. "And I don't know how else to take it. You made a mistake. Christ, you're human. Do you love her?"

"Of course not," Clinton said.

"You made a mistake, then, that's all. I don't want it to happen again, but I do understand it."

Susan's voice had become almost sickly sweet, and Clinton knew now that something unpleasant was coming. They had been married long enough for him to understand at least that much.

"What do you want?" he asked.

Susan blinked, but said nothing.

"Do you want a divorce?"

Susan just stared down at him, the smile slowly leaving her lips. "No, I don't," she said softly, at last. "Our marriage is all right. It's been strained, but it's all right."

"I'm sorry," he said.

She shook her head. "Don't be."

"If there's anything I can do to make it up to you, Susan . . . ."

"There is, Clinton," she said. "There definitely is."

"Yes?"

"You're going with me to Frank and Cheryl's tomorrow night," she said.

Clinton shook his head, but Susan reached out and ran her fingers through his hair.

"Yes, you are," she said. "It'll be loads of fun. And you're going to enjoy yourself. Or at least you're going to appear to enjoy yourself."

"He's crazy," Clinton said.

''No, he's not. And you will be coming with me,'' she said. She got up, went across to the bar, and then turned back. ''Was the little bitch any good, Clinton dear?''

Clinton just stared at her, a sick feeling in his stomach.

''Did she have firm little tits? Did she have a tight little pussy for you? Was she a good fuck, Clinton?''

''I'll go with you tomorrow,'' he said at last, hanging his head. He could not take any more of it. ''I'll go.''

Cheryl was frightened, now that she had actually done it. There had been no problem with the girls. Aunt Harriet's was much better than any old party anyway. But how Frank was going to react when he found out was beginning to worry her.

The bus had left at four fifteen exactly, and Cheryl had followed it in the van for a few blocks, somehow afraid that it would turn back. But then she had pulled over as she watched it head out to the Interstate.

Now, a half hour later, she was home. She poured herself a glass of wine, turned on the television and tried to concentrate on a game show, but she couldn't.

Frank was going to be furious. And rightly so, one part of her mind told her. But another part held a fear that this could set him off on another of his insane rages.

Two weeks ago the neurologist that Frank had been seeing had given her the telephone number for a psychiatrist in private practice.

''But I really think you should wait before you consult with a psychiatrist,'' he had said. ''However, the choice is yours, of course. Yours and your husband's.''

Monday, she told herself now. If Frank went off the deep end tomorrow night, she would definitely call the psychiatrist on Monday.

She had just sat down in front of the television when a car pulled into the driveway. She jumped up and went to the window as Frank got out of the car, spoke to the three men inside, then started toward the house. The car backed out onto the street and took off.

The front door opened and closed. ''Hello,'' Frank

called out.

"In here," Cheryl said, trying as best she could to compose herself. She wasn't ready for a fight yet. Not yet.

Frank came into the living room, a grin on his face, but he looked tired. "Thank God, it's Friday," he said, coming across the room. He kissed her on the cheek. "What're you drinking?"

"A little wine," she said nervously.

"I'm going up to change clothes. Why don't you pour me a brandy?" He turned and headed back out to the vestibule.

"Okay," Cheryl said.

She went over to the bar, and poured him a stiff shot of brandy. Before the accident he'd drink brandy and water with plenty of ice. Or, during the summer, gin and tonic. But never straight booze, without even ice. Now he drank it like water, with little or no effect.

She set his glass down on the small table by his favorite chair, switched the television set off, and then sat down on the couch with her glass of wine.

When Frank came back downstairs, he was wearing a pair of corduroy trousers, a sweatshirt and sneakers. He slumped down in his chair, picked up his glass and took a deep drink.

"What a bitch of a week," he said, laying his head back.

"Have you finished the specifications for the new hospital?" Cheryl asked, trying to be conversational.

"Hell, no," he snapped. "Every goddamned time we send the book over to them, they find something else to bitch about. I told Lon that the next time they wanted something changed we should tell them to shove it up their asses."

Cheryl sipped at her wine. Her hand shook, and Frank finally noticed her nervousness.

"What's the matter with you?" he asked.

"Nothing," she said. Not now. Not now. She had visions of him jumping in the van and chasing after the bus, and bringing the girls back.

"Something's wrong," he said. "Did you have a bad day? Something happen with the girls at school?" He looked over his shoulder toward the kitchen. "Where are they?"

"Gone," Cheryl said softly.

Frank turned back to her. "What?"

Cheryl set her glass down on the coffee table. "Gone," she said. "I sent them away."

"Where?"

"Harriet's."

Frank's eyes had narrowed into slits, and his complexion had visibly darkened. "Why did you do that?" he said evenly.

"I didn't want them at the party tomorrow night," she said defiantly. She was having trouble looking him in the eye.

He got up from his chair and came slowly across the room to her. For a moment Cheryl was terrified of him. He seemed barely able to control his anger.

"You sent them away because you didn't want them to come to a Halloween party?" he said, his voice rising. "My God, woman, you're crazy. You're the one who needs to see a shrink. What the hell did you tell Harriet?"

"Don't shout at me," Cheryl replied.

"Shout?" Frank roared. "I should be screaming from the roof. What the hell's the matter with you? What the fuck did you say to the girls? Your father is crazy and you've got to run away now?"

"I'm afraid of you, Frank," Cheryl shouted.

Frank started to say something else, but he clamped it off.

"I'm afraid to death of you," Cheryl continued. She really was, but she didn't know what she was saying now. The tears were welling up in her eyes, and her knees were weak. "You're not yourself anymore. I didn't know what to do, but I didn't want the girls watching you kill some poor rabbit."

"Christ," Frank swore, but the anger had gone out of him.

"Don't you see? Ever since the accident you've been different. I don't know what to do anymore." She was crying now.

"Take it easy, babes," Frank said as he reached down for her, but she shrank back.

"No," she wailed.

"Cheryl, for Christ's sake, it's me. Frank. Your husband. I'm not going to hurt you. I'm not some monster."

"Oh God, Frank," Cheryl sobbed, and she let herself go limp as Frank gently pulled her to her feet, and enfolded her in his arms. He felt strong, and warm and masculine, and very comforting.

"It's all right," he said soothingly as he held her close.

"I'm sorry, Frank," she cried.

"It's all right, babes," he said. "I understand what you've been through. And I'm not mad about the girls, just a little hurt, that's all. But I do understand."

"I didn't know what I was doing," she said. "I just kept thinking about you killing that rabbit. And about the girls. They're so young and innocent."

"It'll be all right," Frank said softly. "You'll see, it'll be all right."

Cheryl's tears began to subside, and she looked up into her husband's face. He was smiling.

9

Klubertanz pulled off the busy Pacific Coast Highway about 3:00 P.M. and parked his rental car just on the shoulder. The sand dunes here sloped about thirty feet down to the beach, where the gentle waves rolled up on the shore, one after the other.

The funeral had been yesterday, but only a handful of people had shown up for it, all of them new friends Sylvia had made here in California.

The man she had written him about, the one who loved the kids and was going to make the perfect husband, was nonexistent, as it turned out.

Her friends had known nothing about the man, characterizing Sylvia as a great person, but very lonely. Never went out on dates. Totally devoted to her job and her children.

Dead end there, Klubertanz thought morosely. Everywhere were paths that led nowhere.

The mechanic at the Highway Patrol garage had been even less help.

"There wasn't a thing wrong with that car, lieutenant," he said.

"Steering, brakes, tires?" Klubertanz hammered at the man. Anything. He needed something.

"No, sir. Wasn't a brand-new car, but it was in good shape."

Another dead end. Still no answers. Only more puzzles.

Traffic had been light, the investigating officers said. Weather was beautiful, sunny, mid-seventies.

"There weren't even any skid marks, lieutenant," one of the officers said. "I'm sorry, but her car just went off the road, hit the sand, rolled three times, and then caught fire. It's a bitch."

More dead ends.

The only witnesses they had found could tell them nothing of help, either. No one had really seen anything.

"I was just passing a truck about half a mile back, when I saw this Chevy flipping end over end down to the beach, and then it exploded," one of them said.

Slowly Klubertanz turned his gaze away from the beach, to a spot fifty yards farther up the road, where twin furrows, etched deeply in the sand, led from the highway down to the beach.

He got out of the car and pocketed the keys as he moved slowly up the highway.

No skid marks. No bumps or potholes. No sudden dips in the road. The apron at the side was wide, and in good repair. No loose gravel, or rocks, or sand. No possibility of spray from the ocean below.

At the spot where Sylvia's car had left the highway, Klubertanz crouched down, scooped up a handful of the sand from the furrows and held it up to his nose.

There was no smell. Just a neutral odor. No gas or oil or brake fluid. Nothing to indicate a malfunction of the car. Nothing.

He straightened up, tossed the sand down, and then went down the side of the sand dune, to where the car had first flipped over. A huge hole had been gouged in the sand; fifteen yards away there was a second gouge.

Standing there, he could envision the crazy, twisted path Sylvia's car had taken from the road, finally ending on its top in flames below. The sand was blackened, glass and other debris still there. The California Parks Department would not be out until early next week to clean up the rest of the mess.

Klubertanz could visualize Sylvia and the kids being slammed around inside the car as it flipped end over end. Screaming. Panic stricken. And then the fire. The heat. The searing flames.

He suddenly turned away, unable to look any longer.

And after while he trudged wearily up to the highway, and then back to his car.

It was time to go home, he thought, one hand on the top of the car as he looked out across the ocean. His wife and children were buried. There was nothing left for him here. Nothing.

It was a little after 4:00 P.M. by the time Klubertanz got back to his motel near the airport. He took off his jacket, poured himself a drink, and telephoned Republic Airlines to confirm his reservations tomorrow back to Chicago, and then Madison.

Taking his drink into the bathroom, he stripped and climbed into the shower, where he let the hot water stream down on his body. He felt battered, as though he had been in a dog fight.

It was going to take a very long time to get over this, if he ever did. In the meantime, he was a cop, and back in Madison he had work to do. It was time he got to it.

When he was finished in the shower, he dried off and dressed in clean clothes. He'd have dinner here in the motel, then a few drinks at the bar before turning in.

As he was pulling on his shirt, his telephone rang. "Klubertanz," he said, answering it.

"Lieutenant Klubertanz, I've been trying to reach you all day," a familiar voice said. It was a long-distance call.

"Father Ferrari?" Klubertanz asked.

"It's me," the priest said. "I heard the terrible news about your wife and children just this morning."

Klubertanz sat down on the bed.

"I tried to reach you at your office, but your Captain Miller, told me what had happened. I'm terribly sorry for you, my son. I know how you must feel."

"Thank you, Father," Klubertanz said. "But is there trouble there?"

The phone was silent for several seconds.

"Father?" Klubertanz said. "Are you still there?"

"Yes," Monsignor Ferrari said. "There was another desecration of our altar last night."

Klubertanz could feel a little thrill playing up his spine.

"Was anyone . . . hurt?"

"No," the priest said. "No one saw a thing. But there was another inscription. This in blood again. It's why I tried to contact you."

"Was it the same Latin words?"

"It was in Latin," Monsignor Ferrari said, his voice soft, and again there was a hesitation.

"What is it, father? What'd it say?"

"Do you know what day this is?"

Klubertanz was confused. "Saturday."

"Halloween," Monsignor Ferrari said. "All Hallows Eve. The traditional night of celebration for witches."

Klubertanz started to say that Halloween was for children, but he stopped himself. "Do you think there will be more trouble tonight?"

"All the children's stories of witches, demons and dark spirits on this night are based on historical fact, lieutenant. In the dark ages, in Europe, this was a night of slaughter. No one went out. Everyone locked themselves in their homes to await the sunrise. Stay indoors. Please. Do not go anywhere."

"What was written on your altar, Father?" Klubertanz asked, suddenly cold.

"It didn't hold any meaning for me until I spoke with your captain," the priest said.

Klubertanz said nothing. It was as if he was suspended in time.

"Your wife, was her name Sylvia? Your children, Stewart and Melissa?"

"Yes," Klubertanz heard himself saying.

"Domine Deus," Monsignor Ferrari said softly. "Stay put tonight, lieutenant. The names of your wife and children were written on my altar."

The room was spinning. "What else was there, Father?" Klubertanz said. "Were there any other names?"

Silence.

"Father?"

"Mine," the priest said. "But be careful, son."

After the priest hung up, Klubertanz immediately

called his department back in Madison. It was after six there, and he automatically got the desk sergeant.

"This is Klubertanz," he snapped.

"Lieutenant? Are you back, sir?" the man said.

"I'll be back tomorrow. But I want a twenty-four hour guard put on Monsignor Dominic Ferrari, immediately. Good Sheppherd church, just off the square."

"Got it," the sergeant said. "First thing in the morning. I'll . . . ."

"Now!" Klubertanz roared. "Right now. This instant. On my authority."

"Yes, sir," the sergeant said, flustered. "Whatever you say. What are we looking for?"

"Someone is going to try to kill him."

10

Cheryl looked at her wristwatch; it was just 8:00 P.M. She got up from the couch.

"It's time," she said.

Marion Martin looked up at her, then glanced nervously at her husband. But Fred smiled reassuringly, and they both got up.

"This is crazy," Clinton said, but Susan shot him a harsh glance, and they, too, got to their feet.

All evening it had seemed as if the house lights were getting dimmer. Cheryl had asked Frank about it, but he had just laughed. Now the corners were in darkness, and a chill permeated the air.

"Cheryl?" Susan said.

She looked up. They all stood around her. Marion and Clinton looked uneasy, but Susan seemed almost excited, and Fred had had a grin on his face ever since he had arrived.

For a seeming eternity, Cheryl just stood there, unable to move. But then she was sure she could smell burning candles, and she knew that Frank was ready.

"Downstairs," she finally said, and she turned and slowly led the way through the house to the basement door.

At the top of the stairs she hesitated again.

"Frank?" she called down. "Are you ready for us?"

There was no answer. From the head of the stairs she could see the flickering lights of candles; the smell of hot wax was strong.

She started down the stairs, one step at a time, her hand trailing on the banister, the others behind her.

At the bottom she stopped again. "Frank?" she called,

but still there was no answer, and she moved softly through the darkness, turning the corner into the rec-room.

The scene was horribly familiar. A pentagram had been drawn on the carpeting with some kind of luminous paint. At each of the corners was a lit black candle, and in the center of the figure was a plastic model of a human skull.

The couch and easy chairs had again been arranged in a semi-circle across the pentagram from the card table, over which was draped a black cloth. On the table was a straight razor, the blade open.

Frank was across the room, doing something behind the bar. When he looked up and spotted the others, he smiled.

"Is everyone here?" he asked.

He seemed normal, the thought flashed in Cheryl's mind. He was wearing a sweatshirt; his hair was tousled, his eyes dancing.

She nodded, and Susan pushed past her.

"Come on in," Frank said, moving around the bar. "Sit down. Everything will be ready in just a minute or two."

Susan seemed almost disappointed.

"Why don't you mix everyone a drink?" Frank said to his wife. He went around the pentagram.

"I thought . . . ." Cheryl started, but she couldn't finish it.

The others came into the rec-room and took their seats.

"Go ahead and have a drink. I've got to go upstairs for a moment. But I'll be right back," Frank said, and he left.

Cheryl could hear him hurrying up the stairs, and then she thought she could hear him whistling. This wasn't going to be so bad tonight. It was just a game. That's all. Just a game, she told herself.

She mixed them all drinks, poured herself a glass of wine, and sat down on the couch between Susan and Marion.

"Have you got any aspirin, Cheryl?" Marion asked.

"Headache?"

"One's just starting . . . ." Marion began, but then there was a loud thump upstairs in the kitchen.

"Frank?" Cheryl called, looking toward the door.

"Accipe potestatem offerre sacrificium Asmodeus, Missasque celebrare," Frank's voice came from the stairway.

"Sounds like Latin," Clinton said.

"Lucifer, Asmodeus, Astaroth," Frank chanted, and they could hear him coming down the stairs. *"Tam pro vivis, quam pro defunctis. In nomine Astaroth,"* Frank said from just around the corner. His voice was low now, menacing, and Cheryl could feel the gooseflesh rising on her arms and legs.

"Frank?" she said again.

"Shut up," Susan hissed.

Frank stepped around the corner, and Cheryl's stomach flopped over.

"What the hell . . . ." Clinton sputtered.

Frank was nude. His body glistened with red oil, highlights reflecting and dancing across his chest from the flickering candles. In his hands, outstretched in front of him, was a small black cat.

"Accept, oh unholy Father, of the almighty and eternal damned, this black host," he chanted as he moved slowly around the pentagram, the muscles on his back and in his legs rippling.

"Accept this offering which I, Thy unworthy servant, offer to Thee, my living and true God of darkness, for my innumerable sins, offenses and negligences."

He reached the table and raised the struggling cat high over his head.

Cheryl was mesmerized. She could not take her eyes off him. He seemed larger than life. More powerful.

"This offering is for all here present, and for all Your faithful servants living and dead, that it may avail me and them of the true knowledge of life and everlasting service to You."

The room was quiet for a long second.

"Astaroth!" Frank screamed, and he slammed the cat down on the table with one hand, while with his other he snatched up the open razor.

"Asmodeus!" he screamed, and he slit the cat's throat, blood suddenly pumping over the table, the cat howling, struggling, scratching Frank's arms and chest as he once again raised the animal off the table.

"Lucifer!" Frank shouted. With his free hand he reached behind him and grabbed something.

With mounting horror, Cheryl could see that it was a small glass, and Frank was catching the cat's blood in it, the dark red fluid pumping from the animal's throat, thick and repulsive.

The cat's struggles finally ceased, and Frank laid the carcass on the floor behind the table, then held the half-filled glass in both hands high over his head.

"For this is the chalice of Astaroth's blood, of the everlasting book of the damned, and the mystery of the dark faith, which shall be shed for all of us," he said, turning his back to the others.

A flash of lightning, followed by a clap of thunder, shook the house, rattling the windows.

"As often as ye shall do these things, ye shall do them for a commemoration of all the spirits that dwell within us," Frank said.

It was raining now; Cheryl could hear it pattering against the basement windows.

Frank lowered the glass of blood and drank deeply of it. Cheryl's stomach was flopping over, and yet she could not take her eyes off his back.

He mumbled something that she couldn't quite catch, then set the glass down, stepped around the table, turned, and looked directly into Cheryl's eyes.

He had an erection, his penis thrusting huge and straight. He raised his right hand and beckoned to her.

This wasn't really happening, she thought, horrified. Her cheeks and ears felt warm, her stomach fluttered and her knees were weak, yet she still could not take her eyes off him. He was half-covered in the animal's blood.

"Cheryl," Frank said softly.

She shrank back in the couch, the tears coming to her

eyes. ''Frank . . . please,'' she cried softly.

''Cheryl,'' he repeated.

She forced herself to turn away from him and look at Marion and Fred. They both were staring at her, almost as if they were in a trance. Susan was smiling, and Clinton was shaking his head.

''God . . . ,'' she said, turning back. Frank still stood there, his right hand out toward her, and she could feel herself standing up, as if she had no control over her own muscles.

''Yes,'' Fred said softly.

She went around the pentagram and stopped directly in front of her husband, who was smiling. He reached out and unbuttoned her blouse, slipped it off her shoulders and tossed it aside. Next he reached around behind her and undid her bra, tossing it aside as well.

It was cold in the rec-room, and Cheryl could feel the others' eyes on her back. She was frightened of what Frank was doing, and deeply ashamed that she was allowing it.

''Beautiful,'' Susan said from behind her.

Frank took her arms, and gently guided her down to the carpeted floor, and when she was lying on her back, he took off her shoes, and then undid the waistband of her slacks, sliding them and her panties down around her hips, and then off.

She looked over at the couch, and the others were all staring at her. Frank got down on his knees and spread her legs, as she tightly closed her eyes.

''No, Frank. Not like this,'' she said softly.

''For Asmodeus, the guiding spirit,'' Frank said, and he entered her, thrusting deep and hard, causing Cheryl to cry out in pain.

''Sonofabitch,'' Clinton swore.

Frank was pounding deep and brutally into Cheryl, but the pain had gone, leaving her numb. It would be over soon, she kept telling herself. She would endure, and in the end even the shame would pass.

She thought she heard Marion cry out, but the blood was pounding in her ears as Frank's motions came harder and faster. She had never known him to be so large, to penetrate so deeply.

"We're going," Clinton shouted, his voice coming to Cheryl from a distance.

Susan was saying something, arguing, and again Clinton shouted, as Frank suddenly thrust deep, then stopped, his body shuddering.

Someone was going up the stairs, Cheryl could hear that over the noise of the wind and rain outside, and then Frank was withdrawing from her, his weight suddenly off her body, and without opening her eyes, she rolled over on her side, clamping her legs tightly together.

"Why, Frank?" she cried to herself. "God . . . why this . . . ?"

Her head was spinning. Her body felt bruised, and she was very cold, lying there on the floor. Her thoughts focused on the girls, who were safely in Minneapolis. Now she thanked God that she had sent them away.

Someone, it sounded to Cheryl like Susan, moaned. She turned her head and opened her eyes onto a vision from hell.

Fred and Marion were making love on the floor three feet away from her, Marion's breasts large and flattened. Beyond them, near the couch, Susan was nude, on her hands and knees, Frank on his knees directly behind her, grasping her hips, while he made love to her from the rear.

Sweat streamed down his face and chest, his eyes were closed, and he was pounding faster and faster, Susan rearing back to meet his thrusts, as she lowed like a cow.

Part Three

THE SABBAT

December

1

Klubertanz emerged from the university library and stopped long enough to button up his overcoat against the chill wind before he headed back toward the Square.

Now that the university was on Christmas break, State Street Mall was relatively deserted of students. But farther up the street, the stores were busy with people doing their last-minute Christmas shopping.

He passed a woman dressed in a Santa Claus outfit, the Salvation Army tripod next to her as she rang a little bell. He dropped a dollar in the kettle without breaking stride.

''God bless you,'' the woman said mechanically without looking at him; the bell continued its mournful clanging.

It was Thursday. There were six more shopping days until Christmas, but Klubertanz wasn't in the spirit. For the past five weeks, since he had returned from California, he had been like a man possessed, his life consumed with worry for the safety of Msgr. Ferrari, and work on the case.

There had been no attempt on the old priest's life, nor had Klubertanz uncovered any leads on the murders, although he felt he was making some progress.

Captain Miller and the others in the department believed that Klubertanz was following Osborne's suggestion, and was looking for a psychotic person or persons. In reality, he was working along a completely different line.

He had learned in several discussions with Msgr. Ferrari, and with a dozen bookstore owners here in town, as well as from his own readings, that black magic and the occult were very popular subjects in Madison. There were several bookstores dealing exclusively in that sort of thing, and the libraries had a good selection of material.

Working completely alone, Klubertanz was checking customer lists from all the bookstores, and questioning librarians about the people who frequented those shelves. He was looking for a connection, any connection, no matter how slight, between the names on his list and the ambulance drivers or Sister Colletta.

So far he had drawn a blank. Each day the list seemed to grow longer. And each day he missed his wife and children even more.

It began to snow lightly, and Klubertanz lowered his head against the wind as he continued up toward the Square.

A wild goose chase, Capt. Miller would call it if he knew what was really happening. And perhaps the man was correct. Perhaps he was chasing unrealities. Yet he could not help himself.

Slowly, over the past weeks, he had become completely convinced that the three murders were related, although he still had difficulty in swallowing the idea that the inscription of his ex-wife's and children's names on the altar at Good Shepherd was anything more than a sick practical joke.

"Stan, for Christ's sake, are you deaf?" a woman shouted behind him.

Klubertanz looked up, and then over his shoulder. Brenda Wolfe, wearing no coat, and clutching a linen napkin in her hand, stood in the entrance to the Ovens of Brittany restaurant.

He walked back to her. "Do you always run around in the winter without a coat?" he said.

She took his arm and led him into the restaurant, the atmosphere inside warm, delicious compared to the chill wind outside.

"I was just having an early dinner. Alone. I saw you walking by."

He took off his coat, hung it up by the door, and joined her at a small table near the large windows.

A waiter came immediately. "Would you care to see a menu, sir?" The restaurant was crowded. Mostly with young people.

Klubertanz hesitated. He really didn't want any company right now, and in fact had been avoiding Brenda ever since his return from California. He knew it hurt her, but he did not want to impose his grief on her. Not until he was better able to handle it himself.

"Please do, Stan," Brenda was saying.

"I should get back to the department."

"I don't have the plague, and if you don't want to talk about anything important, I'm good at inconsequential bullshit."

Klubertanz had to smile, despite himself, as he looked into her warm, smiling face. There was concern there for him, as well; he could see it in her eyes, and it touched him.

"All right," he said, looking up at the waiter. "But first bring me an Irish coffee. It's cold out there."

"Yes, sir," the waiter said, and he was gone.

For awhile they sat in silence, staring out at the passers-by, but then Brenda looked across the table, and reached out for his hand.

"I'm really sorry for you, Stan," she said with compassion. "And I understand why you've been avoiding me for the past month or so. But it wasn't necessary."

Klubertanz was having a difficult time meeting her eyes. The restaurant suddenly seemed too warm, and overcrowded.

"But I think you should talk about it," she continued.

"Not now," he said.

"I don't mean right this instant, but perhaps later this evening we can go someplace quiet."

Klubertanz managed a slight smile. "Thanks for the offer."

"But?"

"I really do have a desk load of work to get at."

She withdrew her hand from his, and a minute later the waiter was back with Klubertanz's drink, and a menu. He quickly glanced at it, ordered an omelette and a croissant, and when the waiter was gone again, lit himself a cigarette and sipped at the laced coffee.

"We'll get a conviction on the Turner case," Brenda said, breaking the second awkward silence between them.

"It was open and shut," he said mechanically. "She was wearing an engagement ring, she had been raped, and all her friends said she was a quiet, prim little girl. Her fiancé tried to jump the gun. It's happened before."

"Still nothing on the ambulance drivers and the nun?"

Klubertanz looked up, his jaw tight. "Not yet," he said.

"Still following your earlier theory?"

He nodded. He wondered what she would think if she knew what had been written on the altar at Good Shepherd. Monsignor Ferrari had ordered the second inscription cleaned, and had not told anyone about it except for Klubertanz. Captain Miller would have insisted that it meant the murders had been committed by a crazy. Monsignor Ferrari believed differently, and so did Klubertanz.

But who else would believe it? Who else would swallow such a story?

Brenda seemed exasperated. "Goddamn it, Stan, you can't clam up like this. You've got to talk it out with someone."

"Talk what out? Syl and the kids? Or the murders?"

"Everything."

"I'm not ready."

"You should be. You're damned near a basket case. It's a wonder you can get anything done."

Klubertanz looked away again. No one out of the department had gotten wind yet that a patrol car was almost always near Good Shepperd church. Watching. Waiting for anyone strange to show up.

He had played hell with Capt. Miller over it, arguing that, since the nun had been killed there, it was possible that the "crazy" might try for Msgr. Ferrari. It wouldn't wash much longer, but he had to keep trying.

"If you want me to leave you alone, say so, and I'll bug out," Brenda was saying. "If you want me to shut up, tell me, and I will. But don't just shut me out like this."

Klubertanz focused on her again. "Have I been that bad?"

"Terrible," she said. "Honestly, Stan, I'm worried about you."

"Me, too," he said.

"I'll fix us dessert at my place," she said.

The work could wait until morning. "You don't know what you're letting yourself in for."

"I think I do," she said, a knowing smile on her lips. "But even if I'm wrong, I'm a big girl. I'll take my chances."

It was late, past 8:00 P.M., when one of the grad students poked his head into Clinton Polk's office.

"Do you want me to stay and help with the analysis when it comes up from the computer, Doctor Polk?" the young man asked.

Polk looked up. "No, you can go, Greg. They just called; it won't be ready until morning."

"Anything else I can help with?" the young man asked. Ever since the Regents had come through with new grant money for the project, everyone in the department had treated Polk with a new respect. Forgotten was the botched DS 19 experiment, and there had even been some talk on campus about the Nobel Prize.

And yet, Polk felt like a man trudging through life on quicksand, while all around him the countryside was beautiful and solid.

After Frank Rader's party last month, Susan seemed to be a changed woman. No longer did she become argumentative with him when they didn't make love. Forgotten was the incident when she had caught him in bed with Vicki Karsten. And she had moved out of the guest room, back into bed with him.

Which was fine with him, because twice now he had found himself late at the lab with the girl, and both times they had made love. She had seduced him, he told himself the first time. He really could not help it. But when the second incident occurred, he had stopped telling himself anything.

A part of his mind told him that his life was all wrong. He knew the right path to take, but something seemed to be pulling him in the opposite direction.

At home, everything was strained, except on Wednesday nights, when he and Susan, as well as Fred and Marion, met at the Raders' for dark ceremonies.

Frank had killed another cat, a black rooster and a black rabbit. Each time at the end of the ceremony they all made love with their wives on the floor.

In fact, Clinton thought now, staring up at the grad student in the doorway, it was the only time he and Susan made love anymore.

He shook his head.

"Are you all right, Doctor Polk?" the young man asked.

"Just a little tired," Polk said, sitting back in his chair. "I'm going to pack it in, myself."

"Yes, sir," the student said. "Good night."

"Good night," Polk said, and the student left, closing the outer lab door a second later.

For several moments Polk remained where he was seated, listening to the silence. Then he got up and crossed the lab, opened the door to the corridor and looked out. The building was quiet now, everyone home for the night. Even the janitors wouldn't be on this floor until well after midnight.

Clinton closed the door and looked across the lab, back at his office, goosebumps on his arms.

What had made the Regents suddenly change their minds and extend his grant money? Frank would say it was his dark ceremonies. Fred would agree. Doctor Willis had thought it was a miracle, and Vicki Karsten said she had known all along that he would get his money. But he had no rational explanation.

The DS 19 experiment failure should have been the clincher as far as the Regents were concerned. Even Dr. Willis had been deeply disappointed in him.

Slowly Clinton went back to his office for his overcoat.

Whatever the reason, he thought, the renewed grant money had given him a new lease on life . . . at least as far as his professional life was concerned. And he had made a silent pact with himself that this time there would be no screw-up. This time his research would be letter-perfect, significant. By spring the breakthroughs they were all waiting for would actually come about. He no longer would be the scientist on the verge. He would be the scientist with a major discovery to his credit.

He had started out the door when the telephone rang. For just a second he hesitated, but then he turned back and picked it up on the second ring.

"Doctor Polk," he said.

"Hi, Clinton," Vicki's soft, sensuous voice came over the line. Polk's stomach flopped.

"Hello, Vicki," he said. "Did you want to talk to someone? The others have already gone."

"Good," she said. "Because I wanted to talk to you."

"Me?" Clinton said, sitting on the edge of his desk. He looked at his watch. It was past eight thirty. He had not gotten home for the last two nights before 11:00 P.M.

"Yeah," she said, chuckling. "You. I was just lying here, alone, wondering how it would feel to have you next to me. On my own bed."

Clinton's mouth was dry, and before he could reply, the girl went on. "My roommate is staying with her boyfriend tonight. I was just wondering if you could stop over. Maybe for just an hour or two."

"I don't know," Clinton said, although he did know.

"Please?" she said. "Just an hour, or even a half hour?"

He took a deep breath and let it out slowly. "Are you still on Mifflin Street?"

"Christ, no," Vicki said. "We moved out of that dump a couple of months ago, after the fags got wiped out. We're on East Johnson now, two blocks off the Square."

"I'd have to leave by ten thirty."

"Good," she said. "I'll have a drink waiting for you." She gave him the street number, and then hung up.

He slowly put the phone down, his hands sweaty. This could not continue to happen. And yet he did not know how to end it, or even if he really wanted to end it. The fact of the matter was that Vicki was incredible in bed. She made him feel so much like . . . like a man.

He smiled to himself, flipped the lights off, and left the lab, his step light, his heart racing.

2

Despite the Wednesday night sessions, despite everything Frank Rader had promised, and despite the fact that Fred Martin really wanted to believe in the ceremonies, it looked as if the Milwaukee contracts would never come through.

He had gone out on a limb as far as was humanly possible, still with no results. He had bribed Peppinger and a dozen minor officials in the government, with no results. He had, with Friedan's approval, shaved their costs and inflated their promised performance to the absolute limits, still with no result.

It was shortly before noon on Friday. Fred Martin sat behind his clear desk with absolutely nothing to do for the remainder of the day. Under normal conditions, with his work finished, he'd take the rest of the day off. The long weekend. But now he was afraid to leave. Afraid of what might fall apart.

The contracts had come through all right, unsigned of course, and he and Friedan had signed them and sent them back to Milwaukee.

For the next ten days everyone in the agency had been up. Happy. Bright. The talk about making Fred a full partner had been solidifying; as Friedan had said; "Everything is coming up roses. A whole goddamned garden full."

But then the ten days had turned into twelve, and then fifteen and twenty, still with no word from Milwaukee. Peppinger and the others had once again been out to Fred's calls. Letters had gone unanswered. All communications had ceased.

"Patience," Frank Rader had told him. "It will come to pass. But you need patience."

Fred sighed deeply. Patience he had. Or at least he had always thought he was a patient man. But now the gnawing at his gut had become almost too much to bear.

The intercom buzzed, breaking him out of his thoughts, and he hit the button with a shaky hand.

"Yes?"

"Fred, come into my office, would you?" Friedan said.

"Be right there," Fred said, and he released the switch.

For a long moment he sat without moving, the fear inside of him black and monstrous. Was this it? Had Peppinger called Friedan and said no deal?

He got to his feet, straightened his tie, buttoned his suitcoat, and left his office.

Down the plushly carpeted corridor, Fred knocked once on Friedan's door and went inside.

Roland Friedan was a short, dapper man, with thinning, white hair and a small, trim mustache. He was standing at the large, green-tinted window in his expansive office, staring down at the city, when Fred came in and closed the door. He turned around, an expression that was hard to determine on his face.

"I was just thinking about skiing," Friedan said.

"Skiing?" Fred asked, coming across the room to the huge, leather-topped desk.

"Yes. Phyllis and I wanted to go north next weekend for a little skiing up at Telemark, but it doesn't look as if we're going to make it now."

"There hasn't been much snow yet this year."

Friedan managed a slight smile. "It's not that," he said. "It's this Milwaukee thing."

Fred's heart thumped. "I don't know what the hell happened. I've done everything I possibly could . . . ."

Friedan waved his hand. A gesture of dismissal. "I know what happened, Fred. I know exactly what happened."

This was it, then, Fred thought. And curiously, he was calm about it. Deep in his heart he had known the deal would fall through. And now he couldn't even bring himself to be frightened of the legal consequences that would probably follow.

"What can we do?" he asked.

Friedan laughed out loud. "What can we do?" he asked. "Well, for starters, get ready for five years of hard work."

Fred just looked at the man.

"This afternoon I'm going to issue a press release announcing not only the Milwaukee deal, but your promotion to full partner in Creative Sales, Inc."

"It came?" Fred asked softly. "They signed the contracts? We have them in hand?"

Friedan slid a bulging file folder across the desk. "Twenty minutes ago. Lock, stock and barrel. Five million for five years, with escalators and renewals, as well as bonuses for above-standard performance and results."

"It came?" Fred repeated. He felt stupid. He could think of nothing else to say.

"You did it, Fred!" Friedan shouted. He came around his desk and pumped Fred's hand. "By Christ, you actually pulled this off."

Fred looked into the man's eyes, his knees suddenly weak. "Jesus."

"Jesus is right," Friedan said, and he helped Fred to a chair. "Just sit tight and I'll pour you a drink. Looks as if you could use one. I know I sure as hell can."

While Friedan was busy at the bar, Fred kept thinking about the work he had done over the last year on this deal. The late evening meetings in Milwaukee and here in Madison, handing money over to men whose names were well known by the public. Trips to Acapulco. Booze. Women.

Christ, they had gone way out on a limb. But it had worked. It had actually worked.

He looked up as Friedan came back with their drinks, and handed him his, then perched on the edge of his desk and raised his glass.

"To Creative Sales and a very long and profitable future."

Fred raised his glass and numbly drank some of the scotch. "I hope to hell I never have to do anything like this again."

Friedan's expression darkened. "Don't ever say that to anyone at any time," he snapped. "We did what we had to do, and it worked. It's the cost of doing business."

Patience, Frank Rader had told him. And he had a vision now of Frank holding a black cat over his head, slamming it down on the table, and slitting its throat.

"Asmodeus," he said to himself.

"What?" Friedan asked, and Fred looked up sheepishly.

"It's nothing," he said. "Just thinking to myself." He raised his glass again. "To Creative Sales. And believe me, Roland, this is just the beginning."

"That's the kind of talk I like to hear. Especially from my partner."

Fred finished his drink and then stood up.

"Another?" Friedan asked.

"Not now," Fred said.

Friedan finished his drink, then got to his feet. "I'm taking us to lunch at the Edgewater."

"I'm going to have to take a rain check on that one, too, Roland," Fred said. He could feel the strength building inside him.

"Why?"

"There's someone I have to tell about this."

For a moment Friedan drew a blank, but then he grinned. "Marion," he said. "Of course. Take the rest of the weekend off. There's plenty of time for us to celebrate."

Fred went to the door, but he turned back to Friedan.

"We're never going to talk about this again, but I'll tell you this much. There was a hell of a lot more to this Milwaukee deal than anyone will ever know."

Friedan looked serious. "And I don't want to know, Fred. All that matters now is that you pulled it off."

Fred nodded, then left Friedan's office and went back to his own, grabbed his overcoat, and told his secretary he was leaving for the day.

Outside, the day was bright and sunny, but very cold, the temperature well below freezing. Fred hurried down the street to the parking ramp where he kept his car. It had worked. It had actually worked. He wanted to sing and dance down the street; it was only with the greatest effort that he kept himself in control.

He reached his car, got in, raced out of the ramp, sped around the Square and out over the causeway toward the south side.

Within six months they'd buy a new car. Probably the Mercedes that Marion had fallen in love with a few years ago. Within a year they would begin shopping for a new house. Probably in Maple Bluff. Shortly after that, they would become members of the country club. Vacations in Europe. New clothes, new furniture. The whole kit and caboodle, as he had told Marion a hundred times.

Within ten minutes he had pulled into the parking lot of Solar Products, Inc., just as Frank Rader, carrying a briefcase and a cardboard box, barged out the front door.

Fred rolled down his window and pulled up beside Frank. "Just stopped by to pick you up for lunch."

At first it seemed as if Frank hadn't heard him, and he kept walking, his head down, a dark expression on his face. He was so close Fred could have reached out and touched him.

"Frank?"

Rader looked up suddenly, and stopped. "What the hell are you doing here?"

"I came to take you to lunch. I've got some good news."

Rader just stared at him. But then he nodded. "I can use some," he snapped. He came around the car, shoved his things in the back seat and then got in beside Fred.

"Where do you want to go?" Fred asked. There was definitely something wrong.

"I don't give a shit. Anywhere I can get a drink."

"Can you take the rest of the day off?"

Rader looked at him. "I can take the rest of my life off. I was just fired."

Fred had driven to the parking lot exit, and he waited as a taxi pulled in. "What?"

"The sonofabitch fired me. Just like that, told me to get out. Because I wasn't kissing his ass."

"That's terrible."

"Terrible? It's the best fucking thing that's happened to me in two years."

"What are you going to do?"

"Do!" Frank shouted. "Drive that bastard right into the ground, that's what I'm going to do."

Fred stared at his friend for a long moment. He and Frank had never been really close, but lately, since Frank had begun his ceremonies, Fred had come to depend upon him as the Rock of Gibraltar, a steady hand, a shoulder to lean on, someone to look up to and seek advice from. But now it seemed as if Frank was pulling apart. It gave Fred a shaky feeling.

He pulled out of the parking lot, drove back to the Beltline and headed slowly into town. Frank stared silently out the windshield.

"You're a good engineer," Fred said after a few minutes. "Maybe you could start your own business."

Frank started to flare, but then he calmed down. "It's a thought," he said. "But there isn't enough money for that."

"I could possibly help out with that. The Milwaukee contracts came through today."

"I knew they would," Frank said absently. "But there still could be some trouble, in that."

Something clutched at Fred's gut. "Trouble?" he asked.

Frank looked at him again. "We're not out of the woods yet, my friend. My getting fired proves that. And Clinton still hasn't come over to our side, although he did get his grant from the Regents."

"What kind of trouble?" Fred asked, his old fears rushing back.

"We both know how you managed to ramrod that contract through down there. What if some snoopy newspaper reporter gets the story? Or perhaps the Justice Department takes a closer look?''

Fred was very cold.

''There's only one thing left for us to do,'' Frank was continuing. We're going to have to fight fire with fire.'' He looked up, his eyes bright. ''We've all been pulling in separate directions, that's the trouble. That's why we're losing. And we will lose unless we do something about it. Believe me, we will lose.''

Fred's legs shook so badly he was having trouble keeping a steady pressure on the gas pedal.

''Monday is the twenty-first,'' Frank said. ''The Witches' Festival. For centuries it's been one of the single most important gatherings.''

Still Fred could say nothing. He was mesmerized.

''Don't you see, Fred? Monday is our big chance. If we can weld ourselves together into a solid unit . . . a coven, if you will . . . nothing will be able to stand in our way. We'd be too strong.'' He looked away. ''Christ,'' he said in awe. ''Christ.''

''You're right,'' Fred said. ''We're going to have to do it.''

Frank looked at him, a smile on his face. ''How about Marion? Will she join us?''

''Yes,'' Fred said.

''Fine. Then have her make black robes for all of us.''

Fred was confused, and it showed on his face.

''You know, like choir robes, only with hoods on them.''

''What kind of material?''

''It doesn't matter. Silk, cotton, anything, just as long as it's black. Solid black. She can sew, can't she?''

Fred nodded. ''She made a lot of the baby's clothes.''

''Good,'' Frank said, half to himself. ''Eight o'clock Monday night. We'll have a full-blown sabbat, by God, and no one or nothing will ever get in our way again. We'll be too strong. Everything will be ours.''

''Everything,'' Fred mouthed the word. ''Everything.''

3

It was just three thirty, and Susan Polk was climbing out of the bathtub, when she heard a car pull up in the driveway. She went to the window: Frank Rader was climbing out of the driver's side of Fred Martin's car.

She watched him cross in front of the car, and then stop in the middle of the driveway. Fred evidently wasn't with him. He looked up and saw her in the window and smiled, then moved out of sight below to the front door.

She quickly dried herself off, put on a little powder, pulled on a terrycloth robe and hurried downstairs.

Frank had let himself in, and he stood just inside the vestibule, watching her as she came down the stairs. He was smiling.

"You certainly look happy enough," she said, reaching the bottom.

Frank took off his overcoat and laid it on the hall table. His tie was loose and his hair was disheveled. To Susan, he looked rugged and very masculine. Her stomach was fluttering.

"Is Clinton at the lab?" he asked softly.

She nodded. "He probably won't be home until late," she said, her voice husky.

"How is it going for him?"

"Good, I think. He hasn't said much. But the Regents did extend his grant money."

"It won't last," Frank said. "The bottom is going to drop out for him."

Susan said nothing. She could not take her eyes from his.

"Is he still bedding his assistant?"

She nodded. "He was with her last night until nearly

midnight, but I didn't say anything to him."

Frank came forward and glanced into the living room. "Fix me a drink. We have to talk."

"Is something wrong?" she asked, slightly disappointed.

"It could be, unless we get ready for it."

Susan went to the living room bar and poured him a stiff shot of brandy.

When she turned around, he was seated on the couch, his legs out in front of him as he lay back. She brought the glass over and sat down beside him.

He took a drink and sighed deeply. "I had lunch with Fred. His Milwaukee contract has finally come through, but he's heading for trouble, just like Clinton. Something is going to happen with the Milwaukee people, just like it is with the Regents."

"How do you know?"

Frank smiled knowingly. "I know," he said. "This morning I was fired."

"Frank!"

"It's all right," he said. "I knew it was coming. I was getting ready to quit anyway. I think I'm going to start my own business. I didn't like the way Surret was doing things."

That's what she liked about him, Susan thought at that moment. He was so damned calm, so confident. Being around him made her feel safe, protected.

"But we're going to have to get ready for all of this or we're going to be in some serious trouble."

"Next Wednesday night . . . ," Susan started, but Frank cut her off.

"Our Wednesday night sessions are fine as far as they go. But I told Fred the same thing I'm going to tell you. We've not been pulling together. It's been me up on a stage doing a little performance each week. No one else has really participated."

The comment stung. Susan had felt for some time now that she was someone special to Frank. Someone special in his ceremonies.

"You've been fine, Susan," Frank quickly added. "And so has Fred. But the others are a disruptive influence on what I'm trying to do." He took another drink. "Christ, all I'm trying to do is help us. Guarantee good futures for us. You'd think they'd see at least that much."

God, he was wonderful, Susan thought. Her legs were weak.

Frank sat forward and put his glass on the coffee table, a serious expression on his face. "Monday is the twenty-first. It's the Winter Festival. We're going to meet at my place. Will Clinton cooperate?"

Susan nodded.

"No, I mean will he *really* cooperate? None of this is going to work without everyone's help. He has to be a participant."

"He'll participate."

Frank smiled. "It's settled, then," he said. He seemed to think of something. "Have you ever done any modeling in clay?"

"In high school," Susan said. "A couple of pots."

"Marion is going to make us black robes. Over the weekend I want you to pick up some modeling clay and make three small human figures. Can you do that?"

"I don't know," Susan said.

"They don't have to be perfect. Just as long as they are at least recognizable as human. Don't worry about making them works of art."

"Sure," she said. "I can do it."

For a long moment Frank looked into her eyes, his serious expression beginning to soften. "You've been very good through all of this," he said.

She felt tingly all over. She could not say a thing.

He reached out and caressed her cheek with his fingertips, an electric shock running through her body with his touch.

"You and Clinton haven't been making love except Wednesdays at my house, have you?" he said.

She shook her head. She was moist.

Frank stood up, looked down at her, and then reached

down and pulled her to her feet, into his arms. They kissed deeply, and she could feel his strength flowing through her.

When they parted, he was smiling, and without a word they walked arm-in-arm, out of the living room, up the stairs and into the bedroom, where Frank took off his coat and tie, slipped off his shoes, and began unbuttoning his shirt.

With fumbling fingers Susan undid her robe, let it slip off her shoulders to the floor, and then came into his arms again, his hands all over her body, gently stroking, as he kissed her neck and shoulders and finally the hardened nipples of her breasts.

A moan escaped her lips, and pressing herself against him, she could feel his hardness.

"God, Frank," she murmured. Her heart was racing, and her knees were so weak now she could barely stand.

He picked her up, brought her to the bed and laid her down, then finished undressing. When he came to her, she was almost out of her mind with desire for him, and they made love with more passion than she had ever known.

Like Clinton Polk, Cheryl Rader felt as if she was walking through a dark, dank swamp, the ground underfoot quicksand.

She had lost weight, and her eyes always seemed red and puffy, makeup doing little to hide the lines of stress that were becoming more and more evident each day.

She was concerned about Frank's sanity, of course, yet she had all but given up any hope that he would voluntarily seek help. She had telephoned the psychiatrist that Frank's doctor had recommended, but the man had told her there was little he could do, unless she wanted her husband committed.

Committed? Christ, she had wanted to scream at the man. There was no way possible she could bring herself to do that.

Talking with Frank got her nowhere. Marion was too involved with her own problems to be of any help, and Susan had the hots for Frank, so she would not be a sympathetic ear.

She didn't know what to do anymore. Every Wednesday night she had made sure Dawn and Felicity stayed with friends, but that couldn't continue much longer. The mothers of the girls' friends discouraged sleeping over on school nights.

She opened the oven door, basted the roast she had been preparing, and when she was done with that she went into the living room. It was five thirty, and already dark outside, so she plugged in the Christmas tree lights and stood back a moment to look at it.

An FM station on the stereo was playing Christmas music, and yesterday afternoon she had hung the two dozen Christmas cards they had received so far above the fireplace.

The girls were upstairs in their room, wrapping gifts.

Last year Frank had come home from work the Friday before Christmas, laden with last-minute, unexpected presents. She had made them both a drink, and the girls some hot chocolate, and they had sat around the fire, looking at the tree as they sang carols. That evening had ranked as one of the very best in her memory. So different from this year.

Cheryl stood there, staring at the tree, half-listening to the music, and half-listening for the girls upstairs.

They had been arguing earlier in the afternoon, but were quiet now.

The girls were always quiet now around this time of the afternoon, because Frank was due home at any minute. And whenever he was in the house, the girls strictly avoided him. They kept out of his way, afraid to be noticed by him.

It wasn't natural, and it made her sick at heart.

The telephone rang, startling her out of her thoughts, and she went into the kitchen to answer it.

An unfamiliar woman's voice was on the line. "Mrs. Rader, is your husband at home?"

"No, he's not," Cheryl said, a little clutch of fear in her

stomach. "Who is this, please?"

"Mr. Surret's secretary," the woman said. "When do you expect him home?"

"Any moment," Cheryl said. "When did he leave the office?"

"You haven't spoken with him yet today, Mrs. Rader?"

"No, I haven't."

The woman hesitated a moment. "Well, Frank left the office around noon. He took most of his things with him, but there still is a box of books here that belong to him, and Mr. Surret wanted them picked up before the weekend."

"Just a minute," Cheryl said, confused. "I don't understand what you're saying. What books?"

"I wouldn't know, Mrs. Rader, but Mr. Surret would like them picked up either this evening, or first thing in the morning. The office has been reassigned."

"Reassigned?" Cheryl said, her voice weak.

"Yes, Mrs. Rader, Frank was dismissed this morning."

"Oh, God . . . ."

"Well, if you would pass the message along to your husband when you see him, we would appreciate it," the woman said and hung up.

Cheryl remained where she stood, listening to the dial tone.She had half suspected something like this was going to happen.

Slowly she hung up the telephone, and trudged back into the living room doorway. She stared at the brightly lit Christmas tree, presents piled beneath it.

"Frank," she said to herself, the tears beginning to slip down her cheeks. "Oh, Frank, what's happening to you?"

A car pulled up in the driveway, a door slammed, and then the car backed out.

Cheryl quickly wiped her eyes as the front door opened and closed. A second later Frank came into view.

He stopped when he saw her. His face seemed flushed, his hair was disheveled, and his tie was off, but he seemed happy.

"Something smells good," he said. "Are you cooking a roast?"

Cheryl nodded. "Mr. Surret's secretary telephoned just

a moment ago."

Frank's expression darkened. "What'd that bitch want?"

"You left a box of books in your office. They want them picked up by morning."

He nodded, but said nothing.

"Why didn't you come home, or at least call and tell me that you had been fired?" she said.

"Because I had a lot of thinking to do first," he said evenly.

"What are we going to do now?"

"Fix me a drink, and then we're going to talk," he said.

"Goddamn it, Frank," Cheryl shouted. "What the hell is happening?"

"The sonofabitch fired me, that's all," he snapped. "And I'm glad it happened. Saved me the trouble of quitting."

Cheryl moved slowly toward him. "This has got to stop, Frank. We can't go on like this."

He stood there, watching her. "Go on like what?"

"You know what I mean. You've been different since the accident. And these Wednesday night sessions are insane. The girls are frightened to death of you."

None of what she was saying seemed to register with him. She took a step closer.

"You've got to snap out of it, Frank," she said. "Doctor Willard gave me the name of a psychiatrist . . . ."

Frank reached out and grabbed her by the arms and pulled her to him. "What'd you tell him?"

Cheryl hiccoughed. "Nothing."

"Goddamn it, I want to know!" Frank shouted.

Suddenly it was as if someone had slammed her in the stomach.

"Frank?" she said.

He looked into her eyes, and then shoved her back, turned on his heel and stalked upstairs.

She had smelled a combination of perfume, bath powder and another, unmistakable odor on him. It had been faint, but it still lingered in her nostrils.

Frank had just had sex with someone. This afternoon.

4

A front was passing through southeastern Wisconsin, and the first major snowstorm of the season was predicted sometime later tonight.

Lieutenant Klubertanz, seated alone in his office, shivered as he listened to the rising wind outside. In front of him was the list of names that he had lived with for several weeks now. Until this evening they had provided him with absolutely nothing. But that had changed. Or at least he thought it had.

Frank Rader, an engineer with Solar Products, Inc., here in Madison, had been among the last people Ahern and Shapiro had dealt with before their deaths. He'd known that since the early days of the investigation, of course, but now he'd learned something new about the man. He'd checked the hospital records on Rader's admittance.

Rader had been technically dead for at least three minutes. Dead, Klubertanz thought. A few weeks ago he had seen a special on television dealing with life-after-death experiences. Some of the testimony had been patently ridiculous, but other stories had had a haunting quality to them. Visions of vast arenas filled with people. Foggy plains at night with lights in the distance.

He had shut the television off before the program was completed because it brought back too many thoughts about his ex-wife and children. But now it came back to him.

Rader's name was not on any of the bookstore lists he had seen so far, but that was not conclusive. The stores and libraries did not keep very complete records, and there were dozens of mail-order houses dealing in witchcraft and the occult.

In fact, Klubertanz thought, there really was no reason to suspect the man. He had been in an accident and the City Ambulance Service had picked him up. Nothing more than that. Ahern and Shapiro had picked up hundreds of people over the last year.

And yet, the fact that Rader had been dead for a few minutes, and the fact that the incident had happened so soon before Ahern and Shapiro had been killed, stuck with him.

The hospital had provided Klubertanz with Rader's address and date of birth, and using that, he had checked with the Department of Motor Vehicles for the man's driving record.

Speeding ticket three years ago, and in the accident he had been cited for operating a motor vehicle while under the influence of alcohol. He had pled no contest to the charge, and since it had been his first offense, he had been merely fined.

That's as far as he had taken it, and he still vacillated between looking a little deeper into Rader's background, and dropping it. If Capt. Miller got wind of what he was doing, the man would order him off.

Klubertanz shook his head, gathered up the papers from his desk, stuffed them in a couple of file folders and locked them in a drawer. He put on his sportcoat and headed for the door.

With his hand on the light switch, he stopped a moment and looked back at the telephone on his desk. Then he glanced at his watch. It was just a little past seven. He had promised to pick Brenda up around eight for a movie and drinks afterwards. She had been sweet last night, and she had definitely been a big help. It had almost been cathartic to unload his misery on her, and this morning when he had come into work he had felt like a human being for the first time in weeks.

But he had plenty of time before he had to pick her up.

He went back to his phone and dialed Msgr. Ferrari's private number at Good Shepherd. The priest answered it on the second ring.

"Sorry to bother you so late, Father," Klubertanz said. "But I was just wondering if I could stop by to talk with you."

"Of course," the old priest said. "I'll be in my office."

"You're sure it'll be all right? I mean you don't have other plans?"

The priest chuckled. "At my age you don't make plans, you just take each day as it comes."

"I'll be there in a few minutes. I'm downtown."

"I'll be waiting," Monsignor Ferrari said, and he hung up.

Ten minutes later, Klubertanz let himself in through the side door of the Good Shepherd administration building.

Monsignor Ferrari's office was at the end of the long, dark corridor, light spilling out from the half-open door.

Klubertanz hurried down to it, went inside, and closed the door behind him.

"Stanley?" the priest called from his inner office.

"It's me," Klubertanz said, going in.

The old priest was pouring two glasses of wine. "It must be cold out there."

"It is," Klubertanz said, sitting down across the desk from the priest, and accepting the glass of wine.

The priest sat down, and sipped at his wine. "We're going to have snow tonight. A white Christmas."

Klubertanz managed a smile. "Don't tell me you believe in Santa Claus."

"Of course I do," the priest said, with a twinkle in his eye. "Don't you?"

Klubertanz shrugged. "It's hard to believe anymore."

"That's what makes belief so precious. If it was easy, the rewards wouldn't be near as great," Monsignor Ferrari said. "You're troubled."

"I've come across something I don't understand," Klubertanz said, the words difficult. "Death. What happens afterwards."

Monsignor Ferrari nodded. "The age-old question," he said. "We will sit on the right hand of God, and so be judged.''

''Let's say a person was dead briefly . . . two or three minutes . . . and then was revived,'' Klubertanz said slowly. He felt like a fool, bringing this to the priest.

''I watched that television program as well. Fascinating.''

Klubertanz sat forward. ''I'm serious, Father. What happens to a person during those minutes?''

''I should think you would better ask that of a physician.''

''I mean to a person's consciousness . . . his . . . .''

''Soul?''

Klubertanz nodded.

''We don't know.''

''As simple as that?''

Monsignor Ferrari nodded. ''What have you come up with, Stanley?''

For a long moment Klubertanz said nothing. Suddenly he was having difficulty in asking what he wanted to ask. ''Does the name Frank Rader mean anything to you?''

The priest thought, then shook his head. ''Should it?''

''Is there a possibility he could have a connection, even slight, either with this church or with Sister Colletta?''

''Of course. But was his name on any of the church records you examined?''

''No,'' Klubertanz said. He hadn't really expected anything, yet he was somewhat disappointed.

''Who is he? How did you come up with his name?''

''He's an engineer here in Madison. There was a car accident in September in which he was injured. He may have been dead, briefly.''

The color had begun to leave Msgr. Ferrari's face. ''The ambulance drivers who were called to the scene . . . .''

Klubertanz nodded. ''Ahern and Shapiro.''

The priest took a deep breath, and let it out slowly. ''Do you think he was involved in their murders?''

''I don't know yet, Father. I just don't know.''

''Why is it you came to me tonight?''

Klubertanz was silent.

Monsignor Ferrari got slowly to his feet and went to the window. His office faced the Square, and from here he could see the capitol dome.

"Religion for you, I suspect, is nothing more than a good fairy tale, and witchcraft, a bad one. You don't believe in either."

Klubertanz said nothing.

"And maybe you're right," Monsignor Ferrari said.

A faint flicker of surprise crossed Klubertanz's features, and the priest caught it.

"Don't be surprised, Stanley. We priests are mortal, too, you know. We have our weaknesses, our fears. Our doubts."

"I never meant to question your beliefs, Father," Klubertanz said.

"No, of course not. We're talking here about you. Three murders have been committed. You are charged with the responsibility of solving the crimes and bringing the murderer to justice. You'll do that in any way possible, won't you?"

"Yes," Klubertanz said. His mouth was dry.

"You've come up with the name of a man who was technically dead for a short period. And now you want to know if it is possible that this man had an experience while he was dead, that made him . . . perhaps a disciple of a demon, or perhaps a witch. Possessed him, if you will."

"It's ridiculous, I know . . . ."

"Perhaps not. There simply is no way of knowing for sure." Monsignor Ferrari came over and sat down in a chair next to Klubertanz. "This Frank Rader, whose name you've come up with. Is there anything else that might lead you to suspect him?"

Klubertanz shook his head.

"Is there any reason to suspect that he is involved in witchcraft?"

Again Klubertanz shook his head.

The priest seemed almost sad. "Then I am happy for Mr. Rader, whoever he is, but I am saddened for you." He touched Klubertanz on the sleeve. "But you will find the murderer, Stanley. You will."

"Thank you, Father," Klubertanz mumbled, not sure of anything now, most of all his own abilities as a cop.

The first few wind-driven snowflakes were beginning to fall when Clinton Polk parked his car in the garage.

It had been a long week, and he was dead tired. He and three of his assistants, including Vicki, had worked through the day on the computer analysis of their latest experimental run, finishing up finally around eight this evening. Although the results looked promising, the hoped-for breakthrough still seemed elusive, just beyond their grasp.

He entered the kitchen, laid his briefcase down on the counter and went into the living room.

A fire was burning on the grate, the Christmas tree lights were on, but Susan was not there.

"Susan?" he called out.

"Downstairs," she shouted from the basement.

He hung his overcoat in the hall closet, then went back into the kitchen, where he opened the basement door.

"What are you doing down there?" he called down.

"Be right up," she called. "Fix yourself a drink."

The stairs were in shadow, but a light came from the other side of the basement, near the washer, dryer and laundry tubs.

"Are you washing clothes this late?" he asked, coming down the stairs.

"Don't come down here," she shouted urgently, but he had reached the bottom of the stairs and flipped on the lights.

Susan was sitting at a small table near the laundry tubs, doing something with what looked like lumps of mud. She was wearing jeans and a sweatshirt, a bandana around her head, slick mud nearly up to her elbows.

"Goddamn it, I told you not to come down here!" she shouted angrily.

Clinton came closer and saw that she was working with modeling clay. Two lopsided statues, each about a foot tall, covered with wet towels, stood on the washer, and she was working on a third.

"You're going into sculpting now?" he asked, smiling, trying to be genial. He felt guilty about last night.

Susan brushed a strand of hair away from her eyes with the back of her wrist, leaving a streak of wet clay across her forehead. "Go back upstairs. I'll be right up," she snapped.

"What are you doing?" he asked. Something was wrong here.

"I said, go upstairs," she shouted.

"I asked you what the hell you're doing," he said angrily.

She jumped to her feet and faced him. "You've got no right to ask me anything! You established that last month when you fucked that little bitch from your lab!"

Something momentarily raged inside Clinton, and he lashed out, slapping her on the face with his open palm. Her head snapped back, and she staggered against the small table, toppling the crude statue she had been working on.

The blow stunned Clinton more than it did Susan, and he stepped forward to help her, but she brushed his hands away.

"You've been screwing her right along, haven't you?" she said. Her eyes were filled with tears; a large, angry red mark was already forming on her cheek. "You were in bed with her last night; how about tonight? Did you nail her in the lab? Or maybe in your office, out in front of everyone?"

"Christ, I'm sorry, Susan. I didn't mean to hit you."

"Tell me, Clinton, dearest, does she suck your cock for you? Lick your balls?"

Clinton had backed up a step.

Susan turned, a dreamy smile on her face, and lovingly set the toppled statue upright. "Monday night is the Winter Festival," she said, all traces of her anger suddenly gone.

Clinton just looked at her, open mouthed. None of this

made any sense.

"Monday night is going to be very special. Frank says we're going to have a full-blown black mass."

"No," Clinton protested. He wanted to shout at her, take her by the shoulders and shake some sense into her.

"Oh, yes," Susan said in the same dreamy voice. "After Monday night, you won't have to worry about the Regents or about your research. Everything will fall into place."

"No," Clinton repeated dumbly. His stomach was rumbling, his bowels loose.

Susan turned to him, a slight smile on her lips. Her left cheek was puffy. "You'll lose your grant, unless you do as Frank says."

"Bullshit."

"It's true. Your research is going nowhere, and won't unless you help us, Clinton."

"You're crazy. You're all crazy," he said, backing up another step.

Susan laughed out loud. "Have you ever stopped to ask yourself why the Regents have extended your grant money for as long as they have? Your research work has dropped to nothing. Remember the DS 19 experiment? It'll happen again, and then what will Doctor Willis have to say?"

"Stop it, Susan," he said.

"You're going to lose it all, my dearest husband," Susan taunted. "You can get it up for the little bitch at the lab, but not for me except at Frank's house. Isn't that right, Clinton?"

Clinton backed up another step, but Susan was coming after him now, her face contorted.

"Did you know that Frank came over here this afternoon?" she said, taunting him.

"No!" Clinton screamed, unable to allow himself to hear what he knew was coming. Unable to think. He raised his hand to hit her again.

"That's right," she said. "You can't get it up, but if it makes you feel better, you can hit me again."

''No,'' he shouted, but he hit her, knocking her to the floor.

And then he was on her, like a mad man, ripping her jeans open, and then he had them off, and he tore her panties apart, roughly spread her legs, getting his knees between them as he fumbled with his own trousers.

''Yes,'' Susan was moaning. ''Do it, Clinton, God, yes . . . . .'' She held her hands out for him.

He pulled his trousers and shorts down around his knees, but his penis was still flaccid.

Susan reached out for it, but he jerked back, falling to the side, tears of frustration and humiliation coming to his eyes. ''I can't,'' he cried. ''Oh God . . . I can't . . . .''

Susan jumped up and cradled him in her arms. ''It's all right, Clinton,'' she said gently. ''It's all right. We understand. After Monday it will be better. You'll see. Frank said this would happen, but after Monday it will be okay.''

5

It had snowed all night, and into the morning, not stopping until just before lunch. The snowplows had done an efficient job, so that by early afternoon the streets were all clear. But Madison had been transformed from the end of a gray fall to the beginning of a gloriously white winter.

There had been a rash of fender benders over the night, but no serious accidents. A young man on South Park Street had celebrated the holidays a little too hard and, drunk, had fallen out a second-story window. He was at Madison General under observation, with only minor injuries.

"Other than that, it's been pretty quiet, lieutenant," the desk sergeant told Klubertanz.

"Let's keep it that way. If anything comes up, give Josh a call; I'll be gone most of the afternoon."

"Going shopping?"

"Something like that," Klubertanz said, and he left Police Headquarters, got into his car and headed toward the west side.

For a few hours last night with Brenda, he had been able to forget about his conversation with Msgr. Ferrari, and the name Frank Rader, but this morning he had been compelled to come downtown and do some more checking on the man.

Rader had enlisted in the Air Force August 1, 1956, where he worked as an electronics technician, receiving an honorable discharge in July of 1960. In September that year, he enrolled at the University of Wisconsin here in Madison, in the Physics Department, transferring to the school of engineering two years later, and graduating with his bachelor's degree in electronics engineering in 1965.

He had worked for a couple of small electronic firms here in Madison, had done an eighteen-month stint with Texas Instruments down south, then had returned to Madison, where he had worked with Ohio Medical Products for a couple of years.

After that he had become involved on a part-time basis with a couple of architects here in the city, finally developing the designs for what were called, "electronically controlled, energy efficient," buildings, accepting a position as a prime engineer with a new firm, Solar Products, Inc., two years ago.

Klubertanz had almost dropped his investigation of Rader at that point, but instead, he had called the president of Solar Products at home, just half an hour ago, and had come up with the second anomaly in Rader's existence.

The man had been fired yesterday.

It was just a little after three when Klubertanz pulled into the driveway of a pleasant-looking, two-story colonial house just off University Avenue. It was a nice neighborhood. Neat. Well maintained. Solid middle class.

He got out, pocketed his keys, and went up to the front door. He rang the bell; a chime sounded from inside.

A few moments later the door opened and a pleasant-looking woman, wearing slacks and a sweater, was standing there. "Yes?" she said.

"Mrs. Rader?" Klubertanz asked, reaching for his ID case.

"Yes," she said.

He flipped his case open and showed her his gold shield. "Lieutenant Klubertanz, Madison Police Department."

The woman looked from the badge to Klubertanz. "Is there something wrong? Some trouble, I mean." Her voice was shaky.

Klubertanz smiled pleasantly. "No, ma'am, nothing like that," he said. "You were involved in an automobile accident back in September. I'd like to speak with your husband about it, if I may." He looked over her shoulder into the house. "Is he at home?"

"Yes," Cheryl stammered. "He is. But he already paid his fine."

"I know that, Mrs. Rader," Klubertanz said. "Would it be all right if I came inside?"

Cheryl hesitated for a moment, but then stepped back and let Klubertanz in. He closed the door.

"Could you get Mr. Rader? I'll only take a minute of his time."

"Sure," Cheryl said, backing up. She turned and left Klubertanz alone.

He could hear music playing from somewhere upstairs as he stepped into the living room. Presents were piled under a beautifully decorated tree in front of the window, and above the fireplace, a couple of dozen Christmas cards had been tacked to the wall.

Pleasant room. Normal. Nothing out of the ordinary.

Frank Rader, a tall, husky man with a thick shock of dark hair and intense blue eyes, came from the dining room, a curious expression on his face. He crossed the living room to Klubertanz.

"Mr. Rader?" Klubertanz said, again pulling out his ID case, and flipping it open.

Rader nodded and looked at the badge. "What can I do for you, lieutenant?"

Klubertanz pocketed the case. "I'm sorry to bother you on a Saturday afternoon like this, but I've come to ask for your help."

"Oh?" Rader said coolly. There was no fear in the man's expression or manner, and Klubertanz was mildly disappointed. "My wife said that you were asking about our accident."

"It's not really the accident, Mr. Rader, it's the two ambulance drivers who brought you to the hospital that night."

Cheryl had come back. "Why don't you take him into the study, Frank?" she said.

Rader was angry with her; Klubertanz could see it in his eyes.

"That would be fine. I'll only be a couple of minutes.

But I really could use your help."

"This way," Rader said after a moment, and he turned on his heel, went back out into the vestibule, and, producing a key from his pocket, unlocked a door and swung it open.

Klubertanz followed him into a small, pleasant study that was furnished with a large desk, an executive chair, a small couch and easy chair, a large, professional drafting table, and, along two walls, floor-to-ceiling bookcases.

Books were piled on the desk, on one of the chairs, on the coffee table and here and there on the floor. An ashtray on the coffee table was filled to overflowing.

Frank closed the door, offered Klubertanz a seat on the couch, and then perched on the edge of his desk.

Klubertanz sat down and picked up a book with strange drawings on the front of it. *The Encyclopedia of Witchcraft and Demonology,* by Robbins.

"A fascinating subject," Klubertanz said, his heart racing.

"Yes, it is," Rader said dryly. "Now, what can I do for you?"

Klubertanz put the book down. "I'm working on the murder investigation of Stanley Shapiro and Bruce Ahern."

"I read about it in the newspapers," Rader said. "It doesn't seem as if you've had too much luck."

"Evidently you're not aware that Ahern and Shapiro were the ambulance drivers who brought you to the hospital the night of your accident."

"I'll be damned," Radar said, looking surprised. Again Klubertanz was disappointed.

"At any rate, I've been doing some checking with anyone who might have had contact with them shortly before their deaths. You were one of their last calls."

"I don't think I can be of much help to you on that score," Rader said.

"Oh?"

"You could check with the hospital if you'd like, but I'm told by the doctors that I was legally dead for a brief period there. So you see, I don't remember a thing. I didn't even know who the ambulance drivers were."

"There was a television program the other night about people who've died and come back. Did you see it?"

"No."

"Strange," Klubertanz said, half to himself.

"What's strange?"

"The experience. It must have been strange."

Rader shook his head. "Not at all. As a matter of fact, I don't remember a thing. One minute I was driving home from a party, and the next moment I woke up in the hospital with the doctors working on me."

"You were a lucky man, Mr. Rader."

"Very," Rader said. "Now, if there's nothing else . . . ."

Klubertanz got to his feet and glanced again at the book. "Have you always been interested in the occult?" He struggled to keep his voice calm.

"Since I was a kid," Radar said. "It's sort of a hobby with me."

"Curious hobby."

"No worse than collecting dead butterflies."

"I suppose not," Klubertanz said, and he stuck out his hand. Rader shook it. "Thanks anyway for your help, Mr. Rader. And again, I'm sorry to have disturbed you at home like this. But, as I said, I've been routinely checking Ahern and Shapiro's last contacts."

"I hope you find their murderer," Rader said. "They did save my life."

"Yes," Klubertanz said, turning to the door, but then he stopped as if he had just thought of something else. "By the way, you're not Catholic, are you?"

"No," Rader said. "Lutheran. Why do you ask?"

"Oh, it's another case we've been working on," Klubertanz said. "The rape-murder of a young nun. Happened a short time after Ahern and Shapiro were killed."

"I read about that one, too," Rader said. "Do you think they may be connected?"

"Connected?"

"The three murders."

Klubertanz shook his head. "No, it never occurred to me. What made you think of it?"

A flicker of something other than normal curiosity crossed Rader's eyes. But then he shrugged. "Because you asked me about all three of them."

"I see," Klubertanz said. "Well, thanks again for your help."

He let himself out of the study, and in the vestibule saw Cheryl Rader watching from the living room. He nodded. "Mrs. Rader," he said.

She nodded back. As Klubertanz let himself out, Rader came to the door.

"If there's anything you might think of, I'd appreciate you giving me a call," Klubertanz said. He took out one of his cards, and handed it to Frank.

"I never knew Ahern and Shapiro, and I don't remember anything about that night, so I don't know what help I might be able to give you."

Klubertanz nodded. "Thanks anyway," he said, and Rader closed the door.

Had there been something there, Klubertanz asked himself? He waited on the step for several seconds, and then turned back to the door and rang the bell.

Rader opened the door almost immediately, exasperated.

"I was just wondering if perhaps Mrs. Rader might have remembered the ambulance drivers the night of your accident."

"I don't think so," Rader said, but his wife had come to the door.

"What ambulance drivers?" she asked.

"Sorry to be such a bother," Klubertanz said. "But I was just wondering if by chance you remembered the two ambulance drivers who brought your husband to the hospital the night of your accident?"

"Vaguely," Cheryl said. "I rode in their ambulance with Frank, but it was all such a blur. Why do you ask?"

"They were the ones who were murdered a few days later. Bruce Ahern and Stanley Shapiro."

"Oh, my God," Cheryl said, bringing her right hand to her mouth.

"I'm sorry, I thought you knew."

She shook her head.

"Then you do remember them?"

She nodded, her eyes wide. Her husband seemed angry.

"Is there anything you can tell me about them, that night? What they said, perhaps? If they met anyone in the hospital, or anything like that?"

"No," Cheryl stammered. "It all happened so fast."

"You rode in the back of the ambulance. Which one was driving, and which one was back there helping your husband?"

"I don't know," Cheryl said. "I couldn't even tell you what they looked like."

"All right," Klubertanz said after a hesitation. "I'm sorry to have bothered you." He started to turn away, but once again turned back.

"What now?" Rader was clearly beginning to lose his temper.

"Your car," Klubertanz said. "It was a total wreck, wasn't it?"

Frank nodded, and Klubertanz turned to Cheryl.

"You didn't stay the night at the hospital, did you?"

Cheryl shook her head. "No. I went home later."

"Did you take a cab?"

"No," she said. "Some friends took me home. It was a terrible night for all of us."

"Oh?"

"Our friends lost their baby the same night," Cheryl said.

Klubertanz's stomach flopped over. "I have children of my own," he said. "I can sympathize. Perhaps they might have seen Ahern and Shapiro."

"Not a chance," Frank said. "Christ, their child had just died."

"There might be a slight chance. Perhaps if you could

tell me their names?"

"Listen, lieutenant, . . . " Frank started, but Cheryl interrupted him.

"Fred and Marion Martin are their names. But I'm sure they won't be able to help you."

Klubertanz stared at her. It seemed as if he was floating about three inches off the porch. His head was reeling, his stomach boiling. Finally he nodded. "Thanks for your help," he said, and he turned on his heel and went down the walk, climbed into his car, and backed out of the driveway.

Before he turned up the street, he glanced back at the house in time to see a face appear momentarily at the study window, but then it was gone, and he couldn't be sure if it had been Frank or his wife.

As he turned down toward University Avenue, Klubertanz tried to sort out his thoughts, but it was almost impossible at the moment.

Frank Rader. Deeply interested in the occult. Direct contact with Ahern and Shapiro. Friends with the Martins, whose baby, according to at least one doctor's suspicions, had been murdered. Coincidence?

Klubertanz wondered.

6

Marion Martin stood, fully dressed, in their bedroom, a few minutes past 7:30 P.M., staring at the full-length mirror on the bathroom door. Fred had taken the black robes she had made out to the car, and was waiting for her.

But she could not go with him. Not like this. Not tonight. She could not take any more of Frank's insanity.

"We're going to be late," Fred called from the living room.

She turned and looked toward the open door. Everything seemed to be so far away. The lights dim. Fred's voice sounded as though it was coming from the end of a long tunnel.

"Marion?" he called again.

She had heard a noise from the baby's room that night, but then Fred had awakened, and she was sure he had heard the noise too, and had gotten up to check.

She had lain there, then, half asleep, half awake, waiting for Fred to come back to bed. Waiting for him to crawl in beside her, and assure her that the baby was all right, and go back to sleep.

But he hadn't come back, and slowly she had come fully awake.

But she couldn't have awakened. It had to have been a dream.

She had gotten out of bed, had shuffled down the corridor and had gone into the baby's room in time to see Fred struggling with their baby. He was hunched over the crib. He was angry.

"Marion?" Fred said from the doorway, and she blinked and focused on him, her knees weak, her heart racing.

"I . . . ," she stammered.

He came all the way into the room. "What's the matter, sweetheart?"

"I don't feel so well," she said.

"Nonsense. You're just nervous, that's all."

"I can't go there tonight, Fred. Please don't make me."

Fred came across the room and took her in his arms. He smelled good, and his arms felt strong and secure around her.

"What is it?" he asked softly.

"I don't want to be with the others tonight. Let's just stay home."

"We promised we'd be there. I told you what Frank said about the Milwaukee deal."

She looked up at him. "You can't believe that, Fred."

"It's true. Without Frank we would never have gotten the contract. It would have all fallen apart."

"No," she protested weakly. She had no resistance left. Nothing in her life seemed to be the way it should be.

"Yes," Fred said gently. "We owe him at least this much. But I'll promise you one thing."

"What's that?"

"After tonight we'll probably not go back."

"Really?"

"Really," he said. "It's just that Frank has been so good to us, we have to do this. It means a lot to him."

"Tonight will be the last night?"

"Promise."

Marion looked deeply into her husband's eyes. Kindness there. The same old gentleness. Her dream had been nothing more than a nightmare.

"All right," she said at last.

"That's my girl," Fred said, smiling. "We'll leave as soon as possible, too. We just have to put up a good front. I don't want to hurt Frank's feelings. Not now."

Clinton Polk had called in sick this morning, and had remained home all day, watching television and drinking, so that by 7:30 P.M., when Susan was ready to leave for the

Raders, he was drunk.

She came from the kitchen now with a hot cup of coffee. "Drink this, and then get upstairs and take a shower," she said.

"I'm not going," he said, looking up at her.

"Oh, yes, you are, Clinton," she said. "Drink the coffee."

She turned on her heel and went out of the living room. He could hear her going upstairs.

Since Friday night they had not spoken more than a couple of words to each other, and he had slept downstairs on the couch. Susan had not refused again to sleep with him, it was just that he had been unable to face her up there.

He sipped at the coffee, burning his lip, but he didn't really feel it.

Several times over the weekend, he had thought about calling Vicki. He thought if he could go over to her apartment and they could make love, he would feel better. Feel more like a man.

But each time he thought about it, he shrank away from actually making the call. His life, he figured, was in shambles, or at least heading that way. And he was afraid of accelerating the process.

In fact, he thought now, he was afraid of doing anything. He had not been able to face the lab this morning, and he didn't know whether he would be able to face Frank and the others tonight.

He sipped at the coffee again, and looked toward the kitchen as Susan came back. She had a big grin on her face as she came over to him, took the cup from his hand, and set it down on the table.

"The coffee isn't going to do you much good, is it?"

"I'm not going," Clinton protested, but Susan helped him up from the chair and led him out to the foot of the stairs.

Puppy had been sleeping on the rug near the door, where their black lab used to sleep, and he looked up now and wagged his tail.

Susan laughed out loud. "I don't know who is worse, you or the dog," she said. They still hadn't been able to housetrain the dog completely.

"What's happening to us?" Clinton asked. His lips and tongue felt thick.

Susan's smile died. "You've been having trouble at the lab for the past few months, that's all. We'll get back on the track before too long," she said. "Up the stairs, now."

She helped him upstairs, and into the bathroom, where she sat him down on the toilet, and helped him to take off his clothes. He felt like a child being undressed by his mother.

When he was nude, she helped him into the shower, and then turned on the water.

"I'll be right back," she said, and closed the curtain.

Clinton steadied himself with both hands against the shower stall as the warm water streamed down his head and shoulders. He felt faintly sick to his stomach, and when he closed his eyes the room spun.

He knew that he would do whatever it was Susan wanted him to do. There was no help for it. He still loved her. And even more importantly, he needed her approval.

It was what had attracted him in the first place, his need for acceptance and her willingness to provide. And it was the reason he had gone to Vicki. Whatever he did at the lab was, in Vicki's schoolgirlish terms: "Simply magnificent."

The shower curtain was pulled back a few minutes later; Clinton looked up as Susan reached in and shut the hot water off.

For several seconds nothing seemed to happen, but suddenly the ice-cold spray hit his body, and he reared back, nearly falling in the tub, and Susan had to grab him. She was laughing.

"Christ . . . Christ . . . ," Clinton sputtered, the cold water a harsh shock to his system.

But then she turned the spray off, helped him out of the tub, and began drying him with a thick towel.

"I don't give a damn what you do or don't do over there

tonight,'' she was saying. ''But you are going to stay until I decide it's time to leave. Do you understand what I'm saying?''

Clinton was no more sober than before, but he was much more awake, and he nodded. ''I'm sorry,'' he mumbled.

''There's nothing to be sorry about,'' she said, tossing the towel aside. She led him into the bedroom, where she sat him down on the bed and brought him his socks and underwear.

''I can do it,'' he said, taking the clothes from her.

''Sure?''

He nodded. ''Go down and get the car warmed up. I'll be right there.''

Susan stepped back and looked at him. ''No trouble tonight?''

''No trouble,'' he said. ''Promise.''

''Your coat will be on the kitchen counter. Hurry up, I don't want to be late,'' she said, and left the bedroom.

Clinton sat there, holding his underwear in one hand, his socks in the other. At this point in their marriage, Frank Rader was her hero. The man she looked up to. Whatever it took, he told himself as he began to dress, he would change that. He was not going to lose his wife that easily. Not to some shyster engineer who was good at parlor tricks.

It was a few minutes before eight and Cheryl Rader stood by the living-room window looking out at the lightly falling snow, listening to the nearly absolute silence of her house.

She was more frightened at this moment than she had ever been in her life, although in one respect she felt a huge sense of relief.

Yesterday, after a long, violent argument, she and Frank had come to an agreement about the girls. Frank had gone along with her demand that they never be included in any of his ceremonies. For that, Cheryl had agreed to become a willing participant in what he was doing.

She had telephoned her sister yesterday, promising that she and Frank were coming up the day after tomorrow to spend Christmas, but that the girls would be coming up by bus today. She had seen them on their way this morning.

All during the late afternoon Frank had worked in the kitchen, not allowing her to come in, and when he was finished, Cheryl had expected to find a big mess. But the kitchen had been spotless. There had been a lingering odor of pork, and something else that smelled like cake or perhaps muffins, but he had washed and dried all the pots and pans, and taken the things he had prepared down to the rec-room.

An hour ago he had gone to the liquor store. She was waiting for him to return, and for the Polks and the Martins to show up.

Cheryl didn't want to think about the visit from the police lieutenant on Saturday, but she couldn't help herself. She had asked Frank about it later, but he wouldn't discuss it. And now she found herself dwelling on the incident.

The detective had been good looking. Handsome in a rugged, rawboned sort of way. But in his eyes there had been sadness. Something had happened in the man's life, recently, that had deeply affected him. Cheryl wondered what it was.

The van pulled up in the driveway, and a moment later Frank came up the walk, a box in his arms.

"No one has showed up yet?" he called from the vestibule.

"Not yet," Cheryl said, turning away from the window. "It's not quite eight."

Frank came into the living room, lugging the box. "Put this stuff away, would you? I've got to get upstairs and get ready."

He went into the kitchen, Cheryl right behind him, and set the box on the counter. When he turned around his face was flushed, his eyes bright.

"After tonight everything is going to be a lot better. For all of us," he said.

"You've said that before."

"I know." He took her into his arms and hugged her. She did not resist, nor did she respond.

When they parted, she looked up into his eyes. "What are you going to want me to do tonight?" she asked.

"Not much. Not much at all," he said. He patted her on the ass, and then went upstairs. Cheryl began putting away the ice and liquor.

7

Monsignor Dominic Ferrari slowly regained consciousness, a sick feeling deep inside him and a terribly thick numbness in his throat.

It was very difficult for him to breathe. He tried to clear his throat of the liquid that was blocking his airway, but he was having trouble.

He lay crumpled in a heap on the floor of one of the confessionals in the church his life ebbing out of his body with each pulse of his heart.

"*Domine, non sum dignus, ut intres, sub tectum meum* . . . ." The long familiar words came into his mind. "Oh Lord, I am not worthy that Thou shouldst enter under my roof . . . but only say the word and my soul shall be healed."

He tried to straighten out his legs, but the dark, cramped quarters were too small.

From where he lay he could look up at the tiny screened window that divided the participant from the priest. A large gaping hole had been torn in the fine wire mesh.

"Why?" he asked himself. He could not form the word on his lips, he could not speak at all, but his mind was still alive.

With each weakening beat of his heart, blood gushed down the front of his surplice from the ragged wound in his throat. The priest who had come to him in his office less then half an hour ago had been young, and very nervous, his eyes darting back and forth as if he was afraid someone might break in on them at any moment. When he had telephoned earlier this evening he had specifically asked for privacy.

"Are you in trouble, Father?" Monsignor Ferrari had

asked him. He did not recognize the name, and assumed that the priest was from outside the diocese.

The man nodded. "I've come here to you . . . because I want you to hear my confession."

Monsignor Ferrari's eyebrows rose. "How about your own diocese?"

The man hung his head. "I can't," he said in a small voice.

Monsignor Ferrari got up from behind his desk, came around to the young priest and laid a hand on his shoulder.

"I will hear your confession now, my son."

The priest looked up, fear and infinite sadness in his eyes, as well as something else that was faintly disturbing.

"Not here, Monsignor," the priest said. "Not here. In the church will be better." He looked up again. "Please?"

Again there was something disturbing about the man, but Msgr. Ferrari nodded, and together they left his office and entered the church.

The priest entered one of the confessionals, and a moment later Msgr. Ferrari slipped into his side, sat down on the low, wooden bench, and slid the curtain away from the tiny window.

"Bless me, Father, for I have sinned," the priest began in a low voice, and Msgr. Ferrari leaned forward slightly to hear better.

"A little louder, please, my son."

"Placeat tibi, sancta Asmodeus, obsequim servitutis meae."

Asmodeus, the word flashed through Msgr. Ferrari's brain, and he looked up in stark terror as a hand crashed through the screened window, grabbed him by the throat and yanked him forward.

"Sit nomen Asmodeus benedictum," the priest hissed, and they were the last words Msgr. Ferrari had heard as the man's powerful fingers tore into his throat.

Now, very weak from loss of blood, he knew that he was dying. He knew the face of the monster who had murdered Sister Colletta, the flower of a nun; who had slain the ambulance drivers and who had desecrated the altar.

He knew the face that Lt. Klubertanz sought. He knew!

Slowly, painfully, Msgr. Ferrari managed to turn his frail old body a little to the side, and he reached for the latch on the confessional door. But it was too high, several inches above his fingers, and he let his hand slump back. The tiny effort had caused an even greater weariness to descend upon him.

He was not frightened of death. He was an old man, and for a number of years now he had been prepared for the inevitable; in some ways, he had almost begun to look forward to face his master.

But he did not want to die. Not now. Not with what had been released to the world.

He reached up to his throat and felt the jagged wound where the man had torn his neck apart with his bare hand, the blood flowing, forming a thick pool on his chest.

Asmodeus. The demon. With the bloodied index finger of his right hand he traced the letter A on the confessional door, then brought his finger back to the blood on his chest.

Slowly he raised his hand again and traced the letter S.

Each time he raised his hand, his entire arm seemed as if it was encased in lead. Each time the sickness in his body seemed to grow, and his vision to dim.

He managed to trace an M, an O and finally a D, before he no longer could move.

"Let me be with You, my Lord," the words lovingly crossed his mind. "Forgive me my sins and tresspasses, as I forgive others theirs. Let me sit finally in Your judgement so that I may at last know eternal peace and happiness."

8

In the candlelit shadows of the basement, Cheryl Rader was shivering beneath one of the thin cotton robes that Marion had made for them. The others, seated across the pentagram from the card table, were dressed the same.

Frank had made them take off all their clothes, including their watches, and even their wedding rings, and then dress in the black garments.

"Welcome to the Winter Festival," he said. He stood behind the card table.

He seemed larger than usual to Cheryl; somehow more animated, as if he had gained power and stature from somewhere, as if he was girding himself for a fight.

"We are a gathering of witches," he continued. "Our dedication is to make our lives good by stamping out the evil that opposes us. Tonight we will have our first sabbat. And after this evening, nothing will ever dare oppose us."

He spread his arms out in front of him, raising his hands toward the ceiling. "Asmodeus, our Master, our protector; Astaroth, who loves and guides us, protect us from those who would do us harm."

He looked directly at Fred. "Protect this man against the evil forces that are now gathering against him. Make his days number many and make his life prosperous. Protect him, and vouchsafe his contract with Milwaukee."

There was a beatific glow on Fred's face, and his eyes were glazed. Cheryl felt sorry for him, and even sorrier for Marion, who was taking the brunt of his belief in this insanity.

"For Marion, I ask for peace in her soul, so that she may finally know happiness and comfort. So that she no longer walks in the shadow of her belief that her husband murdered their baby."

Marion gasped. Fred did not react at all.

Cheryl wanted to jump up and tell him to shut his mouth. She wanted to turn on the lights, blow out the candles and wipe the pentagram from the carpet. But she had promised that she would cooperate. For the girls' sake.

"For Clinton, stay the Regents from canceling his grant. Make him see his goal and discover the enzyme that he has coveted for these years."

Clinton, expressionless, glanced at his wife, who was gazing up at Frank.

"For Susan, I seek fulfillment for her desires . . . for her wants and needs."

Cheryl could feel a hot flush spreading from her neck to her face. This was all so unreal. It wasn't happening.

"Finally, for my wife, I seek the end of her fear, before it consumes her."

Cheryl flinched.

"Asmodeus!" Frank shouted. "Astaroth! Hear my plea in this, our hour of need."

The wind was blowing outside, howling around the edges of the house, and Cheryl thought she could hear the distant rumble of thunder.

"I am the master," Frank said lowering his hands. His forehead glistened with sweat, and he was out of breath. "Susan Polk shall be my high priestess, and shall assist me in all that I will do for you."

He held out his hand for her, and Susan glided around the pentagram and joined him.

Frank looked directly at Cheryl, for a moment, daring her to object. She shrank back in her seat, her stomach queasy.

It was only going to be for tonight, she thought desperately. He had promised her. Just this one last time.

"Master," Fred mumbled. He looked like a man on drugs. Cheryl wasn't sure that he even knew where he was at the moment.

Frank came from behind the card table, carrying a

plastic dishpan, which he set down in the middle of the pentagram. Cheryl could see that it was half filled with a black liquid. Ink. Oil.

He went back to the table again, rummaged around in a cardboard box on the floor, and brought out a small wooden crucifix. He laid it on the floor at a spot just within the pentagram.

Susan remained standing beside the card table.

"Who will be first?" Frank asked.

"For what?" Cheryl said.

Frank smiled. "For your baptism." He held out his hand to her. "Come."

Just for tonight, Cheryl told herself one more time, and she got to her feet, and came around the pentagram.

"Don't be frightened," he said, soothingly. "This is for your own good, believe me."

Cheryl looked into his eyes. "What do you want me to do?" Her voice was shaky.

Frank led her by the hand to the crucifix. "Step on it," he said.

She looked down at the cross.

"Step on it," Frank repeated.

Slowly Cheryl moved forward, and put her right foot on the cross.

"Now say: Asmodeus, our protector, help us."

Cheryl looked again at Frank, then back down at the cross. "Asmodeus, our protector, help us," she said in a small voice.

"Astaroth, who loves us, hear our cry."

Cheryl repeated those words as well, and then Frank turned her around, so that she was facing outwards from the pentagram, and told her to let her body completely relax.

"What?"

"Relax, Cheryl," he said. He placed one of his hands on the small of her back, and grabbed her arm above the elbow and gently eased her backwards. At first she stiffened, but then she let herself be guided down to the floor on her back.

Supporting her head over the plastic dishpan with his left hand, he dipped the fingers of his right in the black liquid, and sprinkled some of it on Cheryl's forehead.

"I baptize this woman, Cheryl Elizabeth Rader, in the name of Lucifer, Asmodeus and Astaroth, so that she may gain strength and eternal power from the spirits who guide us."

He lifted Cheryl up to a sitting position and then helped her to her feet. He was smiling.

"Almost done," he said, and he guided her back to the crucifix. "Step on it again."

Cheryl obeyed.

"Now say: The power of the Father, the Son and the Holy Ghost is myth."

Cheryl's stomach was knotting up, and she shook her head. "I can't."

"You will," Frank roared. "the power of the Father, the Son and the Holy Ghost is myth!"

"Frank?"

He stared at her, hate in his eyes, and she could almost feel herself shrinking.

"The power of the . . . Father . . . the Son, and the Holy Ghost . . . is myth," she finally said in a barely audible voice.

Frank grinned. "Welcome home, Cheryl," he said, and he kissed her gently on the lips. "You can sit down now."

Shakily Cheryl stepped outside the pentagram and sat down.

"I'll be next," Fred said, jumping up, and he hurried around to Frank.

Cheryl huddled deep in the easy chair as she watched the others submit themselves to Frank's ceremony. Fred was willing, Marion almost fainted, and Clinton nearly tripped on the candles when it was his turn.

Finally Susan submitted herself to Frank's baptismal ceremony. When she was finished, she baptized Frank, and after he had stepped on the crucifix, denying the power of the Christian Trinity, she kissed him deeply. When they parted, she was flushed.

Cheryl locked her thoughts on Dawn and Felicity.

Frank took the dispan away. Susan brought the three clay statues she had made into the pentagram, where she set them around the plastic skull.

When Frank came back from the table, he was carrying a hatchet. Susan stepped aside as he entered the pentagram and got down on his knees.

"We have enemies," he said, raising the hatchet over his head with both hands. "Death to our enemies!" he shouted, and he brought the hatchet down with all of his strength, smashing one of the statues into a thousand pieces.

"Death to our enemies!" he shouted, raising the hatchet again, and bringing it down on the second statue.

"Death to our enemies!" he screamed wildly, smashing the third.

"Death to our enemies," Susan repeated.

"Death to our enemies," Fred said. And then they were all repeating the phrase, as Frank got to his feet. Even Cheryl found herself drawn into the chant.

"Death to our enemies . . . death to our enemies," they chanted, louder and louder; shouting; Frank and Susan finally screaming the words; until Frank suddenly held up his hands for silence, and everyone stopped.

Cheryl couldn't believe that she had so easily been caught up in the moment. Her insides were boiling, her heart hammering.

"We will pray," Frank said in a subdued voice. "Our Master, Who art in hell, hallowed be Thy name; Thy kingdom come, Thy will be done on earth as it is in hell. Give us this night our daily feast; and help us to be strong as we annihilate those who are weak; and lead us not into deliverance. But deliver us from the God of the lamb."

For a long moment Frank stared at the others, and then he raised his eyes to the ceiling. "So be it," he said.

No one said anything, and Frank looked at them all. "So be it," he repeated. "So be it," Susan said, and the others echoed her.

Sweat once again glistened on Frank's forehead, and he

seemed to be happy. He turned to Susan.

"Now?" she asked.

He nodded, and went back to the table. Susan hurried out of the pentagram, the candles flickering with her sudden movement, and then she went out the door and up the stairs.

Cheryl had watched her go, and when she turned back Frank was standing behind the card table, the gleaming straight razor in his right hand, a large silver goblet in front of him on the table.

"There are strong forces opposing us," he said reasonably. "We must be strong in our combat of them."

Fred was nodding, almost slavering like a dog. They all knew what was coming. Frank was going to kill an animal. But this time, it seemed different to Cheryl. This time, she suspected it was going to be much worse.

They could hear Susan coming down the stairs after a couple of minutes, and they all turned as she came in. In her arms was a small black puppy.

"No," Clinton said, jumping up. It was their puppy. The one that Frank had given them to replace Bo.

"Sit down, Clinton," Susan said sharply.

"You can't do this," he said. He was obviously still drunk, but he was also frightened.

"Sit down, Clinton," Frank said menacingly. He held the straight razor.

"For God's sake, someone do something," Clinton said, turning to the others. "Fred?" he said. Fred wouldn't look up. "Cheryl?"

Cheryl looked at him, her heart thumping. She wanted to help. She wanted to stop this, but she could not. The girls—she had promised. She shook her head.

"There is no God here. You yourself have denied his power," Frank said.

Clinton slowly sank back on the couch. "You can't do this," he mumbled. "He's just a puppy."

"Asmodeus!" Frank shouted. Susan handed him the puppy, and Frank cradled it in his left arm. The animal was confused, but his tail was wagging, and he tried to reach up and lick Frank on the face.

"Astaroth!" he shouted. *"Libra nos, quaesumus, Asmodeus, ab omnibus malis praeteritis, praesentibus, et futuris."*

His right hand moved so fast it was a blur to Cheryl, and suddenly blood was pumping from the puppy's throat. Quickly Frank laid the razor down, picked up the silver goblet, and held it under the flow, catching the animal's blood.

"No," Clinton cried, and tears streamed down his eyes as he held his hands together between his knees.

Frank ignored him as he carefully collected the weakening puppy's blood. And finally the animal shuddered, and then lay still in his arms.

He placed the body on the card table, then held the goblet up in both hands, and raised it over his head. "Creatures of Satan, who bring sin to the world, guide us."

He brought the goblet to his lips and drank some of the blood, and then, turning, held it out to Susan.

She stepped forward, took the goblet in both hands, and drank, her gaze never leaving Frank's face.

Cheryl's stomach was heaving now, and she shrank back as Frank turned around and held the goblet out in her direction.

"I can't," she said.

"You must," Frank said, gently.

Susan came around the pentagram and helped Cheryl to her feet. "It's not as bad as you'd think," she said softly.

"For God's sake, Susan, I can't," Cheryl said. She was nearly vomiting with only the thought of it. Yet she felt as if she had no strength, and she allowed Susan to lead her to Frank.

Susan took the goblet from Frank and raised it to Cheryl's lips.

"Drink," she said. "Just a little."

The rim of the goblet was warm against Cheryl's lips, and she could smell the sickly sweet, metallic odor of the puppy's blood. She tried to turn her head away, but Susan moved the goblet with her, raising it.

And then the blood was at her lips, and involuntarily she gagged, getting some of it in her mouth, and swallowing it.

Susan suddenly let her go, and Cheryl fell back, looking wildly around the room, trying to find someplace to run, someplace to hide. Her stomach was flopping over and over, the bile rising sharply in the back of her throat, mixing with the thick, warm, sickly taste of the blood.

Fred had gotten to his feet. He helped Marion around the pentagram, where they both drank some of the blood as Cheryl finally stumbled back to her seat.

Now that the puppy was dead, Clinton seemed to have lost his last shred of resistance. When it was his turn, he dutifully came forward, drank of the blood, and then returned to his seat.

Frank took another drink of the warm blood, apparently savoring it, and then, in an almost light, jovial mood, he went across the room to the bar, set the chalice down and from behind the bar came up with a large sheet of parchment paper and a drawing pen.

Next he set out six glasses, a bottle of brandy and a bottle of white wine.

Everyone, including Susan, was staring at him, and when he looked up, he seemed bemused. "Why the glum looks? Church is over. It's time for a little fun."

No one moved. There was no doubt in Cheryl's mind any longer that he was completely insane. The accident, or whatever, had driven him crazy. she realized with a start, that she had known this for weeks.

"Come on," he said. He opened the brandy and poured himself a drink, took a sip of it, and then set the glass down. He picked up the pen, dipped it in the goblet of blood, and wrote something on the parchment.

"Cheryl?" He was holding the pen out to her.

She went over to the bar and took the pen from Frank. He had signed his name in the puppy's blood on the paper.

"Sign just below my name," Frank said. He uncorked

the bottle of wine and poured her a glass.

Cheryl dipped the pen in the blood and quickly signed her name below Frank's, then took the wine from him.

"Susan?" Frank said.

"A little brandy," she said, coming up to the bar, and as Frank was pouring her drink, she signed her name.

When she was done, Frank handed her the glass. "Come on, everyone, sign your name up here," he said, and then to Susan, "As soon as they've signed, pour them a drink. I'll get the food ready."

While the others came up to sign their names, Frank laid out the dishes he had prepared earlier in the afternoon, among them bits of deep-fried breaded pork, a clear broth, a plate of what looked like corn muffins, a large tossed salad, rice, and a loaf of unleavened bread. There were paper plates, plastic forks and spoons, but no knives. Nor was there any salt.

"Go ahead and get started," Frank said coming from behind the bar. "I've got something to do upstairs. Be back in a jiffy."

Again everyone stopped what they were doing and watched as Frank picked up the puppy's carcass, and then left the room.

"He's wonderful," Susan said, and Cheryl spun around to her.

Fred who had just signed his name, grinned at Cheryl. "Come on, Cheryl, relax. After tonight, we're all going to be on easy street."

"You're all crazy."

"You've got that right," Clinton said. He tossed back his brandy, and held his glass out to his wife for a refill.

Cheryl stepped back, away from the bar, and looked at them all. Marion stood behind Fred, her eyes moist, her lips quivering.

"Don't you see what's happening here? Don't you see what he's turning us into?"

"What's that?" Fred asked.

Cheryl backed up another step. "I want you all to go home. Leave. Right now."

No one moved.

"Get out!" Cheryl screamed.

Susan started around the bar, and Cheryl turned on her heel, raced out of the basement and up the stairs.

Frank was doing something at the counter by the sink; when Cheryl burst through the doorway he turned around.

He was holding a bloody butcher knife in his right hand, and a strip of meat in the other.

The puppy's carcass, half butchered, was lying on the counter. Cheryl looked from the gruesome sight up to Frank's eyes.

"What's wrong?" he asked.

The room seemed to be spinning, and Cheryl watched through half-closed eyes as the floor came up to meet her.

"Cheryl," someone said. It seemed like Frank's voice, but it came from a great distance.

And then there were others around her, holding her hand, and then she felt that she was being carried. Downstairs.

When she opened her eyes, she was lying on the couch in the rec-room; Marion Martin, a dull, vacant expression in her eyes, stood above her.

"Are you all right now, Cheryl?" she was saying.

Cheryl blinked and looked beyond Marion. The others were seated at the bar. They were all talking and laughing as they were eating.

Again the bile rose up in Cheryl's stomach, and she reached out for Marion. "He was butchering the puppy up there."

"I know," Marion said softly. "He cooked it. They're all eating it now. They made me have some. But I spit it out when they weren't looking. I just had some wine and the muffins." Her voice was slurred, as if she was drunk.

"Marion?" Cheryl said. She managed to sit up. "What's wrong with you?"

Marion shook her head.

"Sleeping Beauty is awake," Fred shouted from the bar, and everyone laughed.

He and Susan got off their barstools and came over to the couch.

"Feeling better, Cheryl, sweetheart?" Susan asked. She was barely suppressing a laugh.

Fred took Cheryl by the arm and lifted her to her feet. "Come on, the feedbag is on."

Cheryl shrank back. He was drunk, too. "No," she said.

"Come on, Cheryl, you're missing all the fun," Susan said. She took Cheryl's other arm, and she and Fred led her over to the bar where they made her sit up on one of the stools.

Frank was grinning stupidly. He set a paper plate in front of her, poured her a glass of wine, slopping some of it on the bar, and then waved his hand toward the plates and bowls of food. "The feast," he said. The others laughed. "What would madame like to try first?"

In the center of the bar was a plate with several strips of meat. Cheryl's eyes were drawn to it.

"Perhaps some bowwow beef?" Frank said, lifting up the plate.

"Bowwow beef," Fred mimicked, and he laughed so hard he nearly fell off his stool.

Susan began barking like a dog, and Fred and Frank both joined in with her.

Cheryl reached out and grabbed a muffin from one of the other plates, and took a bite. It tasted like cornbread, actually quite good, and she managed to swallow the first piece. She took a small sip of her wine.

"Eat it up, like a good girl," Frank said, a silly grin on his face. "And you won't have to eat anything else." He held up his right hand, three fingers extended. "Scout's honor."

Cheryl quickly finished the muffin.

"One down, one more to go," Frank said, and he gave her another.

"I don't want any more," Cheryl said.

"Just one more," Frank insisted. "Then you won't have to eat anything else. Just one tiny weeny little muffin.

That's all."

Cheryl forced herself to eat the second muffin, everyone watching her, and when she finally had it down, they all cheered, and Frank poured her another glass of wine, then leaned way over the bar toward her.

"Everything will be better in just a little while, babes. You'll see."

His eyes were glazed, and held a faraway, almost dreamy look. When he backed away, he took a deep drink of his brandy, then set the glass down and went to the stereo.

"Music," he said. "It's time for a little dancing."

The card table had been shoved back against the wall, leaving a fairly large space for a dance floor on the other side of the pentagram. When the music came on, it was some rock tune that Cheryl didn't recognize. It was probably one of the girls' records.

"Care to dance?" Frank asked, coming back to Cheryl.

She shook her head. She was still feeling a little light headed, and her stomach was still queasy. If only this night were ended now. She wanted to be in her own bed, warm and safe.

Frank helped Susan off her barstool and led her across to the dance floor, where Fred and Marion were already dancing. Susan came into his arms. Although the music was very fast, they danced as if it was a very slow tune.

Clinton had gone around behind the bar where he poured himself another drink, and took one of the muffins.

"Have another biscuit," he said.

Cheryl shook her head. She was feeling a little dizzy.

Clinton was suddenly beside her. "Stomach a little upset?" he asked drunkenly.

Cheryl nodded.

Clinton held the muffin up to her lips. "Eat this," he said. "It'll help. Believe me."

Cheryl took a bite of the muffin, not really knowing what she was doing. It was good, and it did seem to settle her stomach, but the room was definitely beginning to spin now, and the music no longer seemed harsh. In fact, she could feel the rhythmic beat of the tune, more than hear it.

"Any better now?" Clinton asked.

She looked at him. His face seemed somehow out of proportion, but pleasantly so. A small mole on the side of his nose gave him a rakish . . . almost sexy look.

She took another bite of the muffin, and then Clinton set it and his drink down.

"Do you want to dance now?" he asked. His voice was dim, and indistinct.

Cheryl looked over toward the dance floor. Frank and Susan had taken off their clothes, and Susan was kneeling on the floor in front of him, fondling his erect penis. Cheryl giggled, and she could feel a warmth spreading from between her thighs. The room was tilting now to the left, and then to the right; it was a pleasant sensation.

Clinton helped her off the barstool, but instead of leading her over to the dance floor, he took her in his arms where they stood.

For just a moment Cheryl resisted, but then she felt his erection beneath his robe against her thigh, and it seemed as if she was melting, and she let everything go.

"Clinton," she heard herself saying, and she felt his hands on her back, and then on her ass, little electric shocks going through her.

He was kissing her, his tongue darting inside her mouth, and suddenly she felt an aching need for a man inside her. Any man. Clinton.

She drew back, undid the tie at her waist, and let her robe slip to the floor, as the music played on and on.

She was lying on the floor, her legs spread, Clinton's face between them, and the pleasure was coursing through her body in time with the music. She seemed to be flying higher and higher, her heart hammering, her chest heaving.

"Yes," she cried. "Christ, yes! Yes!"

Part Four

CANDLEMAS EVE

February

1

It was as if a deep haze had settled over Madison, Wisconsin. Christmas, which had promised to be one of the best ever because of the upswing in the nation's economy, had turned out to be a bust. It seemed as if the lights of the city were slowly dimming, and everyone held their breath waiting for them to go out.

New Year's Eve was worse. Drunk-driving arrests were up seventy percent from last year; five people were killed in three separate automobile accidents that night; and early the next morning, a house on Madison's south side burned to the ground, killing a mother on ADC and her five children. Two days later, the father committed suicide by hanging himself in the county jail, where he was spending time for nonsupport.

The weather had turned against the people as well, newscasters calling it the worst winter in recent memory. Temperatures of twenty and thirty below zero were not uncommon through January and into early February, alternating with days in the low teens when the snow would blow down from the Canadian plains.

The American Automobile Club reported to its directors that, for the first time in many years, their automotive help division was actually losing money. No one's cars would start, and crews were out on calls twenty-four hours a day, seven days a week.

Madison Traffic officers Bob Tollefson and Dick Egan, who had been partners for seven years, sat in their patrol car in the parking lot of Doctor's Clinic, watching the late-night traffice along South Park Street.

It had been a quiet swing shift, their worst call a suspected breakin at a nearby liquor store. The owner had returned to check on something, and had accidentally tripped the alarm.

They had been in the parking lot for the better part of an hour.

"What time is it?" Tollefson, behind the wheel, asked.

Egan looked at his watch. "Eleven oh four, on the button."

"Fifty-six minutes and we can turn this heap in."

"Do you want to stop someplace for a drink afterwards?"

"Sounds good," Tollefson grunted.

A dark green Chevy, its left rear quarter panel smashed in and nearly rusted away, one of its headlights out, the other badly out of alignment, came weaving up the street, nearly hitting the center island, and then sped toward the Beltline Highway.

Egan sat up. "A customer."

"Yup," Tollefson said, putting the cruiser in gear and pulling out of the parking lot as he flipped on the red lights.

Egan got on the radio and informed dispatch that they were in pursuit of a suspected OWI, heading south on South Park Street.

They caught up with the Chevy in a couple of blocks and, as Tollefson was about to flip on the siren, the car ahead of them suddenly sped up, and halfway through an intersection turned right.

"Shit," Tollefson swore as they skidded past the intersection. He snapped the car in reverse, screeched backwards and, hitting the siren, turned down the dark back street, as the tail lights of the Chevy turned the corner down the block.

Egan was on the radio, informing dispatch now that they were giving chase.

Tollefson swung the cruiser around the next corner at high speed, nearly losing the back end, but the Chevy's tail lights were nowhere in sight.

At the next intersection he slammed on the brakes and backed up, swinging the car around.

"Tricky bastard," Egan said. The green Chevy, its lights out was parked in a driveway leading to a small house.

Egan unsnapped his holster, his bowels loosening slightly, as Tollefson pulled up behind the Chevy, blocking its escape.

Egan quickly explained the situation to dispatch, and then he and Tollefson got out of the cruiser. They both drew their service revolvers. Tollefson headed around to the driver's side of the car while Egan hung back to the right, standing in a half crouch, ready to bring his revolver up if there was any trouble.

The cruiser's lights were still flashing, and in the distance Egan could hear the sirens of the backup units he had requested. He had also seen, out of the corner of his eye, that some people had come out of the house next door, and were standing on their porch, watching.

Tollefson cautiously approached the car. The driver's window was down, despite the cold, and when he was about three feet away, someone shouted from inside.

"Don't shoot me! Don't shoot! I don't have a gun."

"Out of the car!" Tollefson shouted.

Egan raised his revolver in both hands, his right thumb on the hammer, ready to draw it back.

The car door slowly swung open, and a husky man got out, his hands raised over his head. He was wearing dirty tan slacks, hunting boots, a thick sweater and a bulky carcoat. For a moment he stood there, weaving back and forth, obviously drunk or high on something.

"Turn around, place your hands on top of the car, and spread your legs," Tollefson snapped.

The man slowly complied. Egan moved in, holstering his revolver. He quickly frisked the man. Tollefson covering him. He came up with a long hunting knife in a belt sheath.

Egan held it up to the light. There were stains around the handle. He backed off, his heart beginning to accelerate again, pulled out his flashlight and examined the knife under its beam. The stains looked like blood.

Egan handed the knife to his partner and then moved in toward the man again as he took out his handcuffs.

Pulling one arm back at a time, Egan cuffed the man, and then turned him around. His eyes were glazed, but there was no smell of liquor on his breath. Pot, probably, Egan thought.

He quickly read the man his rights, as the first of the backup units, lights flashing, siren blaring, pulled up behind their unit, and two officers jumped out.

Tollefson holstered his weapon, and locked their prisoner in the cruiser's back seat, as Egan looked inside the Chevy.

The interior of the car reeked of marijuana, and in the ashtray Egan found the distinctive ash. The glove compartment yielded nothing but the usual junk, matches, an out-of-date insurance card for Larry Triggs, 703 East Mifflin Street, and a clothespin whittled down into a roach clip.

"What've you got here, Dick?" one of the backup officers asked.

In the distance they could hear still another siren as another backup unit approached.

Egan grabbed the keys from the ignition and got out. "Don't know yet," he said tersely.

He went back to the Chevy's trunk as Tollefson came up.

"Looks like blood on the knife," his partner said.

Egan looked up and nodded. "Could be he's a hunter."

"Hunting season is over with."

"Yeah," Egan said. He inserted the key in the trunk lock, and the lid rose.

A sickening smell wafted up at Egan. He stepped back, gagging.

"Christ," someone swore from behind him.

Egan flipped his flashlight on and shone the beam into the trunk. There was a big bundle of what looked like fur, or some kind of a blanket, stuffed in one corner. Egan stepped forward and carefully pulled one end of the bundle up, and then flipped it over.

The fur had covered a hatchet, a meat cleaver, a long, curved butcher knife, and a thin steel crucifix at least eighteen inches long. Everything was covered with blood.

For a long time Egan stared down at the gruesome sight. Then he turned and looked into his partner's eyes. "Better get the BCI van out here, and have dispatch get ahold of Lieutenant Klubertanz."

Instinctively they both glanced over at the man locked in the back seat of their cruiser. He was staring at them, a grin on his face.

2

It was early morning, still dark and very cold, when Clinton Polk came slowly out of a very deep sleep. Ever since Frank's wild ceremony just before Christmas, Clinton and his wife had gone back to sleeping with each other, although they seldom, if ever, made love. He no longer had any great desire for her. A couple of times a week he would stop at Vicki's apartment, and they would go to bed. Sometimes they showered together, a couple of times she had fixed him dinner, and once he had even taken the girl to Chesty's, a student bar, one of her favorite hangouts.

Susan didn't seem to give a damn any longer, what he did. She was regularly sleeping with Frank Rader. They all knew it, but no one seemed to care, except for Cheryl. But Cheryl wasn't saying much of anything. At the Christmas get-together she had had sex with everyone, including Susan and Marion.

Frank had laced the corn muffins, the soup and the breading on the pork with marijuana, and the party had gone on until nearly noon.

Lying now in his bed, Clinton wondered what had awakened him. He reached over for Susan, but she was not there. He sat up.

She was at the window, looking out at the snow that had been falling all night.

"What's wrong?" Clinton asked softly.

"Listen," she snapped.

"To what?"

"Shut up and listen. Outside. At the front door."

Clinton cocked his head and held his breath. After a few seconds he gave it up.

"I don't hear a thing."

Susan turned around as he switched on the bedside light. Her face was pale, her eyes wide, and her lower lip quivering.

"What the hell is it?" Clinton said, flipping the covers back and getting out of bed.

"It's at the front door. Scratching there."

Clinton crossed the room and reached out to her, but she shrank back.

"Don't," she said in a small voice. She was wearing a sheer nightgown, and she was shivering. Clinton suddenly wanted her.

"Come on to bed," he said gently.

"Can't you hear it?" she shouted.

"Hear what, for Christ's sake? You were dreaming."

"No," she said, backing up against the windowframe. "Something is at our front door. Scratching to get in."

Clinton just looked at her for several long seconds. "You're crazy," he said, and turned back to the bed, but Susan grabbed him by the arm.

"Clinton, please! There's something down there!"

"What's down there?"

She shook her head. "I don't know. I'm afraid."

"There's nothing . . . ." Clinton said, but Susan cut him off.

"There it is! It's Bo. He's come back."

"Bo is dead."

"Our dog is down there."

"Christ," Clinton swore. He pulled away from her and went out into the corridor. There he held his breath, listening for the sound that Susan thought she had heard.

For a second or two he could hear nothing, and was about to turn back, when there *was* something at the front door. Suddenly he was cold, the hair on the nape of his neck prickling.

He listened. It came again. A soft scratching at the front door. Gentle, but insistent. Bo, their old black lab, had destroyed the finish on the bottom half of the storm door by scratching to get in after his evening outings.

But Bo was dead. The vet had performed an autopsy on

the animal, and Clinton had retrieved the body and buried it in their back yard. Months ago. The dog was dead.

The scratching continued. Softly. And now Clinton thought he could hear a dog whining outide. Whining to come in out of the cold.

He stepped farther out into the corridor, groping for and finally finding the light switch. He flipped it, and the lights came on upstairs and down.

Susan appeared at the bedroom door, and he glanced over his shoulder at her.

"You hear it?" she asked.

He nodded, then turned and started toward the stairwell.

"Where are you going?"

Clinton stopped and looked back at her. "Downstairs."

"No. You can't. Call the police."

"And tell them a dog is scratching at our front door?"

Susan brought her hand to her mouth. "Let's call Frank, then. He'll know what it is."

"Crap," Clinton said. He went to the head of the stairs. The scratching sound was much louder now.

He started down. Susan rushed out of the bedroom, after him. "Call Frank first," she cried. "Please?"

"Stay here. I'll just take a quick look."

Susan came down the stairs after him, one hand on his back.

It was definitely a dog scratching at their door. Clinton could hear its distinctive whine now. And it did sound like Bo.

At the door, he turned the lock and reached for the doorknob. The scratching suddenly stopped.

"Clinton?" Susan mewed like a baby.

He turned the knob and slowly opened the door.

Bo, their old black lab, was lying on their porch. Dead. Long dead. Its body rotted and covered with dirt from the grave in their backyard.

Susan screamed and slowly collapsed on the vestibule floor as Clinton slammed the door and, with shaking hands, snapped the lock in place.

Marion Martin awoke with a start, her heart racing. There was something wrong, something drastically wrong, she could feel it, thick in the dark bedroom.

She rolled over to snuggle with Fred, but he wasn't there. His side of the bed was empty, the covers thrown back, and she sat straight up.

"Fred?" she called weakly. But there was no answer.

She flipped back the covers, found her slippers, and got up. She grabbed her robe from the chair and went to the door.

"Fred?" she called out again, this time a little louder.

The house was almost pitch black. Quiet. Ominous.

She had felt this way before. A few months ago. And that night came vividly back to her, as she stood looking down the corridor, trying to penetrate the darkness.

The living-room clock chimed four times, and then was silent.

"Fred? Are you here?" she called timidly. She was frightened.

There was no answer. After a few seconds, she worked her way down the hallway to the open bathroom door, where she hesitated before continuing down to their baby's room.

The door was closed, and she reached for the doorknob, but then could not bring herself to turn it. She was truly afraid of what she might see if she opened the door. She wanted Fred to be here with her, right now. Frank and his ceremonies had made them all crazy, and the thought of what they had done last month at his house even now brought a blush to her cheeks.

It was filthy. Beyond the killing of the poor, defenseless puppy, they had all acted like animals, and she had been no exception.

"Dear God," she whispered to herself. "What is happening to me?"

She wanted to turn away from the door. Fred was probably in the kitchen, fixing himself a sandwich or having a glass of milk. Often he got up in the middle of the night for a snack. He would come back to bed soon.

Instead, she turned the knob, and slowly opened the door. There was a small light on. It came from the frilly little table lamp with pink and blue markings on the shade atop the bureau by the closet.

For a terribly long second, Marion stood there blinking, unable to focus on anything. But then she was seeing Fred. His back was to her. He was bent over the crib. And just as in her dreams, he was struggling with a tiny bundle.

"Oh, God . . . ," she barely breathed. This could not be real. It could not be happening. The crib was in the attic. Fred had put it up there weeks ago. And the wall-paper had been paneled over, the bureau and the little lamp stored away in the garage.

It could not be happening.

She took a half-step into the room, and a baby cried, the sound piercing her heart.

"Fred!" she screamed, and then she could feel herself falling to the floor, her world going soft and gray, the light fading away, and her own cries coming from a great distance, mingled with another voice. A familiar voice.

"Marion . . . Marion?"

It was a familiar voice, soft, brushing across her senses like the light touch of a feather.

Someone was patting her face, holding her up in a sitting position, and reality came back to her like water being poured through a funnel, and she finally opened her eyes and looked up.

Fred was there with her. Holding her in his arms. "What happened?" he asked her.

She felt safe and very secure with his arm around her. But she was confused. What had happened to her? She had no recollection.

"Are you all right now?" he asked.

She nodded, and he had started to help her to her feet when everything came back to her in a blinding flash, and she jerked away from him, slumping back to the floor and knocking her head against the doorframe.

"Marion," Fred said sharply, and he grabbed her again, and pulled her to her feet.

"The baby!" Marion screamed. "You had our baby!"

"What are you talking about?"

"Our baby! The crib . . . ," she started, but then she realized that the hall light was on, and she could see everything in the baby's room.

The crib was not there. The dresser wasn't by the closet; there was no lamp. The paneling on the walls gleamed dully in the indirect lighting. The room was empty. Empty.

But she had seen it. She had seen Fred. He was killing their baby.

"What's happening to me?" she wailed. "God help me."

Cheryl Rader had come to the realization that Frank would probably never stop his insane ceremonies without outside help. But the psychiatrist she had spoken with had told her she had only two choices in the matter: She could either talk Frank into volunteering for such help, or she could have him committed. The last could only be done on a court order, and then only if she could prove to the judge that Frank had become a menace to himself or to society. Yet, deep in her heart, she had always known that such a thing was totally impossible for her. She just could not commit her husband to an asylum. She couldn't.

The only other alternative, then, was to talk Frank into seeing a psychiatrist on his own. And it was to this end that Cheryl had decided to devote herself.

It was dawn and Cheryl lay in bed thinking about Dawn and Felicity and Frank. The girls had been gone a month now, and she missed them terribly. But after the crazy ceremony just before Christmas, there had been no other choice for her but to send them away.

The day after they had returned from Minneapolis she had confronted Frank with her idea.

He had smiled and joked, but Cheryl had been insistent, and Frank had finally put down the newspaper he was reading and looked across the table at her. The girls were outside playing in the snow.

"What exactly is it that you want, Cheryl?" he asked. His voice was cold, and devoid of emotion.

"I called a private boarding school today," Cheryl began hesitantly. "The St. Martin Academy, up in Beaver Dam."

"A Catholic girls' school?"

"No," Cheryl said. "It's nondemoninational and coed. They're sending me the brochures and an application blank."

"What brought this up all of a sudden?" Frank asked. There was a slight smile on his lips.

"It's not all of a sudden. It's just that . . . ."

"Just that what?"

Cheryl looked directly into his eyes. "I'm afraid of you, Frank. Afraid of what you've . . . of what you're doing."

"So you want to send the girls away from me?"

"Yes," Cheryl snapped.

"In exchange for what?"

Cheryl looked at him. He wasn't joking. He was *bargaining* with the girls!

What could she give him that he didn't already have?

"I . . . ." She stopped, sick at heart. She simply did not know what to say.

Frank leaned forward, his elbows on the table. "We're going to have more trouble around here," he said. "A lot more trouble before everything settles down. So I'll make a deal with you."

Cheryl waited.

"We'll send the girls to the private school. We'll try it for a semester. We still have enough savings to swing it."

Still Cheryl held her silence, but her heart was hammering.

"On one condition," Frank said.

"Yes?" Cheryl mumbled.

"I want your cooperation. Your complete cooperation in everything I'm trying to do."

Cheryl nodded, afraid to say anything at all.

"You're going to be my willing, devoted wife. If not, I'll pull the girls out of that school."

Cheryl's back bristled, and she sat up. "They're your daughters, for God's sake, Frank. What the hell are you saying?"

Frank's expression softened. "It's not like it sounds," he said. He seemed almost hurt. "I'm trying to help us all here. That's all. Just a little longer and we'll all be on easy street."

"I don't give a damn about easy street," Cheryl shouted. "I want our old life back."

Frank shook his head. "I wish it was that easy, babes. But believe me, I'm trying."

The bargain had been struck, but now, lying here in bed, Cheryl wondered if it had been necessary. Since that morning Frank had seemed like his old self, like he had been even before the accident. Happy, relaxed around the house, and yet ambitious to get back to work.

Shortly after New Year's he had spent a day downtown having a professional résumé typed up, and had sent out copies to at least three dozen firms, some of them as far away as Milwaukee.

Within ten days he had begun getting replies; he had been out on seven interviews already.

His spirits had seemed much better, too, during the past weeks. Last Sunday morning he had even made pancakes and sausages, like the old days.

No longer did he seem consumed by his studies into the occult. And no longer was he drinking as much as he had.

But it just wasn't the same without the girls. And Cheryl was looking forward to summer, when they would be home again.

She smiled to herself, and looked over at Frank in the growing morning light. He was sleeping peacefully, but he looked pale, a strand of his dark hair over his forehead contrasting sharply with his skin.

She rolled over and reached out to brush the hair away from his eyes. Her fingertips touched his forehead, and her hand recoiled.

His skin was cold to the touch. Ice cold.

She sat up and looked down at him. His eyes were not fluttering. His lips were still.

She pulled the covers back partway. His bare chest was white, just like his face. And it was not moving. It was not rising and falling.

Cheryl reached out and touched his chest. "Frank!" she said. His skin was ice cold, the flesh almost rock hard.

He was dead.

"Frank!" she screamed, throwing the covers all the way back and scrambling out of bed to grab the telephone on the nightstand.

Frank's chest heaved, and his right leg began to jerk spasmodically.

She stepped back.

His eyes began to flutter, and his mouth began to work, as if he was trying to say something.

Chery could do nothing but stare at him, the telephone to her ear, the dial tone humming.

"Asmodeus, protector of Your loved ones," Frank mumbled, and he opened his eyes. A moment later he sat up. Slowly his head swiveled to the right and he looked up at Cheryl.

Cheryl screamed, dropped the phone, and backed up a couple of steps. It wasn't Frank. The man on the bed *was not* Frank.

Slowly, as if he was a machine, the man swung his legs over the side of the bed and rose to his feet, his expressionless gaze never leaving Cheryl. Then he started slowly toward her.

She continued backing up until she was against the wall. She wanted to run. To scream. She could not move.

When he reached her, he raised his right hand and touched her face, his fingers warm now. He was going to kill her. It was not Frank. He had been dead.

For a seeming eternity the man just stared at her. Then, slowly, as if his face was an animated drawing, his features changed, softened, and he smiled.

"Were you having a dream, babes?" Frank asked pleasantly.

3

Tom Jankowski, the young court-appointed attorney, had finished with the suspect by 8:00 A.M. He stepped tiredly out of the interrogation room, his tie loose, his jacket over his arm.

During the long night, Lt. Klubertanz had studied the arresting officers' reports, and had reviewed all the reports on the murders of Ahern, Shapiro, Sister Colletta and Msgr. Ferrari, as well as the physical evidence files.

Jankowski joined Klubertanz at the coffee machine down the corridor.

"Is there an extra cup in there for me, lieutenant?" the attorney asked.

Klubertanz looked up and handed his cup of coffee to Jankowski. "Finished in there?"

Jankowski nodded. "For now." He sipped at the hot coffee. Klubertanz plugged another thirty-five cents into the machine.

"Does he want anything? Breakfast? A couple of hours of sleep? Cigarettes?"

Jankowski shook his head. "He just wants to get it over with."

Klubertanz collected his coffee from the machine and straightened up. He glanced toward the interrogation room, his insides boiling. He wanted to get at the kid right this instant. He wanted to pound him into the wall. Get the truth out of him. But all night he had been telling himself to slow down. Calm down. Nothing would be accomplished by blowing his stack. But it was damned near impossible to slow down, because every time he did, he saw the frail body of Msgr. Ferrari, his throat torn, crumpled in a bloody heap in the confessional. And all night he kept thinking about Frank Rader. Could he have been so wrong?

"I'm asking for the preliminary hearing at two this afternoon," the attorney said. "I don't have to bullshit the troops here, lieutenant. My client has admitted to the murders."

"All four of them?"

Jankowski nodded. "I'll seek at least a ninety-day psychiatric examination."

"Innocent by reason of mental defect." Klubertanz said.

The attorney laughed tiredly. "Shit. Triggs is as loony as a Mickey Mouse cartoon. He thinks he's the devil, or some sort of spook, or demon."

"What?" Klubertanz snapped, his hand shaking. Some of the coffee slopped out of his cup.

The attorney shook his head. "Ask him yourself. He'll tell you everything . . . over and over again."

Klubertanz dumped his coffee in the wastepaper can.

Captain Miller strode up the corridor to them. He looked grim.

"Have you talked with him yet, Stan?" he asked, looking pointedly at Jankowski.

"I was just going in."

"I'll be in the observation room," Jankowski said. He nodded to both of them, then turned on his heel, and went down to the room next to Triggs. A one-way mirror and an intercom connected the two rooms.

"The DA says the preliminary hearing will be set for two this afternoon," Miller said. He seemed worried.

"The boy attorney already told me," Klubertanz said. "He also told me that Triggs is confessing."

Miller ground his teeth. "They're going to cop an insanity plea, aren't they?"

Klubertanz nodded.

"Do you want me in there with you, Stan?"

"No. I want to talk to him alone."

"Take it easy," Capt. Miller said, after a slight pause.

"I know that you and the priest were close, but don't blow anything now."

"I won't."

Captain Miller glanced toward the interrogation room. "Osborne is coming down this morning; he'll want to see the kid. And there must be fifty newspaper and TV reporters upstairs."

"How the hell did they find out?"

"I don't know. But before you talk with them, make damned sure you know exactly how far you're going to go. This one is too big to screw up now. I'll send the steno down when you're ready."

"Yeah," Klubertanz said. "I'll see you when I get out."

"I'll be in the observation room."

Klubertanz grabbed his file folder and yellow tablet from where he had laid them on top of the coffee machine, went down the corridor, nodded to the uniformed cop at the door, and went inside.

The room was small, the ceiling and walls covered with acoustical tiling, except where the observation mirror was set three feet from the floor. The only furnishings were a small, gray, steel table with two chairs.

Larry Triggs sat at the table, his hands folded calmly in front of him. He had not slept since his arrest last night, but he did not seem tired. His eyes were bright, and he looked alert, although he was filthy dirty.

"Good morning, Larry," Klubertanz said, forcing himself to smile as he sat down across the table from the young man.

"Who are you?" Triggs asked.

"Lieutenant Klubertanz. I'm senior detective in the Homicide Division. Is there anything I can get you before we start?"

Triggs shook his head. "Do you want them in the order I snuffed 'em, or can we start with the cunting nun I fucked?" He was grinning.

Klubertanz smiled. "Let's talk about Bruce Ahern and Stan Shapiro."

"Those faggots!" Triggs snapped.

"What's the matter, Larry, wouldn't they suck your cock?"

Triggs' face turned a mottled red, and he slammed his beefy fist on the table top. "I'm no queer! I fucked the nun."

"Before you killed her?" Maxwell had reported that the nun had been sexually abused *after* she had died.

Triggs laughed. "Before, during and after. Great piece."

Careful, Klubertanz told himself. "Why, Larry? Why'd you kill her?"

"They used to beat me," Triggs said, his voice suddenly subdued. His mood swings were dramatic.

"Who used to beat you?"

"Those cunting nuns when I was in school! That's who."

"Why did you kill Ahern and Shapiro?" Klubertanz asked. He wanted to keep the kid off balance.

"I was at the Pirate Ship, and they were there, hittin' on me."

"Why'd you go there?"

"I wanted a drink."

"So Ahern and Shapiro just come up to you at the bar, and then what?"

"I didn't know their names," Triggs said disgustedly. "But it was the little one. He came up and sat next to me and asked if he could buy me a drink. I told him to fuck off, but he wouldn't go."

"He didn't leave you alone, did he?"

Triggs shook his head. "Then the other one came up and put his hand on my . . . shoulder."

"On your shoulder, Larry?" Klubertanz asked, sitting forward. "Or was it on your leg?"

"My shoulder, goddamnit. What the hell are you trying to do to me?"

"Then what happened?" Klubertanz asked.

"I followed them home. They were walking, but I used my car. Had to circle around the block a couple of times."

"And you killed them that night?"

Triggs laughed. "What do you take me for, a fool? Of course I didn't kill them that night. Someone would have remembered me from the Pirate Ship. I was smarter than that. I waited two months, and then I killed them." He giggled. "Do you know what I did? I cut their cocks off and stuffed them down their throats."

"What were you doing in the confessional?" Klubertanz asked, shifting his line of attack again.

"Telling my confession."

Klubertanz opened the file folder. On the first page was some of the material on the black mass that Msgr. Ferrari had given him. Whoever had killed the nun knew the litany.

"Accipite et manducate ex hoc omnes," Klubertanz said, struggling with the Latin words.

"Your pronunciation is terrible," Triggs said.

Klubertanz said nothing.

Triggs shook his head. *"Hoc est enim corpus meum,"* he snapped, the Latin coming easily to his lips. "For this is my body."

"You were an altar boy?"

"Goddamn right."

"Why did you kill Monsignor Ferrari?"

"Because Asmodeus ordered me to do it!"

"Like he ordered you to kill Ahern and Shapiro?"

"Yes, the nun . . . ." Triggs stumbled over the words. "No . . . the ambulance drivers. I mean . . . ."

"What do you mean, Larry?"

"What are you trying to do to me?"

"Find the truth, that's all, Larry." Klubertanz sat back in his chair. "How about Sylvia, Stewart and Melissa?" he said softly.

"What?"

"How about back in October, Larry? Were you out in California, by any chance?" An image of the funeral he had attended crossed his mind.

"I've never been to California," Triggs said. He seemed confused. Disoriented.

Later, Klubertanz thought. ''Did Asmodeus order you to kill Ahern and Shapiro, then?''

''Yes . . . yes he did.''

''Where did he tell you this, Larry? At his home?''

''No . . . I mean . . . .''

''Where then, Larry? Did you meet him downtown?''

Triggs screamed like a mortally wounded animal, the high-pitched, keening sound inhuman, and his entire body began to shudder and flop as if he was having an epileptic fit.

''Medic!'' Klubertanz shouted, jumping up from his chair. By the time he reached Triggs, the young man had thrown himself on the floor, smashing his head against the edge of the table.

''Medic!'' Klubertanz shouted again. He pulled off his belt, quickly folded it over, and got down on the floor next to Triggs. The door burst open and several people rushed in, one of them, helping hold the young man steady while Klubertanz stuffed the belt in his mouth so that he wouldn't swallow his tongue.

''Ambulance is on its way,'' Capt. Miller was shouting.

Triggs voided in his trousers, the stench in the small room gagging them all. Jankowski had to leave, but Klubertanz remained where he was, with one of the other cops, holding Triggs down so that he would not cause any further injuries to himself.

There were too many things wrong with Triggs' story. Klubertanz was convinced that the young man had been telling the truth as far as it went, but he was leaving out two important details. Asmodeus . . . the demon . . . or a man? And, the names of his wife and children. Monsignor Ferrari had found their names inscribed in blood on his altar. But it hadn't seemed as if Triggs knew about them.

4

Clinton Polk parked his car behind the Biochemistry Building, but he didn't bother to lock the doors as he usually did. Nor did he hurry up to his lab, although he was an hour late for work.

Someone had dug up poor Bo's body from the shallow grave behind the house, and had placed it on their front porch. It had been some sort of a gruesome practical joke, probably pulled by whoever had poisoned the animal in the first place. They'd never find him.

Later in the morning, after it had gotten light outside, Clinton had dressed, and then managed to scoop the dog's rotted body into a large, plastic garbage sack. He took it back to the garage, to the trash cans.

Then he went behind the garage.

A pick and shovel lay beside the shallow hole in the ground. Whoever had done this had gone to a lot of trouble. The ground was frozen solid.

But why, Clinton had asked himself all morning. Why do such a thing? There seemed to be no reasonable answer.

Susan had gone back to bed, and was still sleeping when Clinton left, finally, for the lab.

It was Friday. He planned on leaving work early and talking Susan into going out for a movie and dinner. They had not done that for a couple of months. And at this moment they both needed the diversion.

Clinton stepped off the elevator as Dr. Willis was coming down the corridor.

"There you are," the older man called out. He didn't seem very happy.

"Good morning," Clinton said.

"Come on down to my office, Clinton, there's something I have to say to you," Willis said.

They rode downstairs to the first floor in silence, then entered Dr. Willis' large cluttered office.

"There was some trouble at the house this morning, that's why I'm late," Clinton said, but Willis waved it off as he closed his office door behind them.

"I'm glad I caught you before you got to your lab," Willis said. "I wanted to save you at least that embarrassment."

"The Regents?" Clinton asked softly. Frank had said there would be trouble.

Doctor Willis looked away. "Yes," he said. "Your grant has been canceled."

"What do they want, another report?"

Doctor Willis looked back, a pinched expression on his face. "It's more serious than that, Clinton."

"What the hell do they want out of me?" Clinton said, raising his voice.

"There's no need to shout. It won't do any good."

"Sorry," Clinton mumbled.

"I always thought we were friends, Clinton, but this came as a complete surprise to me."

"Is this about the DS 19 experiment?"

"Partly," Willis said. "The board was disappointed over that, needless to say. That and your recent performance in the lab, but even those things could have been accepted."

"There's more?"

"You've been fired," Willis said. "The board found out that you and one of your student assistants have been . . . have been having an affair."

Clinton slowly let out the deep breath he had been holding. It had come finally, as he had known all along it would. And he had no defense for it.

"You can appeal, of course," Dr. Willis was saying, but Clinton turned on his heel and left the office.

He took the elevator back up to the fourth floor, and went down to his lab. He was not surprised. If the tables had been reversed, and he had been on the Board of Regents, he would have voted the same way. But it hurt. In his heart he knew that he had a real contribution to make to science. It was just that over the past few months he had somehow gotten off the track, and as hard as he tried, he couldn't straighten things out.

Vicki Karsten and two of his other grad students were in the lab when he came in. They looked up at him.

He managed a slight smile. "Could I speak with you for a moment, Vicki?" he said.

She came across the lab to him, her nostrils flaring, her eyes wide.

"Vicki, I'm sorry . . . ." Clinton began. The girl slapped him in the face.

"You sonofabitch," she said loudly. "You miserable sonofabitch." She brushed past him, out the door, and the other two students followed, leaving him alone.

His left cheek stinging, his face flushed, Clinton let his gaze take in the lab.

He had spent a lot of hours here. Good hours. Exciting times of discovery. For a while, when they were talking Nobel Prize, he had basked in the glory. Although he had never taken it seriously. He had been on top of the world. On top.

Slowly, he turned around, left the lab, and went downstairs out to his car. Before he climbed in, he looked up at the fourth-floor windows. He had wanted to grow old here. Become department head, maybe even Dean of the College. The venerable old scientist. Professor emeritus Polk. On all the *right* committees. Invited to all the *correct* functions. *The Clinton S. Polk Biochemistry Building.*

Polk fought back the tears as he got in his car and slowly drove off campus.

He had never considered having an affair with one of his students. In fact, the idea had been totally repugnant to him. And yet, it had happened. Even now he didn't quite know how it had come about, although he had enjoyed that, too.

Past the Veterans Hospital, Polk turned down a side

street toward the lake, finally pulling into the Raders' driveway.

Frank was the one person who would know what had happened, and why, Clinton thought. As he got out of the car, Susan came out of the house. He wasn't surprised to see her here.

"You were fired, weren't you?" she said, reaching him.

Clinton looked from his wife to the house, and he nodded. "I just came from the lab." He looked back at her. "What'd Frank say?"

"He knew about it. And he even knew about poor Bo," she said. "I came over in a cab. I had to talk with him."

"What do we have to do?"

"He wants us all back here tonight," Susan said. "He'll explain it all to us then."

Again Clinton looked up at the house. A few flakes of snow began falling from the overcast sky, and he shivered.

A few minutes before noon, Roland Friedan stormed into Fred Martin's office, and threw a Madison newspaper down on the desk. His face was red; his hair was mussed and his tie was loose.

"How could you let this happen?" he shouted at the top of his voice.

With shaking hands Fred picked up the newspaper. "What's wrong?" he asked.

"It's there," Friedan yelled. "Read the sonofabitch!"

Fred looked down at the newspaper, his heart immediately skipping a beat. Peppinger's photograph was on the front page, beneath the banner headlines: MILWAUKEE OFFICIAL RESIGNS OVER BRIBERY CHARGES.

"You told me that you had it covered," Friedan shouted.

"Shut up a minute," Fred heard himself saying. He quickly scanned the story.

Mayoral assistant Dwight Peppinger had been charged with accepting bribes from a number of firms dealing with the city of Milwaukee, the story reported.

An examination of his bank accounts and inventories of

his personal expenditures over the past two months had revealed more than $100,000 in unexplained income.

Peppinger's attorney had refused comment, other than stating that there were a lot of people involved.

Fred focused on those last words. Nowhere in the story had Creative Sales, or his own name, been mentioned. But the statement from Peppinger's attorney indicated that if his client was going to fall, he was going to take everyone else with him.

He looked up at Friedan. It had happened, just as Frank said it might. But for once in his life Fred wasn't paralyzed with fear. He was angry. Angry with Peppinger, who not only had been too stupid to hide the money he had received, but had to practically admitted his guilt.

"I want to know what the hell you're going to do about this?" Friedan asked. He was shaking with rage.

Fred folded the newspaper, dropped it in the waste basket, and got up. "If Peppinger is fool enough to get himself into this kind of a mass, that's fine with me. But we're not going to be involved."

"What?" Friedan sputtered. "How can you say that?"

"I'll take care of it, Roland. Don't worry yourself about it."

"We could all be up on criminal charges."

"And will be, unless you lower your voice," Fred said, coming around from behind his desk. He grabbed his overcoat from the closet.

"Where are you going, for Christ's sake?" Friedan shouted. "You've got to stay here. We have to straighten this out!"

"I'm going home, and I suggest you do the same," Fred said. At the door, he stopped and turned back to Friedan. "By Monday, everything will be straightened out. I promise you. Just keep your mouth shut."

Outside it was bitterly cold, and it was snowing. As Fred hurried to his car, he kept seeing the headlines. Frank had told him that a battle was coming. A big battle, but one that they would ultimately win.

A month ago he would have been frightened out of his

mind by this latest development, but this noon his step was confident, almost jaunty. They would win. Frank had said so.

If Peppinger did name names, his would be at the top of the list. If he was convicted, he would probably be sent to prison.

Frank would have to be told.

Fred drove unhurriedly across town, pulling into the Raders' driveway ten minutes later.

Frank came to the door almost instantly. "I saw the headlines," he said.

Fred smiled. "I thought I'd better check with you, just to make sure."

"I want you and Marion over here at eight o'clock sharp."

"Are we going to have another ceremony?"

"Not tonight," Frank said. "But everyone is going to be here. We have a lot of work to do."

"You can say that again," Fred said. "I've taken the rest of the day off. Friedan is going crazy down there. Can I come in for a drink?"

"Not now," Frank snapped impatiently. "I've got too much to do this afternoon . . . that is, if you want me to help."

"Sorry," Fred said, backing up. "I don't want to interrupt anything. Marion and I will be here at eight on the button. Should we bring anything?"

Frank shut the door without answering him. For a few seconds Fred just stood there; then he turned and went back to his car.

"The hell with it," he told himself as he backed out into the street. A long, leisurely lunch and a few drinks were just what the doctor ordered.

Cheryl Rader felt as if something very heavy was on her chest, making it nearly impossible for her to breathe.

She stared across the table in Charlie's Restaurant, not wanting to believe what Marion had just told her. But after what she had gone through with Frank this morning, she knew she should.

"When I woke up, Fred was standing there above me," Marion was saying.

"What did he say?"

"Nothing. He told me that I had been having a nightmare," Marion said. Her complexion looked sallow. "When I opened my eyes, the crib was gone. The room was empty."

"You were dreaming."

"I want to believe that, Cheryl, but I saw it. Even her little lamp was there on the bureau. It was there!"

Cheryl reached across the table for her friend's hand. It was cold and moist. "Maybe you were really having a nightmare."

"But I saw it, Cheryl. It was so clear."

But impossible, Cheryl thought. A roomful of furniture could not be moved that quickly. Nor could a dead man come back to life. She took a deep breath.

Should she tell Marion what had happened with Frank this morning? She decided against it now. The poor woman had troubles enough of her own. She had still not gotten over the death of her baby. No one would, this fast. Telling her would accomplish nothing.

Cheryl smiled weakly. "Eat your salad before it wilts."

"What's happening to me, Cheryl?" Marion asked. "What's happening to all of us?" She looked around the busy restaurant. "Ever since Jessica died . . . it's been all so crazy. So mixed up. Confused." She looked back. "And now Fred is in trouble."

"What kind of trouble?"

"I'm so ashamed," Marion said.

"What trouble is Fred in?"

"It was on the radio this morning. There's a man in Milwaukee who works for the mayor. He's been charged with accepting bribes."

"What does that have to do with Fred?" Cheryl asked, not understanding.

"Fred is the one who bribed him."

"My God," Cheryl said softly.

"If they find out it was Fred, they could send him to jail, Cheryl. He couldn't take that. He's not a criminal."

"Of course he isn't," Cheryl said, her mind spinning. This morning, Frank had been busy in his study. When she had asked him what he was working on, he had told her off-handedly that Clinton and Fred were in serious trouble, and were going to need his help.

"Have you talked with Susan today?"

Marion shook her head. "What am I going to do?"

"Eat your salad," Cheryl said absently. Frank would be planning another sabbat. To combat their enemies, he would say. But despite her promise to him, she didn't know if she could go through with it.

"Cheryl!" Marion said sharply.

Cheryl blinked. "Take it a day at a time, Marion. It's all any of us can do. If we can manage today, we'll worry about tomorrow when it comes."

When they finished their lunch an hour later, Marion insisted on paying. Cheryl suspected it was because Frank was out of work, and Marion, who always seemed to worry about everyone else but herself, wanted to help.

Outside it was snowing heavily, although there wasn't much wind.

"Be careful driving," Cheryl said. "These roads will be slippery."

Marion nodded. "Are you going to be home tonight? Can I call you?"

"Of course," Cheryl said.

They hugged, and then Marion crossed the street to the parking lot, as Cheryl watched her. She was a lovely woman, but Cheryl was afraid she would never be her old self again.

Cheryl was afraid of more than that.

5

"The preliminary hearing is being held over until Monday afternoon at two," Brenda Wolfe said. "Triggs will be out of the hospital by then."

"Is it epilepsy?" Klubertanz asked. It was a little after 1:00 P.M. They were in his office.

"For our sake, I almost wish it was," she said. "But Osborne called me just before I came down. He said Triggs' fit was almost certainly psychotically induced."

"The kid is crazy."

Brenda nodded. "And he's your murderer."

"There's no doubt of it," Klubertanz said softly. "His fingerprints were all over Ahern and Shapiro's apartment, on the altar at Good Shepherd, and in the confessional booth. The weapons were the ones used, and the kid admitted he killed them all."

"Neat," Brenda said.

"Yeah."

"But you're not convinced."

"I'd be a fool not to be. The bastard killed them all."

Brenda took a cigarette out of her purse and lit it. "So where do you go from here, Stan?"

"Nowhere. The police work is done. It's up to you now."

"Bullshit," she said mildly. "I know you better than that. And I'm worried about you."

"Touching," Klubertanz said sarcastically, and he was instantly sorry for the remark. It had hurt her. "I didn't mean it that way, Brenda."

"Sure you did," she said. "But I'm a big girl, I can take it. What I can't stand to see is you beating yourself to death. Why, Stan? Triggs is your boy. What the hell are you looking for?''

Klubertanz held his silence, remembering the telephone call from Msgr. Ferrari on Halloween. He had not reported their conversation. And now that the priest was dead, no one else knew about the inscription on the altar that night. Larry Triggs had not known about it. Only the person who had written it knew.

''If there's something that could affect the outcome of Triggs' competency hearing, you're going to have to tell me sooner or later. Why not now?''

Klubertanz also remembered Maxwell's puzzlement over the autopsies. Monsignor Ferrari's body had been in the same shape. Stiff with rigor mortis. Impossible, yet consistent.

''Don't clam up on me, Stan. I'm a friend, remember?''

''I'm not ready yet.''

''There is something, then,'' she said. ''An accomplice?''

''Not yet.''

''Goddamnit, Stanley.''

Klubertanz got to his feet and came around his desk to her. ''How about dinner tonight?''

For a long moment Brenda said nothing, but then she managed a smile. ''My place. Seven thirty.''

''I'll be there,'' Klubertanz said. ''White wine, or red?''

''Rosé,'' she said, and she left his office.

After Brenda was gone, Klubertanz grabbed his coat, got his car and headed out University Avenue, arriving at the Raders' house fifteen minutes later.

He parked on the street across from the house and sat staring at it, the engine ticking over softly, the heater pouring out its warm air.

Larry Triggs had committed four murders. But he knew nothing about the fact that Sylvia's and the kids' names had been written on the altar at Good Shepherd. Nor had anything been found in Triggs' apartment that would indicate he had ever heard of them.

Klubertanz knew there was absolutely no reason under the sun for him to suspect Frank Rader. No reason at all. Yet he shut off the engine and crossed the street.

The door was opened before he could ring the bell, and Frank Rader was standing there.

"I wondered if you were coming in, or if you were just going to sit out there in your car," Rader said, stepping back.

Klubertanz came inside; Rader closed the door behind him.

"Care for a drink?"

"Sounds good."

"Brandy?"

"That's fine." Klubertanz followed the man into the living room.

"Have a seat, lieutenant," Rader said, going to the bar.

Klumbertanz unbuttoned his jacket and sat down. "It's cold as a bitch out there."

"It's supposed to snow all weekend," Rader said. He brought Klubertanz his drink, sat down and raised his glass. "Cheers."

"Thanks," Klubertanz said, raising his glass. Then he took a drink. It was good.

"I suppose I should offer you my congratulations."

Klubertanz raised his eyebrows. "Oh?"

"It was on the radio. They said you had caught the murderer."

"He's only a suspect," Klubertanz said off-handedly. "I don't think he's guilty."

Rader said nothing.

"After every murder we get half the crazies in town giving us their confession."

"I suppose," Rader said distantly. "The radio newscaster seemed to be convinced."

"They only know what we tell them. They have to guess at the rest," Klubertanz said. He took another sip of his drink. "What kind of brandy is this?"

Rader shrugged. "I don't know. Cheryl usually buys it."

"Cheryl?"

"My wife."

Klubertanz looked toward the kitchen. "Isn't she home?"

"What can I do for you, lieutenant? Or is this a social visit?"

"To tell the truth, Frank, we're kind of stumped on this case. We're at a dead end. And I could use some help."

"Help?"

Klubertanz finished his drink and set the glass down on the table beside him.

"Another?" Rader asked.

"Not for me, but go ahead."

Rader finished his drink, and went to the bar, where he poured himself another stiff shot. "What kind of help?" he asked, coming back.

"Last time I was here, you told me that you were interested in the occult. Demonology, and things like that."

"A passing fancy, that's all."

The last time Rader had said he had been interested since he was a kid. Why was he lying now? "I thought it was a hobby with you?"

"It is, sort of. But what does this have to do with the murders?"

"That's the only thing we do know for sure," Klubertanz said. "Whoever killed those four people has to be totally crazy. He believes that he is some kind of a disciple of the devil. Asmodeus, or Astaroth, or something like that."

Rader did not react.

Klubertanz was somewhat disappointed. "You don't happen to read or write Latin, do you?"

Something flashed in Rader's eyes that time, but then he laughed out loud. "That's a hell of a question," he said.

"Just wondered," Klubertanz said. He got slowly to his feet. "Sorry to have bothered you, Mr. Rader."

They shook hands at the front door.

"You're not Catholic, are you?" Klubertanz asked.

"You asked me that once before."

"I forgot."

"I see," Frank said, opening the door.

"Well, thanks for your help, anyway, Mr. Rader," Klubertanz said. "If you should think of anything . . . anything at all . . . give me a call, would you?"

"Sure," Frank said, and Klubertanz headed down the driveway. Frank closed the door behind him.

At the street, Klubertanz stopped and looked back, half expecting to see Rader at one of the windows, but he wasn't. Klubertanz turned and started across to his car.

The Raders' blue van came down the street and pulled up beside him.

He went around to the driver's side as the engine died and Cheryl Rader got out. Her eyes were wide, and she looked definitely frightened.

"Good afternoon, Mrs. Rader," he said. She just stared at him. She was holding a bag of groceries. "Perhaps you don't remember me. I was here before. Lieutenant Klubertanz?"

She nodded, and for just a moment he wanted to hold her, to comfort her, to tell her everything would be all right. She reminded him of his ex-wife.

"I just stopped by to ask your husband for some help. The last time I was here, I noticed that he was interested in witchcraft."

Cheryl nearly dropped the bag of groceries, and Klubertanz had to reach out to help her.

"Are you all right, Mrs. Rader?"

She nodded after a moment, but she was shivering.

Klubertanz pulled out one of his cards and slipped it in the grocery bag. He glanced at the house.

"If there's anything I can do for you, Mrs. Rader, anything at all, please call me," he said. She was staring at him. "Day or night," he said softly. "My home phone is also on the card. I'd like to help."

6

Five hours later Cheryl stood in the middle of the rec-room, staring down at the shag carpeting. The lights were on, and there was no mistaking what she was seeing . . . or more accurately, what she was not seeing. There were no traces of melted wax on the carpet, there was no pentagram; in fact, there were no signs anywhere that the room had ever been used, or would be used tonight, as anything but a rec-room.

Frank was upstairs getting ready. He had told her that he had invited the others over, and she had been sure that it was for another of his ceremonies.

But if Frank was going to stage one of his ceremonies, it apparently wasn't going to be down here.

She stuffed her hands in her sweater pockets, and felt the card that the detective had given her. She had plucked it out of the bag when she was putting away the groceries, but had not looked at it.

Something in the man's eyes, and something in the way Frank had reacted to him, frightened her.

"I do nice work, don't I?" Frank said from behind her, and she jumped.

"You startled me," she said, turning around as he came into the rec-room. He was smiling.

"You were a million miles away."

"I came down to see if everything was ready."

Frank looked around the room. "We're not going to do anything tonight. Just talk."

He seemed a little wistful.

"How'd you get the carpet clean?" she heard herself asking.

"The Pentagram was drawn with watercolor. It washed

right out. But I had to use a grease solvent on the wax.''

''You could never tell anything had happened . . . .'' she said, letting it trail off.

''What did Klubertanz say to you out in the driveway?''

She flinched. ''Nothing much.''

''He put something into the grocery bag,'' Frank said. ''What was it?''

''Nothing,'' she repeated.

Frank just stared at her, a slight smile on his lips.

Finally she pulled the card out of her pocket. ''This,'' she said, handing it over.

Frank took the card, glanced at it, and then put it in his pocket. ''What'd he say to you?''

''He told me that if I needed any help, I should call him.''

''Cute,'' Frank said. ''I wonder what he had in mind. Maybe helping you with your shopping, or maybe with the housework?''

The doorbell rang. Frank ignored it. ''What else did he say to you?''

''Nothing,'' Cheryl said, and the doorbell rang again. She glanced beyond Frank toward the stairs. ''Someone is here.''

''It's just Susan and Clinton,'' he said. ''They'll come in.''

Cheryl heard the door open.

''Anyone home?'' Susan called out from upstairs.

How had he known?

''Fix yourselves a drink. We'll be right up,'' Frank shouted, without taking his eyes off Cheryl. She was suddenly very cold. ''Lieutenant Klubertanz will not be coming back here,'' he said. ''So forget his name. You won't be seeing him again.''

Cheryl could say nothing.

''Is that clear?'' Frank snapped.

She nodded. ''Yes, Frank.''

He smiled. ''Fine. Let's go up, then, we've got a lot of work to do.''

The doorbell rang again; Susan shouted that she would

get it. By the time Frank and Cheryl reached the living room, the Martins were just taking off their coats.

Frank went to the bar and began mixing them drinks. Fred was beaming; he pecked Cheryl on the cheek as she took his coat. He smelled of booze.

"Funny," he said, gazing across the room at Frank. "It's cold out there, but I didn't even notice it on the way over."

"Is it still snowing?" Cheryl asked.

"Yeah." He moved off to join the others at the bar.

Cheryl and Marion went out to the vestibule to hang up the coats.

"What's going on?" Marion asked, a catch in her voice. She seemed pale.

"I don't know," Cheryl said, keeping her voice low. "But it's not going to be another of his ceremonies. He told me that he just wanted to talk to us."

"I'm scared, Cheryl. Real scared," Marion said. She looked toward the living room. "Something's going to happen. I can feel it."

Cheryl had been feeling it all day, too.

"Come on, you two, I want to get started," Frank called from the living room.

"Coming," Cheryl said, closing the closet door.

She and Marion sat down on the couch next to Fred. Susan perched on the arm of the chair by the fireplace, and Clinton sat across from her, next to Frank, who was standing, a drink in his hand.

"We have arrived, at long last, at our final battle," Frank began. His voice was soft, barely audible, but there was an intensity in his words that startled them all.

The house was suddenly deathly still. Even the fire on the grate seemed subdued.

"Even at this hour, our enemies are gathering to defeat us. It has come down to a matter of survival."

Susan was gazing at Frank in open adoration; Fred was licking his lips; Clinton was wide eyed, and Marion was trembling.

"We are a fledgling force. Our wings still are untried on

the winds of the dark forces that mean to destroy us, that mean to drive us out of our protective alliance, that mean to murder us."

Cheryl could feel her heart hammering in her chest.

"The powers that oppose us are afraid of what we have become, or what we will soon be capable of. We cannot sit idly by and let them destroy us. Asmodeus is on our side."

"Asmodeus," Fred mumbled the word.

"Shut up," Susan snapped.

Frank continued as if he had not heard the exchange. "Fred did not kill your child, Marion. But I know who did, and why."

Marion gasped, and brought her right hand up to her mouth.

"Oh, God," Cheryl whispered to herself. She was heartsick. And frightened. And cold.

"Are you willing to help me drive your child's murderer into everlasting agony?"

Tears were streaming down Marion's face, and she seemed to be sinking back into the couch.

"Are you willing to help me?" Frank roared.

"Yes," Marion whimpered. "Yes . . . yes . . . ."

"Are you willing to help me, Fred, to avenge your baby's death, to guarantee your continued protection from prosecution?"

"Yes, master," Fred said slavishly.

"Are you willing to help me, Susan? To be my chosen handmaiden?"

"With pleasure," Susan said, the words rolling sensuously from her lips. Cheryl shuddered; she concentrated on the girls, on Dawn and Felicity.

"Clinton," Frank said. "Your research has been denied. Will you fight for it? Will you lend your strength to our purpose?"

"Anything," Clinton said. "I'll do anything."

Frank's gaze turned to Cheryl, and her breath caught in her throat. "Yes," she croaked.

"You lie!" he bellowed.

"I'll do whatever you say, Frank. I promise. You have to

believe me. Please." The girls were safe. Dawn . . . .

"Swear it on the lives of your daughters."

"Frank?"

"Swear it," Susan said.

Cheryl looked over at her.

"Swear it," Fred said, and Cheryl's gaze shifted to him.

"Swear it," Clinton said mechanically.

"Yes," Cheryl said, nodding her head. "Yes, Frank, I swear it."

"Then so be it," Frank's voice boomed. The lights went out; only the flickering flames in the fireplace illuminated his face.

"We will celebrate the black mass," he said, his eyes larger than life, his voice boring into Cheryl's brain. "It will be a celebration of what we have become. A celebration of our absolute power."

Cheryl had a sudden, overwhelming longing to be with the girls. To hold them closely, and to assure them that everything was going to be all right.

"Monday is Candlemas Eve. We shall leave this place for another, more secure, fortress, where we will hold a three-day sabbat. From that time forward, through all eternity, we shall be one with Asmodeus . . . we shall have absolute power over our enemies."

No, Cheryl screamed silently. She had to see the girls first.

"Fred and Marion shall provide the provisions. The pork, the beef, the turnips, the whiskey," Frank was saying. "Susan and Clinton shall provide the beasts . . . the black puppy, the rooster, the rabbit. And Cheryl and I shall provide the setting."

7

Saturday morning broke overcast and very dark. At nine, streetlights throughout Madison were still on, motorists drove with their headlights, and storefront windows were still lit up. It had snowed all night, and it looked as if it would snow all day. Forecasters were calling for a further deterioration in the weather through the weekend, with a sixty percent chance for a major winter storm to develop by Monday.

Driving downtown, Klubertanz was in a foul mood. Captain Miller had called earlier this morning asking him to come down to the office by 9:30 A.M., but he had refused to say what he wanted to talk about.

It was one more piece of shit, Klubertanz thought glumly, in an already overloaded pot.

Last night he and Brenda had argued bitterly about the Larry Triggs case, and they had both ended up saying things that they shouldn't have. She had accused him of living in a fantasy world.

"You're Mr. Macho cop," she had snapped shrilly. "And if anyone doubts your magnificent judgment, you kick them out of your life . . . just like you did your wife."

The remark still stung, because there was some truth to it. But he hadn't been thinking that straight last night, and he had lashed back at Brenda, calling her a hardline libber bitch, who would die an old maid because she wasn't woman enough to attract a man.

He had tried to call her this morning, to apologize, but her line was busy, and he supposed she had taken her phone off the hook.

It didn't matter anyway, he thought. It just wasn't

going to work for them. In many respects his job did come first, and she was too demanding and too competitive ever to settle down.

Still, he thought, he did have a feeling for her, and he did respect her, so he owed her an apology.

He pulled around behind the City-County Building, parked his car, and went upstairs.

Captain Miller was in the duty room, waiting for him.

Without a word, Klubertanz followed him into his office, the three or four officers in the duty room suddenly very busy behind them.

"Coffee?" Miller asked.

"I could use a cup," Klubertanz said, closing the door.

Miller poured them each a cup from the coffee maker behind his desk, handed Klubertanz his, and then sat down. "Have a seat, Stan."

Klubertanz slumped down across from Miller, and sipped at his coffee.

"You look like hell, do you know that?" Miller said.

Klubertanz had to smile. "I feel worse, believe me."

"I believe you. And I also believe that you're a good cop."

"Am I on the carpet?"

"Not yet, Stan, but if Internal Affairs gets hold of this, you will be. And they'll beat you to death."

Klubertanz took a deep breath, and let it out slowly. "What's the bottom line? Whose feathers have I ruffled?"

"John Q. Public, in the person of an engineer by the name of Frank Rader. He phoned yesterday afternoon with his bitch. I tried to get you at your place, but you weren't there."

"I was out," Klubertanz said dryly. "What's Rader's complaint?"

"Harrassment, for starters. Scaring the hell out of his wife. False accusation."

"Anything else?"

"Drinking on duty. He says you accepted a drink from him."

Klubertanz had to smile. "It was a pretty good brandy."

"We've got our murderer, Stan. And Sylvia running off the highway was nothing more than an accident. No connection."

Klubertanz very carefully set his coffee cup on the edge of Miller's desk. There was a roaring in his ears, and his hands shook. "What did you say?"

Miller was alarmed. "What the hell's the matter with you, Stan?"

"What'd you say about Sylvia?"

"There's no connection between her accident and the murders here in Madison. I mean, it's just too fantastic."

Klubertanz's breath was coming shallowly now. "What makes you think there was a connection?"

"There wasn't . . . ." Miller stopped. He was obviously frustrated.

"You said there was no connection. What brought it up in the first place?"

"You did."

Klubertanz shook his head. "No, I didn't. I haven't said a word here about Sylvia and the kids."

"I don't mean here. I mean with Rader. You asked him about it."

"No, I didn't." Klubertanz thumped his fist on the desk and jumped up. "No fucking way did I mention Sylvia's accident to that bastard."

"Sit down," Miller said.

Klubertanz just looked at him, a single thought screaming through his brain.

"You must have mentioned the accident to him. Maybe you didn't even hear yourself. Things like that do happen."

"No," Klubertanz said.

"Then how the hell would he know about it?"

"Because he killed the nun," Klubertanz said. "Because he killed Ahern and Shapiro, and Monsignor Ferrari. And somehow, Sylvia and the kids."

"That's crazy, Stan, and you know it. We've got our

confessed murderer. Motive, means and physical evidence. Jesus Christ, what the hell more do you want?"

"The real murderer."

"We've got him," Miller said, and Klubertanz started to protest, but the captain overrode him. "For the sake of argument, let's assume at least that Triggs is the murderer, and Rader put him up to it for some reason."

"You're goddamned right he put him up to it," Klubertanz shouted.

"All right, all right, just bear with me for a moment."

Klubertanz said nothing.

"Aside from the first question that pops into my mind . . . mainly, what's the man's motive . . . I've got to ask what all this has to do with Sylvia's accident?"

"Right after the accident, when I was in L.A., Monsignor Ferrari telephoned me at my motel. It was Halloween. He told me that the altar at Good Shepherd had been desecrated again."

"I don't remember seeing that in any of the reports."

"It wasn't there, because Ferrari didn't tell anyone but me, and I didn't report it."

Miller's eyes narrowed. "What are you saying to me, Stan? Was this Rader character involved?"

"Up to his ears, but I didn't know it at the time."

"Then . . . ."

Klubertanz held up his hand, and Miller stopped.

"There was writing on the floor of the apse. In blood."

"I don't think I'm going to like this," Miller said.

"In Latin. Another message from the demon, Asmodeus. But this time there were four names."

Miller seemed to be holding his breath.

"Sylvia. Stewart. Melissa. And Monsignor Ferrari."

"Jesus," Miller said softly. "That's why you asked Triggs about it. I didn't know what the hell you were getting at."

"No one but the murderer knows about it."

Miller shook his head. "Wrong," he said. "The only person besides you and the priest was the one who wrote it. Which does not necessarily make that person the murderer. Just someone with a sick sense of humor."

"For Christ's sake, captain!"

"For Christ's sake, nothing, Stan. What the hell have you got here? Someone desecrates an altar, writes the names of your ex-wife and children there, and that makes him a murderer?"

"How would anyone have known?"

"It was in the *Capital Times*. A small article on the back pages. 'Madison cop's ex-wife and children killed in a California car accident.' Anyone could have read it."

What Miller was saying made sense, of course. Yet, Klubertanz could not accept such a simple explanation.

"There's too many holes in your version," he said.

"And yours leaks like a sieve, Stan. Listen to reason, for God's sake."

"Or?" Klubertanz said.

A pained expression crossed Miller's face. "Or I'll have to relieve you, pending a departmental investigation."

Klubertanz shook his head. Maybe Brenda had been right last night. A hundred percent right. Maybe he was nothing more than a macho cop with an inflated sense of his own importance; with a feeling of infallibility.

Slowly he pulled out his ID case, flipped it open, and looked at the plastic identification card with his photograph, and at the gold shield. Then he closed it, and gently laid it on Miller's desk.

"You can't be serious about this," the captain said.

Without a word, Klubertanz removed his service revolver from its stiff leather holster beneath his coat, opened the cylinder, removed all six shells, and laid them and the gun on the desk, as well.

"I'm relieving myself from the force," he said softly.

"If you approach Rader again, without just and sufficient cause, I'll have to arrest you."

"I hope it doesn't come to that, captain," Klubertanz said. "I sincerely hope not." He turned, left the office, and went out to his car.

Were Brenda and Capt. Miller right?

No, he thought firmly. No.

8

Marion Martin stood in the bathroom, staring at the untidy jumble of bottles and toothpaste and razor blades in the medicine cabinet.

Sleeping tablets. Their doctor had prescribed them for her after Jessica had died, but she had only used them a couple of nights. They made her drowsy too fast, and then completely knocked her out for at least ten hours.

That was with two tablets. What about four of them, she asked herself? Or ten of them, or the entire bottle?

She reached up for them, but stopped short, her hand trembling.

Actually swallowing the pills would be the difficult part. But after that she would just fall asleep. Fall asleep and never wake up. But what if she dreamed? What if she had another nightmare about Fred and the baby? What if the nightmare went on and on, forever? Would she be able to handle that?

She withdrew her hand and hung her head. If she died like that, this afternoon, she would never know what had really happened that night. What if Fred had really killed their baby? He would escape if she destroyed herself now.

But did she want to know for sure? She looked up again at the bottle on the top shelf. The label seemed to be mocking her; seemed to be daring her: Reach for me if you can, release is just around the corner.

Life had been so simple, growing up in Mankato, Minnesota. But it wasn't simple any longer. Nothing was simple now. It was all beyond her.

At the very least, her husband was a criminal. He had bribed people. And at the very worst, he was the murderer of their child.

Slowly, she closed the medicine cabinet, her image in the mirror swinging around, but she looked away, unable for the moment to face herself.

She left the bathroom, and in the corridor looked down toward the baby's old room. The house was quiet. Fred had left an hour ago to do the shopping for Monday's ceremony. Twice she had tried to telephone Cheryl, but both times there had been no answer.

Marion moved toward the baby's room, a step at a time, her outstretched hand brushing against the wall.

Jessica had been a good baby. She never cried much, not even when her diaper was messy. When it was time for her feeding they would go into her room, and she would be lying there wide awake, waiting patiently for them.

A couple of feet away from the door, Marion stopped, unable to continue.

Fred had been such a proud father. He had brought a 35-mm camera with all the attachments, and went through at least two rolls of film a week at first.

They had laughed a lot then. Sometimes in the evening, lying in bed together, they would talk about what Jessica would be like when she grew up.

"Just wait, Frederick, until she goes through puberty. Teenage girls are worse than pregnant women."

Fred just laughed. "I loved you when you were pregnant."

"Just wait," Marion said. "The first time a boy brings her home late . . ."

"I'll break the little bastard's arms," he said in mock anger.

There were tears in Marion's eyes now as she stepped up to the door and opened it. God, they had been so happy in those days. And it had only been a few short months ago.

For the briefest of moments, what she was seeing simply did not register on Marion. But then, like the sudden illumination of a lightning strike, the image of the room burned itself into her mind.

The clown print wallpaper was back. The baby's bureau, with the little lamp atop it, was against the wall.

And the crib stood in its old spot.

It was an hallucination, she told herself. She was dreaming this again.

She stepped all the way into the room, her heart pounding. There was a bundle in the crib. Wrapped in a pink blanket.

"Oh God," Marion whispered, her breath coming rapidly.

She moved closer, and she could see a few thin wisps of blonde hair.

"Jessica?" she whimpered, moving to the side of the crib.

Her hands were shaking very badly as she reached into the crib and gently pulled the blanket back.

It was a doll. Life-sized. With blonde hair, and a little rosebud mouth.

Marion backed away from the crib, her hands at her mouth to hold back a scream.

It wasn't real. The thing in the crib was not Jessica.

She turned and ran out of the baby's room to their bedroom, where she picked up the telephone and dialed.

It was too much. She could not handle this any longer. No one could.

The telephone was answered on the second ring.

"Cheryl? Oh God, Cheryl, is that you?" Marion screamed.

There was a silence.

"Cheryl?" Marion whimpered. "Please?"

"I know what you're going through, Marion," Frank's smooth, well-modulated voice came over the line.

Marion's eyes widened, and her stomach flopped.

"It won't do to get yourself upset like this, Marion," Frank continued. "Hold on until Monday. On Monday it will all be better. I promise you. Monday."

At St. Martins, Cheryl Rader walked toward the gymnasium with one of the school's assistant directors, a young woman in her early twenties.

"It's our big midwinter dance," the woman was explaining. "The girls have been in the gym all day, decorating."

"Are Dawn and Felicity there?" Cheryl asked.

"If they're not, they're in the kitchen." The woman, whose name was Betsy, looked at her watch. "Some of them have probably started on the snack trays. We'll have at least two hundred people here. Will you and Mr. Rader be able to join us? A lot of the parents are planning on being here."

Cheryl shook her head. "I don't think so."

"Perhaps you can make it for the Spring Fling. It's in April. You'll get the notices."

"Sure," Cheryl said.

They reached the gym. Hard rock was blaring from a radio on one of the bleachers. A couple of girls were up on a tall stepladder, hanging mesh baskets of balloons, and a dozen other girls were taping bunting on the walls. Dawn and Felicity weren't among them.

"Hold on a sec, and I'll look in the kitchen," Betsy said, and she hurried across the gym and out another door.

This morning the urge to come out here and see the girls . . . see them with her own eyes, and make sure they were all right . . . had become overwhelming.

Frank hadn't asked where she was going when she left, and she had not volunteered the information.

The forty-mile drive to Beaver Dam had taken her longer than she expected; the snow that had been falling since yesterday had made the roads very slippery.

"Mom . . . mom!" the girls shouted from behind her, and Cheryl turned to see Dawn and Felicity, wearing sweatshirts, bluejeans and sneakers, bounding down the corridor, Betsy right behind them.

Cheryl hugged both girls, and then kissed them on the cheek. "I'm so glad to see you two," she said.

When they parted, Cheryl looked up. Betsy was standing there, an odd expression on her face.

"Would you like to take the girls to the reception room? I could bring you a cup of coffee."

Cheryl smiled but shook her head.

"Did Daddy come with you?" Felicity asked.

"No, not this time, sweetheart," she said. "Maybe next time."

"He was here Thursday," Dawn said. "But when he didn't come yesterday, we thought maybe . . . ."

Cheryl had turned cold. Thursday. Frank hadn't said anything about coming up to see the girls. And the way Dawn had said it made it sound as if Frank had come here often.

"You thought maybe what, sweetheart?" she asked.

Both girls were suddenly fidgeting. Betsy had moved off down the corridor, and when Cheryl looked her way, the girl was just disappearing around the corner.

"You know," Dawn said.

"No, I don't know," Cheryl said. "Has daddy been up here a lot?"

"Every day," Felicity chirped, but then she bit it off, as if she wasn't supposed to tell.

Dear God, every day. "It must be a surprise. Daddy didn't say anything to me about it," Cheryl said weakly.

Dawn and Felicity each took an arm, and led her away from the open gym doors.

"Are you feeling okay, mom?" Dawn asked. She sounded solicitous. Almost grown up.

"I'm fine."

"Are you better now?" Felicity bubbled. "I mean, if you're feeling better, daddy says we can come home."

Cheryl's knees were weak.

"Daddy says this school is a bad place for us. He says we should be home," Felicity continued.

"Can we come home soon?" Dawn asked.

"Don't you like it here?" Cheryl asked. She had to force herself to sound and appear calm.

Dawn shrugged. "It's okay, but we like it better the way it used to be."

So do I, Cheryl wanted to say, but for the moment she could not make any words come to her lips. She just stood there staring at the girls; staring into their open, innocent eyes. What was Frank doing? She had promised him that she would cooperate. He had agreed that he would leave the girls out of this. She had promised. So what was he doing?

"Are you all right, mom?" Dawn asked. "Do you want to sit down?"

Cheryl managed a smile, and she shook her head. "I'm just fine, dear," she said. "Daddy and I are both going to come up next week."

"I love you, mom," Dawn said.

"Me, too," Felicity chirped.

9

Cheryl was awake when the alarm went off at 7:00 A.M. on Monday, but she feigned sleep as Frank reached up and shut it off.

He got out of bed, and even with her eyes closed Cheryl knew that he was standing at the foot of the bed looking at her. Watching her. But then he moved off, and she could hear the bathroom door closing, and a second later the water running, and she opened her eyes.

When she had returned from the school late Saturday afternoon, he had been preoccupied, and somewhat agitated, and she had known that it was the wrong time to bring the subject up. He had gone to bed early.

All day yesterday he had been locked in his study, coming out only when dinner was on the table, his eyes red rimmed and puffy, his complexion pale.

She was sure his headaches had returned. When she had asked him about it, however, he had slammed his fork down, shoved his plate aside, and stormed upstairs to bed.

Cheryl had not gone up until after the ten o'clock news, and then he had been sound asleep.

Day by day, she told herself now, listening to Frank in the shower. She would take each day's problems as they came.

The shower stopped a couple of minutes later, and the bathroom door opened. Cheryl closed her eyes.

Frank rummaged around in the closet, and then she heard the rustle of clothing as he got dressed, and smelt his aftershave as he came near the bed. Finally he crossed the room, and then there was silence.

She waited several seconds longer, then opened her eyes.

Frank stood at the bedroom door looking at her, a lop-sided grin on his face. He was wearing his heavy wool hunting slacks and a thick sweater.

"You'd better dress warmly, it's going to be cold up there," he said. "I'll put on the coffee. Do you want some breakfast?"

"No," Cheryl said.

"Well, shake a leg. Everyone's going to be here in less than an hour." He went downstairs.

Cheryl pushed the covers back and got out of bed. She went to the window. The snow had not let up all night, and now the wind was beginning to pick up, blowing it into long, sloping drifts. She shivered. It *was* going to be cold up at the Whitefish Point house. Cold, and lonely, and frightening. But she had endured since September. The three days in Door County would pass.

She went into the bathroom where she brushed her teeth and took a quick shower.

She dressed slowly in her dark green leotards, bluejeans, turtleneck shirt, thick sweater and her winter dress boots. She ran a brush through her hair, straightened up the bathroom, made the bed, and threw their dirty clothes in the hamper.

Then she took a deep breath and went downstairs.

Frank was finishing some bacon and eggs when Cheryl came into the kitchen and poured herself a cup of coffee.

"There's still some bacon left," Frank said. "You sure you don't want me to fix you some breakfast?"

"I'm not hungry," Cheryl said, leaning against the counter. She sipped at the hot coffee.

"Okay," Frank said. He sat back in his chair and looked up at her, a faint smile on his lips. He was so goddamned handsome, Cheryl thought. And usually so gentle and understanding.

"The girls said you were up to see them on Saturday," he said.

Cheryl almost dropped her coffee cup. "When did you talk to them?"

"I called yesterday afternoon to see how they were

doing. I've been up there almost every day for the past few weeks. Haven't had much else to do."

"They told me," Cheryl said. "They also asked me when I was going to be feeling better. They want to come home."

"I want them home, too."

"Why did you tell them I was sick?"

"I didn't tell them that you were sick. I told them that you had been a little upset lately, that's all. And you have been. It's the reason we put them in that school in the first place."

He made it sound so reasonable. "Why'd you call them yesterday?"

"We're going to be gone for three days; I didn't want them to worry if they tried to get hold of us and couldn't."

For a long moment, she just stared at him. Since Saturday afternoon she had been sure that Frank was going to suggest the girls come along with them. "I thought . . . ," she started, but she bit it off.

"You thought what?" Frank asked. "What's the matter?"

"Nothing," Cheryl said, the ache in her gut subsiding. She pushed away from the counter. "Have you packed the van yet?"

He shook his head.

"Before you do, you'd better lay out the clothing you want to take. I'll do up the dishes here and then pack our things."

Frank got up and came over to her. Smiling, he took the cup from her hands, set it on the counter, and then took her in his arms.

At first Cheryl resisted, but then she let herself go. God help her, she still loved him.

"It's been a rough few months for all of us," he said softly. "But you've taken it the hardest."

"I'm scared, Frank," she said, looking up into his eyes.

"I know," he said, nodding. "I know. I've told you more than once that our troubles would be over very soon, and that we would all go back to normal. But this time it'll work. You'll see."

"I was worried about the girls," Cheryl said.

"Don't. They'll be fine while we're gone. Promise."

For a moment they just stood like that, in each other's arms, and then Frank kissed her tenderly, the way he used to.

"Do we have to go?" she asked softly.

He nodded. "It's important."

The doorbell rang.

"Dark blue Chevrolet, Impala," Klubertanz said into the microphone. He wiped the steamy car window with his coatsleeve, and held the binoculars up to his eyes. "Wisconsin, Y-Z-7-7-dash-5-3-6," he said. Klubertanz lowered the binoculars as he waited for the make.

He had been parked diagonally across the street from the Raders' house since early this morning. Yesterday he had had no luck. Neither Frank nor his wife had left; and no one had come. Until now.

A gunmetal gray BMW sedan came around the corner, passed Klubertanz and pulled in behind the Chevy in the Raders' driveway.

Klubertanz raised the binoculars again, and watched as a man and a woman climbed out of the car and went up the walk. They rang the bell; the door opened and they went inside.

The radio blared: "Unit 483 Alpha. Chevrolet, Impala, blue, license YZ 77-536."

Klubertanz raised the microphone. "Roger."

"Registered to Martin, Frederick N., 453 Fond Du Lac Terrace. White male, forty-two, five feet ten, a hundred ninety-seven pounds, brown eyes, brown hair. No holds, no warrants, no previous convictions."

"Ten-four. Need a make on a BMW sedan, gray, license, Wisconsin HERCAR . . . . spell . . . H-E-R-C-A-R."

The dispatcher repeated the license, and again Klubertanz settled back to wait.

Fred Martin. Madison General Hospital. A secret autopsy had been performed on his three-month-old baby at the hospital's request back in September. Suspected murder.

Nothing had come of it, but Klubertanz had not forgotten the name. It gave him gooseflesh now.

It was snowing quite heavily, and the wind was whipping down the street. Except for his police radio and the activity across the street, it felt as if he was alone, in an empty city.

"Unit 483 Alpha. BMW, TI 2000, gray, license H-E-R-C-A-R."

"Roger," Klubertanz said. Rader's garage door was coming open.

"Registered to Polk, Clinton, S., 1710 Van Hise Avenue. White male, thirty-nine, six feet, a hundred eighty-seven pounds, blue eyes, light brown hair. No holds, no warrants, no previous convictions."

"Ten-four," Klubertanz said, and he hooked the microphone back on its holder.

Two men came out of the garage, one of them going to the Chevy, the other to the BMW. They both pulled out suitcases and went back inside. They were moving in.

They came back out again. This time Martin took a cardboard box from his car and returned to the garage. Polk was doing something in the back seat of the BMW.

Klubertanz raised his binoculars and watched as Polk straightened up, a small black puppy in one arm, a perforated cardboard box with a handle in the other, and went into the garage.

A dog, and probably some other kind of animal in the box. But why? What the hell were they going to do, and why the menagerie?

What in Christ's name was going on here?

Cheryl came out of the kitchen as Clinton was handing over his car keys to Frank. The wind howled through the open garage door and it was bitterly cold. Fred, Marion and Susan were already in the van, and Clinton climbed in behind the wheel.

"You're not coming with us?" Cheryl asked her husband. She felt as though someone had kicked her in the stomach. The girls. She was afraid he was going to go back on his promise.

"I have a couple of things to do before I can leave. I'll follow you up in about an hour," Frank said.

She was frightened out of her mind. "I want the truth, Frank," she said breathlessly.

"What the hell do you want out of me?" Frank shouted. "Jesus fucking Christ! I've got a couple of things to do here at the house. I'll be right behind you."

"I'm not going to play games with you now, Frank," Cheryl said, lowering her voice. "I want you to stay away from the girls. If I have to call the cops, I will. But stay away from the girls."

Frank looked her straight in the eye. "I want to have a sabbat tonight. And I want it done right. There's a couple of things I forgot to pack."

"We'll wait for you."

Frank shook his head. "They're books I don't have. I've got to go down to the library and get them."

"We'll all go."

"Goddamn it, Cheryl, you're going to do what I tell you to do, or I *will* go up and get the girls! And there's not a goddamned thing you can do about it. Everyone up there thinks you're nuts."

The puppy in the back of the van whined, and Cheryl jerked that way. Dear God. What *could* she do?

"You're all upset for nothing," Frank said, much calmer now. "I won't be an hour behind you. Susan and Clinton know what to do to get everything ready. You can help them."

She knew he was lying. She knew it. He was going to get the girls. Suddenly she thought of the detective, Klubertanz. If she could call him . . . he had said he wanted to help. He would know what to do.

"Come on, Cheryl, get into the van," Frank was saying.

Not now, though. Frank would stop her. They would be

pulling in for gas or something. It was a five-hour drive. She would call then.

Cheryl climbed up into the van, and Frank smiled.

"That's a girl," he said, and then he looked beyond her to Clinton. "The roads are going to be pretty shitty, so take it easy. There's a shovel, some sand, and a set of chains in the back."

"We'll be okay," Clinton said. His eyes seemed glazed.

Frank slammed the door. Clinton started the van, backed out of the garage and out to the street. The garage door came down, and Frank went into the house.

Klubertanz had gotten a clear look at the van as it passed him, and Frank Rader had not been in it. But his wife had been there, in the front passenger seat. She had seemed very frightened.

Rader had sent them all away. And by the looks of it they would be gone at least overnight. But today was a Monday, not a weekend or a holiday, which meant Clinton Polk and Fred Martin were taking the day off. Wherever they were going, whatever they were going to do, it had to be important. He waited a full five minutes before he got out of the car. With his head bent low against the harsh wind, he hurried down the street, and up to the Raders' front door.

Frank Rader had known about Sylvia and the kids. How? His wife was frightened. Of what? The Martins, whose baby had died mysteriously were involved, along with another couple. Involved in what?

Monsignor Ferrari had suspected that a gathering of witches existed in Madison. Were these that group?

He rang the bell. A grim-faced Frank Rader opened the door.

"Good morning, Frank," Klubertanz said brightly.

"What do you want?" Frank snapped. He had on a winter coat and hat, and he was holding a small nylon overnight bag.

"Going someplace?"

"I asked you what the fuck you wanted, Klubertanz."

Klubertanz let his voice go deadly flat. "You have the right to remain silent, you have the right to . . . ."

Rader laughed. "Bullshit. You're no longer on the force."

"Don't try me, Rader," Klubertanz said, his muscles bunching up.

"Get the hell out of here. Leave me alone, or I'll call the cops and have you arrested."

"Be my guest," Klubertanz said. He glanced at the overnight bag in Rader's left hand. "That might take a while though. Probably make you late. The roads are getting pretty bad."

"Shit," Rader said. He put the overnight bag down, turned on his heel and disappeared into the living room.

Klubertanz stepped inside the vestibule, closed the door, and quickly opened the overnight bag.

There was nothing inside except two black garments with white trimming. Quickly he took one out. It was a choir robe; the white trim formed a cross on the front. It was too small for an adult. Poorly made.

He stuffed it back inside the bag, then straightened up and went into the living room. Frank was on the telephone.

"Yes, he's here now," Frank said. "Of course." He was smiling as he held the phone out. "Captain Miller would like to talk to you."

Klubertanz crossed the room and took the phone from Frank.

"Good morning, captain," he said.

"Stan, for God's sake, what the hell are you doing?" Miller shouted. "If he presses charges, he'll have your ass."

Klubertanz looked at Rader and smiled. "Yes, sir," he said. "You're damned right I'll stick with it."

"What?"

"I understand, sir, thanks for your help," Klubertanz said and he hung up the phone.

"Nice try," Frank said. "Now get out of my house."

Klubertanz just stood there, staring at him.

"Either leave now, or I'll call him again and have a warrant sworn out for your arrest."

How far could he afford to push it? If he was arrested, Rader and the others would gain enough time to get their stories straight, and cover up any evidence linking them to the murders.

Frank reached for the phone.

Klubertanz turned, walked out of the living room, and left the house. He could feel the man's eyes on his back as he walked down the street, climbed into his car, and drove off.

At the corner, before he turned right, he looked in his rearview mirror. Rader was climbing into the BMW.

Klubertanz sped up and, at the next corner turned right again. He could either follow Rader to wherever he was going, or he could go back to the house.

He turned right again, and up the block he slowed down, barely nosing the Alpha into the next intersection as the BMW's tail lights disappeared down the street in the opposite direction.

For a long moment, Klubertanz sat there, wondering about the puppy that Polk had been carrying, and about the overnight bag Frank had taken with him.

Why hadn't he gone with the others? And why hadn't the others taken the overnight bag with the robes?

Finally, Klubertanz turned right, going down the block and into the Raders' driveway. As he went up to the front door, he pulled the set of lockpicks from his pocket.

10

It was well after 11:30 A.M. when Klubertanz came up from the rec-room and headed back to the vestibule. Now he had been through every room in the house, except for the garage and the study.

He had found nothing to indicate that Frank Rader was anything other than a devoted, loving husband and father. Absolutely nothing, except the suspicion that the girls were no longer living at home. Most of the clothes had been gone from their bureau and closet.

Where were they? How long had they been gone? And more importantly, why had Frank and Cheryl sent their daughters away?

The study door was secured with an expensive lock, and it took Klubertanz nearly five minutes to open it. When the bolt finally slid back, he straightened up, pocketed his lockpicks, and slowly opened the door.

The curtains were drawn, and the study was in darkness. Klubertanz reached inside, found the light switch, and flipped it on.

"Bingo," he said softly.

The place was in a shambles. Books and magazines lay everywhere. The desk had been pushed to one side; some sort of five-sided figure was painted on the carpet. At each corner of the figure was a half-melted black candle, and at the center was the skull of some kind of animal. Probably a dog, Klubertanz figured. Stuck in the desk top was a long, slender dagger with a black handle. And painted on the far wall, in what appeared to be blood, was the single word ASMODEUS.

Conscious of his own heartbeat and his own breathing, Klubertanz picked his way carefully over to the desk.

The chair had been tipped over, as if Rader had jumped up in a hurry. Klubertanz set it upright, then wheeled it around behind the desk, and started to sit down.

There was something in the darkness under the desk.

He took a small penlight from his pocket, switched it on and directed the narrow beam into the leg well. His stomach instantly tightened into a knot.

Sealed in a clear plastic garbage bag were the bloody, headless, disemboweled remains of a black puppy. It looked as if it had been . . . butchered.

Klubertanz switched off the penlight and looked up at the inscription on the wall.

Frank Rader was insane, there was no doubt about it.

Klubertanz's eyes moved back to the skull at the center of the pentagram. The man had slaughtered the puppy, cut off its head, and then cleaned the fur and flesh from the bone.

He sat down at the desk, careful to keep his feet away from the plastic bag. Frank Rader was crazy. He had killed a puppy. He had an interest in witchcraft. And he was a liar.

But a murderer, too?

This room was the man's sanctuary. His stronghold. If there was an answer, it would be here.

The desk had two drawers to the left, three to the right and one at the center. Klubertanz slowly opened the center drawer.

A tray held pencils and pens, paper clips and rubber bands, as well as a roll of postage stamps. Farther back in the drawer were dozens of business cards, most from engineering and architectural firms; an odd assortment of loose keys, a couple of pipes, pipe cleaners and a Zippo lighter, a pocket compass, a bookmark, a two-year-old pocket calendar, and about fifty cents, mostly in pennies.

The top drawer on the left contained several blank pads of paper, along with a small drafting set. The bottom drawer was empty.

Nothing. Nothing.

Klubertanz opened the top drawer on the right side. On

top was a small book, the title stamped in gold: *The Black Mass*. Under it were a leather-bound appointment book and a checkbook.

He took all three out of the drawer and set them on the desk. He opened the second. It contained some typing and carbon paper, but nothing else. He opened the bottom drawer. It was filled with newspaper clippings. The top few dealt with the arrest of Larry Triggs on suspicion of murder; others dealt with the murders of Ahern, Shapiro, Sister Colletta and Msgr. Ferrari. Two covered the auto accident in California in which Sylvia and the children had died.

Klubertanz stared at the clippings for a long time. Rader had made the connection. But it still didn't prove him the murderer.

Nothing here yet justified breaking and entering. Nothing here, yet, that he could take to Capt. Miller. Not yet.

He switched on the desk lamp and picked up *The Black Mass*. There was a thumbprint in blood on the first page.

After the title page and introduction came a litany. In Latin down the left-hand column, and in English down the right. "Accept, oh unholy Lucifer, almighty and eternal spirit, this black host, which I, Thy unworthy servant, offer to Thee, my living and true protector . . . ."

The hairs were rising at the nape of Klubertanz's neck as he thumbed through the thin book, stopping here and there at the names Asmodeus and Astaroth; Balberith and Sonneillon; Carnivean and Gressil. A hundred demons, each with its own dark power.

Something caught Klubertanz's eye. He was in a chapter headed SACRIFICE:

> After Beelzebub has consumed the sacred species, the newly ordained supplicants receive the highest order of sacrifice of like rank; dog to dog, rooster to rooster, hare to hare; man to man; the preparation of each being the same.
>
> However, the rank, as well as the offertory prayers, shall be determined wholly by the nature and appropriate hier-

> archy of the forces opposing the coven. Imminent death, destruction or exposure, of course, demands the ultimate offering . . . the body and blood of man.
>
> Even within this hierarchy there are appropriate ranks as well; the least effective being a male adult, the most effective being a female child . . . .

Klubertanz closed the book.

There had been at least four murders already. Were they contemplating another?

He opened the appointment book and quickly flipped through it, very conscious now of the passage of time. It had been several hours since they had left, and there was no telling what they had already done, or what they were getting ready to do.

The book was filled with names and dates and cryptic comments, some of them understandable: dinner F&M . . . dinner at the Martins; girls' B-day . . . his daughters' birthday. But there were other notes that made little or no sense, and several telephone numbers with no names next to them.

Klubertanz took some paper out of the top left drawer, then went back, in the book, to the pages just before each murder, and copied down every note that made no sense to him, and every anonymous telephone number.

Four telephone numbers seemed to repeat themselves. He picked up the phone and dialed the first. It was answered after one ring: "Madison Public Library."

Klubertanz hung up, then dialed the second number, letting it ring ten times with no answer. The third and fourth numbers connected him with the University of Wisconsin's main switchboard, and with Solar Products, Rader's old employer.

He dialed the operator, and when he had her on the line, he identified himself, then gave her the number that hadn't answered. "Need a name and address for it, please," he said.

"Checking," the operator said.

While he waited, Klubertanz gazed around the room. There was more here, a lot more. And before he was finished he'd know all there was to know about Frank Rader.

The operator was back. "That number is listed to a Mr. Lawrence Triggs, 703 W. Mifflin Street."

Klubertanz had expected almost anything but that. "Jesus," he said softly.

"Sir?"

"Nothing," Klubertanz said. "Thanks for your help." He hung up the phone, and sat there staring at it. After a moment he let his gaze shift to *The Black Mass.* Larry Triggs had committed the murders after all. But under Frank Rader's direction. Possibly with Rader's help.

So where the hell had he gone? What the hell was he planning now?

He looked at his watch. It was noon. Black magic was a nighttime affair. All the murders had been committed at night, or very early in the morning. There was still time. But not much.

With shaking hands, Klubertanz opened Rader's checkbook and quickly looked through the stubs. Mortgage payments, gas and lights, groceries, liquor store, telephone bills, a few for cash, several to bookstores and mail-order houses, other day-to-day expenses. But then, early last month, Rader had written a check for more than two thousand dollars to the St. Martin Academy. The daughters?

He glanced again at *The Black Mass*. The man was a homicidal maniac, but was he so crazy that he would involve his own daughters?

Klubertanz picked up the phone and got the operator. "This is Lieutenant Stanley Klubertanz, Madison Police. I need the listing for the Saint Martin Academy."

"For information dial . . . ."

"This is an emergency, operator," Klubertanz said. "Please hurry."

"Is that a Madison number?"

"I don't know."

"One moment, please."

The black choir robes in the overnight bag had been

small. Small enough for thirteen-year-old girls. Christ.

"Saint Martin Academy is listed in the Yellow Pages. It's located in Beaver Dam, Wisconsin. Shall I dial it?"

"Yes, and hurry."

Beaver Dam was only forty miles or so north, and Frank had left the house hours ago. He'd had plenty of time to drive up there, and take them out of school.

The number was ringing, and then a woman was answering. "Saint Martin's."

Klubertanz forced himself to slow down. Forced a calmness into his voice.

"Good afternoon," he said. "I'm a friend of Frank and Cheryl Rader's. I understand Dawn and Felicity are students at the academy."

"Yes, sir?" the woman said cautiously.

"I'm trying to locate Frank, but he's not at home. He's not there visiting his girls by any chance, is he?"

"You just missed him, sir," the woman said.

"Do you know if he was returning home?"

"No, sir, I couldn't tell you. He didn't say."

"Perhaps one of the girls might know," Klubertanz said.

"They're not here. Mr. Rader took them out of school."

Jesus, Klubertanz said to himself. Jesus Christ. He slammed the phone down, waited a second, then picked it up and dialed Madison Police Headquarters. Captain Miller was going to have to understand that Dawn and Felicity were going to be Frank Rader's next victims. They were going to have to find out where Frank had taken the girls.

He only hoped they had enough time.

In less than six hours it would be dark.

11

The Door County house was a three-story, Victorian-style mansion that had been built in 1905 by a successful Great Lakes commercial fisherman. Shortly after he died, commercial fishing on Lake Michigan had gone drastically downhill. The lake had always been in delicate ecological balance, but finally, overfishing, the lamprey eel and industrial wastes had nearly destroyed it. It hadn't been until the sixties and seventies that the answers were found.

No one on Wisconsin's Door County peninsula, which jutted sixty miles out into Lake Michigan from Green Bay, wanted or could afford the old house, and the county took it over for back taxes. It had stood empty from 1950 until the Raders bought it five years ago.

They had thought it neat and kind of wild to have their very own mansion, but they never used the upper floors, just downstairs, as a lake cabin.

"Our own baronial retreat," Frank had called it.

The girls loved the place, and when the Polks and the Martins visited, they enjoyed it as well, although Susan had said it was probably haunted.

There were no jokes now, however, as Clinton slowly maneuvered the van down the snow-clogged road to the house. The trip up, which normally took around four and a half hours, had taken them nearly nine hours, and it was dark already.

Outside of Oshkosh, Highway 41 had been blocked off by the Highway Patrol because the snowplow crews had not been able to keep up with the drifting snow.

Cheryl had brightened up when she thought they'd have to return to Madison, but Clinton had pulled off to the side of the road, put the chains on the back tires, and headed through the city, around the road block.

Cheryl hoped that Frank would not be able to make it with Clinton's car.

They had stopped at a gas station in Green Bay, but Susan had followed Cheryl into the restroom, and then back out to the van, so that she had been unable to telephone the detective.

The road wound its way down through the trees toward the lake, and, fifty yards from the huge house, came out into a lake clearing. Normally, at that point, the view was dramatic. The house, with its many brick chimneys, its dormers and gables, its portico and the iron gate in front of the wide front porch, rose majestically above the sand dunes. Beyond it another fifty yards was Lake Michigan, stretching away to the horizon.

On a summer day, there always were several sailboats in sight, and on a clear evening the stars out here seemed so brilliant and so huge, you could almost reach out and touch them.

But there was nothing visible now, as they came out into the clearings, except a vague, hulking shape through the blowing snow and darkness, and Clinton struggled to keep the van on the narrow roadway.

"The electricity is off," Cheryl said, suddenly thinking of it. "We can't stay here tonight."

"Frank told me that he called and had it switched back on," Clinton said.

They came around the circular drive, and Clinton had to gun it at the last moment to get through a deep snowdrift, and the van shuddered to a halt at the iron gate.

Clinton shut off the headlights and sat back with a deep sigh. It was utterly dark here. "I hope to hell they've got the roads plowed before we have to go back."

"You did a good job, honey," Susan said from the back seat.

Cheryl was staring at the dark house. She didn't want to go in. It seemed so terribly isolated and ominous now, considering what Frank was going to make them do.

"I hope Frank makes it okay," Fred said.

"He will," Susan said with confidence. "He will."

The voices around her seemed very far away to Cheryl as she continued to stare up at the house.

"Fred and I will go inside and get a fire started," Clinton said. "You girls bring our things in."

"You'll have to stay in the living room," Susan said. "Just for a couple of hours. We'll stoke up the kitchen stove, and before we go to bed we can get a couple of bedroom fireplaces going."

Clinton switched the engine off and started to open the door. Cheryl turned around in her seat and grabbed him by the arm.

"No," she shouted. "We can't go in there."

"Why not?" Clinton asked, looking at her.

"Can't you see what he's doing? What he's turning us into?"

"Take it easy, Cheryl," Susan said from the back seat.

"No!" Cheryl screamed and grabbed for the keys in Clinton's hand, but he shoved her back, and then slapped her in the face, the back of her head bouncing against the window.

"Clinton!" Marion shouted.

"Shut up, all of you," Clinton snapped savagely. "Until Frank gets here I'm running the show. And you're all going to do exactly what I tell you."

Cheryl's face stung from the slap. She had counted on him and Marion to help her.

"Do you understand what I'm saying, Cheryl?" he shouted, spittle flying from his lips.

She nodded. "Yes."

Clinton stared at her for another long second, and then he, too, nodded. "Good," he snapped. "Now get this goddamned van unloaded, and fix us something to eat. I'm hungry and tired, and I'm not going to put up with any more of your shit."

As he opened the door, the van instantly filled with the howling wind. He pushed through the iron gate and up the walk onto the front porch. Fred followed Clinton into the house. A second later the lights came on inside, and then the porch light.

"Let's get this stuff inside, before we freeze to death," Susan said, and she got out and opened Cheryl's door.

Cheryl looked at her. There was no friendship or warmth in the woman's eyes. Just hardness, and a slight edge of amusement.

"Coming?" Susan said.

Cheryl looked beyond her, up to the house, as the living-room lights came on. Then she stepped down out of the van, into the incredibly cold wind and swirling snow. Susan pulled a box of groceries out of the back and thrust it into her arms.

"Have them start the kitchen stove right away. We can heat up some soup to go with our sandwiches," Susan said.

The groceries were heavy. Cheryl stumbled and almost fell twice as she pushed through the deep snow and slowly mounted the three steps to the porch.

The outside door was open. Cheryl stepped into the small entryway, but she could not bring herself to open the inner door with its frosted glass window.

"Go on in," Marion said, right behind her.

Cheryl looked over her shoulder. Marion was just as frightened as she was.

"Don't make them mad at you. Clinton will just hit you again."

Cheryl bit her lip. Awkwardly, she fumbled with the inner door, getting it open, and she and Marion stepped inside.

Straight ahead, the grand staircase rose to the second floor. Behind it was the door to the kitchen. To the left, double doors led into the formal dining room, and to the right, through a wide archway, was the huge living room, with its massive natural stone fireplace that dominated an entire wall.

The house had been stripped of furnishings before they had purchased it. The first couple of years they had brought up a number of items they had picked up at garage sales. But the nouse was still essentially empty. And dead cold now, although Cheryl could smell woodsmoke.

Fred came out of the living room, a grin on his face. "Did it with one match," he said. "I'll get a fire started in the kitchen, too."

"We'll heat up some soup," Cheryl said.

"Great. I'm starved."

Cheryl and Marion followed Fred past the staircase, and into the huge, tiled kitchen, furnished with a butcher block table, an icebox, and a mammoth wood-and-coal-burning, six-plate range.

Fred flipped on the overhead lights, and began stuffing newspaper and kindling into the stove's firebox. Cheryl and Marion set their boxes on the table.

Susan came in a second later and put a couple of grocery bags on the table.

"Stay here and get the soup on," Susan told Cheryl. "Marion and I will bring the rest of the things into the living room."

Cheryl glanced at Marion, then nodded.

"God, it's cold in here," Susan said, shivering, and she and Marion left the kitchen.

Smoke was coming from the open plate on the stove, and Fred glanced over at Cheryl.

"The chimney has to heat up before it'll draw," he said. Like Clinton, he had a glazed look in his eyes. He glanced down at the nearly empty woodbox next to the stove. "I'll have to get more wood from the living room," he said. He smiled at Cheryl, then left the kitchen.

She stood by the table for a long moment, but then she hurried over to the counter by the large tin sink and opened the top drawer. It was filled with silverware and cooking utensils, including half-a-dozen sharp knives.

She glanced over at the kitchen door, and then quickly grabbed one of the knives, opened her coat, pulled up her sweater, and stuck it in the waistband of her jeans.

If Frank showed up with the girls, she would take them back to Madison in the van. Or at least down to Sturgeon Bay, where they could stay the night in a motel. And no one would stop her. Not Clinton, nor Susan. Not even Frank.

12

The crew from the BCI van had gone through the Raders' house with a fine-toothed comb. Two other crews were going through the Polks' and the Martins' homes. Captain Miller had pulled a few strings downtown, and had managed to convince a sympathetic Circuit Court judge to issue the search warrants for all three places.

But as of 6:00 P.M. they had come up with nothing that would indicate where the three couples had gone.

APB's had gone out on the State teletype network with descriptions and license numbers of the Raders' dark blue van and the Polks' BMW. So far neither vehicle had been spotted.

Captain Miller had been speaking on the phone, and when Klubertanz came in from the garage, he put the phone down, looked up, and shook his head. "Nothing yet, Stan. But with weather like this, it's no wonder. Did you find anything in the garage?"

Klubertanz shook his head as he crossed the room to the liquor cabinet. He poured himself a stiff shot of brandy, and tossed it down, then poured himself another. "Do you want one?"

"No, and you shouldn't, either. We're all going to have our asses in a sling unless we come up with something more than we already have."

Klubertanz turned on the captain. "What the hell are you talking about? Christ, he had Triggs' phone number in his book. He called him at least ten times that we know about."

"I'm sure other people besides Rader spoke with Triggs on the telephone. It doesn't make them accomplices to a murder."

"Four murders," Klubertanz corrected. "At least. And possibly two more tonight, unless we can stop them."

The telephone rang, and Capt. Miller picked it up. "Miller."

Klubertanz was tired. His eyes felt like someone had poured sand in them, and his mouth tasted foul. The brandy wasn't helping much.

As Capt. Miller was speaking on the phone, Klubertanz went over to the fireplace. On the mantel was a framed photograph of Frank and Cheryl Rader and their two daughters. It was summer, and they were all smiling, posing in front of a huge, ramshackle old house, behind which was a very large lake or the ocean.

Klubertanz stared at the photograph for a long time. They looked so happy. It could have been that way for him and Sylvia and the kids. But it hadn't worked out. And now there was no chance of it. No chance at all.

"I'll be damned," Miller was saying, and Klubertanz looked over at him. "What about Polk, anything on him or his wife?" the captain asked, looking up. He held up a finger for Klubertanz to wait. "Yes?" he said. "When?" And then, "All right, good work, Smitty. Anything else turns up, give me a call here." He hung up the phone.

"What'd Smitty dig up?"

"You know the bribery thing down in Milwaukee?" the captain said.

Klubertanz nodded.

"Fred Martin was indicted this afternoon on twenty-seven counts. The warrant for his arrest just came through on the teletype."

Klubertanz whistled. "And Polk?"

"He was fired from his job at the University on Friday."

"Why?"

"He was screwing one of his lab assistants."

"An interesting combination . . . Rader, Martin and Polk," Klubertanz said. "No hint where they might have gone?" He glanced up at the photo on the mantel again.

"Not a clue."

Not a clue, Klubertanz said to himself, but then his

breath caught in his throat, and he set the brandy glass on the mantel, and reached up for the framed photo.

''We're just going to have to wait and see what the APB's turn up,'' Capt. Miller was saying, but Klubertanz wasn't listening.

He slid the cardboard out of the back of the frame, then pulled the photograph out. On the back side was stamped: DOOR COUNTY PHOTOHAUS, STURGEON BAY, WIS.

''What have you got?'' Capt. Miller asked. He came across the room.

''I don't know,'' Klubertanz said, turning the photo over. ''Does this look like Door County?''

Captain Miller studied the photo for a long moment. ''Could be,'' he said.

''The lake side, or the Green Bay side of the peninsula?''

''What difference does it . . . .'' Captain Miller suddenly understood what Klubertanz was driving at. ''Do you think they went up there? To this house?''

Klubertanz looked up. ''It's possible, isn't it?''

''Anything is possible, Stan. But it's a long shot.''

''It's the only shot we've got,'' Klubertanz said, his stomach in knots again. He brushed past the captain, hurried out of the living room, crossed the vestibule and looked in the study. Two of the BCI crew were going through the bookshelves. They looked up when Klubertanz came in.

''Where's Urban?''

''Downstairs in the rec-room. They're dusting,'' one of the men said.

Klubertanz hurried back through the house and took the stairs down two at a time.

George Urban and three other lab men were lifting prints from the bar when Klubertanz burst through the doorway.

''Need your help, George,'' Klubertanz shouted.

Urban, who was the BCI crew supervisor, was a huge, ponderous-appearing man, but he had an exceedingly quick and orderly mind. He put down the equipment he had been using and came around the bar.

''What do you need, Stan?''

Captain Miller had come downstairs too.

''Household papers, bills, canceled checks, shit like that? Where is it all?''

''Up in the kitchen for the most part. Some in the study, but you've already seen that, and a bit in the front bedroom,'' Urban said. ''What is it you're looking for?''

''House payments. Mortgages.''

''This house or the mansion?''

Klubertanz just looked at the man for a second. ''Jesus,'' he said. ''The mansion. Is it up in Door County? Sturgeon Bay, maybe?''

''Close,'' Urban said. ''A place called Whitefish Point. Off County Trunk T, about five or ten miles north. They've been paying on it for the last five years. Banquo Mortgage Company here in Madison. Not a bad deal, $158.50 a month . . . .''

''Come on and show me where the papers are. I need an address,'' Klubertanz snapped.

Urban looked away again, then nodded. ''County Trunk T, north of Sturgeon Bay. Fire number 1742.''

''A big house?''

''Like I said, a mansion.''

Klubertanz turned to Capt. Miller. ''That's it.''

''You think they went up there?''

''I don't know where else they'd be. It's worth a shot.''

''I'll call the Door County Sheriff's Department, see if they can send a unit out there to look around,'' Captain Miller said.

''Fine. Meanwhile, I'm going to drive up.''

''What the hell good will that do?'' Captain Miller protested. ''I doubt if you'd make it up there in this weather, and even if you did, it's out of our jurisdiction.''

''I'm no longer with the force, remember?'' Klubertanz said.

Miller was clearly exasperated, but it was also clear that he knew he couldn't really do anything about it.

''At least let me make the call first.''

''I'll monitor Tac One, in my car. The sooner I get started, the sooner I'll get up there.''

''Goddamn it, Stan . . . ,'' Miller sputtered, but Klubertanz was already out the door and heading up the stairs.

13

Cheryl was alone in the warm kitchen, drinking a cup of tea, when there was a commotion at the front and she could feel a cold draft from the door.

She set her cup down, checked the knife in her waistband for the tenth time, and hurried to the kitchen doorway.

Frank, his hair tousled and snow covered, his jacket open, stood in the front hall. Susan, Clinton and Fred were with him, while Marion hung back by the living-room archway. But the girls weren't there. He had not brought the girls with him! The relief was almost staggering. Cheryl broke into a smile. Her worst fears had been groundless. The girls were safe.

"Sorry I'm late," Frank was saying, his voice a little hoarse, "but the roads are getting bad."

"We were starting to worry about you," Susan said.

"I'm here now. Where's Cheryl?"

"In the kitchen." Frank looked beyond her to the kitchen doorway.

Cheryl stiffened.

"Fix me a drink, will you, babes?" he said. Then he turned back to the others. "You can all get into your robes. I'm going to change upstairs. Then we can get started."

"You haven't had a chance to eat anything," Susan said.

"I'm fine, Susan, thank you," he said gently. "But the sooner we get started, the sooner we'll be safe." He looked toward the front door. "Even now they are gathering against us out there."

Cheryl hadn't moved. Tomorrow, somehow, she would

get to a telephone and call for help. Tonight had to be endured.

''Is everything ready?'' he asked.

''We've got an altar set up in the living room. And another table for food. The animals are there, the pentagram has been laid out, and the candles are ready for lighting.''

''Good,'' Frank said thoughtfully. ''Did anyone bring a radio? Have you been listening to the news?''

''No,'' Fred said nervously.

''They've issued a warrant for your arrest.''

Marion stifled a cry, and Frank looked over at her. ''It's nothing to worry about,'' he said. ''After tonight the charges against him will be dropped, and a public apology will be issued.''

''You're crazy!'' Marion screamed. ''Fred, can't you see it?''

''Tie her and gag her,'' Frank snapped.

''No,'' Marion cried, stepping back.

Cheryl could feel her heart hammering.

''Then keep your mouth shut,'' Frank said deliberately.

Marion said nothing. Frank turned to Susan. ''Why don't you help Cheryl check the silverware drawers in the kitchen, and make sure all the utensils are in their proper place? Especially the knives. We wouldn't want to have an accident.''

Christ, he knew! But how?

''Sure,'' Susan said, and started toward Cheryl.

''Marion, I want you to go in and change your clothes now,'' Frank said. ''Fred, I don't want you to worry about anything tonight. And Clinton, you've done a good job for me. I want you to know that within ten days the Regents are going to order your reinstatement.''

Susan had reached Cheryl and held out her hand.

Cheryl looked past Susan at Frank, who stood there watching. How had he known, she asked herself. It was impossible.

''Don't make it difficult for yourself,'' Susan said, half under her breath.

Slowly Cheryl raised her sweater, pulled out the knife and

handed it to Susan. "I'm sorry," she said in a small voice.

Susan took the knife. "It's all right now, Cheryl. Why don't we fix Frank his drink, and then get ready?"

Cheryl turned back into the kitchen and poured Frank a large glass of straight brandy. Susan put the knife back in the drawer by the sink.

Together they went out into the main hall, and then into the living room where Frank was looking over the arrangements.

A large silver pentagram had been painted on the faded old rug, in front of a library table draped with a black altar cloth. Fred and Clinton were lighting the candles, and the room was reasonably warm from the roaring fire in the fireplace.

Frank took his brandy from Cheryl, drank it down, and then handed the glass back to her. "I'm going upstairs to change now," he told them. "I'll be back in five minutes. I want you all to be ready. We'll begin at once."

No one said a thing, and Frank smiled at Susan. "We'll begin with the rooster, and work up from there. Get everything ready."

"Yes," Susan said dreamily, and Frank turned and strode out of the living room.

Susan went across to the couch, where the black robes had been unpacked, and began getting undressed. Clinton and Fred joined her a moment later.

Cheryl glanced at Marion, who was standing by the fireplace, and then looked toward the main hall. The crackling fire and the howling wind outside were the only sounds she could hear. She could feel the fear and tension building up inside of her.

Something bad was going to happen here tonight. It was thick in the air. Something very bad.

"Let's go," Susan said, and Cheryl looked over at her. She was completely nude, the nipples on her breasts erect from the cold. Fred was looking at her, and he had an erection. Clinton didn't seem to mind, nor did Marion, who had joined them and was half undressed.

They were all crazy.

14

It had taken Klubertanz the better part of an hour to drive from the Raders' house to his apartment, change his clothes, put the chains on the Alpha's rear wheels, and then pack a shovel, some sand, and a couple of extra blankets in the trunk.

The wind was shrieking wildly now, blowing snow everywhere. Out in the country, away from the streetlights, it would be almost impossible to see more than a few yards. Yet Klubertanz knew that it would be impossible for him to sit here in Madison and wait for morning.

He left the car running, the heater on full blast, as he hurried back up to his apartment one last time, to get a bottle of whiskey and an extra flashlight.

Just as he was about to leave, the telephone rang, and he stopped at the door, debating whether or not he should answer it.

The phone rang again.

"Shit," he said, and he went back into the kitchen and grabbed the phone on its third ring. "Who is it?" he snapped.

"Me," Brenda Wolfe said. "Still mad?"

"No. As a matter of fact, I tried to call you, but your line was busy. I wanted to apologize for being such an asshole."

"I had it off the hook," she said. "And you *are* an asshole, but so am I. Do you want to come over?"

"I can't tonight. I'm working. In fact, I've got to go right now."

"Bullshit," Brenda said. She had been drinking, Klubertanz could hear it now in her voice. "Either come over here now, or you can kiss off, Stan. I'm tired of waiting around for you."

"You don't mean that."

"Yes, I do," she said.

Klubertanz shook his head. He could not handle ultimatums. "Bye," he said softly, and he hung up the phone. There would be time to straighten it out when he got back, he thought.

He went outside to his car, the wind penetrating even his heavy parka, climbed in behind the wheel, flipped on the headlights and windshield wipers, and headed toward the highway north. There was no other traffic, not even the snowplows, on the roads.

He flipped on his radio, turned up the volume and switched to the Tactical One channel. "Headquarters, this is 483 Alpha, how do you copy?"

"Roger copy, 483 Alpha. Captain Miller wants to talk to you. Hold on while we make the patch."

Klubertanz laid the microphone on his lap, unzippered his parka and settled back in the seat. It was going to be a very long night. And out here, driving now, he wasn't at all sure that he would make it even ten miles, let alone all the way up beyond Sturgeon Bay, a hundred and eighty miles north.

He kept seeing the look on Cheryl Rader's face as she had passed him in the van. She had been frightened; she had looked helpless. She knew that something was going to happen tonight. But he wondered if she realized that her daughters were going to be involved.

Klubertanz doubted it. He thought Frank had remained behind to pick up the girls in secret. Which meant she would not have gone along with him.

"Until 483 Alpha," the radio blared.

Klubertanz picked up the microphone. "Roger," he said.

"Stan, this is Miller."

"What'd they say up in Sturgeon Bay?"

"We can't get through. All the phone lines are down."

"How about the State Radio net? Can we relay a

message through them?''

''We're trying that now, Stan. Where are you?''

''Just passed under the Interstate bridge. I'm heading out 151.''

The radio was silent for a moment. ''You'll never make it tonight.''

The Alpha shuddered as a gust of wind caught it, and he had to swing left around a large snowdrift. Miller was almost certainly correct, but he was going to have to try, nevertheless.

''I'll check with the State Radio at Fond Du Lac,'' Klubertanz said. ''But keep trying to get through to Sturgeon Bay.''

Again the radio was silent for a long moment. ''Good luck,'' Capt. Miller finally said, and Klubertanz shook his head. It wasn't he who needed good luck this night.

15

Cheryl was cold beneath the thin black robe. She sat on the couch between Fred and Clinton. Marion sat in a chair, and Susan stood by the black-draped table across the pentagram from them.

The black candles were lit, the tiny flames reflecting dully off the white plastic skull at the center of the pentagram. And from time to time the rooster, lying on the table with its legs tied, would cackle.

It had been fifteen minutes since Frank had gone upstairs to change, and they all listened now for sounds from above. But there was nothing except the crackling of the fire on the grate, and the moaning of the wind outside.

They were so isolated up here, Cheryl thought. So alone. So dependent upon whatever Frank wanted to do.

She couldn't help but think of how it had been with them a few short months ago. But with that thought came others. The step-by-step disintegration of their lives came clearly to her now, and she shuddered.

"Asmodeus!" Frank shouted from the front hall, and they all looked that way, Cheryl's heart thumping.

"Astaroth! Lucifer! Protect us in our hour of need."

"So be it," Susan said, her shoulders back, her head high, a slight smile on her lips.

Frank appeared in the archway, wearing nothing but some kind of shaggy fur cape over his shoulders, held around his neck by a thick gold chain. His body gleamed with oil, and he had painted a large red cross on his chest.

He spread his arms, his hand raised upwards. "Smother the enemy of weakness within us. Destroy our enemies without. Bolster our courage so that we may be strong enough for the most difficult tasks ahead."

A strong gust of wind roared down the chimney, fanning the already high flames, and sending a plume of ash and smoke into the room.

"Veni, Creator Lucifer," Frank spoke the Latin words clearly. "Come, take possession of our souls."

Fred and Clinton were paying rapt attention to Frank; Marion had her eyes tightly closed.

"Take possession of my soul," Susan said softly. She undid the buttons at the front of her robe, pulled it off her shoulders and let it fall to the floor.

They were all watching her. She picked up the rooster with both hands and held it above her head. "Accept these sacrifices in the name of our Master, Lucifer," she said.

Frank moved slowly into the room and at the table took the rooster from Susan. He held it over his head, turned to the others, and began to squeeze with his powerful hands.

"This fowl, unworthy of Your notice, oh Great One, I give to Olivier, the Prince of the Archangels in the third hierarchy."

The rooster was struggling wildly, its innards and body fluids being forced from its beak and anus as Frank relentlessly tightened his grip.

"For Olivier, Prince of the Archangels," Susan said, her eyes bright.

The rooster's body burst, its bones breaking, and its blood running down Frank's forearms. He tossed the creature aside.

"So be it," he said.

Susan ducked down behind the table, and came up with a small black rabbit. She handed it to Frank.

Cheryl couldn't move; it was as if she had been mesmerized.

Frank held the rabbit over his head, and began to squeeze.

"For Carreau, Prince of Powers, in the second hierarchy, I give to Thee this unworthy beast of the forest."

Stop it, Cheryl screamed silently. She could not even move her lips.

"For Carreau, Prince of Powers," Susan repeated, and the rabbit shuddered once as Frank's fingers penetrated its sides, blood and gore mixing with the rooster's on his arms.

He tossed the carcass aside, and Susan ducked behind the table again, and this time came up with the tiny black lab puppy.

"No," Cheryl whimpered. They all ignored her.

"For Sonneillon, fourth in the order of Thrones, lowest in the first hierarchy, I give to Thee this unworthy beast of the hearth." Frank raised the puppy in both hands, directly over his head. The little animal licked Frank's hands, its tail wagging.

Suddenly, without warning, Frank slammed the animal to the floor with all his might.

"Frank!" Cheryl screamed. Her paralysis was broken. She leaped from the couch before Fred or Clinton could stop her, and ran to the puppy. It was still alive.

Frank shoved her back, sending her sprawling, raised his right foot and brought it down on the puppy. The animal's body split open with a sickening sound.

"For Sonneillon!" Frank bellowed.

"For Sonneillon," Susan repeated.

"For Sonneillon," Frank bellowed again. Fred and Clinton repeated it.

Frank had an erection. The killing had sexually excited him.

"The chalice," he said.

Susan rummaged around behind the table, finally coming up with the large, silver chalice they had used before. She set it in the middle of the table.

"The instrument," Frank said. He was staring down at Cheryl.

Susan came up with a straight razor. She opened it and laid it beside the chalice.

Frank smiled. "The moment for which we have all striv-en is here."

There were no animals left alive.

Cheryl started to crawl backwards, away from Frank. His

eyes seemed to burn into her head.

"For Olivier, we slew the rooster; for Carreau, the hare; and for Sonneillon, the canine. What then for Lucifer, our Master?"

"What then for Lucifer, our Master?" Susan chanted.

"What manner of beast or fowl for the Mighty One?"

"What then for the Mighty One?" Susan asked.

"What shall we offer, in order that our enemies shall be defeated?"

"What shall we offer?" Susan asked.

Cheryl got shakily to her feet and dared a glance at the couch where their clothes were piled. Her purse was there with her key to the van. If she could get her keys . . . .

"For Lucifer!" Frank shouted.

She took a step backwards, toward the couch.

"Mommy?" a small voice called from the front hall.

Cheryl spun on her heel. Dawn and Felicity, both of them wearing long, flowing black robes, stood in the entryway to the living room, their eyes wide, their mouths open.

"No!" Cheryl screamed, darting toward her daughters.

Frank was quicker. His right fist slammed into her shoulder, knocking her off her feet.

"Run!" she screeched. "Run and hide!"

16

In Beaver Dam snowplows were lined up along the street, like tanks waiting to go into action. Cars were buried beneath piles of snow, and long drifts shifted up the deserted main street under the onslaught of the intense wind.

A full-scale blizzard, the Madison radio stations were calling it. The worst in forty years.

Madison Police Dispatch had tried to raise Klubertanz ten miles back, but their transmissions were breaking up too badly for him to make any sense of them.

He drove slowly through town, and on the other side sped up as much as he dared.

The forty-mile trip up from Madison had taken him two and a half hours. At this rate it would be morning before he made it to Sturgeon Bay. And although he knew he was going to be too late . . . whatever they had planned would be done tonight . . . he still had to try.

Just beyond the town, Klubertanz looked into his rearview mirror to see a police cruiser, its red lights flashing, pull up behind him.

He cautiously let up on the gas, and lightly pumped his brakes, the back end slewing around despite the chains on the rear wheels.

When he had the car stopped in the middle of the empty highway, he set the parking brake, got out, and hurried back to the cruiser. He climbed in the back seat.

"Lieutenant Klubertanz?" the cop driving asked.

"Yeah. Did Captain Miller call?"

"Yes, sir," the other cop said. "Asked us to keep a look-out for you."

Klubertanz just looked at them. They seemed embarrassed.

"He asked us to talk to you."

'Well?"

"Ah . . . sir, he asked if we couldn't get you to stay here in Beaver Dam for the night, or at least until the snow lets up."

"Not a chance," Klubertanz said tiredly. "Did he say anything about the phone lines up to Sturgeon Bay?"

"Yes, sir. He said to tell you that the lines are still out, and so far he's had no luck with the State Police Radio net. I think one of the relay towers might be down."

Klubertanz nodded. "How are the roads south of here?"

"South?"

"Yeah, back to Madison."

"Closed, sir."

"And I suppose they're closed to the north, too?"

"Yes, sir," the driver said.

"Fine," Klubertanz said. "I just made it from Madison on closed roads; I guess I'll try to get a little farther north."

"Ah . . . well, sir, your captain told us to . . . ."

Klubertanz smiled tiredly. "Tell you what," he said. "I'm going up to my car to get my things, okay?"

Both cops nodded uncertainly.

"And I imagine your jurisdiction doesn't go beyond the city line?"

"No sir."

"Fine. Have a good evening, then." Klubertanz climbed out of the squad car and worked his way back to his car.

The flashing red lights behind him went out at the same time he released the parking brake, put the car in gear and continued north.

17

For a long moment the girls remained in the archway. Then they turned and sprinted around the corner.

"It was you!" Marion screamed, jumping to her feet. "You killed my baby!"

Frank glanced at her, and then started toward the archway.

Marion suddenly leaped forward, raced across the living room and jumped on Frank's back like a madwoman, screaming and clawing and biting at his neck.

"It was you!" she screamed again.

Cheryl jumped to her feet, her right shoulder aching from Frank's blow and leaped at him, nearly knocking him off his feet.

"Stop them!" Susan shouted.

Fred reached them first, and he dragged his clawing, screaming wife away from Frank, ripping the black robe down her back. But then he had his arms around her, holding her securely.

Frank's left arm slammed into Cheryl's chest, knocking her to the floor, her head banging against Clinton's leg.

Then Frank turned on Marion, who was struggling in her husband's grasp. He doubled up his fist and smashed it into her face. Cheryl could hear a flat, cracking sound; it was Marion's jawbone breaking. Blood sprayed from her mouth and trickled down her nose. Her eyes rolled up in her head, and her knees sagged.

Fred was rocked backwards by the force of the blow.

"Asmodeus!" Frank bellowed.

Fred looked, wide eyed, from his wife's battered face to Frank's, twisted in anger.

"That's enough," Clinton said, and he stepped quickly

over Cheryl, shifted his weight to his left foot, and swung at Frank.

''No,'' Susan shouted.

Frank easily ducked Clinton's punch, stepped to the right and, bunching his fists together, slammed them with all his strength into the side of Clinton's head.

Clinton was lifted off his feet by the blow, and he crumpled in a heap on top of one of the pentagram candles.

''Astaroth! Asmodeus! Lucifer!'' Frank shrieked. ''Help us in our hour of need!''

There were tears streaming down Susan's cheeks now. She looked radiant. ''Yes . . . oh, yes, Frank.''

Frank looked at her for a long second, then stared at the others, no recognition or emotion in his eyes. His rage had vanished. He suddenly wheeled around and loped out of the room.

Polk was groggily getting to his feet as Fred gently laid his still unconscious wife on the floor. He was shaking.

''Marion. Oh, God, Marion, what have we done?''

Cheryl sat up, and then somehow managed to stand. The room was spinning.

Blood was streaming down Clinton's face from his right ear, and he was shaking his head.

Cheryl took an uncertain step toward the archway.

Susan leaped past them, the straight razor in her hand, and stood in the archway. ''No one leaves this room,'' she shouted.

Fred rose. ''Someone help Marion,'' he said.

''She deserved it,' Susan shouted.

Fred turned on her. ''You bitch,'' he hissed, and lunged at her.

''Look out, Fred!'' Clinton shouted.

Susan slashed out with the razor as Fred's fingers curled around her throat, and they both fell to the floor.

Clinton was there a split-second later, and he grabbed Fred by the shoulders and flipped him over. Susan scrambled backwards, the straight razor no longer in her hands. Fred's intestines seemed to flow like liquid out onto the floor from a huge gash in his belly.

"The girls," Cheryl screamed. The room was still spinning.

Clinton turned. "Find them and get the hell out of here," he snapped. "Take the van into town and get the cops. I'll keep Frank busy."

"No," Susan screamed.

Cheryl sprinted back to the couch where she pawed through the clothes, finally finding her purse.

Susan was scrambling toward Fred's body, trying to find the razor. Clinton shoved her backwards, out into the main hall, as Cheryl found her purse, dumped its contents on the floor, and snatched up the van keys.

"Frank!" Susan screamed. "They're coming!"

Frank bellowed. It sounded as though he was in the kitchen.

Cheryl started forward. One of the girls screamed. It seemed to come from the kitchen as well.

"Dawn?" Cheryl screeched, racing for the archway. "Felicity?"

Clinton had made it out into the main hall, past Susan, who was getting to her feet, and a second later Cheryl was right behind him.

Before Susan could stop either of them, they had reached the kitchen.

Frank was in front of the butcher block table. He was holding a huge meat cleaver over his head. His eyes were wild, spittle drooled from the corners of his mouth, and he was laughing maniacally.

"Oh God, Frank!" Cheryl cried.

Frank reared back against the table, raised his head, and screamed in perfect imitation of the girls.

Somewhere in the house, upstairs perhaps, the girls screamed for their mother. Distracted, Clinton looked up, and at that moment Susan darted past Cheryl and grabbed her husband by the arms.

"I've got him, Frank!" she screamed wildly.

Frank leaped forward and swung the meat cleaver down. Clinton spun around to avoid the blow. Susan just managed to looked up as the heavy blade missed Clinton and buried itself in the top of her skull, sending blood and large pieces of white matter splattering everywhere.

The force of the blow jerked her body violently to the left, and Frank staggered backwards, losing his grip on the weapon.

Cheryl spun around and raced out of the kitchen, through the main hall, and up the stairs. Behind her in the kitchen she could hear the sounds of a terrific struggle.

She reached the second floor landing. "Girls?" she shouted.

"Up here," one of them screamed.

Upstairs. Cheryl flew down the corridor, skidded around the corner and took the stairs up to the third floor. The girls appeared at the railing.

"Mommy?" they both cried.

"We're getting out of here, darlings. Come on!"

"I can't," Felicity whimpered.

Cheryl grabbed Felicity's arm, and half pulled her down the stairs, Dawn racing with them.

Frank bellowed downstairs.

"What's wrong with daddy?" Dawn cried.

"He's sick," Cheryl said, trying to keep her voice low.

They had reached the second floor and the three of them hurried to the head of the stairs, and started down.

Brandishing the meat cleaver, his body covered with blood, Frank came out of the living room. He saw them, and started up.

"Daddy!" Felicity screamed in terror.

Cheryl pulled the girls behind her and shoved them back up the stairs. "Run, girls! Hide!"

Frank bellowed again, his voice deep and hoarse, as Cheryl turned back and prepared to leap down on top of him. If she could knock him off balance, he might hurt himself in the fall. The single thought crystallized in her brain. It was the girls' only chance now.

"Mommy!" Felicity cried.

"Run!" Cheryl screamed, and she tensed her muscles, ready to leap.

Suddenly Clinton was in the hall, and he started up the stairs, a fireplace poker in his hands.

Frank raised the meat cleaver. Cheryl backed up, stumbled and nearly fell. Clinton came up behind Frank, swung the poker overhead with both hands, and slammed it with every ounce of his strength into the back of Frank's head.

Frank was knocked sideways, blood splattering everywhere. His right hip hit the railing, his body flipped over it, and he seemed to hang there for a long, terrible moment, before he plunged down to the parquet floor below, hitting with a sickening thud.

Clinton and Cheryl stared at each other. There was a huge gash in Clinton's side, the blood pumping out in rhythmic spurts.

"Get help," he said weakly, stumbling sideways against the railing.

The girls came back to the head of the stairs, to Cheryl, who was staring in horror over the railing.

Frank was still alive. His legs were moving. And he was trying to crawl forward to where he had dropped the meat cleaver.

Clinton looked down and saw him too. "Get out of here," he said, and with a massive effort he started down the stairs, the fireplace poker in his right hand.

Cheryl herded the girls down the stairs behind Clinton. At the bottom, as Clinton staggered toward Frank, they raced toward the front door.

"Cheryl," Frank shouted as they reached the door. She jerked it open.

"Help me, Cheryl," Frank said in a normal voice.

Cheryl turned around. Frank stepped past Clinton, who was leaning, nearly unconscious, against the banister.

"Help me," Frank pleaded. He raised the meat cleaver as he came forward.

Felicity screamed, and slumped to the floor in a faint.

"Help me," Frank laughed.

With his last bit of strength, Clinton swung the fireplace poker like a baseball bat. It hit Frank in the neck.

Frank bellowed, and turned on Clinton, swinging the meat cleaver, missing him by several inches.

Clinton shoved the poker in Frank's face, knocking him momentarily off-balance. "Run," he shouted.

Cheryl scooped Felicity off the floor, and she and Dawn opened the outer door, and staggered out onto the porch and down into the blizzard. Behind them they heard a blood-curdling scream.

A tremendous gust of wind nearly knocked Cheryl off her feet, and when she regained her balance, she looked back up at the house.

Frank stood in the open doorway, his face a grisly mask of blood. "Come back," he shouted over the wind. Cheryl, still holding Felicity in her arms, staggered backwards.

"Come back, girls," Frank called, and then he turned around, and Cheryl could see that the fireplace poker was sticking out of the back of his skull.

Clinton was right there, and in one terrible, swift motion, Frank buried the meat cleaver in Clinton's face, nearly splitting the skull in two.

Cheryl staggered another step, as Frank dragged Clinton's body away from the door, and into the house.

18

It was dawn. The wind had subsided, the snow had stopped, and already to the northwest the sky was beginning to clear. The temperature had plunged to eighteen below zero.

The Whitefish Point mansion stood dark and silent, only thin wisps of smoke rising occasionally from two chimneys, as six snowmobiles, each carrying two heavily dressed men, parked at the end of the long driveway from County Trunk T.

Klubertanz had recognized the house from the photograph as soon as his snowmobile had come out of the trees and into the clearing.

He had finally arrived in Sturgeon Bay two hours ago, but it had taken all this time for him to convince the local authorities that there could be a problem out here, and then to round up the men and equipment.

Smoke was rising from behind a hummock of snow in front of the house. Klubertanz tapped the driver of his machine on the shoulder, and pointed that way.

The man nodded, and headed over the big snowdrifts, pulling up behind what they could now see was the Raders' blue van. The other snowmobiles pulled up, too.

Klubertanz climbed down and plowed his way through the snow toward the van. The engine was running. Someone was inside the vehicle. He only hoped that whoever it was had had enough sense to come out periodically and clear the snow away from the exhaust pipe.

As he crawled over the last big drift, near the rear of the van, he could see that the snow *had* been scooped away. The tailpipe was clear.

Around the side of the van, several of the other men

from the County Sheriff's Department helped him clear the snow away from the door. The others went up to the house and went inside.

They reached the door handle, and Klubertanz flipped it up and slid the door back. Cheryl Rader, huddled between her daughters, looked up in terror. After a moment she smiled. "Lieutenant Klubertanz, isn't it?"

Klubertanz nodded. "The girls . . . are they . . . ?"

Cheryl looked down at them, then back up. "They're sleeping," she said. "Thanks for coming."

"How did you know to clear the exhaust?"

"Frank told me what to do if ever I was stuck alone in a car, in a snowstorm."

Someone shouted something from the front porch of the house.

"I think they're all dead in there," Cheryl said.

"Your husband?"

Cheryl nodded. "He went crazy after the accident. Can we get out of here now?"

Someone else was shouting something from the house.

"In a little while. I'll get you and the girls some warm clothing. We'll have to take you down to Sturgeon Bay by snowmobile. All the roads are closed."

"That's fine," Cheryl said. "I'm glad you're here."

"Be right back," Klubertanz said, and he climbed out of the van. Before he went up to the house, he went around to the rear of the van. The exhaust pipe was still clear. Then he climbed over the big drift.

Two of the Door County deputies were on the porch, vomiting. A third stood, white faced, by the open door; he wasn't looking inside.

Klubertanz trudged up on the porch.

"Christ . . . Christ," the deputy by the door said. He looked up at Klubertanz. "Christ," he said again, weakly.

Klubertanz took a deep breath, then went into the house.

There were two large pools of blood in the main hall. Someone had walked barefoot through them, and there were bloody footprints everywhere.

He stepped around the nearest patch of blood and then into the living room. The sight there stopped him dead in his tracks, his stomach flopping over and the bile rising sharply in his throat.

Clinton and Susan Polk, Fred and Marion Martin, were hanging from the ceiling by their ankles. Their bodies had been slit open from crotch to chin. Their organs had been scooped out of the body cavities, and were lying in glistening piles beneath them.

Klubertanz was suddenly conscious of the fact that he was here alone in the house.

He unzippered his heavy parka, and pulled out the .357 magnum he had brought with him.

Someone was behind him.

He spun around.

"Jesus Christ," the sheriff's deputy said, looking from Klubertanz to the bodies and then back to Klubertanz.

"Frank Rader," Klubertanz said, lowering his gun. "He did this. He's got to be here someplace. Let's find him."

"Yes, sir," the deputy said, backing out of the room.

Klubertanz glanced back at the bodies, then left the room and went out onto the porch. He holstered his weapon.

Two other snowmobiles were coming up the driveway as the deputy was organizing his people for a thorough search of the house and grounds.

Klubertanz had an odd feeling about this one. Somehow he didn't think they would find Frank. He didn't want to believe in the supernatural, and yet, with everything that had happened, he just didn't know any longer.

"How about the woman and kids in the van, lieutenant?" one of the deputies asked.

Klubertanz stepped down off the porch. "Just look for Frank Rader. I'll take care of them."

"Yes, sir," the deputy said, and Klubertanz headed to the rear of the van to make sure that the exhaust pipe was still clear.

Epilogue

TWO YEARS LATER

It was a few minutes before five in the afternoon of a lovely fall day, and Lt. Klubertanz was about to knock off for the day when Capt. Miller called him into his office.

The nightside duty briefing had already been held, and most of the late-shift officers were out on patrol. Lately, Fridays seemed to be the big night of the week, and a lot of the guys were pulling overtime to help with the extra work. Klubertanz hoped that he wasn't going to be stuck with weekend supervisory duty again. He had pulled it three weekends in a row.

Klubertanz knocked lightly on the captain's open door, and Miller, seated behind his desk, looked up and waved him in.

"Just got something from the FBI over in Detroit that I thought you'd better see."

Miller handed him a single sheet of paper. It was a Fugitive Sighting Report, which the FBI routinely sent out to the originating law enforcement agencies in flight-to-avoid-prosecution cases.

The name on the top line caused Klubertanz's heart to skip a beat, and he slowly sat down.

Five horribly mutilated bodies had been discovered in a cabin in a remote section of Upper-Peninsula Michigan, near the small town of Gulliver.

The investigating officers said that the five appeared to have been killed in some kind of occult ceremony. The locals said that strange things had been happening in and around the town over the past two years.

Frank Rader had been positively identified by a number of people in Gulliver, who described him as pleasant, but somewhat peculiar. His bloody fingerprints had been found all over the cabin.

It was happening again. It was beginning all over. Klubertanz looked up into Capt. Miller's eyes. "I'm going home."

"I understand," Capt. Miller said. "If we get anything else, I'll call you."

"Thanks," Klubertanz mumbled. He went back to his office, grabbed his jacket, and hurried down to his car.

All the way through town, and out to Nakoma on the west side, Klubertanz kept remembering in vivid detail how it had been that day in Door County two years ago.

They had searched every square inch of the house, and the grounds down to the frozen lake, without finding any sign of Rader.

After ten days of looking, the Door County Sheriff's Department had finally given up the search. The case was shuffled back to the Madison Police.

In late spring after all the snow had melted, a second search had been initiated in the vicinity of the Whitefish Point mansion. The theory was that Frank had frozen to death out there someplace, and his body had been covered by snow. But no trace of him had been found, and the FBI had begun its search.

Now it was starting all over again.

It was five thirty by the time Klubertanz pulled up in front of his pretty two-story contemporary on Doncaster Drive. Don Briggs, his next-door neighbor, was raking leaves, and he waved. Klubertanz waved back, then went up the walk to the front door. His hand shook as he reached for the doorknob. He was being stupid; he knew it, and yet he couldn't shake the feeling of imminent disaster.

He took a deep breath, let it out slowly, and then went inside.

The house was quiet.

"Cheryl?" he called out. He took off his jacket and hung it in the hall closet. "Cheryl?" he called again. "Girls?" But there was no answer.

He stepped into the living room and his heart nearly leaped into his throat. The room was a shambles. There was blood everywhere. The carcass of their Irish setter was lying in a bloody heap on the coffee table. Its head had been cut off, its belly split open, and its insides scooped out and flung around the room.

"Oh, God," Klubertanz barely breathed. "Oh, God . . . Cheryl?" he screamed. He pulled out his service revolver and raced into the dining room.

There was blood all over the walls, and printed in blood, on the mirror above the buffet, was the single word ASMODEUS.

"Cheryl?" Klubertanz shouted again.

Cheryl screamed in the kitchen.

A deep, black darkness welled up within Klubertanz as he flew across the dining room, kicked the kitchen door open, half off its hinges, and stepped inside.

Frank Rader, dressed in a bloody hunting shirt, khaki trousers and hunting boots, stood by the sink, an axe in his right hand, a demonic grin on his distorted features.

"Help," he screamed in a perfect imitation of Cheryl.

"Where are they?" Klubertanz said, a sudden, deadly calmness descending upon him.

Rader just laughed.

"Where are they, you bastard?" Klubertanz raised his service revolver and cocked the hammer. "What have you done with them?"

Rader laughed again, raised the axe with both hands and started slowly forward. "You can't kill me," he said. "I'm immortal. Nothing can kill me."

Klubertanz stood his ground as Rader continued toward him. "Where are they?"

Rader raised the axe higher over his head, and lunged.

Klubertanz fired. The shot caught Rader in the chest, and he staggered backwards, a look of surprise on his face.

Klubertanz fired again, this time hitting Rader in the neck. Blood splattered everywhere. He fired a third and fourth time. Both bullets hit Rader in the head. He stumbled against the kitchen counter and started to go down.

"Where are they?" Klubertanz shouted, and fired the last two bullets at Rader's body. "Where are they?"

For a long time then, Klubertanz stood where he was, looking down at Rader's body. He thought he could hear someone outside shouting something, but it didn't matter any longer. Soon he was going to have to search the house. Cheryl and girls were here somewhere. Probably in the basement.

He laid his empty revolver on the counter after a while, and then looked up as he heard sirens in the distance.

Maybe he wouldn't search for them. Maybe he didn't have the stomach for it. Maybe he couldn't handle it. He loved them so much.

He turned and shuffled out of the kitchen, through the dining room, past the dog that Rader had killed and butchered, and then out into the hall. He opened the front door as three squad cars pulled up in a screeching halt.

Don Briggs and his wife, along with several other neighbors, stood on the sidewalk looking up at him.

Several uniformed police officers were piling out of their cars, and were racing up the walk toward him. Two of them had their guns drawn, and one was carrying a shotgun.

He could hear the police radios in their units, blaring messages from dispatch. In the distance he could hear another siren.

"What happened, Stan?" one of the cops shouted.

Klubertanz stepped out on the porch as the first cop reached him.

"Stan!" Cheryl's voice screamed his name from down the block.

"What the hell happened?" the uniformed cop shouted.

Klubertanz shoved him aside. Cheryl was running across the street toward him. The girls were right behind her.

They were safe! They hadn't been home! They were alive!

"Cheryl!" He was running down the walk, the police

officers shouting at him, his neighbors stepping fearfully aside.

Then she was in his arms. "What is it? What happened?" she cried.

"You're all right! Oh, God, Cheryl!"

Dawn and Felicity were there now, too, hugging him, and it *was* all right. It *was* over, finally. Frank was dead. For certain. There was no way he could come back to harm them.

"We heard shots," Cheryl said.

Klubertanz looked deeply into his wife's eyes, and there was an instant, silent communication between them. She looked up toward the house, her face pale.

"He . . . ." she began.

"It's over, this time."

She looked again into his eyes.

He nodded. "Nothing will ever hurt you or the girls. I promise."

She wanted to believe him. He could see it in her eyes. But she was frightened that it was starting all over again.

He held her then. Closely. He suspected they would both be frightened for a long time to come . . . for a very long time . . . . But they had each other. They would manage.

AUTHOR's NOTE

This is, of course, a work of fiction. So I have taken some liberties. My apologies to the city administration of Milwaukee, and to the Madison Police Department. Everything I wrote about you good people, is totally a figment of my imagination.

But, and it is a very important but, witchcraft, the occult, and black magic, are endeavors best left alone. What I have portrayed could happen.